MW01241216

THE FERRYMAN'S TOLL

The Ferryman's Toll

AN HOURGLASS NOVEL

Daniel James

Copyright © 2024 Daniel James

Bottled Lightning Press

This is a work of fiction. Names, characters, places, and incidents either are the product of the author's imagination or are used fictitiously. Any resemblance to actual persons, living or dead, events, or locales is entirely coincidental.

All rights reserved. No part of this book may be reproduced or used in any manner without written permission of the copyright owner except for the use of quotations in a book review.

Cover design by Hampton Lamoureux at TS95 Studios

Interior design by Olivia M. Hammerman

ISBN: 978-1-3999-7339-7 (paperback)

PROLOGUE

In the forgotten concrete bowels of Elzinga Asylum, Dr. Julius Sharp watched the sedated woman slumped before the pedestal, atop of which sat the maker of monsters and madness: the Eye of Charon. It was an abominable thing, not made for this world of science and reason; like most of the things Julius had witnessed and assisted in creating down here.

The woman, garbed in prison overalls, her former beauty now a wasteland of scars, was once known as Dolores Ricci before becoming a number in a maximum-security penitentiary. Now, she had entered a whole new prison. She moaned mindlessly in a sedative's chemical grip. The Eye glared from its pedestal in the center of the large, clammy chamber, its severed mercury-tinted tendrils twitching steadily. Scrutinizing the mortal subject cast before it, it became a blazing oculus of hellish, otherworldly light.

Julius had the bearing of a man in the company of hungry tigers. As a renowned psychiatrist and head of this hospital, he had long ago developed an air of pensive and analytical study. But in these moments, it was a cheap mask. Standing beside him in this ceremony was a looming muscular figure whose reputation had been chilling long before he had lost any remaining essence of humanity: the Hangman, Charon's greatest work.

Julius adjusted his spectacles, using the motion to peek at the savage killer brooding next to him. The Hangman stared at the woman in typical mute fashion, but there was something else hidden deep in his gaze, something that would prove invisible to a stranger: a curiosity not for violence, but something else.

Julius scribbled something on his small notepad and quickly slipped it inside his suit jacket, giving a furtive glance about the centuries-old stone-and-iron cellblocks, patrolled by the silent dark-suited guards stationed here to watch over him and this infernal program.

He inhaled wearily and watched in despair as the Eye of Charon fashioned the body and mind of Dolores Ricci into something only fit for worlds of teeth and bloodshed.

I

Clyde swam deep, the pull of sleep dragging him through viscous layers of dreams, of memories, each one peeling away to reveal an ever-greater mystery beneath it all. Darkness took him, one as absolute as the deepest oceans, and then it delivered him. The sensory oblivion started to wane. A rainbow prism of light radiated softly upwards from the fathomless depths, and Clyde sank towards it. It was a city, a *continent* of glorious light, a shimmering jewel of every imaginable color amidst the infinite darkness of unconsciousness.

Even in sleep, a part of Clyde was awake, and he knew exactly where he was.

The Median.

An immaterial place. The halfway realm between Life and the dead planes of Erebus. Median was a domain of sleepwalkers, where the glowing threads of every living soul bound together to create an ever-expanding kingdom of sleek spires and gables, hills and roving pastures. Clyde knew the place, but he didn't know how he had arrived here unaided. Previously, his visitations had been dependent on another individual, one who was both a man and something other. The man was called Spector, a former thief of mystical reliquaries turned Hourglass specialist. The *other* was Ramaliak, Spector's ram-headed avatar and an ancient lord of dreams with a mysterious connection to the rulers hidden somewhere deep within this slumbering realm.

Those first dives into the Median had been part of Clyde's training regimen at the Indigo Mesa facility in New Mexico, a requirement due to his specific ability to tether the soul of another to his own. The conditioning had taken time, the diving procedure exhausting and dangerous to a novice, having to plunge through the tiers of the dreaming imagination and the catalogues of memory before piercing through to the innermost tier of the Median. But with Ramaliak at his side, Clyde had finally gotten there. And he had learned the limits of his power: he could bind one soul to his own. Only one. An occupancy taken up by his deceased best friend, Kev. But now, somehow, he had made the voyage alone, something he had never done or been able to do before.

He touched down on the pulsing threads of neon acres surrounding the outer limits of the metropolis and watched the knitted souls thrum with warm life. His hand moved upwards to worry at his forehead, his fingers revealing his own soul, a light-blue thread unspooling slowly into the knitted landscape. He moved his hand away, and his soul thread dissipated like blue chalk dust. In the times Ramaliak had guided him to this forbidden place, the only living thing Clyde had witnessed besides himself and his Sherpa was the endless thread count. And it was this quietness that currently troubled his lucid mind. Ramaliak had previously hinted at the presence of other beings in this realm. Clyde cast his gaze about, worrying that powerful dreamers, rulers, lawmakers, or beasts might be watching him, a trespasser, a potential meddler with no diplomat present to parlay his presence here in this enchanted land. The stillness exuded threat.

How the hell had he slipped up and fallen through the outer tiers? Had some form of unconscious muscle memory guided him back to this hidden place?

Dreamers could die if careless. Spector had told him so. And souls, Clyde knew from experience, could be destroyed too, their vibrant threads turning black like burned wires, the individual truly lost, not living nor wallowing in Erebus. Some place beyond death.

Clyde wanted to leave.

Had to.

Now!

He turned, surveying the sparkling hills and flats and distant tree-studded valleys glittering off towards the horizon. He wasn't sure how to exit this realm without Ramaliak at his side. His eye became drawn to a point on that far-flung tree line. Somewhere in that vast gleaming forest lay the golden soul threads of his older brother and estranged father, both former US Marines, felled in different wars, each of which had been waged by greedy instigators whose well-polished shoes were never troubled by dirt or blood. Clyde's inability to braid their souls to his own, thereby anchoring them to the living plane, remained a point of quiet discontent for him.

Something moved along the horizon. And it wasn't alone. The things, whatever they were, remained too far away to distinguish clearly, but more of that creeping dread oozed through Clyde like cold oil. The pressure mounted, so much so that he was struggling to breathe. He imagined dying in this place, his own soul thread becoming snipped. A fixed length would remain woven into the tapestry as tribute, while the remainder of his soul would be shunted to Erebus like an unwanted frayed end, taking Kev right back there with him. That awful place of ravenous soul eaters and endless survival. He still couldn't breathe and felt himself losing control, unable to move, fixed to the spot for the mysterious residents to capture or kill. He screamed for Ramaliak, screamed in outrage at this stricture. His screams trailed off, unanswered, to parts unknown.

With a dropping leg, Clyde jerked awake, a sheen of sweat on his forehead. The nightmare fell apart in his hands as he tried to rethread it back together. All he recalled was the fear. He glanced at the loaded handgun in his loose grip, a habit he acquired shortly after joining the NYC head office in response to the ominous atmosphere brought on by the increased number of assassination attempts on Hourglass personnel. Clyde always made sure the gun's safety was on before closing his eyes; the last thing his boss needed was his staff assassinating themselves.

He reached for the phone on his bedside unit and checked the time. 19:48. He had woken up before his 8 pm alarm. He would have enjoyed another ten minutes, but at least he managed to get a few hours' sleep before the mission. The past weeks had caught up to him. His heavy eyes were sluggish, rolling across the shadowy army of Funko Pop! dolls lining the graphic novel-laden shelves and desk of his bedroom. Following the mission briefing earlier, he had wanted some quiet time to unplug from the job and draw, but after getting back to his apartment, he could hardly keep his eyes open. He tended to keep his illustrative artwork saved on his computer or squirreled away in one of his dozen or more sketch pads.

Before life's great curveball, he had wanted to be a comic-book artist more than anything. To call it an obsession would be an understatement. Now it felt as though he was always struggling to carve out the time to work on his creator-owned project, and anytime he did manage to pick up a pencil, he found escape from the job near impossible. He had been working on something since accepting his official post at the Madhouse—New York's head Hourglass office—an ongoing project of sorts that could be considered stress-relief: a pyramid of killers, gradually taking up more wall space. Each illustration depicted an assassin dispatched by the Cairnwood Society—chiefly Edward Talbot, a mid-tier member who ran a lot of their regional work—to wreak bloodshed and havoc against Hourglass. Clyde had reimagined them in his skillful comic-book style, arranging them in a pecking order in accordance to their deadly capabilities.

Near the top was a man wreathed in flame and smoke, his face an etching of ash upon a burning ember head. This was Bai Li, the serial arsonist who had torched an agency safehouse, killing a team of agents and their ward in the process as a means of calling out Clyde and the rest of Hourglass's local strike team. Next to this hot-tempered individual was a figure colored in hues of green and yellow: Charles Niedermeyer. Hailing from St. Louis, Missouri, Niedermeyer was a serial killer whose work as a pest control exterminator afforded him ample opportunities to test out various toxic substances on his victims across three states. When the FBI finally closed the net on him, he had opted out of lethal injection in favor of the gas chamber and was on his way to said appointment when a group of well-armed and highly organized unknowns—presumably Cairnwood affiliated—ambushed the US Marshal transport and absconded with him. Li, Niedermeyer, and the several others rounding out the pyramid's lower tiers were now all dead. But Clyde didn't sleep any easier with them in the ground because one killer had continued to elude him. The one at the peak of the pyramid, drawn larger and more domineering than the others.

The Hangman.

The agency's number one target, and the one who had placed all local and regional Hourglass staff in a state of heightened caution. Also, the one who had Clyde sleeping with a gun in his hand, but Clyde wasn't sure what good the gun would do him if the Hangman actually paid him a visit one night. Still, peace of mind.

The Hangman was a dark presence of muscle and killing wire, whom the agency had been hunting since he'd butchered each member of the previous Madhouse strike team one by one, even though each of them had been highly experienced and gifted with an extraordinary skillset. Hourglass still had next to no intel on him, and his sightings had become sporadic since the former team's elimination, though certainly not sporadic enough for Clyde's liking.

Clyde looked away from the pyramid on his wall, sat on the edge of the bed, and tried to compose himself for the upcoming mission. Without bothering with the lamp, he placed his handgun under his pillow, got to his feet, pulled on a Venture Bros. T-shirt, and slowly left his bedroom into the dark apartment. It was open plan, lots of space and exposed brick. He kept his drawing board set up before the window; the view of Brooklyn's McCarren Park was a welcome reprieve for tired eyes. The apartment was a little sleeker and more executive than he was accustomed to. After Director Trujillo, the top of Hourglass's totem pole, had offered Clyde and Kev's services, along with senior agents and teammates Ace Tremblay,

Rose Hadfield, and the ghost trio comprising her Intensive Scare Unit, to Deputy Director Meadows at the New York branch, Clyde's generous annual salary had been supplemented with the added bonus of this new residence. It certainly beat the old place he and Kev had shared on Myrtle Avenue. Unpacking was still a work in progress, though; the apartment—and mainly his bedroom—was still filled with various cardboard comic boxes and unpacked bric-a-brac. Along with his essential artist supplies, he'd made sure to keep all other agency-issued firearms away from the clutter: an automatic shotgun in the closet, a few flashbangs under the sink, several other items to ward off unwelcome houseguests.

He stared out the window at the city teeming with life and electric light and caught his reflection in the glass. Deep-brown skin, athletic physique; he'd trimmed down his loose and kinky hair but kept the scraggly beard. It still didn't seem real, as though this life was also part of the dream. Everything had moved so fast since finishing his training at Indigo Mesa. He had been a scrawny artist desperate to find an *in* into the comic-book business, subsisting on junk food and obsession, and existing in a state of shock over Kev's return from the grave.

Now he killed monsters and those who served them. He fought a covert war that didn't officially exist. And he used to be such a pacifist. But that was before Rose had knocked on his and Kev's door—Hourglass was nothing if not stringent on monitoring individuals with extraordinary abilities, and harboring friendships from beyond the grave was one such ability that fell under that category.

Clyde had never wanted anything to do with any type of military or federal service but had accepted Rose's conditional offer for Kev's sake and some answers. Call it compromise. Call it compartmentalization. It boiled down to the same thing: Clyde, like his brother, Stephen, and his estranged dad, was a soldier at heart. He had just needed to find his war. But unlike Stephen's or his dad's, Clyde's was a war that had to be fought. It wasn't for the few, but the many. The people he had killed were human only as a technicality. They were black-hearted cutthroats, bean-counters, and doom-bringers for the Cairnwood Society. Of course, the world was full of plenty of other threats on a near-permanent basis, but it was Cairnwood that Hourglass regularly dueled with. That said, it still surprised him how quickly he had made peace with all of this. He had only been an official agent for a month, and what an ass-puckering whirlwind of a month it had been.

At least he was back home in Brooklyn and not stuck at Indigo Mesa or another US state HQ; Director Trujillo could have even posted him in Canada since Hourglass was also the premier paranormal peacekeeping agency operating north of the border. He supposed he could thank the Hangman for that.

He glanced down at his latest sketches on the drawing board, bathed in ambient city light. It was a dynamic portrait of heroes and vile villains, these ones fictional. A part of him wished he could just stay here and work on the drawing some more, but the clock was ticking. The surveillance teams would still be in place, monitoring the site of the upcoming infiltration until Clyde and the others arrived.

He went into the small kitchen, had a glass of water, and then poured some lukewarm coffee from the pot into his Green Lantern mug. With his back to the counter, he closed his eyes and tried to clear his mind. Opening his eyes, he found himself staring at the laptop on the counter, along with a small black USB stick, some of the contents of which had become an endurance test of sorts. The USB held not only the files of each of the five former strike-team members, but also the various crime-scene photos and, in a few instances, the camera footage of the Hangman slaying them. The killer was quick, relentless, and remorseless. The video files were awful to watch, but Clyde couldn't resist. It was near enough a nightly ritual in the beginning, but now it was still at least once a week. He told himself that it was research, wanting to understand the enemy: how he moved, how he acted, any possible weakness to exploit. But each death happened so fast and easily that it was impossible to garner anything of value from the videos or the crime-scene information. He turned the laptop on, was greeted by a Deadpool wallpaper, and slipped the USB in. He avoided the Madhouse forensic department's grisly collection of photographs and desultorily scrolled through the files of the deceased Hourglass agents.

Carmen, Traci: former DEA agent. San Antonio, Texas. (Spark—concussive energy blast generation.)

Gries, Louie: former CIA agent. Fort Collins, Colorado. (Lycanthrope—survived a chance encounter with a lunar cult member while stationed in Hungary.)

Koepenick, Scanlon: former civilian. Des Moines, Iowa. (Spark—photon manipulation.)

Lafayette, Rochelle: former civilian. Baton Rouge, Louisiana. (Conjuror of ectoplasmic Senegalese wrestlers—Lafayette was the keeper of a burial mask belonging to the Senegalese Wolof tribe.)

Lind, Julie: former police officer. Atlanta, Georgia. (Spark—density manipulation.)

The three agents designated as Sparks were what worried Clyde the most. Agency intel was quite sparse on the exact origin of such individuals, with most of the information being collated from various ancient texts and cultural myths, but what Clyde did know was that their genetics were infused with some form of otherworldly energy, granting them various unique and powerful abilities. His teammate Ace, for example, was a cryokinetic. Being a massive fan of Chris Claremont's run on X-Men, a foolish part of Clyde still couldn't resist but fan-boy out on occasion, noting how his life had become a comic-book of sorts. But he was quick to dismiss such notions. This was reality, not a comic-book adventure. The pain and the death and the repercussions were very real to him and his team. And knowing that agents with such abilities had been dispatched with ease forced him to think about how he might stack up against Hangman if they crossed paths. Because he was no Spark.

He checked the time on the computer screen. 20:00. He switched the computer off, finished his coffee, then poured the last of the pot into his mug, taking it with him to the apartment across from his. Clyde needed the caffeine to drag him out of the slump these past weeks and that stressful sleep had left him in. He briefly wondered if Kev had experienced any stressful dreams lately, then axed the thought. Of course he didn't. Kev never bothered sleeping.

2

It was true ghosts could sleep. If they were so inclined. Spector had disclosed this to Kev during his training at Indigo Mesa—being the original agency HQ and nerve center responsible for watching over the borders between Life and Erebus also made the facility the de facto spirit central—but he hadn't explained the relevance or necessity of a ghost catching forty winks. That first time in Spector's office, Kev had wallowed in the upper tiers of sleep, the quizzical amalgamations of his imagination, and the archives of memory that helped inform them. It was there that Kev came to face his personal fear of wasting his second chance in the same way he had wasted most of his mortal life. And so, from that point on, Kev was content to forsake such trivialities as sleeping.

He was too keyed up anyway. There was too much to think about. It had been this way since he first came back from being shot dead in a liquor store hold-up four months ago. He died a young man, slightly bookish in appearance, with glasses and a husky body that had not been used to the rigors of exercise in his corporeal days.

While Clyde was obsessing over the Hangman and the murdered strike team, Kev had been tending to his own obsession. Photocopied printouts floated in mid-air before him, arranged in a neatly organized sheaf. Some could call what he was doing self-torment. Some perhaps might call it a fool's errand. Kev called it necessity.

The pages were a selection of his own scrawled notes and copies of the poorly translated passages—including a pictogram story—taken from an immeasurably ancient text titled *Origins of the Dread Paradigm*, an infuriatingly sparse account of what some believed to be the collapse of Heaven. A war of deity-like beings from the frontlines of life and death that had culminated in the current and bleak status quo: the unchallenged rule of the Order of Terminus, the nine mysterious and brutal monarchs who presided over what is known as Erebus or, more colloquially amongst the Hourglass shooters, the Null. The Null is what awaits every living soul: saint, sinner, or somewhere in-between; there is no escaping it. At least not forever. Kev's first official assignment had taken a sudden and unexpected detour to the outer rims of that dreaded place, but as much as it troubled him in its lethality and its inevitability, he had come to believe that somewhere in all of its uncharted horror, it held the means to re-create a peaceful afterlife.

The Firmament Needle.

A single vital apple seed buried amidst a blighted orchard.

Kev believed this because of a brief but unforgettable encounter with a Russian monk during that same mission, an ex-KGB necromancer called Konstantin Kozlov. Every day since then, Kev found himself thinking about the intrigue surrounding Kozlov: a mortal man well acquainted with death who had forsaken his own life for a noble cause. Truly the noblest of causes. Choosing to wander the dead wastes in search of the Needle. Had the monk learned of any enticing leads in his pilgrimage? Was he even still alive, or had Erebus claimed his flesh, blood, and soul?

A ripple of air flicked through the sheets as Kev jostled a largely useless map front and center. Calling it a map was pushing it. So much empty space. Erebus—the Null—had the potential to be limitless in size. And yet, a growing part of Kev ached to return there, to somehow, miraculously, catch up to Kozlov and aid him in his search. Because what greater purpose could one serve than locating the means to build an eternal bliss? Instead, here he was, dealing with asshole dark-art assassins and local disputes.

There was a knock at the door. Kev removed his thick glasses and rubbed his eyes, a habit that had followed him from death back to life. With a flourish of telekinesis, he shuffled the papers into a neat stack at the foot of a large, fully-stocked bookcase. Kev's apartment was otherwise almost entirely devoid of furnishings, except for a large flat-screen TV, a PlayStation, a single standing lamp, which was currently lit in the corner of the room, and a couch to melt into.

'Come on in.' Even if Kev hadn't been expecting Clyde, he could feel the connection between his soul and Clyde's strengthening in proximity. Plus, Clyde was the only neighbor Kev was chummy with. Being a dead guy made it tricky to socialize outside of work. He heard a key sliding into the lock, and Clyde entered the bare apartment with his coffee.

'Crap sleep.'

At first Kev wasn't sure if Clyde was asking a question or making a confession, but surely Clyde knew by now not to bother asking him whether he had rested.

Kev saw how drugged Clyde looked with his half-lidded eyes. But they weren't half-lidded for long, peeling open a little more at the sight of the stacked photocopies by the bookcase.

'You should let it go, man. At least for now.'

Kev had heard this more than a few times now. It sometimes felt like he was the only one on the team who wanted to focus less on trading blows with Cairnwood and more on finding a way to spare the living the atrocities of hell.

'That's rich coming from the guy who dabbles in Hangman snuff movies.' Kev sighed and drifted over to the couch, switched the PlayStation on with nothing more than a thought, and floated two control pads over. He watched Clyde check the time on his phone and make a few decisive tongue clicks before accepting the controller and dropping onto the couch.

'What the hell, we can spare half an hour.'

'I thought it would be simpler than this. The job. Stupid, right?' Kev said. He loaded up their ongoing campaign. 'I dragged you into this line of work—'

'You're tethered to me. It's because of me that you're back here and not in the Null.'

'And again, great big thank-you for that, but—'

'No buts. I chose to come back and work with Hourglass. You didn't force me to.'

'Granted. Still, things escalated so much quicker than I ever would have thought. I wanted a reason to exist. Spend my second chance doing something worthwhile. Do some good. And then right out the gate, first mission, I hear there might be something out there that can make exis- tence more than a glorified waiting room for hell. If we only knew for certain whether the Needle is real or some fable.'

Clyde starting sniping psychos from an elevated position, allowing room for Kev to charge in and use his special move. Even in their leisurely pursuits, they worked as a strong team. 'Kozlov sure as shit thinks it's real, to do what he did. A whole damn cult of them believed it to be real.'

The concentrated rattling of controller buttons and the game's music and joyous chaos settled over them for several beautifully distracting minutes.

'Get that guy there,' Clyde said.

Kev had killed him before Clyde had even finished talking. 'Check it.' He gestured to the loot dropped by the enemy.

'Bitchin' rifle.' Clyde picked it up.

'It's the lack of certainty that makes me itch. My gut tells me Kozlov isn't just some wild-eyed zealot, but I'd like to know for sure.' Kev didn't want to bother Clyde with excessive shop talk before a mission, but he always experienced an urge to discuss matters of the Null after rereading his notes.

'You think the brass know more than they're letting on about the Null?'

'I'd be more surprised if they don't,' Clyde answered. 'I might be- lieve in their cause, but Hourglass is still a government agency. Layers of bureaucracy, and secrets upon secrets. And we're still new blood. What the fuck do we know about the big picture? But for now, it's a compromise we both have to accept to do what we do.'

They had made pretty good headway into the level, engrossed in the serotonin fix of gameplay, before Kev broached his thesis. 'I keep coming back to the arrangement between Hourglass and the Order of Terminus, about the specifics of the truce. You've been quiet about it, but I know it can't sit well with you any more than it does me.'

The Hourglass credo stated its involvement in tackling any supernatural force that intended to harm the welfare of the living and their souls, including the policing and protection of the borders between life and death. But Kev and Clyde knew very little of the agency's directorate and otherworldly politics. It was one thing to protect the souls of this world from malevolent threats, foreign and domestic; otherwise, it seemed as though the Hourglass brass was content to remain locked in an eschatological stalemate that favored the Order.

Clyde nodded, a glint of uncertainty in his eye. 'I've thought about it. But honestly, I can't say I'm informed enough to make any judgement on it.'

Everything Kev knew on the subject of Erebus's ruling houses he'd gathered from another journalistic puzzle piece from Indigo Mesa's library. The tome, *The Diminished Equinox*, had been about as much use as a very old doorstop for Kev's needs, but it had provided the names of the Order's constituents:

The House of Fading Light
The House of Silent Screams
The House of Red Thorns
The House of the Blue Carapace
The House of Strange Fates
The House of Wise Stones
The House of the Glowing Reel
The House of the Celestial Spiral
The House of Cold Stars

But it was the name of one house in particular that continued to nag at Kev: The House of Wise Stones. It was purely conjecture on his part, but it wasn't entirely baseless. Director Trujillo's ancestry was entwined with the Coyotero tribe of Western Apaches, a tribe with a special kinship to a mystical and ancient race known as the hoodoo, the silent and timeless stone people native to New Mexico. For reasons unknown to Kev, Trujillo had become some type of flesh and stone hybrid, presumably sometime around his transition from CIA operative to founder of Hourglass.

'What about the House of Wise Stones?'

'What about it?'

'The hoodoo. They're stone and I'd say they're pretty damn wise, wouldn't you? They may be mute, but they communicate. They can grant passage over to the Null; they built that giant hourglass beneath the desert with Trujillo so they can explicitly time the duration of a traveler's journey while over there.'

Clyde had seen the impressively constructed hourglass first-hand on an unofficial assignment. 'I doubt they built it. You think those blocky hands are capable of such finesse?'

Kev didn't let the technicalities sway him. 'My point is, they're guardians between the living and the dead. They're wise, that's irrefutable. So—'

'So you think for some reason Trujillo and the hoodoo are playing for the same side as the Order?'

'I'm not saying their goals are aligned with the Order's, but they could be a bigger part of the whole cosmic balancing act. Hourglass, us, we're one side of the fence, but maybe the hoodoo are also affiliated with that particular House of the Order. They could be ex-members, working in a liaison capacity.'

Kev knew he was in one of his rabbit-hole moods, digging and digging, and that Clyde was beginning to disengage.

'You know I'm with you on this, man,' Clyde said. 'Literally till death and beyond. But if you're thinking about going to Meadows or even Trujillo and asking again if the hoodoo or somebody might know anything about the Needle or Kozlov, then I'd say you're wasting your time. We've been through all that and only got stonewalled. They're not obligated to explain everything to us. That's the business of intel. These are issues for another time. I don't know when, but it's not now. We're still only runts in the agency.' Clyde turned to look at Kev, nodding slowly until his friend caught on. 'But we're on the inside now. Official. We keep our eyes open, ears to the ground, and play the game. The long game.' He glanced at the screen and blew a psycho's head apart with his sniper rifle, then turned back to Kev. 'And hopefully one day, we might find some concrete evidence pertaining to the Needle beyond the enthusiastic beliefs of some mad monks. But in the meantime,' he dropped his pad next to him, gulped his coffee dregs, 'all we need to focus on is finding Talbot and shutting down this boogieman operation of his before the whole New York department comes under siege from—'

'An army of boogiemen?'

'I was going to be more specific and say a couple more Hangman-caliber assassins, but sure.' Clyde raised his knuckles for a fist bump. Kev saved the game, dropped his pad, and raised his own ethereal blue fist and bumped, transferring a portion of his telekinetic spectral energy into Clyde.

Clyde stood up, his fist momentarily glowing like an X-ray. 'Cool. Now let's get our asses in gear.'

3

Clyde carried a sound-suppressed semi-automatic rifle in his gloved hands, with two sound-suppressed pistols fastened to his body armor, and he even had a combat knife, a few frag grenades, and several flash-bangs. Such armaments would have offered most people a modicum of ease under the circumstances, but he still felt underdressed for this party, especially since he currently found himself depowered for reasons unknown; Kev hadn't even been able to enter the building, a complication their briefing hadn't accounted for. Clyde had even lost the charge he had stored back at Kev's apartment.

From the outside, it was just another warehouse in Queens, New York City, but two facts made it stand out: first, it was the only property in the moribund area of Willets Point that had received some quiet, privately-funded renovating; second, and most importantly, recent intel from one of Hourglass's forensic accountants identified the warehouse as a dummy corporation for the Cairnwood Society.

Clyde slowly paced down the bare tunnel, the strip lights starkly il-luminating beige-painted brick and yellow steel doors. The atmosphere of this place, the very air itself, seemed to carry an odor of anxiety and expectant death mixed-in with the more typical scents of dust and old paint. His eyes darted about, taking in every locked steel door and brick recess. It was the lack of cameras that really had him spooked. It was either sheer arrogance on Cairnwood's part—or rather Talbot's—or there was a very good reason why cameras were not a necessity.

Good security.

Deadly.

The stuff of nightmares.

'Anything, rook?' Ace spoke into Clyde's ear via comm-link.

Clyde flinched at the voice. Wound too tight. He stopped at the corner of the corridor and took a quick peek-a-boo around the corner, not wanting to risk getting his head shot off by a waiting gunman. Gunman...he should be so lucky. The adjoining hallway was clear.

'Nothing piled on nothing,' he replied softly. 'But there's something here somewhere. I know it.' Clyde felt the presence growing stronger, an uncomfortable sensation like that of a dozen cold dead hands pressing down on him, squeezing him. Suppressing him. The force keeping Kev from entering the premises. Kev, his best friend. The generator of their shared power. His teammate. His back-up. His responsibility.

Ace mumbled gruffly in agreement. He was a rough sort, his frequent long silences interspersed with grumbles or ex-hockey player trash talk. 'Fucking wimps. They want us divided for a reason. Think it'll make us easier pickings. Whoever's doing this is in for a fucking rude awakening.'

Clyde wished he felt so confident. The perks of being a Spark and not a currently handicapped Level 1 necromancer. He started down the next long corridor. He made it to the end untroubled and found a yellow steel door with a vertical slit of glass. 'I got a stairwell going into a basement.'

'Nothing bad ever happens in basements.' A third voice. Rose.

'Got a stairwell here at the west end too,' Ace said.

'We doing this?' Clyde asked. Keeping his finger along the trigger guard. 'Rose and I aren't at full strength here, and we don't know what's down there.'

'You pussying out?' Typical Ace.

'I'm playing it smart. Our intel didn't mention there was some type of PLE jammer on-site.'

PLE: Post-Life Entities. Official agency parlance for ghosts. Back-up teams of traditional agents surrounded the premises. No supernatural perks, only the best hardware and training a well-funded shadowy government agency could buy. The reconnaissance teams couldn't identify or even pinpoint the cause of the ghost jamming, but a nifty handheld radar toy had provided them with a glimpse through the large storage depot. The radar permeated most building materials except metal. Aside from the various steel doors outside and within, it was a brick structure. The radar had shown no signs of movement. Not even a mouse. If there was a hostile presence here, it was certainly of a very limited size. But the building's parking lot held a pair of Harley-Davidsons, and a few mid-range Hyundais and Fords. Clyde didn't suspect Talbot or one of his cufflink cohorts would be present, being the sort to only travel in a higher class of car or with a chauffeur, but those vehicles had owners, and those owners could still be here somewhere.

'Even if we find the source down there, we don't even know what *it* is, or if we can knock it out,' Clyde continued. 'And if this suspiciously empty place has anything to do with the assassins being sent after the agency, then we're at a significant tactical disadvantage going down there without Kev and the ISU.' The Intensive Scare Unit was the unofficial nickname for Rose's grisly army buddies, but it had stuck when Kev minted it.

'The nerd makes a good point, Ace,' Rose added.

Ace snorted. 'It's just a jammer, kids. If it's a gizmo, we break it. If it's a type of hex, we grab the conjuror and I'll shove an icicle up his tailpipe. This is us getting paid.'

Clyde shook his head at Ace's big-swinging-dick attitude but stayed silent. He thought about the reinforcement squads surrounding the site. A trickle of sweat slowly coursed down his spine, and he was sorely tempted to get Deputy Director Meadows on the line and have him dispatch a few more guns to search the place with them. But Clyde and his team were the tip of the spear, even if he and Rose had been temporarily reduced to little more than another pair of gun-slinging agents. All they had to do was dismantle whatever was interfering with their skillsets, and Clyde would feel a whole lot better.

He waited a full half-second before taking the plunge. 'Okay, snowman. You convinced me.' He tried not to think about the Hangman hiding somewhere down there. 'I'm moving into the stairwell. And Ace? If I die down here, I'll find a way to come back and haunt your ass.' To little surprise, he found the door unlocked.

'Just another Monday, kid.'

'Heading for a freight elevator,' Rose said. 'Don't do nothing stupid without me.'

Clyde edged into the amber-lit concrete stairwell. Just by standing at the top of the stairs, he felt a noticeable surge in pressure running along the knot twining Kev's soul thread to his. The jammer was definitely down there somewhere. Moving quietly, he counted ten landings before finding a door at the bottom. A pool of blood had seeped in from the other side. Clyde took a few shallow breaths and moved towards the door's small square window; it was dirty, but clear enough to provide a glimpse into a very large sub-basement. He pressed down on the handle gently, the door opening quietly on oiled, well-used hinges. A corpse had been slumped against the other side of the door and sagged into his path. It was a burly security guard, blood-soaked and with a look of complete horror etched onto his face, the lackluster light turning his eyes into pools of shadow. Clyde recognized the guard's company logo on his shoulder: CSS. Citadel Security Solutions. The same well-funded, morally misaligned assholes he had faced during his first outing. And just when he'd been starting to hope that any skeleton security staff would be composed of nothing more than rats and spiders.

Breathing slowly through his mouth, Clyde stepped over the body onto a metal walkway, holding his rifle up and scanning the large room, which opened up and stretched out to the right of his position. It was enormous, easily four stories high and probably half the length of a football field, awash in pools of eerie amber light, and with cobwebbed pipes snaking along walls and towards the ceiling.

The pressure increased within him, its alien magnetism continuing to rebuff Kev's entry. It was a violation. Frankly, it was now beginning to piss him off. He moved quietly towards the head of the stairs, spotting a few more dead bodies, one lying on the floor between him and a circular security hub occupying the center of the huge room. Another sat, legs akimbo, against a wall, chin resting on his bloody chest. The security hub was manned by a couple of bored-looking CSS guards, eyes glued to phone screens or some fascinating crack in a wall, untroubled by the corpses of their own men.

Before starting down the metal stairs, Clyde noticed what looked to be a huddle of bikers grouped around a fold-out table near a smoky far corner of the room, quietly playing cards, swilling beer, and exhaling enough blue poison to rival Detroit in its heyday. These details quickly became secondary to Clyde as he surveyed the back wall of the basement, his eyes scrolling up two tiers of what appeared to be prison cells, or as good as, only sans iron bars. He counted sixteen in total, but only one of the bottom-tier cells held an occupant, a lithe woman, he believed, her details obfuscated by distance, murky light, and wild hair cascading down her face in dark tangles. Was she floating? Her body appeared to hang forward from invisible wires at a near forty-five-degree angle, and all about her cell lay the remains of what could have been another five security guards, though it would be hard to tell until all the severed bits and pieces were accounted for. One of them even appeared to have been splattered across the floor like a large spill of engine oil and red paint.

A movement registered in the corner of Clyde's eye. A large brute slipping through a door and looming at the top of a short flight of stairs opposite him, a hockey jersey pulled over his body armor, and his favorite 1980s hockey goalie mask covering his face. It was always a comfort to know Ace was by your side. He didn't bother with firearms. He did just fine without standard-issue agency hardware.

Neither of them spoke over the comm-link; even their whispers might travel in this tall, narrow box of a room. They met in the middle of the walkway, shared a nod, and started down the stairs. Clyde kept his rifle sight fixed on the fed-up pair of guards. Their movements seemed a little off, a little jerky. Not to mention their apparent disinterest in their slaughtered pals, which was callous even for mercenaries. But Clyde's interest in them was purely out of proximity. It was the three bikers boozing and playing cards, their impersonal monosyllabism barely audible, who troubled him most. In Clyde's admittedly limited experience on the job, the bikers didn't seem the sort to get hired by a wealthy group like Cairnwood, not for rank-and-file security work, at least. That was what they paid CSS for. Which meant they were likely more than they appeared. He cut a glance at the anti-gravity woman in stasis, her cell ten yards or so from the bikers' table. Looked like the agency intel was on the money. This must be where Talbot had been storing his jacked-up lackeys.

Last week was Bai Li, the fire-breathing arsonist who had torched an Hourglass safehouse in Brooklyn. What shade of freak would the coma-tose woman and these bikers prove to be?

Clyde and Ace exchanged a weary glance as they approached the guard hub. Were they being intentionally ignored by the two guards? Ace's fists turned glacial blue, and the drop in ambient temperature caused a chill to run through Clyde, cooling his nervous sweat. The cement wall off to their left had a cage with some high-powered weaponry, but most of the equipment in there was for control rather than execution: cattle prods, flashbang grenades with launchers, a strange rifle Clyde had never seen before, which ended not in a barrel but what looked like a Tesla coil, various heavy-duty restraints, and what might be sedative darts; some of these pacifiers lay scattered about the room.

A few cautious steps later and Clyde understood why the hub guards were so utterly oblivious to the two intruders marching down on them. They were not bored. They were dead. Gray-skinned and white-eyed, blood still dripping from the puddles in their seats. Their motions were even more erratic up close, repeating the same bland, poorly coordinated tasks on a fixed loop. They reminded Clyde of crappy fairground animatronics.

Clyde glanced at Ace, tipping his head towards the bikers' table roughly twenty yards away, spewing a fog of cigar and joint smoke. Just when Clyde was thinking they must be blind or utterly indifferent to his and Ace's presence, one of the bikers peered over another's shoulder then, eyes pinning Clyde, and with an unheard comment, the three of them dropped their cards and stood up. One of them was such a physical freak it gave Clyde a start: a tall man whose whole anatomy was stretched out as though he had been halfway pulled apart by horses, his limbs grossly elongated. However, it was his head that repulsed Clyde the most, its deformation, the skull and features compressed and stretched tall into a crude shape. It reminded him of a steam whistle. Clyde had seen more than his fair share of eyesores in his short time as an Hourglass agent, but this guy was a real contender for the top spot.

Cocksure and loose, the bikers lined up before Clyde and Ace, cracking knuckles and rolling necks. The fact that they were empty-handed and dismissive of Clyde's assault rifle or the fact that Ace's hands were casually sculpting two large frozen gauntlets from thin air only confirmed Clyde's estimation that they were not here to simply play blackjack and look intimidating.

'Look at this, boys. It finally happened. A conjugal visit.' The biker in the middle was a man of gristle and sinew, with long black hair. A teardrop tattoo ran from one eye. The breast of his leather biker cut had the words *PRESIDENT* stitched above his name, *ANSELMO*. 'Now if I had to guess, you're the assholes who got us in this shit. But hey, I'm not complaining. Second chances and all.'

Clyde kept his rifle locked on the prez. 'You more of Talbot's lab rats?'

'Talbot...Talbot? That the English faggot? I overheard the name, heard him talking once or twice, but can't say I had any personal dealings with the guy.'

'That you?' Clyde tilted his head back towards the fresh corpses locked in their pointless pursuits and wasn't sure if their bored mimicry of life made him feel safer or more on edge. The disruptive influence dampening his necromantic ability had grown more intense, thrumming like an overheating generator. It wasn't a trinket or some conjuration jamming Kev's presence; it was one of the three thugs assembled before him. Now more than ever he suspected that this would be the fight he didn't walk away from. Without Kev, he was only a man with a gun.

Outmatched.

'Those poor fucks? Not our doing.' Anselmo pivoted at the waist and gave an amused smirk at the floating woman hovering there, as still as a department store dummy. 'Pretty cool though, huh? The new girl doesn't seem to be fitting in too well with the rest of us. She spends most of her time giving the brick wall the stink eye, but something set her off...oh, I don't know'—he consulted his cohorts—'a few hands ago?' The other two gave gallows grins and nodded. 'And she just put on the best show I've seen in years, killing all those dumb fucks. It was funny at first, watching them run around with their little zappers and needles and shit. Then I just felt kind of bad for them. Those two sorry fucks at the desk mainly. Meat puppets. Something's calmed her down now, though, but I don't know what. I do know it wasn't those piles of guts and their zappy sticks. Anyway, not that this hasn't been a welcome visit and all, 'cause believe me when I tell you we've gotten a little stir-crazy down here, especially since your people have been so busy mowing down our other poker buddies. And sadly, she's not the poker type.' Another smirk at the floating witch. 'Okay, I'm hearing the whispers again.' Anselmo's fingers twirled about his temple. 'Looks like we have a new game on our hands, fellas. Our spooky warden's tellin' me we need to show you some creative violence.'

'Fuckin' right,' said the huge, bald enforcer to Anselmo's right. His leather biker cut designated him as the club's *SGT AT ARMS*, below which was the name *GRIM*.

'Nothin' personal,' Anselmo added. 'We just owe a favor. And you're interrupting my beer.' That got a few chuckles from Grim and the fleshy pipe-headed crony whose biker patch provided his role and name as *ENFORCER* and *ROAD RASH*.

'Before we do this...' Ace brought his ice-slab fists up into a boxer's stance. 'Who are you assholes? Just so I know whose beer I'll be drinking.'

Anselmo smirked and gave a smug little turn, just enough to show his back and the name of his biker crew: Dukes of Purgatory.

'The only thing you're gonna be drinking is my piss.' Grim planted one big motorcycle boot forward, the flesh of his bare muscular arms and smooth-shaven head turning a dull-gray hue before settling into a shimmering polished chrome finish, and his deep-set eyes shone like green traffic lights above a midnight road.

Road Rash started to angle his way towards Clyde, which was when Clyde noticed the biker's forearms slowly altering themselves into meaty exhaust pipes, the cylinders so large they'd likely roar like gas-guzzling lions. Anselmo coasted back to his table and grabbed his unfinished bottle of beer, content to let his men warm things up.

While Ace and Grim moved in for close-quarters combat, Clyde squeezed the trigger, and several bursts of scorched lead sped towards Rash, who responded by belching a thick, noxious cloud of gas. It was like the discharge of a dozen city buses on a hot day. He then raised his bizarre body-horror exhaust-pipe arms into a firing position. Clyde, squinting through the roiling toxic vapors, strafed and fired, moving clear of the gas while aiming for the figure obfuscated by the murk. Two deafening booms, like the loudest engines on Earth backfiring, shook the room. The exhaust pipes peeking out from the flesh holsters of Rash's arms were actually some weird form of organic shotgun. Clyde was unmarked, using the drifting mass of dirty particulate to briefly mask his movement, but the blasts had obliterated large chunks out of the security hub and decapitated one of the corpse dummies. Rash was dangerous, but it wasn't due to his intelligence or strategizing, though he was certainly passionate in his wrath, his cannon barrels thundering again and again, making him a human death machine. Clyde stayed low, seeking his target, burst after three-round burst honing in on the elongated stickman slowly taking shape within the dissipating smog. There was nothing in the way of adequate cover, only open space, making this a foolish and desperate shoot-out, but Clyde wasn't about to turn and sprint back for the cover of the guard hub, risking a spine shredding from Rash's buckshot. He had to close the gap, get in close enough to knock aside those cannon-booming arms before they reduced him to puree. His movements were trained by repetition but guided by fear and instinct. Without Kev to round out his skillset and level the playing field, this was a fight he shouldn't be engaging in.

He stepped in with another rapid burst into Rash's chest, emptying the mag. The biker-creep barely shuddered from the impacts. Clyde swung his rifle stock to bar the aim of Rash's left arm, then cracked the heavy polymer stock into his opening jaw, keeping him from belching another fog of carbon monoxide. It bought Clyde a second or two, just long enough to pull his combat knife and slam it towards the cylindrical temple of Rash's head. The blade's tip impacted at a perfect angle but didn't penetrate, only scraping off a layer of Rash's skin. Going for the head wasn't always a guarantee. Rash swung his right arm like it was a lead pipe, slamming into Clyde's armor and staggering him. The right arm's barrel followed Clyde, and he rolled under the boom a split second before it could blow him in half. He came up into a crouch, seized Rash's left gun-arm and fought it into an arm lock. Clyde wasn't strong enough to wrestle this freak, but he only needed to keep his leverage for another second or two. He saw Rash levelling his right cannon at his head when the biker swore in panic. Clyde had wedged a fragmentation grenade into the ugly maw of the long gun. With a shuffle-step, Clyde got behind Rash and unloaded both pistols into the back of his long head; the bullets couldn't penetrate, but they still had enough kick to pitch the biker forward into a drunken stumble. The grenade went off with a muffled bang, the devastating damage being redirected into the torso of Rash. The enforcer faceplanted, pouring blood-speckled smoke from mouth and both barrels.

Amped-up on adrenaline and coughing any residual airborne filth from his lungs, Clyde holstered his pistols and reloaded his rifle, but he didn't draw on Grim. For all of Grim's threat and imposition, Ace was proving himself a much more skilled hand-to-hand combatant than the metal-skinned thug; Clyde knew first-hand how much it sucked to fight Ace, having been trained by him. Grim fought with determination and anger, a hostility that only grew with his impatience as Ace stayed in the pocket, slipping and bobbing as the chrome-plated fists whooshed by, then returning his own frosty flurries to ribs and jaw. Grim all but roared in frustration, hurling haymaker after haymaker in an attempt to shatter Ace's hockey mask and most likely the skull beneath. After a moment, Ace seemed to grow tired of his game and lowered his hands as if in surrender. Grim's green go-light eyes showed no mercy, and he swung again, almost falling over in the process. His boots had been frozen solid to the concrete.

'Quit fuckin' 'round, shit heel. FIGHT!' Grim was bending at the waist, hammering at the deep freeze trapping his shins.

'We just did. You lost.' Ace delivered an uppercut so powerful that it shattered his right gauntlet into powdered ice. Grim's green beams shut off, his eyelids lowered like steel shutters, and he sagged forward into Ace. Ace clapped his palm over Grim's broken jaw, which hung open like busted machinery, and froze the air within his mouth and throat, a growing obstruction choking the would-be assassin. Grim seemed to be verging on semi-consciousness, slowly regaining his senses but too powerless to resist. It didn't take long, the sub-zero temperature freezing his internals doing more damage than the choking.

Anselmo sat with his boots up on the card table, a cloud of pot smoke pouring from his nostrils. He crushed out the joint, finished his bottle, and dropped his legs. 'That's a pity. Rash was always an asshole, but I considered Grim a true brother, even without the MC patch.' He brushed aside the folds of his leather cut, revealing what looked like a motorcycle headlamp growing from between his pectorals. 'But it's cool. The highway to hell is a never-ending ride.'

The headlamp shone brightly, blindingly so at first, and a wild chorus of growling engines and riotous whoops permeated the air, causing a deafening din that reverberated off the walls. It was a disorienting effect, and it took Clyde a few moments to comprehend what was happening. Riding out of Anselmo's chest lamp along a yellow road of light came a wave of dead bikers: gunshots, junkie-eyed, truck-smashed, and one even fatally axe-wounded. Clyde noticed Road Rash and Grim amongst the posse and realized he must be looking at all the brethren Anselmo had lost in a lifetime of gang warfare, drug overdoses, and bloody police encounters. So that was the prez's power: his body was a kind of soul battery, storing the essences of his dead highway soldiers inside him before they could catch so much as a glimpse of the dystopic ever-after that was the Null. The ghost raiders left the despairing road of light and commenced circling Clyde and Ace.

Clyde watched the path of a few ghostly machines partially skirting through the walls without impediment. Anselmo wasn't through with his party trick; the veins of his forearms began to glow with oil and brimstone. A spectral chopper materialized between his legs, its damned engine rumbling like the belly of some hungry mechanical stallion.

And as quickly as it began, it stopped.

The cycle of ghost thugs vanished into faintly glowing wisps, the roar of their engines leaving with them. Anselmo's bike erased itself from the physical world, a fact he registered with a look of stunned confusion.

Coinciding with this unexpected turn, a flood of relief washed through Clyde; the jammer's effects had suddenly diminished. That meant Anselmo was the jammer, a traffic controller for spirits. Kev would be on his way here very soon, as would the ISU, but it seemed as though the short battle was over.

It seemed to Clyde that Anselmo had forgotten all about him and Ace, showing far more interest in the woman suspended in her cell above a pile of gore and limbs. To Clyde, she still looked to be asleep.

Clyde blew into his hands, still feeling the December chill of Ace's earlier activity, and that's when he noticed the reason for Anselmo's confusion. A series of red shimmering threads were now being slowly drawn out from his spine and limbs. Bloody puppet strings guided by an invisible marionette cross-brace.

'What...the...fuck!' Every word was a Herculean effort for the biker prez, his teeth clenched in agony, jaws locked as tight as his body.

Clyde saw the suspended woman twitch, a small movement akin to a muscle spasm, but it was the first of her awakening. She had a lithe build. Raising her arms leisurely, she could have been either puppet or puppeteer. She lifted her head to the ceiling of her cell, and her wild black hair fell away to reveal a doll mask, ceramic or bone, it was hard for Clyde to tell, but it was painted with an expression of almost sinister coyness. She stepped tentatively from thin air onto the concrete, leaving her confines and moving with a slow grace towards them. She started to move her arms in smooth circles; the motion made Clyde think of the old folks he'd sometimes see doing Tai Chi in the park. But this was no Tai Chi. The movements performed a much darker purpose. A group of stick-thin and featureless alabaster mannequins, ghastly in their motions, rose from the ground around Anselmo's boots, wrenched up from some unknown hell by barely glimpsed strings.

'The elevator's got no power.' Clyde was so enrapt by the scene before him that Rose's voice in his ear made him bounce on his toes. Rose couldn't get down here from her position. Clyde had half a mind to tell Ace to haul ass back to the stairs before pulling the pins on the rest of his grenades and tossing them at the contorting female and Anselmo. But why was she attacking one of her own instead of them? Wasn't she aware of who they were or why they were here?

What happened next happened very quickly. The mannequins climbed up Anselmo, chattering and clinking, helping to tear out his arteries and veins like a glistening scarlet wire mesh. The mess was almost as horrific as his howls of agony, which, mercifully, were short-lived. The blood-soaked puppets vanished back through the floor as though they'd had their own strings clipped. The doll-maker didn't waste time acknowledging the remains of Anselmo but shifted her blank mask to Clyde and Ace.

Clyde gripped his rifle a little tighter, then eased up, seeing the doll-maker's hands fly up to her face as she doubled over with a migraine.

A migraine shared with Clyde.

Behind the wall of throbbing pain, something moved inside Clyde's mind. Gently at first, slow and meek, perhaps troubled by its situation. It was a presence both alien and curious. Clyde didn't understand how he knew this, other than an innate sense of being scrutinized by something ancient and formidable. An image of chaos swirled in his mind, a ravaging storm of wind and light and dust, and as quickly as it arrived, the presence and the image departed.

The ragged-clothed puppeteer was not so lucky. Shrieking in agony, she beat at her temples and, doubled over, ran for the sealed freight elevator near the cells. Things only got weirder: just when it seemed like she was about to run headlong into the steel grating, a giant semi-transparent form enveloped her slender, agile body and crashed through the elevator door as though it were crepe paper. Clyde was about to put it down to his eyes being irritated by Rash's lingering particle matter, but he could have sworn the large form was that of a giant stuffed gorilla. A monstrous green cuddly toy with a banana peel for a tie.

Ace lifted his mask, revealing the frown of someone shaking off a skull-splitting thought invasion. 'Any thoughts on what just happened? Because that wasn't a hangover.'

'Rose,' Clyde said, 'forget coming down here. Something's on its way up to you.'

'Hey, you take the jammer down? Sarge and the ISU are here.'

'Good, you might need them. Some doll-woman-ghost-gorilla inbound. You'll see.'

The semi-transparent figure of Kev rocketed down through the ceiling.

'About damn time,' Kev said. The natural bluish tint of his appearance was marred somewhat by the amber lighting, except for the bullet hole in his chest, which remained a deep cobalt. He glanced about at the various corpses and the smashed-open elevator door. 'What did I miss?'

'Discount Donkey Kong.'

* * * * *

Agent Rose Hadfield had been on her way back from the unpowered freight elevator when she heard a distant crash and the groan of tortured metal. The noise seemed to be coming from somewhere deeper in the building. The basement, sub-basement maybe. It was around this time that her impressively sculpted shoulders and arms became invigorated, the sensation spreading all through her trim solid core and down her huge muscular thighs all the way to her calf muscles. Sure, she'd been an impressive physical specimen before all of this, a competitive power lifter who'd joined the army. But after a near-death experience, which blew her old squad to pieces during an ISIS skirmish in Syria, she'd discovered a strength fit for a demigoddess, the collective grief and anger of her demised war buddies fueling her muscles like a paranormal performance enhancer. Her possession of such strength wasn't dependent on geographic proximity to the ISU trio, but she liked their company. And right now, her muscles were telling her that the PLE jammer was down, and her body was once again the occupied barracks for the ISU.

There came a noise of rapid scrabbling speeding its way up the elevator shaft, and with the building lacking a second floor, it was coming straight towards her. The metal door crumpled outward, tearing from the frame and taking a good portion of the surrounding brickwork with it. The swirling brick dust veiled what emerged, but Rose could have sworn it was a gigantic stuffed monkey. Yet as the dust cleared, there was no giant monkey. Just a woman in white—more gray, actually—a patient's hospital gown? The woman's long dark hair fell away, showing Rose the painted mask hiding her face. She stared at Rose for a few moments as if assessing a threat. Rose was only five-foot-five, and despite not even tipping the scales at 130 pounds, her statuesque frame had a tendency to give others pause. Plus, she had a combat shotgun braced in her hands. Rose stared back, making her own assessments. The masked woman reached to her forehead, as though in response to a pounding headache.

Times like these made Rose grateful for dead allies. Sergeant Connors and Privates Barros and Darcy surged through her with a brief sensation like warm rain trickling down her spine. She sensed their concerns and internal chatter from within the interstitial command center advising her that the woman was a hostile. Another devil-jazzed freak for Talbot to unleash upon Hourglass.

But she wasn't attacking them yet. And she hadn't killed Ace or Clyde.

Rose lowered her shotgun an inch. 'Are you okay?'

Nothing.

'We can resolve this peacefully.'

Agency intel had posthumously revealed that the other assassins had been less than saints in their former lives. All had been career criminals, and one had been the subject of a three-state manhunt before being apprehended by the FBI. But intel had lacked any deeper knowledge on the creation of these exceptionally dangerous individuals and the means of their recruitment. The other enforcers had been very clear and motivated in their intent to kill all things Hourglass, but this woman only seemed confused. Was Talbot also selecting innocent civilians?

'We can get you help.'

The woman suddenly jolted to life, her body sealed tight within that bizarre holographic monkey thing. Rose brought the shotgun to bear and squeezed the trigger. Pale arms sprouted from nowhere, hands snatching at the gun barrel and spoiling her aim, the blast pulverizing one of the rail lights and a chunk of cement in the ceiling. The playful smile of the humongous monkey grew in size as it bounded forth, four paws pummeling the ground. Rose looked about in surprise as the pale wooden arms became pale wooden bodies, puppets climbing out of spaces within thin air to wrest Rose and hold her steady.

They didn't have enough puppets for that.

Rose shrugged them off, picking one up to smash into another. But that was all she had time to do. Somewhere inside that goofy giant monkey, the doll-woman swung her left hand out in a backlash. Monkey see, monkey do. The paw smashed into Rose like a speeding bus, sending her crashing through the brick wall into the large empty lot outside the building. The tarmac was still warm from the day's stifling heat. If Rose had been an ordinary woman, they would have been scraping and jet-washing her off the brick. Dazed but fighting-fit, Rose rolled over and jumped back to her feet. She was hearing the ISU running through potential strategies when several of the featureless mannequins crowded about the hole in the wall, peeking around the broken edges as if to observe Rose. The yellow-orange floodlights of the parking lot shone on their smooth faces. They backed away respectfully as their creator stepped out into the open, the monkey-suit vanishing once more.

Rose clenched her fists and had a sudden desire to pile-drive the toy-making skank into the asphalt. The doll queen made a half-hearted twirl, luxuriating in the warm night air. Her white slippers left the ground as invisible wires carried her up, up and away, running and bounding through the air.

Rose watched her vanish over some adjacent warehouse rooftops and was about to call it in to the perimeter teams keeping watch when she saw them already piling into view with lots of animated hand movements and order-relaying. They had aerial drones and a chopper in the area that should be able to track her. Feeling none too pleased with how the brief fight had gone down, Rose kicked a chunk of brick like a soccer ball and watched it sail like a missile across twenty yards of open lot before putting a big dent in a dumpster and then disintegrating. She fixed her platinum ponytail and waited for Clyde and the others to catch up.

4

Dolores Ricci alighted onto the debris-littered rooftop of a debris-littered building, releasing her invisible strings. The presence in her head persisted, imposing itself with an ever-increasing strength. She didn't know the intruder's purpose or its name, but she recognized its voice, ordering her to submit herself wholly.

And she feared it.

There was quite a bit she didn't know about these last few...what? Was it days? Months? It might have been years for all she knew. Her conscious self, along with her history and her very identity, had been reduced to a hazy sequence of gaps and perplexing imagery. Her graceful fingers tapped lovingly at her mask. She had chosen her persona of Doll-Face, of this she was quite sure. Some part of her told her that it was important. It was her rock and her protection. But for all its worth, it couldn't keep the chilling commands from reverberating throughout her head, leeching her autonomy like a scalpel performing a lobotomy, each slice a memory, each slice a sliver of her independence.

Her fingers went numb, robbing her mask of her caress. Her arms tingled with pins and needles, the lean and taut muscles feeling as though they were empty skin sacks filling up with cement. Her dark eyes stared fiercely out upon the desolation of Willets Point, the "Iron Triangle": a vast industrial area composed mainly of automotive repair and salvage shops, junkyards, and abandoned squalor awaiting the city's long-promised urban renewal.

It was as though she was hanging on by her nails, each one peeling back and breaking, the slippery floor sloping into an ever-increasing gradient, pitching her into the black void below. She couldn't fight it, as much as she tried. It was incredible she had made it this far, this long, against its will. But her knees were beginning to bend, her back arching over, the constant fog of confusion and concealment rolling in across the banks of her mind. Even her mannequins, even her old friend Banana Panic, couldn't help her now. She collapsed into a heap on the filthy roof.

* * * * *

A large figure, terrifying in both shadow and light, landed on the roof with a soft grace that was unfitting for his size. It was a man. Had *been* a man, but how much remained was debatable. He was clad in boots, dark pants, and a black T-shirt that strained against his pumped-up physique. The skin of his muscular arms was pale as bone, but how much of it was on display at any given moment depended on circumstance. Coils of barbed wire slithered around his thick forearms like adders seeking sustenance, slithering back into the flesh without spilling a drop of blood. His whole head was a tangled nest of living barbed wire, so densely layered and articulate that it was capable of mimicking the expressions of the man's true face underneath. The razor-sharp cocoon peeled away rapidly, wire by wire, until only several of the most stubborn remained hitched to the pale, blonde man's cheeks, jaw, and scalp, like earthworms stranded on concrete. He moved over to where Doll-Face lay, and something that might have been compassion peered out of his almost black eyes. Dolores murmured as though lost in a bad dream.

Squatting down slowly, the man placed a large hand on her back, stir-ring her. He knew her exhaustion. He had served others in his life, their violent wills in tandem with his own dark nature, though he remembered little of such relationships now. For now, there was only the one voice. The one preaching silence and compliance.

Except...

That one time...?

No.

Yes.

Now and then it was like there was another voice, quietly muttering from the shadows of his trapped mind, speaking of dangerous things. Rebellion.

He might have heard it whispering just then too, but as quickly as it arrived, it disappeared. Rejected by the ruling voice guiding his will. His diminished psyche was loathe to accommodate anything other than the Master's voice. The Master had a name. Many, he perceived, but none it admired more than Master.

Doll-Face sat up in a ragdoll pose, hunched over, staring at the roof between her splayed legs. Her mind was a black space. Nothing but the call to return echoed inside her skull. Wires pulled her to her feet, and her dancer's agility quickly returned to her limbs. She looked at the huge, frightful man before her, as if sensing some commonality between them.

Together they turned to watch the approach of several aerial drones sweeping across the blighted wastelands. The nest of barbed wires quickly formed over the man's face and head as he stepped to the edge of the roof. Together, the Hangman and Doll-Face cut their way across the shadowy landscape of urban ruin like a pair of midnight blades, beckoned home by a shared lord: Charon.

5

Clyde and Kev met Ace outside their apartment building, his van rumbling with the rhythmic thunder of Geddy Lee's bass guitar and Neil Peart's drumming. Clyde was happy his building didn't have a concierge to trade a sheepish smile with. The van was custom painted in true 1980s heavy metal D&D, complete with swords, demons, magic, valiant barbarians, and some dubiously dressed warrior babes standing before a hellish landscape. The ironic part was that Ace—and Rose too, to be fair—referred to Clyde as a geek or nerd because of his passion for comic-books. But this van! Jack Kirby on a crucifix—just look at this shit!

Ace was hunched over the wheel, all but tapping an imaginary wrist-watch. 'Let's rock 'n' roll, sweethearts.'

It was an hour's drive from Brooklyn to the Madhouse in Oyster Bay, Nassau County.

Clyde could feel the heat already starting to rise in the city, and it wasn't even 8 am yet. He jumped into the van with Kev. Ordinarily, Kev could have passed through the van's door to materialize on the inside, but when out in public he was nothing if not cautious when it came to his conduct. It was one of the reasons why he continued to dress in outlandish outfits that hid every inch of his bluish self, even if the overall effect was the look of a blind person getting dressed in a laundromat. He was a hair's-breadth from wearing a full Halloween costume, or perhaps a burka, every time he stepped out the door. His go-to disguise was all the more conspicuous for the weather: fleece-lined bomber jacket, old jeans and sneakers, aviator shades, wool-eared trapper hat, and a scarf wrapped around the lower half of his face. Clyde had spoken to him about finding a less ridiculous outfit for his public wanderings, but Kev never listened.

As per routine, Ace gestured to the second coffee in the cupholder. A caramel latte for Clyde. Also as per routine, 'One of these days you should splash out and buy your own ride.'

'And pass up another opportunity to be caught dead in this thing?' Clyde reached for his coffee and awaited a verbal retaliation from Ace, but instead the ex-hockey-thug-turned-departmental-AC-unit mumbled a few choice words and focused on the sweet sounds of Rush.

They were a band Clyde could do without, especially since he recalled several training sessions involving Ace beating the living shit out of him to their back catalogue. But he didn't give Ace too hard a time about it. They were his fellow countrymen after all, and probably eased some of the frost giant's homesickness. Ace steered the van onto I-495 East and put his foot down.

* * * * *

The Madhouse was a suitable moniker for the local Hourglass branch. Six floors and two vast wings of mostly original red brick extended from a large central building, complete with a cloistered entryway.

Formerly known as the Baxter Institute, the building had shut down in the 1940s due to underfunding, and the sadly all-too-common-for-the-era industry scandal of malpractice. The former psychiatric rehabilitation center had since been refitted into a state-of-the-art covert department for arcane espionage, intelligence, and, when required, wet work.

Accessible from secure private roads only, the large facility showed no outwardly visible signs of what it had become. But if somebody skillful or crazy enough managed to gain access to the hundred acres of open fields and glimpsed the edifice, they would naturally presume it to be just another dreary government institute. Totaling nine floors, including a basement and two sub-basements, the Madhouse had enough personnel to choke a shakylliris, a realm-hopping meat grazer larger than a sperm whale, according to a bestiary Kev had borrowed for some light reading. The building also extended back into the bay, where a very large private dock and airfield sat on concrete stanchions over the water.

Ace slowed the van to a stop outside an iron gate beneath a big stone archway. An electronic eye housed in the stone post scanned Ace's van, along with his, Clyde's, and Kev's credentials, before the gate quietly slid open. Ace continued along the path towards the expansive parking lot, sliding the van into a free space next to Rose's big red Jeep Wrangler. A couple of armed security guards double-checked and scanned their IDs again at the entrance.

As the pair of bullet-proof glass doors parted for them, they were greeted in the spacious lobby by a walking-talking reminder of the Baxter Institute's grisly and sensational closure: Dr. Martin Schulz. A jagged, crackling body of yellow electrical energy, he could maintain his original human appearance—that of a middle-aged man with a paunch and a thoughtful face, and a half-halo of hair around his bald head—so long as anger or any other powerful emotion didn't fuzz him into a static garble. Somehow, he was able to ground himself without becoming a hazardous electrical storm for the staff or the building's electronics.

Schulz had been the resident authority on psychiatry during the dark night of violence that closed the Institute's doors in 1943. A proponent of electroconvulsive therapy, Schulz had been working tirelessly with a schizophrenic patient who was adamant that a demon lived inside him. The doctor had been trying to chase the devil away with an electroshock session when a riot broke out in the hospital. Many patients and staff lost their lives in the tragedy, including Dr. Schulz, who, during the chaos, had found himself at the mercy of the "possessed" patient, who managed to overpower the doctor and administer him a lethal voltage.

While PLEs are very real, none of the dead from that controversial night had managed to escape the Null to haunt the living...and as for Schulz, he wasn't technically a ghost. But since he had seemed so intent on sticking around, Deputy Director Meadows had offered him a job when the Madhouse first opened its doors, allowing the venerable doctor to become the house psychiatrist and also act as the HQ's one-man power supply, regulating and interfacing with the intranet and the security system, including the lethal countermeasures; of course, back-up generators were present should something go awry.

None of the top brains at the Madhouse quite knew exactly what he was, and the few things Clyde had overheard were filled with the expected mindboggling jargon that made him stop caring. Perhaps Schulz was the product of a demon. When you've seen hell with your own two eyes, such things rarely raise an eyebrow. Maybe one of these days Clyde might strike up a conversation with him at the water cooler.

'What's crackling, Doc?' Kev asked.

'Good morning, gentlemen. Another busy day, I presume?' Schulz had been nothing but cordial to them since their posting, but the buzzy reverb of his voice couldn't help but lend it an ominous tone.

'I hope so, or I just got out of bed for nothing,' Ace replied.

'They're waiting for you in the forensics suite.'

* * * * *

The forensic department was in the R&D wing on the fourth floor. The lab was a curious blend of cutting-edge science and sterility, transplanted with the sort of outlandish set-pieces that Clyde associated with the arcane sci-fi extravagance of 1950s pop culture: the standard microscopes and spectrometers sharing the large lab with monstrous lasers, strange mechanical pods, and crystal-powered machines. He had no idea what a fraction of the equipment was for, but he sure enjoyed staring at it.

Rose was making short work of a strawberry protein shake, and the Intensive Scare Unit stood around jawing like chatty cadavers, the morning light beaming through the three of them like they were pale-blue windows. None of them would be winning any beauty pageants—the heinous wounds they'd received from a bomb blast during a peace-keeping operation in Rojava, Syria, made sure of that. Sergeant Richard J. Connors was the oldest of the three—older than Rose too, for that matter—and could have been a Hollywood leading man in a different life, one where his face hadn't been studded with shrapnel. Private Lewis Darcy was a big refrigerator of a Nebraska farm boy, his innocent face forever marred by his own coughed-up blood, and his guts perpetually hanging out of his abdomen. Then there was Private Savannah Barros, who'd left the mortal world in perhaps the messiest state of all. With her legs missing, and various scorch marks across her body, her apparition was that of a floating torso with arms.

Clyde wasn't sure why a person's ghost couldn't return to this plane in a more aesthetically pleasing manner, but when hell and misery was the final destination, it seemed like a minor cosmic injustice.

While the ISU were stuck with their battle-ruined combat fatigues, Rose was dressed for the weather in a cropped vest and loose shorts, flaunting her muscularity. 'Have a nice sleep-in, guys?' she asked.

'Not all of us get up at six am to bang and clang,' Clyde said, although he had done several miles on the treadmill and some pull-ups in his apartment around 7 am.

'I did my banging last night, clanged the bed frame against the wall a few times if that counts?' Ace added.

'Don't want to know your jerk-off schedule,' Barros said, never missing an opportunity for some bawdy banter, a reflex action for military types.

'I was hands-free. But your mom has a killer grip.'

Barros gave him the finger and a loving smile.

'Lay off him, Savannah. Your momma needs lovin' too,' Darcy chimed in. 'Besides, he's only making up for lost time. Can you imagine what he's had to screw up in Canada?'

'Yeah, a whole lot of elk,' Barros said.

Ace glanced at Barros's missing lower half and smiled like a wolf. 'Say what you will about elk. They got great legs.'

'Shut it down, you chittering nut sacks,' Sarge reined in the two chuckleheads.

Clyde was fidgeting about with a gas tap on one of the benches, waiting for the shit-slinging to finish. He remembered how his brother, Stephen, used to be pretty good with the playground insults, but personally, Clyde could only handle micro-doses of trash-talk.

Rose folded her impressive arms, a small frown of concern on her face. 'Any more of those headaches?'

Clyde tried to relive last night's sensation of something obtruding into his mind, bringing a hazy train of chaotic imagery. Ace shook his head in response to Rose's question, looking carefree, but Clyde was about to mention his unscheduled detour of dreamland prior to the mission before quickly dismissing the idea. They had enough on their plate for the moment without adding issues that might actually be *non*-issues. And he slept like a baby after the debriefing.

Deputy Director Frank Meadows, an aging, solidly built black man with trim iron-colored hair and a general disposition towards glum professional-ism, appeared in the doorway of the adjacent lab, tablet tucked under one arm, finished his briefing with one of the techs, and walked over to stand before the team. He glanced over his shoulder through the Plexiglas window at the other lab techs concluding their investigations. Clyde knew why Meadows was checking on whether the lab coats had gleaned anything useful from last night's corpses: it was regarding the source of their transformation. The arsonist, Bai Li, had gone up like a mini volcano in death, not leaving a great deal of anything useful for the research team to rake over; Niedermeyer had dissipated into a toxic cloud, wafting away on the breeze; and the failed hitmen before them—Darsh Acharya, Donald Rosenberg, and Angela Marquez— had similarly met problematic ends that left nothing for the techs to work with. Clyde stood straight, allowing him to peer across the room through the Plexiglas window. The chilled corpse of Grim lay on a surgical table.

The tech people had thawed him out of his deep freeze, but he remained in his chrome state in death.

'Could make a decent trophy,' Ace mused. 'Can I have him?' The metal man was trapped forever in his dramatic final moments, fists clenched, body wracked in a choking spasm.

The bizarre proportions of Road Rash were propped up on a second table, while a third held the nauseating remains of Anselmo, minus his vascular system.

'So the Hangman continues to elude us,' Meadows said. Clyde found it to be a paradoxical complaint: he certainly wanted Hangman dead, but never wanted to face him. 'At this point, I don't know if this is to taunt us, intimidate us, or if it's for his or Talbot's sadistic enjoyment. But as of now, the best and only lead we have in digging deeper into this—'

'Boogieman Project,' Kev interjected.

Meadows eyeballed Kev for a second or two, then actually seemed to warm to the title. '—If you will, is the identities of these men.' His tablet was connected via Wi-Fi to a large screen in the lab. Law enforcement files on the Dukes of Purgatory flashed up, settling on the mug shot and extensive rap sheet for Ryan Anselmo, followed by those for Franklin B. Grim and Skeeter 'Road Rash' Jones. 'Following identification of their motorcycle club and patch names, we used the interagency database search to glean what information we could about them. Records from the FBI and the Federal Bureau of Prisons indicate that they were recently incarcerated on Rikers Island for heroin transportation and murder charges. That was until one Doctor Julius Sharp, a board member at Elzinga Asylum, paid them separate visits, whereby he determined in his own professional opinion that they were each mentally unfit for the prison gen pop.' Skepticism tainted his words. 'He arranged for their transfer to Elzinga to be under his care.'

'Is Elzinga a legitimate hospital or another Cairnwood shell company?' Rose asked.

'Well, this place used to be legit.' Clyde rolled his eyes about the room in which they stood. 'Look at it now.'

Meadows didn't object, one hand already tapping away to bring up the websites and intel on Elzinga. 'It is legitimate.' Press and documentation pictures of a Gothic fort with some modern tech trimmings crowded the screen. 'But just because they're official doesn't mean they can't be cooking up some dubious work on the side.'

'Looks like a rehab unit for the Hammer Horror monsters.' Clyde skimmed through the paragraphs of information alongside the pictures.

Built in 1752 on Hunter Island, Bronx County, Elzinga Asylum was built as a haven for the growing number of Dutch fur traders and settlers. Dr. Frederik Elzinga commissioned the building to contend with the rising accounts of settlers experiencing extreme psychological malaise, supposedly visited upon them by the medicine man of an unaccountable and bellicose group of Native Americans in response to the Dutch invasion.

Academic journal articles and press releases replaced the institute's history and the images of the forest-dwelling keep, each with positive headlines or thoughtful poses of Dr. Julius Sharp. He was still young, mid-thirties maybe, slim with a dark complexion, smart spectacles, and a neat goatee.

'Now there's a face you can trust,' Sergeant Connors said.

'Looks like a weasel,' Barros added.

'We need to hold off judgement for the moment, at least until all the facts are in.' Meadows lowered the tablet to his side for a moment.

Clyde cut a look from the screen to the deputy. 'I'm taking a swing and saying you need us to snoop around the doc, try to find some connection to Talbot or any other Cairnwood types?'

'Softly, very softly,' Meadows affirmed. 'As I mentioned, Elzinga is an operational mental health facility, and whatever shady extracurricular activities Julius may or may not partake in, we can't risk showing our hand or causing any problematic incidents, be they direct or covert. It's a facility filled with troubled civilians—'

'And criminals.' Ace was blunt.

'Some of them. But not all. And the last thing they'll need is another paranoid delusion about ghosts or spies prowling the corridors.'

'Then the quacks can up their dosage,' Ace said without compassion. 'Those bikers left Rikers as run-of-the-mill pussies, then somewhere between Elzinga and last night they found themselves on a serious power trip. That nuthouse could be wall-to-wall with cons or any other asshole who feels like getting mean and nasty with us. Julius could be running a damn recruitment drive for Talbot.'

'It's a possibility, Ace, but I'm not one for authorizing reckless and unsubstantiated actions,' Meadows said.

Clyde thought about the moral compasses of the other assassins they'd encountered so far. All dangerous criminals, but none of whom had been incarcerated in this state, and therefore no connection to Julius Sharp. 'Any chance the Hangman was a former patient at Elzinga?'

'Unconfirmed, since we have been unsuccessful in acquiring any physical evidence from him. Database-wise, the man's a myth. However, Julius has a brother. Leonard. I don't know how clued-up any of you are in the world of business and entrepreneurial darlings, but Leonard is something of a roaring success. A true rags-to-riches story. I'm not sure where his initial capital came from. There have been rumors of criminal enterprises in his youth, but nothing ever stuck. Whatever the source may be, he used it to start a small local security firm, which went on to become a chugging juggernaut of global corporate security.'

'Cairnwood backing?' Barros asked.

'Unconfirmed. But this'—Meadows tapped a key—'is a red flag.' The logo of Citadel Security Solutions flashed up on the screen, complete with the polite, professional poses of the board members, an ethnically eclectic group, but all white teeth, smart haircuts, and unreadable eyes. 'Leonard's small-scale firm rebranded as CSS several years ago, and he remains the majority shareholder in the company.'

Clyde and the team first landed on Talbot's shit list for sabotaging a very lucrative and morally despicable energy project of Cairnwood's a month ago, which entailed the capture and utilization of fresh souls from the Null. CSS were attached to the project.

'The same private military dick-bags hired for that energy gig,' Rose said. 'Some of the officers we went up against had the sort of jazzed-up abilities you don't get from vitamins and protein powder.' Rose had traded punches with a blonde super-strong lieutenant before hurling him into the giant maw of a soul-sucking sky eel.

Clyde, for his part, had been in a battle to the death with a particularly vile CSS officer inside the staging area of Cairnwood's Brooklyn warehouse, a sadistic killer who tossed used shell casings around, the battlefield mementos stored with the obfuscating and disorientating smoke of warfare and gut-wrenching sounds of slaughtered non-combatants. Collateral. Playthings.

'So we put a pin in Elzinga and start looking into CSS. That energy gig might not have been a one-off job. Stands to reason that they're involved with Talbot's assembly-line assassins,' Clyde said, receiving a full round of agreement from the rest of the team.

Kev thrust a hand up on behalf of himself and the ISU. 'Hey-hey, before we get ahead of ourselves. If I'm going to be sneaking about their main office, I need to know what they're shooting. Do we have any idea if they're still being supplied with those Exorcist rounds?'

During that same Brooklyn warehouse raid, Kev had his beliefs about intangibility challenged when he was shot by a mystically-charged rifle round. It was his second gunshot wound, but unlike the original that had ended his mortal life, he was fortunate enough that the mystical bullet hadn't hit anything vital—if such a thing existed—and the wound eventually knitted itself back together.

'Engaging the enemy used to be a whole lot simpler for us dead folk until those bullets came on the scene,' Darcy said.

'Or maybe we've been getting too soft.' A look of near self-disgust formed on Sarge's shrapnel-peppered face.

'Having so little to work with, we've hit nothing but dead ends in that investigation,' Meadows said. 'A non-starter really. With an extensive list of public and private arms manufacturers, including black market and otherworldly, we're stuck with guesswork about who produced such ammunition. Assume they're loaded for ghost-hunting season, and you won't be surprised.'

'And the rest of us just need to worry about the Hangman and that doll chick,' Ace said.

'Don't forget her damn dirty ape,' Rose griped. 'But are we even sure Little Miss Cuddly Monkey is on their side?' She gestured through the window towards the gruesome corpse of the Dukes of Purgatory's leader. 'I don't think it's unfair to describe her actions as erratic.'

'I guess we'll find out the hard way,' Clyde answered.

Clyde didn't know what was knocking around his and Ace's skulls last night, or causing the doll-woman's psychic disturbance, but he doubted she was some ingénue in all of this. During the debriefing Meadows had disclosed some preliminary observations from the Hourglass forensic team regarding the sub-basement's holding cells. They had discovered that several of the cells bore various indicators of having been occupied by Talbot's former assassins: scorch marks, likely from Bai Li; a few poisoned cockroaches, presumably from Niedermeyer; and hints from a couple of others, essentially confirming that the site had been a holding facility for paranormal killers. No innocent woman would be keeping such company. But what remained unclear was why the assassins appeared to be arriving in such a haphazard fashion, and Clyde wasn't alone in wondering why Talbot wasn't simply stockpiling a large army of monstrous operatives to send at Hourglass's finest en masse rather than the previously solitary assassination attempts. The working theory was that whatever the means of creating them, it was far from perfect. Perhaps the doll-maker's freak-out was further proof of this.

Meadows shut his tablet off and took a breath. 'Before I start to make the calls and strategize any moves on Leonard Sharp and the CSS, I have an announcement to make regarding this squad. You've all been handling this assassin threat commendably, but then I also thought my previous squad were world-beaters.' A look of regret was there, then gone. 'We're up against a very credible threat here, and we need numbers. I'd add another two dozen to your strike team if the assets permitted, but our more exceptional operators are stretched thin at the moment. But I do have one new member for the ranks.'

Kev nudged Clyde in the arm. 'Looks like we're officially no longer the new guys.'

'What are they bringing to the game?' Ace was running a big knuckle against his handlebar mustache.

'Actually, she shares a trait with you, Ace,' Meadows said. 'She's a Spark.'

6

The cresting sun blazed through the boxing gym's windows, turning the twirling dust motes into gold shavings. Leonard Sharp leaned against the corner of the twenty-foot boxing ring, his labored exertions burning with furnace heat. He spat his gum shield into his glove and pawed sweat from his eyes. For a forty-five-year-old man, he was in exceptional condition. A true Spartan, standing six-foot-two and 230 pounds, with a shaved head and goatee that was only recently beginning to show the first traces of silver.

'When he wakes up, pay him double.'

He watched two of his entourage help the ringside physician carry the former top-ranked-boxer-turned-top-class sparring partner out of the ring, just short of fetching a stretcher. The felled opponent wasn't the first respected slugger to collapse under Leonard's fists, and he probably wouldn't be the last. Some CEOs played golf or tennis, but Leonard's lifelong passion was the sweet science. Shaking loose, he stepped out from between the ropes. With some energy left to burn, he moved over to the row of heavy punch bags and, over the sounds of Curtis Mayfield's

"Pusherman," made one dance to his thunder. A torn seam along the leather's side spewed stuffing like a lung coughing up blood. He'd need to tape it up again later.

The gym had the bare-brick, rundown aesthetic Leonard valued, with only the basic equipment required to harness and sculpt a fighter. The greatest pieces of equipment were the heart and the guts, not fitness trends and a juice bar. He liked the atmosphere to be uninviting, intimidating, one that evoked desperation and fanned the flames of determination within any underprivileged fighter striving to escape the ghetto. As a youth, he had been a permanent fixture at Colt's, a brutal proving ground in the Bronx that became the prominent gym for all local aspiring pugilists after the world-famous Gleason's uprooted itself to Manhattan in '74.

But this wasn't Colt's, and it was no longer the Bronx. The past shaped a person, instilled them with certain qualities, ones that, if the person valued them enough, could be carried anywhere in life. There was one luxurious concession in this crucible that Leonard not only allowed but found indispensable: the floor-to-ceiling windows overlooking midtown Manhattan. A spectacular view that reminded him every day just how far he had climbed. And how much he stood to lose.

Midtown: just a piece of the city he once controlled.

'Shit, Len. Looks like you killed that young 'un.' Leonard squinted at the man approaching him. Even with the sting of sweat in his eyes, he recognized the tied-back dreadlocks and the man's unique skin condition. Ronnie "Zebra" Thompson, a tall and imposing African-American man born with a particularly severe case of vitiligo that left his whole body from scalp to toe with pale stripes, watched the stone-cold fighter being hauled out of the gym. Zeb removed his sunglasses and moved slowly about a neighboring heavy bag, moving well, throwing a few gentle taps without wanting to crease his charcoal-gray suit. He made a point of glancing back at the concussed boxer only now finding his legs. 'Is it that bad?'

Leonard thought about the phone call he had received from Edward Talbot last night. 'Just business,' he said between combinations, firing a few stiff jabs and a right cross. A left hook to the body, then the head. 'I need to talk to y'all about how we're going to manage our arrangements going forward.'

'A'ight, well, that's why we're here. The others are waiting in your office when you're ready.'

Leonard's grunts grew more animalistic as his combinations began to change back and forth from speedy flurries to sheer power, the bag convulsing violently. Finally, his fists dropped. Feeling the tension leaking from his muscles along with the sweat, he moved over to the vista granted by the windows, removed his black ten-ounce gloves, and set about peeling off the soiled hand-wraps. He sipped from his water bottle, pulled on a thin sleeveless hoodie, and, grabbing his towel from beside the boxing ring, led Zeb outside. A single step over the threshold took them from a lion's den to sleek, penthouse opulence. With the exception of the gym, the rest of the suite was an open-plan design, bright and airy with tasteful art of pugilists and prized boxing memorabilia tying the room together. Leonard led Zeb back through the suite towards the elevator.

'Is this about the beef with Charlie?' Zeb asked.

'Amongst other things.' Preoccupied, Leonard poked the button for the floor below.

They left the elevator and took a short walk to a spacious, glass-walled conference room where a small assembly of Leonard's most loyal confederates waited, talking easily amongst themselves. All of them were seated around the long table in black leather chairs, except for the one man who stood patiently near the head of the table. Harlan Brink, ex-Navy SEAL operator turned co-founder and managerial head of Citadel Security Solutions. He was the only white man in the room, his rusty crewcut blazing in the sun, and, unlike the rest of Leonard's top earners, he wasn't outfitted in a nice suit and expensive, status-defining jewelry but instead had chosen to conceal his sidearm beneath a simple silk shirt and dark slacks.

'Gentlemen, I apologize for the short notice of this meeting. I know it's early.' Leonard dabbed his face with the towel and sipped his water, choosing to remain standing at the head of the table before his men, all steadfast killers who had traded gang colors for suits, and wished he had taken the time to have a quick shower. But he wanted to get this over with quickly before getting on with his day. 'First...Easton, Whittaker, nice work in handling all this bullshit with Charlie "Horse." You and your boys kept your cool, and that motherfucker was really pushing for a pine box. Luckily it didn't come to that, because you handled your shit.'

'I'm thinkin' I should get into politics, movin' into City Hall. What you think, Len? Think you could endorse me?' Easton asked, receiving a few chuckles from around the table. Slouched back in his chair with cool indifference, golden teeth catching the morning light, gold-ringed hands laced over his stomach, and a small sword tattoo proudly adorning his left cheek, Easton was a street-corner hoodlum who seemed to enjoy fighting his more modern sartorial refinement.

'So Charlie been muzzled?' Whittaker asked. A human boulder with a pencil-thin mustache and a smooth lover's voice to match.

'He's gained a new perspective. Being dangled from the roof of your own restaurant will do that to a person,' Leonard answered.

'Hangman?' Zeb asked.

A look of unease passed like a chill through the hardened gangsters. Leonard even noticed Brink adjusting his posture slightly, lifting his chin a little in attention.

'Nate, yeah.' Leonard still thought of him as Nathan. The Hangman name had been synonymous with Nathan Moore for almost as long as Leonard had known him, but he knew the man behind the gangland legend. 'But it's up to us to make sure Charlie doesn't take this incident to heart, for the sake of our collective interests.'

'You talkin' 'bout extending some olive branch here?' Easton asked contentiously.

'I'm talking about maintaining the smooth operation of our shared enterprise. Things got heated, but we still need Charlie's connections. He answers to me, but without him, we lose our distribution pipeline.' Charlie "Horse" Shen was the "dragon head" of the Black Lotus Triad gang and the link to the East Coast's heroin fortune. 'I accepted responsibility for the Fed-busted shipment and made reparations by sacrificing Anselmo and some of his MC to the Feds. That was me doing things the easy way. Charlie had a sudden attack of ego and went too far, but I was able to have Nate reiterate whose city he is in. Now we need to put this behind us and allow business to return to normal because—here's the rub—should things escalate between us and the triad again, I might not have Nate on hand to pay Charlie another call. Talbot's locked him away again. But we got to the top of this pile the old-fashioned way, with focus and determination. That's what's kept us here all this time, and it will *continue* to keep us here. But...the threat of *the Hangman* can still come in handy if Charlie or any other fool starts pushing boundaries.' He had the whole table in the palm of his hand. 'Business with the Black Lotus goes back to normal. No hostilities. Project power and control, and the rest will follow.'

'I don't know, Leonard. Seems to me that you don't get much more old-fashioned than demons and all that Biblical shit.' Whittaker shifted in his seat. He wasn't attempting to undermine Leonard but had remained ill at ease ever since the shadows had bared their teeth. His basic world of hustling and survival was now a far scarier place. His statement was met with solemn approval.

Zeb had been giving a potted plant a thousand-yard stare before speaking up. 'What if Charlie or somebody else gets a Hangman of their own?'

Leonard gave him a dirty look, not appreciating the complication. 'It won't happen. I'm Talbot's appointed liaison. I'm too well connected in this city, with an overlap of influence that is useful for him and Cairnwood.' Without breaking his hold on their attention, he leaned forward on the table and pointed out the office windows to the Manhattan skyline. 'I owned this fucking city. We all came from the same streets. Those poverty-stricken projects of Castle Hill, just scrawny kids forced into choosing between a life of guns and narcotics or starving to death in some gutter. Most of you have been with me since the beginning and have been integral in helping me take the South-East Sovereigns from the corner to the boardroom. No one is kicking us out of our own damn house.' He thought about his younger brother, Julius, locked away in Elzinga Asylum, selecting candidates for Talbot's sideshow army. 'And if it's any comfort for those of you still in doubt, Anselmo and his boys were killed last night at their holding pen.'

The disciplined stoicism of Brink finally cracked. 'The same team?'

Leonard nodded. The Hourglass team had killed several squads of CSS, including several of Brink's best officer-class contractors, each of whom had been paranormally enhanced.

'Talbot seems to be struggling to reproduce another hitter of Nate's caliber.'

Zeb chuckled. 'That crazy white boy was bad enough when he was just a dude.'

Easton exhaled sharply, rubbing the gang's sword logo on his left cheek. 'Shit, he made me feel like a half-stepper back in the day.'

Leonard knew better than anyone else in the room how ruthless and dependable Nathan had been in his organization's rise. He rubbed his fingers over the old gunshot scar on his chest, a habit that subconsciously reared its head every time he reminisced about the good old bad days.

'I'll never forgive Talbot for doing what he did to Nate, but right now we need to focus on restoring peace to our syndicate. Calm the nerves and any more jumpy triggers—not just Charlie's, but all of our associates— before Talbot begins to question our suitability in keeping our house in order.'

'*Pssht*. More and more it's starting to feel like *his* house, and we're nothin' but that cracker's house slaves,' Easton said, staring out the window.

Leonard understood his anger but also knew it was an overstatement born of frustration rather than fact. Their business largely remained the same, and while Talbot was himself a businessman, his enterprises were focused on avenues that led to much darker and inexplicable things. The only area of professional crossover to date was Talbot's interest in Citadel, which was negligible, at least for the moment. However, his continued use of Julius for his sick little schemes against the covert Hourglass agency did trouble Leonard greatly. He checked the clock on the wall. It was to be another busy day, and he wanted to talk to his little brother. Just to check in.

'This is still our world. No one's taking our crown.' Leonard gently rapped his fist into his open palm and placed the towel about his shoulders. The top earners around the table read the mood: the meeting was concluded, and there was money to be made.

'Get back to work, gentlemen. And don't trample on any Lotus.'

Everybody filed out except for Zeb and the phlegmatic Brink.

'We're going up to see Julius,' Leonard said. 'I'm sick of having nothing but text exchanges with him.'

'He's okay, right? Physically?' Zeb asked. The connotation of his meaning made the atmosphere heavy.

'He's fine,' Leonard stated. 'It's not his physical health I'm concerned about.'

'Do we have an appointment?' Brink asked.

'Fuck Talbot and his appointments. I want to see my brother.' Leonard was quickly becoming a bundle of tension again.

'Jules will be okay,' Zeb said. 'I know it doesn't seem it, him being in that place, goddamn inhuman resources or whatever the shit it is, but it's probably the safest place for him to be. He's found himself on the managerial side. Talbot needs him where he is.'

Brink agreed with a crisp nod. 'He's fulfilling a crucial role for your whole organization. He's doing this for you. Drawing in recruits from the jumpsuit and straitjacket crowds keeps Talbot from considering other options, like conscription from our own talent pool. Captain Agua was a tremendous asset to our firm, and I'm sorry to have lost him to Cairnwood's sabotaged energy deal, but he volunteered for Talbot's program. If not for Julius's placement, we could have our entire CSS personnel, plus your street soldiers, being marched single file into getting some upgrade that could just as soon kill them as make them into a superweapon.'

'That Brit gives off some real old-money slave-master vibes. He's probably already thought about conscription. Chalky motherfucker.' Zeb smirked innocently at Brink. 'I'd say no offense, but look at me.' He gestured to the stripes of his appellation. 'I could make an argument for being black or white depending on the complexion of the room I'm in. But if Talbot does start looking at us, looking for some lowly inner-city element to work on, then I'm sayin' right now that I won't be going quietly. Look at this suit, this watch. Do I look destitute and in need of a handout? I ain't getting drafted. He already took Nathan from us.'

Leonard looked thoughtfully at Zeb and Brink, his closest allies in Nathan's absence. 'He took him because he sensed something in him. Let's be clear, he wasn't wrong in that. We don't know what the fuck Talbot is, but maybe he can sense the killer in people.'

That didn't placate Zeb. 'We're *all* killers.'

'Moore did have a certain sadistic streak in his methods,' Brink said, 'but I think Mr. Thompson has a point. Talbot took him to make a statement, to show that he's just walked in and took something valuable of yours.'

Leonard took a deep breath, then exhaled calmly through his nose. 'I've never backed down from anybody in my life. But I don't know how we fight something like this. I don't see how we can. The wealth and the backing Cairnwood have, magic and who knows what other kind of crazy shit...this is a whole different weight class.'

Brink's expression never changed. 'We do what all successful military campaigns do: gather intel and search for weaknesses. In the meantime, we hold the line.'

Leonard's eyes shifted to the Empire State Building, and he thought of the legacy its designers and builders had left behind: Sharp Industries, his own contribution to the Manhattan skyline, a monumental conglomerate nestled amongst the Financial District's glass and gilded towers. It was the crowning achievement of his corporate life, but it still paled against the majesty of the Empire State Building. Still, Edward Talbot didn't have a tower with his name on it.

Leonard headed towards the door. 'Make yourselves an espresso while I get a shower. We leave in fifteen.'

7

She was guided by punk-rock fury, honing the angry sound of "Sonic Reducer" by the Dead Boys into bright-violet missiles. Clyde didn't understand what he was seeing at first, but he couldn't look away. An East Asian woman with a punk aesthetic, her long black hair streaked with purple and buzzed short on one side, and a pair of wrap-around headphones stood defiantly in the center of the Madhouse's training room, playing air bass but not really. It seemed to be a real enough bass guitar, only one made of pure violet energy. Her fingers galloped across glowing neon strings, the resulting rhythms blasting shockwaves through the artificially-created monsters charging at her.

'Audiokinesis,' Meadows said in response to the team's bafflement. 'The absorption of any sound, which is then stored and converted into physical force.'

Ace looked like a big happy dog at the new recruit's gimmick. 'That's a power *and* a woman I can get behind.'

'You'll be getting nowhere near her behind,' Meadows flatly stated, his voice carrying the weight of paternal threat.

'No offense, Chief. She's too young for me anyway.' He paused a beat. 'She your daughter or something? You get the yellow fever as a slightly younger man?'

Meadows was a long way from the army and the CIA, so he allowed such talk. It was only natural that certain workplace formalities would buckle when you played in the big game.

'She's not my daughter, but she and her family mean a great deal to me. So you keep it in your pants or I'll grab you by that handlebar mustache and knock out what few teeth remain in your head.' Meadows was so casual in his warning he could have been reading out a weather report.

Ace was unmistakably the bigger of the two men, but the much older Meadows had a quiet presence about him. A bad omen.

Ace smiled, showing the gaps in his gum-line, souvenirs from his hockey goon days. 'I knew there was a reason why I respected you.'

With a brash laugh, Rose gave Ace a punch in his arm that would have felled a lesser man, or maybe a tree.

Clyde was captivated, watching the newcomer silently destroy one flesh-hungry beast after another, bobbing her head to the music pumping into her from her headphones. 'What branch is she from?'

'None. This is her first time out,' Meadows said.

The strings of her sound-borne bass guitar were not superfluous or merely a means to anchor her fingers to the flashy weapon, but actually generated musical notes. She wasn't only audibly playing along to the song, she was putting on a show like she was a headline act at some riotous punk festival, stopping the gates of hell with nothing but attitude and the power of rock.

The particular hell in question was being wrought by a training simulator known as the Rorschach, a threat-variable combat test that was largely the product of Schulz, who had helped Meadows's predecessors brainstorm the project, along with some of the mystically-minded faculty. It worked as follows: a part of Schulz's intelligence powered the training room's program, his mind not only watching carefully over the agent's progress but also creating any manner of animal, vegetable, mineral, or monster for the room's enchanted components to fabricate into aggressive, living inkblots.

Clyde and the team had used it since their arrival. It was a little different from how he and Kev had been trained back at Indigo Mesa. The New Mexico branch used the Djinn, which, like the Rorschach, was much more than some agency-contrived tool. The Djinn was, in fact, a very real entity, captured by powerful incantations and stored in the type of hybridized magic-science machine Clyde would never dare ask to be explained. He had just called it the Lamp, like all the other non-tech-heads.

It was a true crash course in Special Forces combat training.

Right now, Schulz's particular assessment was gearing up to a high level with the arrival of a huge thing, a *giant* thing resembling a carrion moth with a scorpion tail, the sort of fever-dream concoction that might lurk in a forest on the verge of death. It beat its shadowy wings with a slow deliberation, their span almost encompassing the whole domed chamber, and reared its segmented onyx tail, the stinger dripping what looked like filthy rainwater. It didn't get much further than that. Clyde watched as the punk chick joyously slid across the floor on her knees, striking a single deep, pulsing bass note.

The symmetrical inkblot fell like liquescent autumn, each black-and-gray smear being absorbed back into the room without leaving so much as a stain behind.

There was to be no encore. The sound-generated bass crackled out of her hands. Schulz appeared in the middle of the room, clapping heartily as though cheering the end of a wonderful theater production.

She turned around and glanced up at Clyde and the team watching from the observation window, raising her arm in a flourish and bowing like a rock star.

She'd been in mortal danger throughout but had made the whole session look like nothing more than a bit of reckless fun.

'What's her name again?' Clyde asked.

* * * * *

'Natalie Mondragon,' the new Spark said. 'And yes, it's a bad-ass last name.'

She was a Filipina, mid-twenties, in ripped jeans with a ripped U.K. Subs T-shirt and jingled with chains and studded bracelets. Her blasé scowl was painted with smudged black eyeliner. Clyde thought she was a knockout.

'That was some show you put on in there. Who needs a rifle when you can make war with music, huh?' Rose said. They were clustered around the marble fountain in the Madhouse's rear courtyard, the pruned elm trees lush and green with their summer coats. 'I don't know where Meadows has been hiding you, but I'm glad he decided to share you with the rest of the class.'

'Me too.' Ace's comment would have seemed innocuous if it had come from the lips of anybody else. Rose gave him another stinging shoulder tap.

'Going through Rorschach's wringer like that, it's impressive that you have no field experience,' Rose added.

Natalie gave a slight shrug, the compliment entering into awkward territory. She seemed to be searching for the easiest way through this thicket. 'My family has baggage. Lots of it. I'm talking fuckin' suitcases full.' She forced a cough, a sharp throat-clear, and used the sound to create a tiny violet dart that whizzed through the air, splitting an elm leaf on a nearby branch. Gesturing to the twirling leaf halves, she said, 'I couldn't ignore who I was anymore. And my dad's tight with the head honcho here, so I've been training in secret. It hasn't been a total summer-school, situation though.' Her hands made a split-second air-bass run. 'Work and play.'

Clyde checked out the tattoos covering her arms. One especially drew his attention: a cartoon skeleton with big bucket headphones, a bass slung over its shoulder like a soldier's rifle, and a beautiful glowing violet aura about its bleached white hands. The great piece made him realize once again how little he'd been drawing for himself lately, not counting his psycho-killer-pyramid pin-ups. It depressed him, how much all this Hangman and assassin business was weighing on his passion. He would make sure to give his floundering comic-book project some love and care when he got home tonight.

'So you play in a band?' he asked. He sat cross-legged on the fountain's rim, using a small twig to make figure-8s in the water.

'Used to. We did okay in the punk toilet circuit. We were called the Trojan Horse Cocks.'

'I love Christian rock,' Ace said, earning a respectable smirk from Nat. 'Never been big on the whole punk scene, though.'

Nat's eyes bounced like rubber balls between his White Snake T-shirt and back to his face. 'Hey, your loss, pal.'

'You local?' Clyde asked.

For all of Nat's outward confidence, she seemed a mite nervous about admitting the next part. 'Greenwich Village.' She said it like it was a dirty confession. 'My dad works at the Philippines Consulate.'

Clyde wondered how much of that factored into why she'd gone down her obvious rebellious live-wire route. 'Nice area. I didn't know civil servants got paid that well. If any jobs come up, tell him to give me a call.'

She feigned amusement. 'He has some old family money to help out.'

'Is your dad a Spark too?' Kev asked. 'Get him down here.'

Nat gave his bizarre wardrobe a humorous appraisal. 'He has the uncanny ability to be a bureaucrat and not die of boredom. But no, he's just a regular old dude.' She chose to time her last words with an eye swipe at Ace.

Kev glanced over at Meadows, who had wandered off a short way down the wide corridor of hedges and trees for some privacy, dappled by the sunlight as he spoke on his phone. 'Those suitcases of luggage you mentioned? You got *any* other Sparks on the Mondragon family tree?'

Clyde knew Kev was fishing for any other tidbit of information on the mysterious Spark phenomena while Meadows was out of earshot.

'You writing a book?' she asked defensively.

'He grows on you,' Clyde said of his bestie.

'So do lice,' she retorted, amused at Kev's hang-up on Sparks. 'So you're not writing a book...is it a Sparks fan club?'

Kev levitated the mirrored shades from his face, revealing the kind, bespectacled eyes underneath. 'They do seem to be one of the great mysteries in this field. I have an interest in them.' He shrugged nonchalantly. 'Shit, who wouldn't? Thought you might know a bit more than I've been able to find out from all the Secret Squirrel types around here.'

Ace made a small ice floe in the water and tossed it towards Kev, who started to casually flip it in the air like a pizza base.

Meadows had ended his call and was on his way back to the group, his black leather shoes silent on the flagstones.

'Drop the bone, Fido,' Rose told Kev.

Meadows was close enough for Clyde to see the perpetual glower in his sharp eyes.

'I hope you're all getting along,' Meadows said, his tone belying his share-circle sentiment. 'Natalie?' He took a seat on the fountain's wide brim, seemingly expecting her to join him.

Clyde and the team listened as the deputy director gave Nat a condensed version of the current agency climate: Cairnwood's local pest, Edward Talbot, and a program of monstrous assassins.

Considering it was her first time out, Nat took it well. But then Clyde's first time had been far from a walk in the park.

Meadows held her attention with a solemn gaze. 'I know your father's feelings on this matter, but I want to make sure your enthusiasm matches his. Don't let the looks of these jackasses fool you.' He gestured to Clyde and the team. 'This is dangerous work of the highest order, and I need to make sure you're ready for this.'

'Cool,' Nat said, stress-free. 'So...I got the gig?'

8

The Tactical Operations Center was functioning at its usual frantic pace, with a few dozen intelligence agents glued to dozens of monitors feeding them surveillance footage of a variety of many low-to-medium-risk operations being conducted throughout the five boroughs. Clyde sat in an office chair inside the central glass cubicle of the TOC's situation room, his team forming a squiggly U-shape around a large desk/touch-screen computer terminal. They were spared most of the broader room's chatter and rattling keyboards from inside here, but not all; the accompanying background office noise still sounded to Clyde like a workaholic's sleep app. The cubicle's large hanging screen contained satellite imagery of the Citadel Security Solutions HQ in Lenox Hill, Manhattan. For a company that specialized in some very shady work, it sure did its due diligence to appear open and trustful from the outside. The HQ's main entrance was set thirty yards back from Park Avenue's busy road and foot traffic by a neat courtyard of shapeless corporate sculptures. As for the building itself, it was a structure of several huge glass boxes, the central and tallest of which was ten stories high. All the boxes fit together in an eye-pleasing conformation, making the building resemble more a flashy convention center than a murky den of top-tier hired killers.

Meadows admired the building on the screen. 'Their website advertises the full gamut of available services, from building security to consultancy and bodyguarding. What it fails to mention is their more unpalatable work. We don't have much on file relating to CSS's executives other than that Leonard Sharp is the founder and majority shareholder, and their head of security is...' Meadows opened a redacted file on screen. 'Harlan Brink. I was able to call in a favor at Langley to get us this glimpse into his profile.' Such favors were an unpleasant affair, but necessary on occasion. With both Hourglass and the CIA being founded on skeleton-cluttered closets and a whole heap of mistrust towards anything and everything beyond their purview, they were oftentimes cautious about favors, being more generally reliant on the standard practice of breaching each other's databases illegally, which was morally acceptable to department brass but a high risk for becoming an interdepartmental, even congressional, powder keg. And so, this time, favors.

The CIA's file on Captain Harlan Brink showed a big, rugged former Navy SEAL in desert camouflage. A list of classified operations from across the globe was blacked out, but Meadows clicked through his little presentation until he arrived at a few departmental correspondence items from the FBI and the DEA, who suspected that amongst Brink's various international dirty work for the CIA was his involvement in taking over an Afghan heroin pipeline with trade links to the US East Coast.

Meadows didn't bother to let the team get up to speed on the Cliff Notes before giving the ending away. 'The heroin pipeline fell into chaos, and no federal law-enforcement agency was able to find anything concrete on Brink's involvement. If the CIA protected him, I wouldn't be gobsmacked. Whatever happened, he returned to the US and became business partners with Leonard Sharp.'

'The keyboard warriors have any luck getting into the CSS servers?' Private Barros had been something of a computer-hacker hobbyist before her short military career went up with a bang, something that Clyde had only learned later, when the whole team were drafted here to the Madhouse.

'Their security software is top of the line, so our cyber security team is having some difficulty in breaching it without leaving a trail a mile wide. This means we can't count on gathering any accurate intel regarding employee records or any red-flag business clients. It also means we can't get an idea of the building's security counter-measures, or listings of on-site personnel.' A little of the hard, no-nonsense bluster fell away from Meadows as he was forced to reluctantly admit another weakness in his departmental game. 'After first getting wind of their involvement with Cairnwood, I tried to get an inside man into their ranks. It didn't go as planned. CSS has stringent employment requirements: specific military connections and the like. Could even be a goddamn secret handshake for all I know. And so I haven't been able to install so much as a janitor in that place. But now that they're more firmly in our crosshairs...' his deep-brown eyes, the color of macadamia nuts and just as hard, seemed to suggest something to Kev and the ISU specifically before encompassing Clyde and the others, 'you'll have to gather up as much intel on this rats' nest as you can from local surveillance.'

Clyde took Meadows's none-too-subtle hint and fixed Kev with a stare. 'It's risky, but if you lose that winter-hobo outfit, you'll be able to traverse through the offices.'

'Providing the building security doesn't have any PLE counter-measures,' Sarge added.

'What are the odds?' Kev asked, the sarcasm flowing naturally. 'I doubt the place is going to be full of mall cops. And I've already been shot once by one of those merc assholes.'

Clyde hated how Kev's intangible state made him perfect for such stealth and recon work, particularly when they dealt with enemies capable of overcoming such an advantage with the novelty Exorcist ammunition. He knew Kev still hadn't worked through the emotional trauma of being shot dead and then brought back as someone trapped on the outside of society. It was the reason he had become some sort of knowledge junkie for all things afterlife. Kev never was much of a people person, existing largely as a one-friend—maybe two—kind of guy, choosing to spend most of his time living inside his own head, but having the option of picking and choosing his level of social involvement taken away from him couldn't feel good. It was the primary reason Clyde had accepted Rose's offer of training at Indigo. Part of him wanted Kev to find a new home.

'Let's put the infiltration idea on the maybe pile for a minute and concentrate on working from the outside in,' Clyde said. 'We could try and get some eyes and ears on Brink, which might help us identify other high-value targets. Learn as much as we can before infiltrating the business. Maybe he'll drop something pertinent to the Boogieman Project.'

Meadows looked puzzled at the name.

'That's the name I coined for this assassin op,' Kev explained. The cubicle lights shimmered across his aviators as he sighed warily. 'And I second observing Brink because I'd be real long in the face if we snuck into CSS HQ only to find a bunch of gung-ho killers planning their next spot of wet-work.'

'I've never had much patience for the spy game,' Private Darcy said. 'But I back watching Brink.' Rose, Sarge, and Barros concurred.

'Couldn't we just grab this Leonard Sharp dude?' Nat asked, her fingers tap-tap-tapping in a restless rhythm against her studded wristband.

'I like your no-shit approach, but before we grab and waterboard a high-profile citizen, we have to consider the angles and ramifications,' Rose said. 'We don't yet know his relationship to Cairnwood. He owns CSS, and some of us know first-hand that a few of those merc assholes were less than human in more ways than one, but he too could be a victim in this. Could be he's getting leveraged by Talbot or some other dickweed.'

'And maybe my front teeth'll grow back,' Ace said.

Clyde didn't disagree with Rose's point, but neither did he find fault with Ace's cynicism. From the feeling of the room, everybody was on the same page.

Meadows brought up a number of street and traffic camera views surrounding the building's intersection, and some aerial drone views surveying the rooftops of adjacent buildings.

Rose, coffee cup in hand, snapped to attention and perused the rooftop vantage points. 'One of those would do nicely for some eyes in the sky.'

'Dibs,' called Kev.

Clyde nodded. 'I'll second his dibs.'

'Café on the street opposite,' Nat pointed out. 'I never turn down a frappé.'

'Well, what do you know? Girl after my own heart,' Rose said. 'Me and the new chick will post up on a table and keep watch on the building's rear.'

The ISU were alert and focused on the numerous camera feeds; death hadn't eroded their discipline and tactical minds one iota.

Sarge gestured to the ramp heading down to an underground parking structure. 'We'll take a little sidewalk plunge and recon the employee parking garage,' he said, volunteering himself and the other two-thirds of the ISU.

Clyde sipped his coffee and glanced at Ace. 'Guess you're on van duty, frosty. Just make sure you take one from the motor pool and not that monstrosity you bought.'

'I like you, Clyde. You've grown on me in our short time together, but you insult the Ice Maiden again and we're going to have a falling-out.'

'What kind of van you got?' Nat asked, her eyes shining with humor and interest.

'Maybe I'll show you the back of it one of these days,' Ace said wryly.

Meadows gave him a look of naked hostility, ending the nonsense.

Clyde sat up, his lower back aching a little from how he'd slept the night before. 'Let's say this place is housing the thing that's turning out wannabe supervillains, what are we supposed to do with it when we find it? Shoot our way out? Blow it up? We're lucky that most of our work involves taking down people who want to remain low profile. The closest we've come to a public shitshow was crashing Talbot's Ivy Lounge soirée. But all those rich politicos and entrepreneurs were happy to scurry back under their rocks afterwards.'

Meadows's face was impassive. 'I sincerely hope I don't need to remind anybody here that we are a covert organization. Theatrics are a last resort.'

'But it's all glass walls.' Nat seemed sincerely flummoxed as to how drama could be avoided in such a place. 'What happens if things get out of hand?'

'We have contingencies to mitigate public awareness of certain sensitive activities, but they're not to be used lightly.'

'Shit, you mean like...' Her hand dipped down from the sky, her lips whistling like an incoming missile.

'Not in such a visible and well-populated area, no,' Meadows said. 'Should the situation reach an undesirable conclusion, our first response will be a textbook smokescreen: terrorist attack, perhaps blame it on some crazy in-house feud. Basically, sling enough shit and see what sticks to the mass media's walls.'

'But what if that doesn't cover it?' Kev asked.

'It's the job of each and every one of you to make certain that never happens.'

'Hey, I get that, I do. But now that we're on the subject, I can't help but wonder how our whole line of work hasn't been exposed by some dope with a phone glued to their hand.'

Meadows played deaf, an increasingly frequent hobby of his when Kev was in the same room, choosing to focus on the wall of monitors. His phone vibrated, stealing his attention. 'Okay, team, I'll leave you to work on the finer details. Rose, run it by me when you're ready.' He turned to leave, then paused next to Natalie and handed her a preliminary ID card. 'Access to the premises, subject to clearance level. You're now official, Natalie.' His mouth worked to say something else, paused, and found a different line. 'You have my every confidence.' And with that, he was gone.

Natalie turned her laminated credentials this way and that as though hoping to find a nifty hologram, but all the black plastic had on it was her surname and first initial, headshot, a bold S2 security clearance level, biometric ID chip, and a simple hourglass design. 'You get free drinks with this?'

Rose chugged the rest of her coffee, crushing the paper cup in what was easily her least impressive feat of strength in Clyde's humble opinion. 'We'll rendezvous at nineteen hundred hours.' She clapped her hands together. 'Now I'm off to put bullets into paper targets of gorillas and dolls. This is your time, people, do what you will. Stay in contact.'

Clyde wanted to get to know Nat a little more, but the old adage of "Don't Shit Where You Eat" flashed through his head on a giant billboard. She gave him a brief lingering look before exiting the glass cubicle with the others, firing some playful abuse at Ace's suggestion to check out his van.

'Mythic?' Kev asked, knowing him so well. Tuesday was new comic-book day. And Mythic Comics & Collectibles was an old haunt of Clyde's in Bed-Stuy.

Clyde watched Nat disappear into the throng of intel agents and sur-veillance jargon. 'Mythic,' he agreed. He turned back to Kev. 'But I should go check on my mom too.'

9

Even in the morning sun, Elzinga Asylum looked imposing. A dark keep of secrets and madness, its crenelated high stone walls gave the impression that it was trying to keep something out rather than hold something in. The ancient woods surrounding it had once been declared ominous by Dr. Elzinga and his fellow Dutch settlers, but whether the fears responsible for such fortifications were genuine or the product of group hysteria and paranoia was beyond the grasp of local knowledge, lost somewhere in the deep forests of folklore.

Beyond the walls and through the grounds, the interior of the main facility wasn't much cheerier, painted in what must have been an intentionally dull hue of overcast-sky gray; with putrid linoleum to match, it told observers to lower their expectations.

It was only 9:30 am but Dr. Julius Sharp had already loosened his slim black tie and rolled his white shirt sleeves up his skinny arms to the elbow. He sat in his unofficial office in the basement of an abandoned section of the hospital. His real office was pleasant enough in its way: mahogany wainscoting, hardwood floor, a fair-sized window, and orderly bookcases. Not this place, though. It was a cement box tucked away in an honest-to-God dungeon prison originally constructed by Elzinga and his petrified villagers.

Nobody official knew Julius was down here, or what *happened* down here. Should any of his colleagues on the hospital board learn of the things that transpired down in this private, forgotten place, it wouldn't end well for them. And Julius didn't want that. It was stressful enough bribing and blackmailing federal judges and prison officials; he didn't want his colleagues getting pulled under with him.

He elbowed aside the leaning pile of psychological profiles cluttering his desk and brushed his fingers across the laptop keyboard, closing the research documents on military sleeper agents and code words before carefully erasing his search history and putting the computer to sleep. A mug of bitter black coffee and a half-full ashtray were positioned on his desk in such a way as to declare their importance to the man's functioning. He had quit smoking three years ago, but it had become an increasingly common response in recent times to succumb to his cravings. Ever since Edward Talbot swooped in from some nebulous corner of the elite stratosphere with money and power and smartly spoken threats.

It was the task awaiting him that troubled Julius. Dolores Ricci, the mentally scarred woman whose face was as ravaged as her mind, had taken to the process. She had survived. But it wasn't her new nature that disturbed Julius now, for she was only the latest in a growing list of test subjects. No, the thing that continued to make him uneasy was the source of the scarred woman's mental subjugation.

The Eye of Charon.

That's what Talbot had called the thing, wearing a straight face all the while. Julius recalled how Talbot had strutted right into this professional world of academia, one in which Julius had studied and worked his ass off to make a name for himself, and within minutes reduced the highly re-vered doctor to nothing more than a lackey. Something between babysitter and recruitment officer. And all it had taken was a brief face-to-face with Talbot and a talk about how things were going to change around here.

Here!?

In Julius's world!

When your brother was Leonard Sharp, that didn't happen. Well, it wasn't Julius's world anymore. And now the Eye was waiting for him outside, silently dominating the central chamber of this old subterranean prison. Further proof that perhaps he should be getting a shrink of his own to gauge the reality within his head and validate whether he belonged on the other side of the locked doors of this place, raving and fantasizing about magic gemstone eyes and dangerous inmates evolving into science-defying hitmen. Perhaps he really was sliding into lunacy; it might explain the near-constant headache he'd endured for the last couple of weeks, a feeling like something had left a shallow imprint on the inside of his skull. Of course, such a symptom could also be the result of ongoing inadequate sleep.

Getting up on his weary legs and fighting a low-blood-sugar head rush, he left the cold cement box of his "office" and started down the large and gloomy stone tunnel towards the central chamber of the dungeon cellblock and his latest subject: Dolores "Doll-Face" Ricci.

She was floating several feet off the floor in the middle of the huge chamber, dangling from nigh-invisible wires but somehow looking comfortable in a cross-legged pose. Those wounded, angry eyes of hers were stark, wide open behind her mask, like yielding portals for the beautiful poison pulsing out from the Eye of Charon. The Eye was the centerpiece of the large chamber, and from its chest-high stone pedestal, it could be mistaken for a piece of incongruous and exotic ornamentation upon first sight, but with a closer inspection, it became evident that it was far more precious than any display piece, but also more disturbing in its design. An emerald iris, stunning in clarity and roughly the size of Julius's fist, sat within a round and robust mound of silver. That was a layman's passing glimpse. The jewel was like no other Julius had ever seen, a stone that came alive of its own accord, a swirling galaxy of hypnotic awe. And the silver...every time Julius looked at it or was forced to touch it, he couldn't ignore the impression that somehow it had once been alive. Had it been some impossible form of living metal, or was it some alien flesh, flash-frozen into this lump of inorganic matter?

Julius glanced at the inanimate form of the Hangman in one of the adjacent cells and sat down in the rickety wooden chair he had positioned roughly ten feet from Dolores and the Eye. His gaze took in the misery of this place: both walls lined with two tiers of iron-barred cells—the upper floor fitted with catwalks and stairs—bare bulbs dangling like suicides from a vaulted stone ceiling, other bare bulbs locked behind mesh cages like prisoners. Everything had been crude and functional when Elzinga constructed this place for the gibbering wrecks of his village, and in the intervening years, very little had been done to soften the depressing design.

Julius checked his watch, tapping one black loafer impatiently. It was chilly down here, but it didn't stop his nervous perspiration from moistening his back and armpits. Being a practical man, one of sound reasoning, science, and logic, Julius never used to believe in fluffy matters such as souls and dark forces, but now, every time he shivered down in this dank hellhole, he couldn't help but wonder if it had been caused by ghosts brushing his shoulder.

This was as much a place of death as it was a crucible of rebirth. The potential subjects came in, selected by Julius based on Talbot's criteria of violence and mental acuity, though there had been a number of willing volunteers who had craved power for willing servitude, such as a number of Leonard's gunslingers from Citadel Security Solutions.

Though for every success, two died. Julius wasn't sure if it was an issue of heart failure or brain embolism; it might even be something else entirely, but Talbot wouldn't allow autopsies for such clandestine rituals due to nothing more than his utter disdain for the subjects. Life was cheap to him. So corpses would be dragged off by his vigilant lackeys and incinerated in an ancient iron boiler elsewhere in the abandoned building, far from the eyes of staff, patients, and visitors; the only eyes in these few derelict buildings were those of Talbot's ever-present and smart-suited goons, those eerily quiet and harsh-featured corpse-burners.

So many empty cells down here. Julius was back down to two patients. It seemed that this operation was doomed to fail. Imperfect methodology. And it kept them from getting a sure-footing in terms of numbers, and when they did have a small pool of killers available, they were quickly slapped down by those government agents who'd caused Talbot to turn the air blue.

Two patients.

And Talbot had bought up that extra holding facility in Queens as though Julius and this large ugly eye would be turning out institutionalized monsters by the dozen.

Such complications brought a silent cheer to Julius.

For all of Talbot's eagerness, Julius believed he was clearly delusional, perhaps even desperate. He'd known the type in his professional circles while coming up. Those so driven and in need of making a splash that they often sealed their own doom—rushed into things, cut corners, engaged in malpractice. Julius only hoped this whole sick machine Talbot was trying to build down here would fall apart and bury him along with it, liberating him and Leonard from this inconceivable subjugation.

He checked his watch again, irritating himself with the repetitiveness of the action. Talbot didn't always warn Julius about his visits. In fact, Julius was almost certain there were times Talbot would drop in unannounced just to throw Julius's plans or schedules into disarray. Talbot liked being the sun in this dark little universe, with everything rotating around him. Still, Talbot had made something of a habit of dropping by on Tuesday mornings, and considering Dolores's display of spontaneity last night, Julius knew he'd be showing up at some point today.

He let his restless eyes settle on the catatonic Dolores and felt a sharp stab of shame. He didn't want anything further to happen to Mrs. Ricci. Well, it was *Ms.* Ricci now, he corrected. She'd been through enough. That was the reason he felt so guilty about plucking her file for this foul endeavor. Unlike those biker morons who had failed Leonard and opted for Talbot's experiment to get out of Rikers—and, against the odds, all surviving the transformation—Dolores Ricci was no volunteer. She had found her way to Elzinga Asylum through the proper channels: a transfer from Bedford Hills Correctional Facility for Women following another violent outburst. There were no shady deals and phony psych evaluations with her. She was a true victim. Her victimhood would be of little surprise to most people. A third-generation mafioso wife, she was essentially destined to be hitched to some wise guy thug. So one could argue that what had happened to her was partly her fault. Why hadn't she run away from the brute when things started to get rough? Leave town. Leave the state!

Alas, she had stayed, and blood had been spilled by the pint.

So no, Dolores wasn't a volunteer, but for Julius she was a necessity. A dangerous gambit he was just desperate enough to play.

And if her actions last night were anything to go by, that gambit might be starting to pay off.

She cried out pitifully. It was the sound of a little girl weeping, and Julius almost wanted to reach out and reach up, to touch her dangling hand. An act of comfort he knew was deeply inadequate. He stilled himself, remaining in his chair on the periphery of Charon's Eye and its observation of Dolores. He watched the Eye's mesmeric light beams continue their alluring pulsing, deep into her helpless gaze. Her mask muffled another sob, and the burning cosmic glow of Charon's pupil went cold, the emerald iris becoming enveloped in a shimmering metal lid. Still cross-legged in mid-air, suspended on those strings, Dolores's head slumped forward into sleep.

Julius wiped a fingerprint smudge from his glasses and stood up with a sigh, casting a furtive glance at Charon's now resting Eye. He didn't know if there was any deeper sentience within the Eye, asleep or awake, but early on into this descent into madness he had discovered, with no small measure of trepidation, that the Eye of Charon could rotate around of its own accord from its seat, as though keeping watch on him and the surroundings. He wasn't sure if those strange mercury-gilded tendrils could function as nascent arms or if the subtle depressions and expansions of the orbital helped shift its weight around, but what he did know was that he didn't want to get close enough to study it.

He walked softly over to Dolores, fearful of her and what she had become because of his choices. His heart galloped in his chest in anticipation of what he was about to do next. Forcing himself to look casual, he made a quick note of the whereabouts of Talbot's sentries, a few of whom lumbered slowly like drones along the upper tier of empty cells, but his chief concern was that "sleeping" Eye. Was it really sleeping? Did it need to sleep? Was it too being observed by other beings on some plane far beyond Julius's ken? Talbot wasn't fond of Julius asking too many questions, but in a world where all the rules had seemingly been thrown out of the window, Julius had to assume that the Eye of Charon could sing a goddamn aria if it chose to.

He gently placed a hand on Dolores's shoulder and leaned into her ear. He had yet to experience any penalties for what he was about to do, and he had to take his chances.

He whispered to her. A brief utterance. Julius had to mentally cross his fingers that the words landed loud enough in her subconscious to weaken the chains Charon had forged.

Finished, he exited the dungeons, happy to be away from the place, and took the stairs up, ready for clean air. As he exited the derelict building the sunlight against his skin made him feel like a vampire in some melodramatic horror movie, and his hands automatically lit a cigarette. Taking his time, he walked away from that place of nightmares, his eyes drifting to the far corners of the asylum's stone-block walls and the dense wood beyond. It was lonely at this end of the hospital's grounds, the bushes and lawns getting primordial ideas.

Every now and then, Julius would spot one of Talbot's emotionless minders sliding out of sight behind an adjunct building or some shrub. He exhaled a puff of smoke into the balmy air, then drew in the pine scent of the green space. He didn't care about the watchers Talbot had set on him, not as long as they didn't catch on to what he was up to with Dolores and his other subject. Sighing, he thought regretfully about the long-term patients he'd been forced to drop onto some of his esteemed and overworked colleagues so that he could march to the beat of Talbot's drum.

Julius's phone vibrated in his pocket. It was Leonard again. Julius swore under his breath; he had forgotten to call him back. Or text him. It was becoming another bad habit. Flicking the cigarette away, he answered the call. Within moments it was clear to Julius that his brother was not in the best of moods, and hearing him explain the situation, he understood why.

Finishing his walk, Julius cut through the side entrance of the asylum's main building, nodding the occasional greeting to a passing doctor or nurse, and met Leonard in the foyer. Julius noticed he'd brought Zebra and Brink with him, and that the three of them had been halted by a few more of Talbot's monosyllabic security. Julius could see that his brother was in danger of letting his courteous philanthropist image fall away.

'Jules, what the fuck's all this?'

These particular guards were new and dressed down in white uniforms, unlike their counterparts in the dungeons, but they carried similar Tasers and batons, which Julius suspected were merely for show, having seen how they effortlessly lugged human dead weight around. Assuming they could be hurt and killed as easily as ordinary men, Julius knew Leonard was capable of doing very bad things to them, regardless of what they were carrying, and without the aid of Zeb and Brink. But assumptions were a dangerous thing.

Julius gave his brother a put-upon look, then glanced over to the reception desk to find the receptionists busy with phone calls and filing. 'New measures. Please don't make a scene.' Leonard stared at the physically imposing men in white, then back to his little brother. 'Talbot doesn't want you coming here.'

'He never said that to me.'

'He doesn't want me getting distracted during office hours.'

'Office hours?' Leonard gave a single hacking laugh. 'I can barely get a hold of you these days. You don't answer your phone, you don't reply to texts.' He inspected Julius's drab and creased clothing. 'Have you been sleeping in this fucking place?'

Julius fought to stifle a yawn, tasting the shit coffee and nicotine that were becoming his staple diet. He didn't dare catch his reflection in the glass of the automatic doors, knowing how bad he must look. If he wasn't careful, his colleagues might start asking him if he was okay. Wouldn't that be hilarious?

'Of course I haven't. I'm just working unsocial hours.'

'You missed the homeless charity fundraiser, missed our last couple of poker nights. What else?' Leonard pondered. 'Oh, that's right, your own damn birthday party.'

That was like a glass of cold water to the face, and Julius realized that he had completely forgotten about his birthday. He seldom cared about getting a year older, but he did remember now that Leonard had mentioned several times organizing a small get-together for him.

'You've become this fucker's slave, Jules. You cool with that?' Leonard stared again at the two guards standing before him, too close, the pair of them unblinking, and he appeared to be considering shoving one guy's hand up the other's ass.

Sadly, Julius knew no such thing could happen. He had witnessed his brother rise from street hood to the strategist who shed his skin and took over a city, but the pond was much deeper than either of them had imagined.

'Don't talk to me that way, Leonard,' Julius warned, then relented. 'This is only temporary. You heard about the trouble in his stable last night?' He lowered his voice. 'Anselmo and his two men, all dead. Talbot's a little rattled, and I'm expecting him to contact me shortly. We're not the only ones who have a boss.'

Leonard looked like he was about to spit on the floor. 'Ah fuck, I'm just all inconsolable about that prick's hardships. Fuck him, fuck his bosses.'

Julius gave him a second warning glance, fearful that his brother's emotional bravado might spur the pair of thugs into reporting the aggressive attitude to Talbot.

'I need to get Nathan and Dolores back on an even keel. Make sure they're responding okay. It shouldn't take too long. I'll see if Talbot shows up, skim through a few more candidate files, and then I'll be out of here. We can grab a drink.' Julius heard the earnestness of his voice and marveled at its optimism. 'What about High Steaks?'

High Steaks. Not only one of the most fashionable and exclusive restaurants in Midtown, but one owned by Leonard.

Leonard still harbored the energy of a belligerent bull, but after a moment he acquiesced. He gave a flat glance at Zeb and Brink, then returned his attention to Julius. 'You call me tonight! When you get out of here. Don't make me come back up here, because one way or another, it won't end peacefully.'

Empty words, Julius knew. His older brother was a man to be feared, but men had had their day in this new world of theirs.

Brink stepped forward, a picture of professional composure. 'I'll stay here on the premises. Keep an eye on things. Zeb can drive you back to the shareholder meeting.'

Leonard thought about it, nodded. 'Call me later,' he told his brother and gave Talbot's goons one parting glare before leaving Elzinga Asylum behind him like it was a bad smell.

Once the automatic doors slid shut again, Brink led Julius a few steps away from the dim-looking guards. 'Has Talbot considered my proposal?'

'Are you sure about this?'

Brink's eyes were clear and determined. He gave a crisp nod.

'When he gets here, you can ask him yourself.' Julius flashed a polite smile at the receptionists and led Brink out of the main building and back towards the derelict structure at the rear of the grounds.

10

Dolores Ricci was buried. Her mind was not her own. Stripped of her volition and her body, her sense of self was now reduced to this quiet echo. She was back in her wedding house, a place that should have been built on cherished memories and love, not fear and abuse. It wasn't the true house, though; it was a replica. Scaled-down, just like her. A doll's house fit for a doll. And the only occupants were herself and her violent tea-party friends.

Dolores moved through the artificial rooms, searching for the source of the whispers. Words she had barely heard, like a gentle wind or the sounds of the house settling, and yet somehow they seemed very important to her. Her memories did a sterling job of furnishing the old rooms in expensive elegance. All the grand furniture and comforts of a high-level mobster's home.

She stopped her wandering, knowing that the whispers had escaped her, and this curiosity brought on a stark realization: What if the whispers had been the manipulations of the thing outside her house? The watcher whose presence kept her inside this house the way a cat keeps a mouse inside a hole. Terrorizing her. Was it toying with her now? Its presence should be filling her with cold black rage, the urge to scream and kill. But she only felt...lost? A little girl afraid of the boogieman in her closet.

Walking through the large dining room, she heard a faint sobbing sound but couldn't locate it. Like a passing wraith, it was there, then gone. It was enough to unsettle her, though, so much so that she suddenly felt the comforting press of Banana Panic's big paw on her shoulder. She reached up and tapped it lovingly, and together they walked in solidarity through this old house of ghosts. In the wide marble foyer, she stopped at the bottom of the beautiful curving staircase, the sound of breaking glass and raised voices stalling her. Like the sobbing, these anxious sounds passed as quickly as they arrived. And now it wasn't only Banana Panic who stood with her, but her full collection of smiling, loving dolls, the ceramic and plastic girls who were always there to listen to her woes. But they were not enough. The thought of the monster at the top of the stairs put cement in her shoes, and all she could do was stare up at the waiting darkness with an open mouth.

Shunning the large, gilded mirror beside the staircase, she slowly approached the netted window next to the attractive front door, steel-lined for security. She parted the netting with a soft, cautious tug, seeing only the wide lawn and sprinklers, the dark neighboring houses, the empty suburban street lit by white sodium lights, lending it an almost sterile air, like a lifeless model town. Still, she felt the sense of claustrophobic terror release its fingers from around her heart.

Could she leave this place? Run from this domestic prison?

Then...

A huge green eye peeled open in the black night sky, larger than any moon, and silently glared down at her with the hunger of an empty-bellied beast.

No, she couldn't leave.

A surging newfound strength rose in her but was quickly beaten back, overcome by older feelings: the helplessness of a child, and of an adult too timid to impose herself on her life.

Rain started to pour down, threatening to wash this dollhouse down the banks into madness.

Outside her head, behind her blank porcelain mask, Doll-Face shed a tear.

* * * * *

The Hangman knelt silently in supplication in a cell adjacent to Doll-Face and the Eye of Charon. His powerful shoulders jumped with the occasional spasm of the bad dreamer. He was walking through the abysmal streets of trash and violence, which he knew like the scars on his palms. A most violent youth, choked with hopelessness. But unlike the cold, hard reality of his upbringing, these spray-tagged streets kept twisting, shifting around on themselves as though he was lost in an ugly slate-gray maze of broken brick and shattered glass. Gunshots rang out in the chill evening air, the sun blinded by walls of ashen clouds. Traversing these old projects in a daze, his Timberlands kicked a crushed beer can against a wall, scaring the life out of a rat large enough to chew through a man's throat with a few quick bites. The size of the animal didn't bother him, especially when a drop of blood landed on his hand like rain. He looked up and almost gasped with sexual delight at the tableau: bodies. Dozens of them, hanging from rooftops and, somehow, even the clouds themselves like the Devil's Rapture, the ragged black shapes bound by nooses of barbed wire, gently swaying in the cold air and leaking their tepid blood.

Hangman felt the barbs stirring about inside him, an artist's urge to create. The deadly wires slithered out of his thick forearms like questing snakes, coiling about his large hands.

Not wanting to be distracted by his baser needs, he tore his gaze from the abattoir in the urban sky and reminded himself that he wanted to find the voice he had heard. It had come to him several times now, words falling from the dirty clouds or tumbling out of an alleyway, spoken by a voice he knew but couldn't place. A man's voice. So familiar but somehow elusive. Time was meaningless here. He was a hamster on a wheel. But if such a thing as time still existed for him, then it seemed like forever since the voice had spoken those intoxicating words, alluding to memories of his past self. The last time he heard that voice it was so quiet, and not speaking to him but to another whose name he thought he recognized: Dolores.

Dolores? That rang a bell, but the gong was too deep, too muffled to resonate with him.

But then...an image imprinted itself over his whole world for a split-second, displacing this trap of cobbled memories and impulses. The outline of a woman, details impossible to discern in the blink. His effort to try and steal the image back was met with the sensation of a small headache.

Above his head, giant tumbleweeds of barbed wire rolled out across the rooftops, blocking out the sky, reel by reel, sealing him down here on these repetitive streets, and any idea of a woman or her name was gone.

Where was he going? Was he trying to get out of here? One building flashed in his mind above all the others: one specific tenement block, painted with a large graffiti symbol of a golden crown girding a sword. It called to him. It was an important part of his life, a period that had sated some of his dark urges.

He watched through the razor sky mesh as that eye opened up again, swirling like putrid green bleach circling a shower drain. It watched him like he was a spider trapped under a glass, and seemed content with his confinement. Nathan willed the living barbs to retreat back into his body, his nest, and with no discernible purpose other than to retread old memories, he continued to walk these streets of violence and desperation.

II

The six-seat Bentley limousine cruised through the Queens-Midtown Tunnel. The trip from the Madhouse had taken the best part of an hour, providing plenty of time for Nat to tell her father, Rodel, all about her newly minted official status as an Hourglass operative. Forty minutes—and several of Rodel's work-related phone calls later—and he was still a wiry ball of pride and excitement.

'I always knew you could do it.' He was a sixtyish man with a neat mustache and combed hair, and having the whole of the plush black leather rear seating to himself only enhanced his slender build. 'Knew you were strong enough to turn things around.'

Nat shrugged, her former bluster and confidence shriveling beneath the praise. From her rear-facing seat, she smirked awkwardly at her dad before choosing to watch passing cars outside the tinted glass. She seemed almost...demure in his presence. 'I didn't get to choose my parents. The power in me. It's not like I can take any credit for having it.'

Rodel waved the modesty away. 'Not the Spark, dear. The—'

Nat waved her own hand. 'Okay, Dad! I don't need to rehash it.'

Rodel settled back, a hint of poignancy dimming his cheer. He stared out the window and sipped a bottle of orange juice from the limo's mini-refrigerator. After a minute or two of comfortable silence, he spoke again. 'As tragic as that was, what happened brought you here. Made you find your strength. And I need you strong.'

Natalie nodded, saddled with weight. She saw the love and compassion in his eyes, but also expectation.

'What are your teammates like?'

Nat gave a light shrug. 'Seem okay, I guess. They're experienced, unlike me. But two of them haven't been at it long either. I just need to make sure I don't slow them down.' Her black-painted nails had gone from tapping speedy rhythms on the polished chestnut paneling to her Coke can, and she absorbed every tinny beat.

'Frank wouldn't have let you join the team, even with your power, if he didn't see your potential as a field agent.' A trace of apprehension entered Rodel's voice. 'But I know what you're like... As proud as I am of you right now, this is a dangerous line of work. I know you're smart and capable, but you're still my little girl, so'—his mouth flashed a bittersweet smile—'you be careful.'

Natalie hardened her exterior. 'I used to play gigs while dodging beer bottles. I got this.' Rodel playfully pretended to throw his empty juice bottle at her. 'Do me a favor, though.'

'Sure.'

'These limo rides need to stop. It's not that I don't appreciate you driving out of your way to help, but if I'm a card-carrying government agent who can kill with noise, I think it's better if you let me take the subway. What's the point in me doing all that training if you keep putting babysitters on me? No more lifts from Daddy. Cool?'

'I can do you one better.' Rodel flashed her a brilliant white smile. Nat waited for him to divulge. 'Seeing as how this is a big day, I thought we'd stop off at a dealership and let you ride home on a brand-new motorcycle.'

Nat almost—*almost*—jumped out of her seat in excitement. Instead, she took a breath. 'As awesome as that sounds—and Christ on a Kawasaki, it's awesome—'

'Don't blaspheme.' He wagged a finger.

Nat made a face of fractional contrition, knowing her dad was only saying it from reflex rather than any genuine religious affront. Spanish Catholicism was deeply integrated into Filipino customs, but Nat and Rodel's branch of the Mondragon ancestry had long since opened their eyes to the existence of a much wider and mysterious pantheon.

'I'll hold off on the new bike for now. Maybe I'll treat myself to one in a few paychecks' time.' Rodel's eyebrows arched up in surprise. 'How about you spring for something to eat instead?'

Rodel started listing several mid- to high-fancy restaurants in Manhattan before Nat shut him down. 'Screw that. Cheeseburgers.'

Rodel shook his head in exasperation and told the driver where to take them. 'You'll never make a good diplomat, daughter.'

12

Clyde was making short work of his steamed crabmeat wontons, enjoying the leafy shade on the sidewalk outside Fat Dragon, a trendy Pan-Asian restaurant in Williamsburg. He had very little tolerance for the anally hip, but he liked the food here, and it wasn't too far from his apartment.

Corrine, his mom, was slowly taking advantage of her day off work and was on her second pineapple juice and sake. Being a Veterans Affairs nurse in Bay Ridge, her tireless work ethic and compassion was sometimes tested, not only by the grief of her patients but a hectic work schedule. She had worked in critical care for a time but now focused on more acute cases, dealing with illness, recovery, and even unofficial counselling by way of being a naturally good listener and shoulder to cry on.

'You're really putting those things away,' Clyde said of her sake-laced fruit juice. 'I hope I won't be piling you into the back of a cab.'

Corrine gave her glass a little shake and smiled. She had a contagious smile, so much so that even middle-age couldn't slow it down, only highlighting it with a web of smile lines around the corners of her eyes.

Her job kept her slim with no shortage of running about, but it was also contributing to the slow fire of gray weaving itself through the once black roots of her curly bob cut.

'I need to make the most of moments like this. Whenever that darn phone rings I'm scared to look at it in case it's work calling me in,' she confided, trying to disguise the stress with sly humor.

Clyde knew she didn't mean it, that she'd rush in to help at a moment's notice, even if she was herself bed-bound and sick. Prior to Hourglass, he had despised all forms of military service to the point where he found it incredibly difficult to empathize with modern-day men and women signing their lives away to die for wealthy sociopaths. Pain sometimes had a way of distorting one's views, and his brother's and dad's bodies lying in the dirt of Cypress Hills National Cemetery was a pain that had also ravaged his mom, but her pain had never coalesced into a bitter edge the way his had, not because she believed in the wars being fought, but because she knew that no matter the politics, these people were laying their lives on the line and somebody needed to be there to help them up when they fell. Clyde hadn't changed his opinion on military service but now felt an acute sadness for the vets his mom treated—and troops the world over—knowing that no matter what horrors they had thanklessly endured for flags and businessmen, the true fight was still waiting for them in the Null.

'How's the eel?' he asked. Grilled eel was something he couldn't bring himself to try. Sushi, crab, prawns, and salmon: there was plenty the oceans provided that he enjoyed eating, but anytime he glanced at eel meat he couldn't help but think of the ugly things lurking in some coral reef, and didn't want any part of them in his mouth. It was a silly thing to get hung up on, he knew. It wasn't like an animal's attractiveness was linked to their taste.

'Fabulous as always.' She took another bite of the grilled meat, and a concerned expression fell across her brow. 'Might have to stop eating it soon, though.'

'Oh? Because the things are so goddamn ugly?'

'I watched this documentary on how the oceans can't sustain the damage of the seafood industry. They're trawling the sea beds until there's nothing left, mass-killing species caught in the nets, even if they're not being eaten.' She pushed the rest of the plate away, leaned back in her chair, and chewed. 'It's appalling.'

Great, now Clyde had to worry about how much humanity was fucking up the ocean just so he could enjoy the occasional bowl of wontons. 'Thanks for ruining seafood for me. We didn't have to come here to eat.'

'Still got sake,' she consoled. 'So how's the job going?'

He sipped his ginger ale.

The job? The job was a necessary lie. Unable to divulge to his mom how he'd come to be working for a secret branch of government, he had been forced to drum up a job that not only explained the finances necessary for him to afford his new apartment but eased her long-running concerns about her only remaining son living as a near-broke illustrator for hire. It was Hourglass policy to protect the loved ones of their agents, but since they couldn't simply appear from thin air and move family members without arousing a considerable number of questions and suspicions, they discreetly implanted agents into the periphery of their lives, surveillance teams or neighbors able to keep watch over them. So having spent the first few days as an official agent fretting over what he could tell her, lightning struck. It was all so obvious: Mythic Comics & Collectibles. His long-time friendly neighborhood comic shop. He had already worked there, pulling in shifts while working on artist commissions, and so it made perfect sense to pretend that he had taken over his friend Brian's position as manager. And thankfully, with his mom not knowing Krypto from Marmaduke, he had plenty of wiggle-room for work-related excuses, not that she would ever drop by unannounced to see him at work.

'Cool, cool. Get paid to talk and hang out, what's not to love.'

Corrine set her gaze to playful scrutiny. 'And here's me thinking a manager would have their hands full.'

'Oh, you know, sometimes.' Clyde sounded almost guilty. 'Ordering titles, dealing with wages and all that drag.'

'Are you still working on that comic of yours?'

'Some.' Another lie, kind of. When he first showed her around his new apartment, he'd made sure to hide any agency-issued firearms and items but had slipped up when she found his recently finished drawing of Hangman—his current pyramid of paranormal killers had yet to begin at that point. He'd automatically claimed that it was a bad guy in his comic-book: *Guns of Metronome*. Definitely *NOT* loosely based on his Hourglass exploits. 'I've slacked off a little lately. Tired when I get home. But I'm going to start dedicating an hour or two to knuckling down.'

'Any cute girls working at the store?'

Clyde humored her with a smirk. The topic of his love life seemed to crop up at least once a year, where, much like the remainder of the eel on her plate, he would be thoroughly grilled. 'I'm not looking for anything right now. Things are a little complicated.'

Now there was an understatement. A warm breeze found him even in the shade, and he glanced across the street to a huge multi-colored mural of a giant octopus with chopsticks in one tentacle. He must have stared at it every couple of minutes, using its artistic merit as cover to give frequent but not impolite glances around the local area. It was troubling to play civilian when you had enemies, particularly with his mom so close, but he trusted the back-up team he had on standby.

When he looked back at his mom, he saw the stalwart wisdom in her eyes.

'You're still young, but don't put it off forever,' she said. 'You can face anything when you have love in your life.'

A shallow cut opened inside Clyde, scar tissue he thought had grown too tough and leathery to open up so easily. Seeing her strength and how she had to pick herself up every day without the love she spoke of at her side made him wish he could tell her what he knew about his dad, Richard. But what good would it do? For all Clyde knew, his dad's soul, perhaps Stephen's too, might have since been destroyed, perished in the Null. It never got any easier, not really, and knowing that death wasn't the true end provided very little comfort.

'What about you? Any stud soldiers got their eye on you at the hospital?'

Corrine gave a bashful laugh, her pain sinking back into the depths of her eyes. 'I'm going to need another six of these'—she lifted her sake— 'before I ever even consider doing anything as foolish as looking for a new man.' The humor, while sincere, quickly evaporated. 'No, hon. Richard was the only one for me.'

Clyde nodded solemnly, not knowing what to say. So he didn't say anything.

He watched Kev, a little way down the street, patiently leaning on a mailbox and tapping his wrist. That was the cue. Time to step out of civilian life and get to work. Paying for their meal, Clyde explained that he had to head back to Mythic to do some work. After forcing the cab fare into his mom's hand, he waved her goodbye and walked down to the street corner where Kev waited. He watched as his mom's pair of assigned agents, both dependable and highly experienced, fell in behind the taxi, tailing it in a bland-looking silver Nissan, which was actually fast as hell, bullet-proof, and equipped to deal with a small three-block war. They would keep Clyde updated about her safe return trip via text message from a secure phone.

Even with Kev's face hidden, Clyde sensed a peculiarity in him. 'You still debating about letting your family know you're back?'

Kev appeared to deflate slightly. 'No. I still can't imagine how I would go about it. How would I even start?'

Clyde went to answer, but Kev cut him off. 'No, I know you'd help, but I still couldn't face it.' Another innocuous vehicle pulled into the curb beside them. A black Toyota, also much more than it appeared. 'They're okay under agency care. Best to leave them to live their lives in peace.' Kev opened the rear passenger seat and glanced at Clyde before sliding in. 'It might be the last time they experience it.'

Once they were in the car, the driver took the swiftest route to a nearby agency satellite office, and from there, the rendezvous point several blocks from the Citadel Security Solutions HQ.

13

Clyde was crouched next to Kev on the roof of a building on 62nd Street opposite CSS, a pair of digital binoculars trained on the executive office suite on the tenth floor, the ubiquitous glass bronzed by the late evening sun. The CSS HQ was even more impressive when seen in person, an almost city-block-sized fortress, though Clyde thought much of it was little more than an extravagance of bland corporate aesthetics with surprisingly little practical use; it made him think of a shopping mall for paid killers. It was either an unusual insistence on openness or sheer arrogance that had so much of the property fitted with two-way glass, though it would undoubtedly be bullet-proof.

Clyde noted the armed guards patrolling the rooftop perimeter: tactical body armor over company uniform and cap, and a model of assault rifle he hadn't seen before. He uploaded the digital footage of the weaponry back to the tech teams at the base and radioed it in to Ace and Rose, both of whom identified the same variety of mysterious rifle in the hands of those manning the lobby and parking structure entrances, respectively. The caliber was unknown, but the general consensus was to err on the side of caution, postulating that their stopping power would lend itself to PLEs, like the ghost-lethal Exorcist rounds they'd encountered the last time they tangled with CSS.

Kev had painstakingly guided a cluster of tiny listening devices through the air and across the street, sticking them on corners of pre-selected office windows, where they would receive any speech vibrations and transmit them into the team's radio receivers. Such procedures were exciting. Until they weren't. 'If we're hoping some asshole just walks past yapping about their super-duper monster-maker, we could be here a while,' he said.

Clyde glanced at him. Without his disguise, the evening light shone through Kev. 'Patience, man.' He slowly swept the lenses across the top-floor offices again, seeing the same suits sitting behind their desks, making calls or hosting video conferences on their computers. The binoculars continued to relay the digital feedback to the tech guys at the Madhouse, where they would compile the data on these individuals for a later date.

No sign of Harlan Brink yet, though.

'Rule number twenty-three: the dead don't need to piss,' Clyde said.

During their pre-Hourglass status, he and Kev had compiled a list of the positive aspects of being a ghost. In hindsight, it was possible that it was all part of a much-needed distraction to keep themselves from suffering a psychological collapse, but even now, it still helped to pass the time.

Kev smirked, gesturing at his ghostly form. 'And just think, one day this could all be yours.' He stared down and across the intersection to where Ace was on Park Avenue, separated from the target building's main entrance by north and southbound traffic; the evening rush hour had come and gone, so visibility wasn't too much of an issue. Ace had made the wise decision to leave the Ice Maiden at the Madhouse garage, borrowing a more discreet second-hand model from the motor pool that was itself a tricked-out beast beneath its unappealing body, just in case an impromptu high-speed pursuit or shoot-out occurred. He was acting casual, slouched at the wheel, sorting through his fantasy hockey league, probably hoping to stick it to Carter in security or Chavez in maintenance—well, probably everyone at HQ involved in the pool, really—while training his sunglasses on the main entrance. The sunglasses were a sophisticated accessory that doubled as binoculars and a digital camera, perfect for observing any interesting comings and goings from across the street. Meadows had made a call to the captain of the 19th Precinct to ensure Ace had a temporary free parking space.

'You need to piss?'

Clyde humored Kev, if only to alleviate a moment's worth of boredom. 'Think I could hit Ace with my piss bottle from up here?'

Ace growled over the comm-link, 'I'll be feeding you piss-flavored ice cubes if you try.'

'Wouldn't dream of it, big guy,' Clyde said. 'Anything on your end, Rose?'

Rose and Nat were sat at an outside table of an upscale cafe on 63rd Street, just across the road from the fort's employee and guest parking garage. Rose was leaning back in her chair, picking at a blueberry muffin, while Nat seemed to be draped over her chair, slurping a caramel frappé. The pair looked as though they hadn't a care in the world other than enjoying the still-bright and warm evening.

'Only further proof that I'd kill myself at an office job,' Natalie said. 'Top floor. Window. Swan dive.'

'Not much activity at the rear,' Rose translated. 'A few tie-and-cufflink types grabbing a smoke and playing with their phones.' Rose spotted a silver Porsche Panamera 4.8 V8 Turbo cruise down towards them. The parking lot's barrier swung upwards in advance, and the car glided effortlessly like a sidewinder snake onto the premises and straight down the ramp, out of sight. 'Scratch that. We got a new arrival, just drove into the garage. Silver Porsche, undoubtedly bullet-proof and filled with assholes. Sarge?'

A short wait. 'Got it,' Sarge confirmed.

Not too far from their position, Sarge, Barros, and Darcy were testing the underground level of the parking structure for any additional paranormal security measures but coming up short: no hexes or barriers or exotic species hungry for protoplasmic ghost-flesh. Just concrete, steel, and security cameras like any multi-storied lot. Cairnwood may well have been outfitting the paramilitary security company with a supernatural operative here and there, and perhaps providing them with the Exorcist ammunition, but that appeared to be where their assistance ended.

'I can confirm it's Brink,' said Sarge. 'He just pulled into his parking space.' Each member of the ISU—plus Kev—was equipped with a special communicator developed by Hourglass. Immaterial in design, the small ear-fitting receiver-transmitters could only be grasped by a living person wearing specialized gloves or implements.

'Run the plate by me again, Sarge,' Rose said. 'We might need to tail this asshole.'

Sarge did as requested, while Darcy and Barros prowled the darker corners of the garage, giving impressed glances at all the other flashy, top-of-the-line cars parked throughout. If they had been capable of interacting with physical matter like Kev, there was a good chance that the CSS goons would be leaving work to find burst tires and scratched bodywork.

'He's heading into the elevator now,' Sarge reported.

'I've still got my eye on the executive offices,' Clyde said. 'Ace?'

'He didn't get out in the lobby,' Ace answered. 'Elevator lights still on. Going up.'

The polished elevator doors finally slid open on ten, and Clyde watched Harlan Brink stride out.

Through the binoculars, Clyde noticed an old scar that wasn't on the man's file photo, starting from just beneath his orange-tinted Oakley sunglasses, crossing his right cheek, and finishing at his jawline. Also: 'Dude looks a little paler than in his file pics.'

'He is ginger,' Ace said. 'And he's not in the Middle East anymore.'

'I get that, but even so, he's looking kind of gray.'

Washed-out color aside, the head of security was casually dressed in a short-sleeve silk shirt, slacks, comfortable shoes, and a shoulder rig with a Sig Sauer P365. Brink shuffled through the huge open-plan hub of the office, mumbling a few things to the posted guards he passed. The bugs planted by Kev picked up the commands as curt dismissals. The guards didn't question their employer; at best they gave surprised glances at each other, then set off for the stairwells or elevators. Brink knocked on the glass wall of one of the occupied offices, leaning in to interrupt two employees from casually tossing a football around as they dealt with a phone call and teleconference, respectively. Brink repeated his brusque order, and within minutes the office ballplayers were ending their calls and logging off their computers. One of the pair tossed a short spiral towards Brink, who caught it and gave the wannabe quarterback a playful punch on the shoulder on his way out of the office. The early finishers spread the boss's orders over their walkie-talkies, and before long the flak jackets and weaponry was being returned to the armory, and a river of expensive cars flooded out of the underground.

'That's strange, right?' Kev asked predominantly to Clyde, but the whole team received the question.

'Not even leaving a skeleton crew security staff? Yep, seems funky for a top-flight international security company,' Rose said.

Brink used a swipe card to access his office and took a seat behind his sleek, minimalist desk. The whole aesthetic made Clyde think of some giant bland robot that had vomited out the building's decor.

Clyde thought about that first paranormally-enhanced psycho he'd fought in the Brooklyn warehouse. Lieutenant Castor. And what about Brink? Did he have any unusual attributes of his own? 'Maybe Brink has some secrets, leaving himself all alone like this.'

'Or maybe what we're looking for isn't here, so there's nothing worth guarding,' Nat said.

'There could be a section of the building we're not seeing. A basement?' Darcy suggested. 'If this is where they're making their boogiemen, I'm betting they'll have more guys down there. I don't see them performing any satanic rituals in an office or staff kitchen.'

'Does anything good ever happen in basements?' Rose asked.

'Me and my buddies used to get drunk in a basement,' Ace said. 'That was always fun.'

'Yo, Sarge, did you say there's no skin-tingling ghost-busting security measures in the building?' Nat asked, her voice lilting with possible bad ideas.

'Confirmed,' he answered. 'There's nothing in the outer perimeter, but the main building is an unknown quantity.'

'I know where you're going, rookie, and I like the way your mind works,' Ace said to Nat. 'How does the ISU feel about touring the interior?'

'Before anybody gets too excited, remember this is recon only, not a black-bag op,' Rose spoke with the last bite of muffin in her mouth. 'There's to be no attempt at deeper infiltration or engagement until we run it by Meadows.'

Clyde continued to monitor Brink as he worked behind his desk. The mic bugs picked up nothing more substantial than some keyboard tapping and paper shuffling. For the most part, the security chief seemed despondent, as though he was putting off doing something.

After another twenty minutes, Harlan Brink switched off his computer and left his office, heading back to the elevators in no clear hurry.

'He's on the move,' Clyde said. 'Back in the elevator.'

The ISU were still waiting in the underground lot, half-entombed in the concrete walls and pillars, eyes on the elevators. Brink's elevator ride down took noticeably longer than his ride up, and Sarge was in the middle of suggesting Brink had kept on going, deeper underground to a sub-basement, when the metal doors opened and deposited Brink.

Clyde ran across the roof to the edge of the building and jumped. He had siphoned a small portion of Kev's telekinesis prior to the recon and now used it to glide and rebound off the walls and the fire escapes into the alleyway. Ace's van rolled up outside the mouth of the alley. Clyde and Kev quickly jumped inside, and Ace merged with the evening traffic, circling the block to close in on Brink's imminent exit from CSS. Rose and Nat had climbed into their souped-up soccer-mom car, and the team's two-vehicle convoy carefully tailed Brink's Porsche north along Lexington Avenue.

After ten minutes of Manhattan traffic and a few close calls casually skimming through red lights, Brink's route led them east down 79th Street towards what would shortly become the busy FDR Drive. It was beginning to feel like a meandering route.

'I don't like this,' Ace said. 'Anyone else feel like we're about to get fucked?'

Rose kept a respectable distance from Ace's van to ensure they didn't move like a collective bunch of overeager novices. 'You think he's leading us to an ambush?' She kept a keen eye on her mirrors as well as the road ahead.

'I think it's just a healthy sense of pessimism,' Clyde said. He saw possible sniper nests all about them and a looming intersection waiting to potentially expel a battering ram of professional killers at them.

His anxiety was premature.

A second or two later, Harlan Brink's armored silver sports car left the road as a huge, internalized fireball pushed it into the air, the incredible pressure of the scorching gas managing to blast the ballistic-proof glass outwards across the street in every direction.

None of the team noticed the CSS drone camera observing them from 150 feet in the air.

14

The clean-up crew arrived swiftly and responded rapidly, cordoning off the street and the burning wreckage of Harlan Brink's car. Dark-suited agency personnel quickly assumed authority from the local police without any posturing or territorial ravings. The NYPD had a quiet liaison high in their chain of command who was quick to shoot orders down the line when Meadows or other trusted high-ranking agents from the local Hourglass branch got in touch, and so, within minutes, the local blues were rerouting traffic and setting up sawhorses to bar the morbidly curious public from getting any closer than the sidewalks. Paramedics were busy loading the wounded collateral into the backs of their ambulances, dealing with shrapnel and burns. Miraculously, there were no fatalities. Ace had intended to douse the flames with ice until the gathering crowd made him cautious. Best to allow the fire department to do it for him.

Clyde and the team were crowding the insides of the mobile command unit with Meadows while forensic techs came and went, lugging equipment, punching in data on computers, and reviewing footage of the explosion from the proximate traffic and security cams.

'Do you think he was murdered, or was this some kind of freaky accident?' Clyde asked.

'What, like he went over a nasty speed bump?' Nat had a mischievous glint in her eye.

'It's possible he was killed because you were made.' Meadows leaned against the countertop with the coffee pot and donuts, a cup of herbal tea in hand, which seemed to be doing little to lift his spirits.

'We didn't have a tail,' Ace said with certainty. He was chewing what must have been a full pack of gum, enough to induce jaw ache in a bull.

Everyone arrived at the same conclusion in a matter of seconds.

'Aerial drone.' Clyde said it for all of them.

Meadows wore an expression that, to Clyde, seemed to suggest that the whole team must have ridden the slow bus to work today. How could they have overlooked something so obvious?

But Clyde wasn't buying Meadows's silent suggestion. 'I doubt his own contractors would have killed him, even if they thought he was being followed. I mean, the dude was the co-founder of CSS.'

'Maybe they thought he was a shit boss,' Nat said.

'I didn't see any projectile hit his car,' Clyde continued.

'Me neither,' Kev agreed.

'So that would mean he's been driving around with an explosive charge fitted to his car? Bit of an extreme contingency in case somebody followed him.'

'Our forensic team will confirm or deny any traces of conventional or abnormal explosive materials, externally or internally.' Meadows sipped his tea. Still looked annoyed. He glanced back towards some of the agents hunched over a monitor. 'Radar picking up anything?'

'No, sir,' answered a skinny man somewhere in his thirties, with a long-term computer-screen complexion and a smart haircut. 'If they were followed by a drone, it's gone back to its nest. Doesn't mean we're still not being watched by a pair of eyes, though.'

'Maybe Brink found himself on the outs with Talbot,' Rose speculated. 'Cairnwood might have sanctioned this. He outlived his usefulness, spat in their eye?'

'Do car bombs fit their style? Does seem a bit more black-ops or crim-inal.' Kev's face was hard to determine now that he had been forced to don his ludicrous outfit again, but it was good he had stashed it in the van judging from how quickly the crowds had poured out of the local storefronts and buildings.

'Their style is doing whatever quietly helps them achieve their goals,' Meadows said. 'They're not going to send a giant bat to swoop down and seize Brink's car in broad daylight. Hypothetically.'

Clyde saw his point. But on the other hand, some of the previous en-counters with the other assassins had veered awfully close to becoming full-blown public spectacles, though whether they were cases of "quietly achieving their goals" gone awry or plain bad recruitment was difficult to tell.

'Does it matter who pushed the button?' Clyde asked. 'If CSS are scrambling around to hide their toys, I think we need to decide quickly on whether we're still going into that big box of mercs to search for Talbot's boogieman machine.'

Rose nodded emphatically. 'I'm with the nerd. I don't see how we have a choice. It doesn't matter what happened to that asshole,' she said, pointing outside to where the techs were nosing around Brink's exploded car. 'We need to stop Cairnwood before they make any more elite killers to send at us.' A look of reticence passed over her face before quickly vanishing. 'I'd say we've handled ourselves pretty well against them up to now, but we still haven't seen hide nor hair of Hangman. And that's really starting to bother me.'

The hyper-capable killer stepped back into Clyde's thoughts like they were a second home, dragging behind him the grisly corpses of dead strike team agents, all more powerful than Clyde; at least the Sparks had been. That was indisputable.

'I'm in no hurry to meet the guy,' he said, 'but Rose is right. I don't like the feeling of treading water while a huge fucking shark continues to circle below us, working our nerves. As nuts as it seems, I'd rather go straight into that place and end this right now if we can. Just to know.'

Ace spat his wad of gum into the wastebasket. 'I'll drink to that.'

'So let's pick a date and time and do this thing before any more unexpected bombs go off,' Kev encouraged. 'Or they make a second Hangman.'

'Or a bitch with a monkey.' Rose was still having a hard time with that loss.

Nat seemed to be mulling something over, arrived at a conclusion, and levelled a peculiar and meaningful stare at Meadows. 'I can do more than tear up inkblots with Schulz. Give me some time with my playlist, and maybe I could shatter that whole building.' Some of the seriousness ebbed from her tone. She made a steeple of her fingers like a calculating hackneyed villain. 'If there are any evil schemers holed up somewhere down there, then that should shake them out. Like shoving a stick into an ant colony. Clear them out and get on in.'

Hearing Nat effectively describe her proposed action as detonating some type of audible warhead was something of a surprise to Clyde. The whole team really, except for Meadows.

'You could do that?' Rose asked, interested and also a little concerned.

Nat, eyeballing the box of donuts, went to answer, but Meadows was quick to kill the suggestion. 'You have potency, but that's a significantly reckless act, Nat. Such an act could incur unknowable casualties. The flying glass alone? Kev couldn't possibly contain such shrapnel.'

'You could evacuate the surrounding areas. That way—'

'Nat, please.' Meadows's tone was gentle, firm, compromising. 'Soon enough you'll learn that we try to operate in confined, controllable spheres until we're left with no other options. And even if this was one of those Hail Mary situations, I'm not sure even you could demolish a building that size, one full of ballistic-proof glass, no less.'

'Just throwing it out there, Uncle M,' she said graciously, helping herself to a glazed donut from the box.

Stone-faced, Meadows finished his tea and sighed in what might have been euphoria for a man of so few facial expressions. 'We're going to be proactive, not reactive. And I need to get consent from the tight-lipped types in Washington before we make any aggressive moves on a private business. Tomorrow night,' he said with certainty, 'you'll infiltrate and leave no stone unturned until we can definitively conclude the presence of Talbot's assassin program.'

Doubt cast its shadow over Clyde. 'Sir, with respect, I know there are correct ways to do things, but shouldn't we strike now while the building's forces are depleted and the chief is dead?'

'I'll refer back to Nat's ant analogy. Depleted doesn't mean the building is vulnerable. Could be a ruse. There is something fishy going on here, and if that place is hiding something unpleasant, I want to exhaust all avenues of investigation before rashly signing off on what could be a suicide mission. Let the heat die down a little. I'll see if the cyber team can get through the company's firewall, perhaps find schematics of any sub-levels and possible supernatural security measures. In the meantime, I'll have surveillance sit on the building for the night, try to see if any other peculiar comings, goings, or blowings occur.'

Clyde nodded, noticing the resounding agreement on the faces of Rose and two-thirds of the ISU for the official order. The eyes of Private Barros, however, held a small flicker of doubt. Clyde still wanted to hit the place tonight, to put the stress of the Hangman to bed, wanted to object further to Meadows's plan, knowing Kev—and perhaps even Barros?— would agree with him. But he decided that unless he was planning on becoming some imprisoned renegade this early in his career, he had best keep his mouth shut.

Meadows stepped out of the command trailer but was quickly caught by Kev.

'Any news yet on those bikers? Trace energy, anything?'

Meadows squinted a little more than usual; his eyes, as dark and rough as tree bark, briefly arced across the surrounding rooftops and the high windows blazing orange with the sun's fading fire. With his curiosity apparently satisfied, his eyes dropped back to Kev. 'When I know, you'll know.'

'Well, are you close?'

'You don't trust me much, do you, son?'

'I'm just inquisitive, sir.'

'Believe me, I've noticed. One day, maybe I'll find you a position in R&D. In the meantime, patience. That's one thing the dead should have in spades.' Meadows glanced about at the clean-up crew loading the Porsche's smoking wreckage onto a tow truck. 'The minute I learn anything pertinent to this assignment, you'll all be sure to know.' His shielded eyes cut to Clyde, still standing in the doorway next to Nat. 'Take the night off, team. Blow off some steam, but no bullshit. Tomorrow night you'll get your wish.' He climbed into the back of a black armored sedan, its red-and-blue dash lights silently flashing, and was quickly gone.

Clyde took the metal steps down from the trailer, the rest of the team filing out after him, apart from the ISU, who vanished to another plane, their command center located somewhere between Rose and who knew where.

Nat turned to Clyde. 'Recon and car bombs. I've had worse first days on the job.'

Clyde couldn't believe how unfazed she was by all of this. 'And tomorrow you'll get to raid a high-security facility potentially filled with monsters.'

Nat finished her donut and shoved her hands in her jeans pockets. 'Cool. You want to grab a beer?'

For a split second, Clyde thought that was a one-to-one offer and fumbled for an answer.

'Always,' Ace piped up.

'I'll buy the first round as long as we move our asses. Too many eyes on us here.' Rose watched the blackened and twisted Porsche being driven away by the tow truck while forensics continued their diligent work in a grid around the car's blast site. 'And this is a school night, so one or two tops, then home.'

'How about five or six?' was Nat's counter-offer.

'We got a big day of prepping and strategizing tomorrow.'

'You can strategize on the bar napkins. Come on, I know a place. You'll love it.' Nat elbowed Clyde lightly on the arm and headed for their loaned rides.

Clyde checked with Kev, who seemed to be going with the flow.

Rose slowly acquiesced. 'Damn, Nat, I hope you don't just turn out to be Ace with a better pair of tits.'

15

The Bottom of the Barrel was a former punk dive in the East Village, now converted into marginally less of a punk dive in the East Village. It still retained an aesthetic of grit and spilt beer from its heyday, but it was from managerial choice and not a constant struggle with rent and maintenance repairs. Despite the rise and fall of the 1970s punk rock scene and its transition into '80s hardcore, the bar and venue had somehow endured to this day.

Clyde and the team were sitting in a booth of red leather upholstery, ripped up and duct-taped, surrounding a table composed of a busted-up speaker cabinet with a stolen large STOP sign acting as a tabletop. Broken guitars adorned the walls like tributes to raucous and successful gigs.

Nat had spoken with the bartender, a middle-aged punk with spiky skunk-dyed hair and bottle-thick glasses, called Wasserman, who was also the manager. Now each team member had a bottle of a potent craft beer called Riot, which Nat highly endorsed.

'Since we might all be dead this time tomorrow, this seems like a cool way to get to know each other a little.' Nat hunkered forward, elbows on the table. Despite her glum prediction, she seemed chirpy.

'You get used to it. All part of the job.' Rose took a deep swig. 'This is not bad.' She then checked the label, which Clyde knew was to see how many calories she would have to burn off for such an indulgence.

Nat gestured to Wasserman. 'His buddies make it. Got a pretty nice kick, huh?'

'I'll have to take your word on that.' Kev sat there, beer-less but not bitter. He continued to survey the place through his aviators. 'Is this place really old or just trying to fabricate a scummy personality?'

Ace chilled his bottle with one large, rough palm. 'I like it. The beer. Not the music. I can't stomach this punk shit.'

Nat gestured at her ear, pretending not to have heard that comment and nodded along to the restless sounds of the Ramones' "I Just Want to Have Something to Do." 'Wasserman ran this place in '77. All the greats played here: Richard Hell, Joey and these guys,' she said, pointing up as if to seize Joey's bored and frustrated voice. Clyde initially thought she was going to cause some micro explosion. 'Patti Smith, Agnostic Front, Cro-Mags.' Her eyes sparkled with enthusiasm, and Clyde couldn't deny that he enjoyed looking into them; there was something exciting and mysterious about her. In fact, he wouldn't mind spending the rest of the night catching some more eye contact with her instead of thinking about storming a stronghold of military contractors and, possibly, the Hangman. 'Wasserman kept this place together with Super Glue and spit for decades.' She rapped her tattooed knuckles on the dented and gouged STOP sign. 'This is all authentic. No posers here.'

Clyde managed to pick out Trojan Horse Cocks on several of the gig posters that plastered every wall, all beset by a near-incomprehensible scramble of felt marker names, slogans, and dirty jokes. 'You play here a lot?'

'A fuck load.' Nat glanced wistfully at the stage covered in wire mesh. Her finger tapped her bottle neck with a few musical clinks as she reminisced. 'Good times.'

Ace raised his bottle in salute. 'You're not dead yet.'

'Who knows?' Rose shrugged optimistically. 'Maybe you'll survive tomorrow night, help us blow this case wide open, and get the band back together.'

Nat returned an ephemeral smirk and swigged from her bottle. 'So, Rosie, how did you end up with the agency?'

Rose offered her the abridged version: a California girl whose air force parents went MIA on mission—now presumed KIA—joined the army, her near fatal stint in Syria, the ghosts of the less fortunate Sarge, Barros, and Darcy, the army shrink, and the subsequent contact by Hourglass.

'I'd love to go to Cali,' Nat admitted. 'The south. Place grew some great punk bands the way bread grows mold. You ever surf?'

'Fuck that! Sharks in there.' Rose laughed a little self-consciously. 'I can't suplex "Jaws" without ground to stand on. What about you?'

'A little. Beautiful place called Siargao, surf capital of the Philippines. My parents like to go back there every couple of years, stay in touch with family and stuff. And it's good for Pops to keep a presence there, working at the consulate. So yeah, ride a few waves, some rock climbing, cave exploring.' Her head quickly swiveled to Clyde. 'What about you? Any surfing in the East River?'

Rose cackled like a surprised Valkyrie, and Ace rumbled the booth with his baritone mirth.

Clyde didn't mind her scoring points off him with a dumb joke. He raised his bottle and took a gulp of beer. 'The only thing I've surfed is the internet...and I can't believe I just said that. And I suck at skateboarding.' He angled a thumb at Kev and broke down how the pair of them landed on Hourglass's radar thanks to CCTV and a few reckless public incidents on Kev's behalf, culminating in the pair of them—mainly Kev—doling out some vigilante justice on a couple of idiots who tried to mug them in the park.

'I had the pleasure of witnessing that.' Rose grinned at the memory. 'I was in town to give them the rundown.'

'Turns out my various slip-ups were collated and forwarded to the PLE specialists at Indigo Mesa,' Kev finished.

'Smacking down muggers,' mused Nat. 'Now that's a satisfying way to land a job interview.'

'It worked out well in the end,' Kev said, his voice humorous behind his face scarf. It was a wonder Wasserman had allowed him entry into this establishment with how he was dressed.

'Okay, last and maybe least, what about you?' Nat asked Ace. 'I heard Canada has its own branch. Are you so bad that even the politest people on Earth don't want you?'

'Nah, just the polite people of Mississauga, Ontario.' He proudly bore his gap-toothed grin, and for such a big, imposing presence, he did have a surprisingly endearing smile. 'Hourglass absorbed the original Canadian intelligence community for all things fucked-up and weird. I was stationed with a team at our HQ, Igloo, but things have been a little quiet north of the border of late, so when these two flashed up on the grid'—he jutted his chin towards Clyde and Kev—'orders came down for me to show Clyde the ropes should he want to stay and get his hands dirty doing something other than reading comics and jerking off.' Clyde gave him a compassionate middle finger and glanced awkwardly at Nat. Ace glugged back the entirety of the three-quarters-full bottle. He shrugged. 'What the hell, I was already in New York when their pick-up was in motion. Not too long after that, all this Hangman shit started, and Meadows needed reliable people here. Call me Mr. Reliable.' His finger made a small rime of ice on the wet ring left by the bottle's bottom.

'I was Ace's "rookie,"' Clyde told Nat, flashing a wink at Ace, then facing her again. 'Looks like that's your spot now, until you notch that first assignment.'

Nat's good-time vibes took a slight dip. 'I can't believe I'm about to become everything I hate, a party-pooper, but should we run through tomorrow night's surprise party? Make sure it's all safe and PG and shit?'

The team leaned in a little closer to talk strategy, not that anybody was likely to overhear anything in the middle of the raucous music, chatter, and drunken laughter.

Rose began. 'First off, we need to factor in that CSS just lost their CO to an unconfirmed party. That'll give us a brief window to strike before they reorganize.'

'For the record, I think Meadows made a bad call by keeping us from moving on that place tonight,' Kev stated.

'Seconded,' Ace agreed.

Kev's concealed face shifted to read Nat's reaction, but she didn't appear to take issue with his opinion. 'No offense, new girl. Is it cool if I talk openly around you? You're not, like...the boss's mole or anything?'

'Would you believe me if I told you?' Nat answered with a calculating squint.

'Depends how cynical I'm feeling on the day.'

As for Rose's opinion, it was all in her eyes, a disciplined acceptance of chain-of-command that had learned to live with top-down decisions. 'We need clearance. Can't just kick the doors in on a "respected business,"' she said with a sneer. 'The big cheese is right. There might have been some falling-out between the contractors and Talbot. We don't know why Brink was eliminated, but it doesn't matter. The loss of a valuable target like him will ensure our window stays open for a while longer.' She used a hand to push away any further in-house political squabbling amongst the team. 'So since we're all fucking clueless as to the actual physical appearance of this power source, I assume we're all in agreement that it isn't going to be a stapler or photocopier?'

The team were all in silent agreement.

'Which means that wherever this power source is, it'll be somewhere more secure than some asshole's cubicle.' She appeared to be struck by a sudden bolt of inspiration. 'I suppose the building's armory is an obvious option?'

'Secure, guarded.' Kev weighed it up. 'And I agree, definitely a better hiding place than some asshole's cubicle. It's also a perfect opportunity for us to check out what hardware they're carrying. See if that new-generation assault rifle comes loaded with supplementary Exorcist rounds or any other tricky armaments.'

'Right, so the smart thing to do is to try and get in there with as little fuss as possible,' Clyde said. 'I wouldn't mourn the death of these scum buckets, but until we know for a fact that they're definitely involved in this assassin thing, I don't want to start a body count.' He still didn't recognize himself when it came to talking about killing, even if it was a necessity. It had become so clinical, black-and-white parameters of a mission's success. His ability to compartmentalize had surprised him after his first kill during the Brooklyn warehouse raid and had only improved since. It was a troubling fact, so he pushed on. 'Kev, if the cyber guys at Mad can't access the site's CCTV or provide us with anything else useful, think you're up for entering through the parking garage elevator shaft, see how far down it goes?'

Kev drummed the gloved fingers of one hand against the arm of his heavy coat. 'What else am I going to get to brag about?'

'Cool. I can try and get in from the roof and work my way down to the armory.' Clyde looked to Rose and Ace for feedback and received nodding approvals from both.

'You need back-up with that?' Nat asked him.

Clyde waited for a few seconds, a rush of thoughts besieging him. He had only recently lost his own amateur-hour status, but did he want an inexperienced agent—regardless of her exceptional power—covering him? He had been that same inexperienced agent less than six months ago, only without the incredible gifts of a Spark, and Ace and Rose had both seen potential in him. Who was he to get picky?

'Yeah,' he answered, and one side of her black-painted lips curved upwards in a smile that held a subtle lasciviousness. Did he read that signal wrong? Maybe she just really enjoyed living on the edge. 'But no punk rock anarchy. Can you handle the silence?'

'You betcha.' Clyde's eyes locked with Nat's for a brief tingling moment. His physical attraction to her was unquestionable, but was it a mutual thing? Could he be that lucky? A Spark who was cozy with his boss... Maybe it was unlucky.

Rose grew a little dubious and irritable with their lack of intel and pinned Kev with a stare. 'We're still fumbling around in the dark. Say you do find a bunker down there. It still won't do us any good unless we know what it is we're grabbing or smashing. Safe bet it'll look like it belongs in some old hag fortune teller's or dusty occultist shop, but what about its size? Its shape, material? The power source could be anything.'

'Shit, it could be a fucking six-headed dragon for all we know,' Ace added, just to calm everyone's nerves. Glancing over the top of the booth towards the packed bar full of punks, he looked impatient for his next bottle. 'You think something like that would go down easy?'

'A hypothetical six-headed dragon? Probably,' Nat said. 'Since it's not real.'

'Point is, Kev and the ISU are sweating ghost-killer ammo here, but there could be other things just as nasty down there. And we'll be upstairs.'

Clyde raised an eyebrow in thought. 'So what are you saying? Let's just hit the place commando-style and take them all down? Fast and loud, no soft infil?'

Rose and Ace shared a similar expression; it spoke of embracing cold, hard facts.

'Let's not fool ourselves, kid,' Ace said. 'Even though we don't yet have all the facts about what we're facing, these CSS douche-drizzles were frontline shooters for Talbot's energy venture. And since we know that stuffy English prick is linked in some way with the Sharps, one of whom owns CSS...' He held his hands out as if in supplication to common sense. 'It's a safe bet we can mop the floor with every last one of them, guilt-free.'

Clyde saw Kev nodding along and knew it wasn't to the body-slamming aggression of Sick of It All.

'And if by some small chance we're wrong, fuck 'em. They're card-carrying professional assholes.' That was Kev's rationale.

Clyde stayed quiet. He couldn't argue with Kev's opinion because technically he wasn't wrong, and he knew it wasn't based purely on the petty fact that a CSS triggerman had put a ghost killer through him back at that Brooklyn warehouse. These were legitimate cold-blooded killers, now with a sideline in working for a cabal of devils.

'What about Sarge, Darcy, and Barros, they want to pitch in?' Clyde asked.

Rose's gaze seemed to regard some distant point in the bar, getting the trio's consensus from their interstitial barracks. 'Three votes for putting the CSS down.'

Clyde sat with that for a moment, not taking it lightly. What did it matter? Everyone was going to hell one way or another. 'Okay then, so we split into teams, designate different entry points, neutralize the on-site personnel, then regroup before scoping out the lower levels.'

'Gives me chills,' Ace said. 'This time tomorrow night, we might have Talbot thinking about another line of work.'

'Let's hold off on the excitement until we bury Hangman,' Clyde said. 'Meadows's last team had three Sparks on it, and we've all seen the pictures.'

'He's a threat, no doubt about it,' Rose admitted. 'But that sick bastard did that by taking them down one at a time. It was a smart move, but together we'll string him up by his balls and treat him like a piñata.'

Nat raised her half-empty bottle in a toast. 'To leading unconventional lives.' That got her a few cynical laughs, and the bottles clinked, except for Ace, who was still staring at the jam-packed bar like a drowning man in need of a piece of driftwood.

To spare him any further pain, they made short work of their beers and called it a night.

16

Leonard stared out of the large bay window of his boardroom. Situated eighty floors atop the sleek Sharp Industries tower, it offered a spectacular panorama. His troubled eyes ventured beyond Wall Street and the surrounding vast expanse of concrete, glass, and steel, the rich lifeblood that made up the Financial District, and settled on the distant blinking lights of the Brooklyn Bridge. The sky was a slowly cooling furnace, the passionate orange-and-red blaze finally fading into a gentle purple. He rolled his neck with a sigh, trying to break the tension in his muscles and enjoying the soft cricking sounds of the motion. The exhaustion from another long day trapped behind his desk in board meeting after board meeting slowly washed over him in a lethargic wave. How he wished the simple concerns of running a multi-million-dollar business empire were the only things playing on his mind.

Julius had gotten back to him. He'd sent a curt text saying he couldn't make that dinner tonight, throwing in a perfunctory apology and explaining that he would be tied up at work. Leonard had attempted calling him back, not to express his annoyance, only his continued concern. He didn't get an answer.

'Mr. Sharp?' A female voice pulled him from his reflection.

Leonard turned towards the slim, attractive figure of his PA, Monica, standing in silhouette at the threshold of his dusky office.

'Yes?' He forced some honey into his tired tone.

'Just to remind you, your meeting for the Fordham Heights regeneration project is scheduled for nine am tomorrow with Mayor Wilson. And your appearance for the Wayward Youth Boxing Program is set for one pm.'

'Thank you, Monica. You should get going. One of us needs to have a social life around here.'

'Goodnight, sir.' She turned to leave.

'Oh, Monica?'

'Sir?'

'Add an extra two thousand to this year's WYBP donation.'

'Of course, sir. Goodnight.'

'Goodnight.'

Leonard leaned into the cool glass, appraising the sprawl of prestigious neighboring tower blocks and businesses spiraling upwards, attempting to match his lofty heights. Good luck to them, he thought. It gets lonely up here.

The door swung open again, and Leonard expected another last-minute reminder from Monica.

It was Harlan Brink, his quick steps conveying urgent news.

'I was going to call, but I didn't want to disturb your meeting.' He stopped next to Leonard, the pair of them framed by the large window, illuminated by twilight and neon. 'Has Talbot been in contact?'

Leonard huffed quietly. 'No. What now?'

'Two things actually. But the first connects to the second.' Harlan paused, trying to find the correct way to disclose some sensitive information. 'I'm enhanced, Len.'

Leonard turned slightly from the window, half his face lost in shadow. 'What?'

'When Captain Agua and the others volunteered, I was tempted too, but for different reasons. I held off for a while, but the way things are moving around here I decided to reevaluate my earlier hesitance. By staying put at Elzinga this morning... Well, it's done now. I know this is something of a gray area, so I was reluctant to tell you my intentions. I—'

'What if they turned you into another fucking dummy like Nathan?!'

'Talbot and I spoke about this before the process. The blank slate is a contingency only. That Eye thing...it can create sleeper cells or leave the subject with their autonomy intact. When Talbot first approached you, Nathan did what Nathan does. So Talbot made an example of him. I suppose it served to show you that he's not to be fucked with by taking him away from you and that he admired Nathan's guts. Apart from that, the mind wipe is on a case-by-case basis. Agua and his three lieutenants were serving Cairnwood interests, so Talbot gave them a modicum of trust. Agua was good, but he had less compunction than some. Maybe he and the others opted for the enhancement for their own personal gain, thinking that they could use it to their advantage when they got back from touring that fucking nightmare country they went into. But I volunteered to strengthen our position. I didn't spend all those years running around killing dictators and drug lords in every armpit of the world to lose everything we have built together. And Talbot needs me since I run the day-to-day operations of CSS. I'm useful to him. His very own box of toy soldiers to play with.'

'The change could have killed you.' Leonard recalled Brink reporting how seven of his shooters were not as lucky as Captain Agua and his lieutenants.

'Except it didn't.' Harlan watched Leonard dismiss his carelessness with a head shake and return to watching the millions of electric lights beneath the purpling sky. 'I did this for the both of us, Len. In a sad way, I had to do this. Like it or not, we're at war now. A war on two sides, potentially, and it's fought by some very unconventional means. I had to become something more if we're to survive this as anything more than slaves or pawns.'

A part of Leonard knew this to be true, but as somebody who had known hell all his life, the realization still unsettled him. 'And do tell, what exactly can you now do?'

'I can make duplicates of myself that explode on command,' he said drily; there wasn't even a momentary flicker of amusement or pride in his disclosure. What sounded like an incredibly lethal and valuable talent was nothing more than a new tool for his belt. 'It's a limited amount at any one time, but it might be effective under the right circumstances.'

Leonard almost asked if these duplicates retained any free will, but decided he didn't want to know. 'And you think by turning yourself into a walking bomb you can keep Talbot and his people from throwing their weight around? They have powers the likes of which we don't understand. More than that, they have deeper pockets than us.'

Harlan did the wise thing and allowed Leonard to think for a moment. 'And this second thing?'

'Somebody has been trying to get into the CSS intranet, and one of our drones spotted Hourglass agents performing surveillance on the CSS building earlier. I had to flush them out to be sure, so I did.'

'I can't believe I'm only hearing about this now.'

'I knew you were busy. You don't have the luxury of hiding behind closed doors when you're the CEO.'

'Fuck me.' Leonard shook his head. 'Doesn't matter, from now on you report to me first. I'm not going to sit by and have my power taken away piece by piece.'

'Understood. Back to the issue at hand. When I called Talbot, he told me—'

'That this was an opportunity.' Talbot stood in the doorway, having let himself in. Leonard didn't like how he sometimes seemed to manifest out of thin air or the strengthening shade like a damn vampire. The shadows continued to grow in the rich décor of his office, encroaching further and further like an opening mouth ready to swallow everything into its obsidian gullet.

Leonard's features hardened and he hung his head with another long sigh. 'An opportunity? For you to uncage Nathan and whatever other monsters you've created?' Leonard's hard eyes sliced towards Harlan for a split second, then back to Talbot.

'I knew you were a bright penny, Lenny.' Talbot smirked. He spoke in a soft, cultured English accent borne from overprivileged breeding, and stood at a lean six-foot, was deathly pale, and yet possessed the kind of movie-star good looks that craftily concealed the unimaginable horrors he was capable of. 'It seems your little quarrel with the Chinese is settled, and more: there is harmony within your teeny-tiny fiefdom. So, of course, I'm going to "uncage" Hangman. Because this latest batch of insects from Hourglass are'—his cheek twitched involuntarily with impatient humor—'getting under my skin. I have a boss too, Leonard. And he has bosses, and they,' his manicured hand windmilled, 'well, you get the picture. I know you don't like working under me any more than I like working under mine, but if we can just achieve some synergy, I think it'll establish a much more comfortable working environment. Don't you?'

Leonard didn't answer. He knew this asshole was just enjoying the sound of his own voice.

'When things go well for me, they'll start to go well for you. I'll be quite frank with you: This opportunity before us, if we can entice these agents into following through with their raid on your security firm, it will produce casualties. We all know what these little bastards are capable of by now. But your employees are trained soldiers. The best death they can hope for is combat. And it won't be in vain. They'll put up just enough of a struggle for Hourglass to believe the building holds what they're looking for—the Eye of Charon, I presume. They'll enter, they'll search, and then—' Talbot slapped his hands together. 'Insects get squashed by Hangman.' He turned to Harlan. 'You can leave, but I don't want you on the premises of CSS, not until after the agents have attacked and are getting hosed off the walls. You're right, I do have uses for you.' Talbot's expression became predatory as he stepped into Harlan's personal space, his eyes taking on a momentary cat's-eye sheen of alien emerald, but Harlan, to his credit, didn't back down. 'However, should you get any foolish notions about biting the hand of your new master, I will castrate you. Clear?'

'Crystal.' Harlan glanced at Leonard, who nodded his farewell, and took his leave.

Talbot joined Leonard at the window, and together, shoulder to shoulder, they watched the magnificence of capitalism's birth. 'A city's skyline... always makes me think of an electrocardiograph. The smaller and less impressive, the weaker the economy, close to flatlining. But a skyline like this, all the bustle and stress of it all, that little green lifeline spiking higher and higher with frantic heartbeats, just like all those fancy buildings out there. All that wealth and opportunity and excitement, it can be bad for the ticker.'

'Why are you really here, Ed?' Leonard massaged his bullish neck.

'You're not to visit Julius when he is working. It distracts him.' Talbot continued to stare peacefully out the window as he delivered the news.

'Run that by me again.'

'His work is too important to be disrupted by your neediness. If he's not taking your calls or replying to your texts, please assume he is busy. Do not go barging in, demanding to see him.'

Leonard kept a gun in his desk drawer, out of habit more than anything, and he strongly considered reaching for it now and unloading it in the smug bastard's face. Would it do him any good?

'Are you really going to stand there and tell me I can't see my brother anymore?'

'No, Leonard. I'm saying you can call him as many times as you like, but if he doesn't answer it's because he is attending to more pressing matters. Don't despair; this isn't a permanent condition. But he does have a good sense for potential candidates, plus the Eye is still in a weakened state, incredible as that may seem. So I need Julius's assistance in restoring its former appetite.' Leonard tensed up; it was a small reaction, but with a body as bulky as his, it was unmissable. Talbot had the nerve to place a pale hand on Leonard's shoulder. 'Don't worry, Leonard, I only meant Julius is helpful for reinforcing some of the subjects' new prerogatives. He's been a tremendous help from the start. The wastes clogging up this state's prisons and asylums are useful subjects for Charon; why throw away any more experienced CSS soldiers on a gamble? No, I'd hate to lose Julius. That would mean leveraging some other prat into his position. So what I need from you is to simply keep your other would-be competitors in line.'

'We all share bloody histories,' Leonard said. 'Especially me and Charlie Horse. The joint venture is only as good as the fear that holds it together, but you and your associates have altered the dynamic by making me little more than another mutt waiting for scraps from the master's table. Some of the things they've heard since you turned up...a lot of them are wondering which scary bedtime stories are bullshit and which carry substance. They don't need to fear me when they could be trying to get you in their corner. The one thing I could still rely on, now more than ever, was Nathan to keep them straight, but I don't have him anymore. You've made him your pet.'

'Are you leading me to believe that you can't maintain control of your piss-ant little syndicate without the presence of one man? Because if that is the case, Leonard, then I can't help but wonder if maybe one of your hungry competitors would be more suited to wearing the crown instead.'

Leonard looked ready to put his fist through the window.

'Look, all I need is you to keep your empire from dissolving,' Talbot said soothingly. 'Otherwise, we have no use for you. An army that wars with itself is of little value to us. You're still on your probationary period. If you slip up, your circumstances may be subject to review.'

Leonard slowly moved his muscular 224-pound bulk over to his high-backed leather chair and settled into it, hearing its familiar creak. Talbot's words suffused tension through him. It was no idle threat. What could he do? He was cursed with humanity. Warm-blooded and weak. Despising the smugness that effortlessly oozed out of Talbot's presence like an un-dulating tide, he tried to look busy and flipped open his laptop.

Talbot studied the look on Leonard's face. 'I understand you're bitter about what happened to Nathan. But we're both businessmen, right? Just consider him a wise investment.'

Leonard fixed his eyes on Talbot and gave a barely perceptible nod. Enmity with no outlet.

'Leonard, if I truly believed you were incompetent in your duties, I would have already disposed of you. But so far, you have proven your worth and earned some good faith.' Talbot's cordial smile grew but was utterly devoid of warmth. 'Your services are more valuable to me without internal politics damaging the foundations. Remember, we're all friends here.' Meticulously, he fixed his tie, preparing to leave for other matters. 'Now I need to check in on your diligent brother. The outcome of this upcoming Hourglass operation could be big for me. You too. If Julius and I can get some traction with Charon's output, we could make some very big waves in the field of enhanced soldiers and private armies. Lots of money, Lenny. Lots.' Turning on the heels of his gleaming dress shoes, he allowed the pool of shadow to take him as he strolled out of the darkened office.

Leonard slapped his laptop closed and spun around in his chair to watch the city canyons illuminate themselves in electric beauty. He tried to call Julius again, just to know that he was okay, but found his desperate call going no further than voicemail. Squeezing the phone in his puncher's mitt, he shook off the depressive reverie and contented himself with the simple fact that Talbot, for everything he was, was pragmatic, and the loss of Julius would be an inconvenience to the effective running of his nightmarish assassin program. Julius was safe. He would try to call him again when he got home. If those super-juiced Feds got buried when they moved on CSS, it might cause Talbot to give Julius a little time off.

17

Julius swiped his ID card across the electronic scanner and opened the sturdy metal door. As he took the stairs down to the sub-basement, his mouth was an unpleasant mix of coffee and nicotine. He popped two mints into his mouth to suck on, craving a shower and his own bed. It had become an involuntary habit of his to avoid his reflection as much as possible, averting his gaze from the thick glass in the doors of the stairwell, and on the occasions he opted for the elevator, he made certain to keep his back to the large mirror. This work was taking its toll on him, and it wasn't only a matter of ethics. Each passing day had him feeling a little more under the weather. He didn't suspect it was a serious malady affecting his health. His post-grad medical background had equipped him with enough knowledge to rule out many health complications, and he suspected that it was all just a concoction of stress, poor sleep, worse food, and a lack of exercise. He couldn't shake that nagging little voice in his head, though, the one that kept postulating on the possible side effects of being in regular proximity to Charon's workings. Could he be exposing himself to some sort of low-grade demonic radiation?

He slammed the door on that thought, locked it, and tossed the key. Choosing to focus on hope, of being the fly in Talbot's ointment, of helping Leonard reverse all of this, and if possible finding a way to atone for all the hell he had helped deliver upon Nathan and Dolores.

Positive thinking: at least that morning's migraine had subsided.

Reaching the bottom, he passed the all-too-familiar faces of Talbot's eerily quiet goons and entered the ancient dungeons of unquiet minds, the large domain of Charon.

Talbot had made one of his brusque phone calls a little earlier. Hangman and Doll-Face were temporarily needed at the Citadel Security building for undisclosed reasons. Apparently, Talbot didn't need Julius to know the specifics other than a CSS transport would collect them shortly. All he needed from Julius was to get them in the right headspace, tell them where to go and what to do when they got there: which was wait and kill any intruders. He felt like a sports psychiatrist for a moment, imagining these unholy terrors sitting on a locker-room bench, and almost giggled out loud at the absurdity of it. Possible delirium, he noted. A sure sign of sleep deprivation.

The Eye rested on its pedestal, closed but never sleeping. A fellow insomniac. Even closed, Julius felt it was watching him. It was a frightening sensation. An atavistic disquiet, as though something grand, unknowable, and malevolent was waiting for him to foolishly slip up. During his brief but tense subversion sessions with Nathan and Dolores, he would scare himself with the possibility that that thing could read his thoughts. But if it could, why hadn't it somehow alerted Talbot of his actions? It needed to establish a hypnotic link with its subjects at first, but after that it was capable of accessing the minds as it pleased. Was it incapable of entering Talbot's mind to issue a warning?

There was another possibility. Charon might be well aware of Julius's subtlety and guile but care very little about the wants and needs of Talbot, so long as it was getting to nibble on a continued platter of souls, sustaining itself and warping the humanity of its hosts.

Regardless of the "sleeping" thing's sentience and possible indifference to these small schemes, Julius still feared his sleight becoming exposed, not for his sake, but for Leonard's, the man who had practically raised him, forced him to pursue the education of academia and not that of the street. If Talbot learned what he was doing, there was a good chance he would find a reason to take it out on Leonard.

Julius approached Dolores Ricci's cell and watched her catatonic form for a few moments. He unlocked the old iron bars and entered, spoke a few rote commands in a practiced neutral tone, and watched as she rose like a wind-up toy. He could practically feel the unpleasant aura crackling off her form as she stood before him. He briefly considered the ravaged beauty concealed by her doll mask and heaps of disheveled hair. He hated himself for using her in this way. He insisted it was a means to an end, hopefully some type of happy one. He instructed her in what she must do. Simple and precise. Then he quietly muttered a sequence of keywords, words important, *vital*, to Dolores's former life, things that had shaped her, for better or worse. Words that should have her dormant mind fiddling with the locks of Charon's control. Julius still felt like a layman defusing a bomb, but so far his actions hadn't blown up in his face.

Her head twitched up minutely, and Julius saw just the barest glimpse of her eyes through the eyeholes of her porcelain mask. They fluttered like those of a sleeper in REM sleep and then opened, as calm and empty as a big blue sky.

He stepped aside, watching as she walked out of the cell to wait in the central chamber, near the slumbering Charon.

Julius left her cell open and crossed over to Nathan's cell, casting an involuntary glance at the statuesque Dolores and the large Eye as he went. The expressionless guards continued to perform pointless perimeter checks of the empty cells like mindless automatons.

Julius unlocked Nathan's cell. The Hangman was on his knees, genuflecting silently, his white skin free of barbs. Kneeling beside him, Julius repeated the instructions and then muttered a second litany of personal phrases.

Hangman's eyes fluttered briefly, trapped in a dream.

'Julius?' A voice.

Julius almost jumped out of his loafers. Talbot stood outside the cell, quiet as a shadow, his eyes narrowed as if detecting the odor of a rotting animal. 'Everything okay?'

Julius stood up, and Nathan did likewise, moving past him and causing Talbot to step aside, leaving the cell to join Dolores and await their collection from CSS.

'Just a little preoccupied. You snuck up on me.' Julius tried to keep the squeak out of his voice. 'I've been trying to narrow down the next couple of candidates.'

'Excellent.' Talbot followed Hangman, inspecting him like he was a used car, hands clasped behind his back and inquisitive eyes wondering at the functionality of the killer. Julius had little choice but to quickly follow suit and trail the pair. 'I'd like to take a look at your new selections soon. They must be interesting to have stolen your attention in such a way.'

Was Talbot fucking with him? Julius felt another bout of the shakes trying to rattle his bones.

'But right now,' Talbot used one dexterous, maggot-white finger to lift Hangman's chin, seeing nothing but eyes as obscured and gray as a pregnant squall, 'there are bigger fish to fry.'

As if on cue, his phone shrilled. Talbot answered, listened for a moment, then ended the call. 'Pick-up's here, boys and girls.'

The Eye remained sleeping, but the Hangman and Doll-Face turned towards the stone staircase. The marionettes of a mad puppeteer.

18

The screams were old and familiar. She knew them well. They were hers. Who she used to be. Weak, begging, imploring. They disgusted her. Dolores was back in her "loving" marital home. Years' worth of tormented crying. The harsh caress of her husband's hands, their vise-like groping and controlling, the wrath of knuckles, mostly in places that couldn't be seen by public eyes, but sometimes a slip-up that left her with busted lips and shiners and excuses. But who cared, really? Who would dare argue with her Sonny?

Even she knew what he was when she first got involved with him. But that was part of the allure. The danger. The excitement. It was a furious red-hot passion, lust without love, and such passions quickly burned out, leaving only the hard, ugly coal of practical arrangements.

Trophy wife.

That was Dolores through and through. Stand there and look pretty at social events. Keep the house clean and be grateful for it. It was a *very* nice house, a big brick beauty in the suburbs of Long Island, away from the whirlwind of big-city business. A beautiful house, but certainly not a home. Serve in the bedroom, don't burn the dinner, and keep that glass of scotch topped up. And when the boys came round to play cards or watch the game, make sure she shows enough leg and ample cleavage, but don't even think about any playful flirting.

Sonny didn't like that.

It was all part of a dance she knew well. One performed to perfection by her mother and her mother before that. Was such blindness embedded deep within their maternal blood? For no matter how much they were drawn towards violent men who existed beyond the very fringes of humanity and compassion, they always seemed shocked when the pain bit deep and the lie of their love fell away like so much cheap chicanery.

Perhaps the expectation of this animus had been bred into the women of her lineage by now.

Dolores remembered it well, how her mom would put all her pain into cooking, cleaning, and being the perfect domesticated homemaker. During the strange and formative years of Dolores's childhood, she had learned to put her own pain into her growing collection of dolls. Her dad had been little more than a stranger in their home, colder than the chains of her old swing set in winter, only offering the barest interest in her when he came home reeking of booze. Instead of words and attention, he regularly threw a doll or a stuffed toy her way. She had grown to love her dolls, though, and learned to confide in them. Particularly Banana Panic. She loved his big goofy expression and the comfort of his warm fluffy body. Holding him tightly, soaking him with her tears, he kept her safe when she heard her mom sobbing from the bedroom next door, sometimes accompanied with the sharp, unmistakable sound of a quick and savage slap.

Every time she heard her mom being beaten like that, or screaming, she had turned to reliable Banana Panic and her tea-party counsel of porcelain dolls. They always accepted her love and kept her warm.

Banana Panic was with her again now, his big fuzzy arms wrapped about her torso from behind, holding her tight and lending her strength as she listened to the endless background noise of her old spousal abuse.

Banana Panic had grown tremendously since her childhood; he was now easily as big as the Disneyland mascots she had always wanted to see as a little girl.

She absorbed his warmth, his power, his purity and solidity of emotion, of friendship, free from the trappings of any sexual desire. The antithesis of Sonny. Wrapped in his fuzzy embrace, staring down at the hardwood floor of her and Sonny's old, shared dining room, she tried to identify the memories connected to her wails, listening to them overlap like an anguished tide. Was she in the bedroom, her face pushed into the pillows? Or was she being backhanded in the lounge because Sonny was tipsy and didn't need her worrying about his drinking? Did he have a hard day at the "office"?

Frozen to the spot, listening to the ceaseless sounds of her hitching sobs and appeals, she unexpectedly heard another voice, one that was also somehow familiar, but from where she couldn't discern. Hadn't she heard it only recently? The distant voice seemed to speak random words to her, but each one somehow managed to resonate deeply, exposing parts of her almost forgotten, moments of personal history tugged tantalizingly from the shadows of this inescapable house and into the light. One pairing of words almost made her cant sideways into Banana Panic's big paws: Leonard Sharp.

She knew that name.

It was the name that had incited so much of her husband's hatred towards the end.

A *lot* of hatred.

Hearing that name stirred something in her, but not the expected dread associated with Sonny. For some reason, it inspired a sense of... *strength*? Power? But how? Banana Panic still held her protectively, and together they sheltered in the large dining room, practically hiding from the hurricane screams.

Leonard Sharp.

Sonny's knuckles and open palms and belt and even a large kitchen knife, still carrying the scent of onions and peppers from the meal she had been cooking but taking too long to finish.

Something else happened.

Sonny's violence ended abruptly because...

Because...?

She couldn't recall. But she felt a surge of strength flowing through her like the heaviest lead. Her echoing screams had ceased, and Banana Panic slowly released her, briefly placing a protective paw on her shoulder. The house had grown quiet and still, like the lifeless model it was. The curtained bay window of the dining room beckoned her. The idyllic Long Island suburb was bathed in moonlight. Beyond the beautiful front lawn and the large willow tree, all the neighboring homes were dark and still as sleepers. But something was off, she could sense it. The neighborhood seemed artificial, model houses and plastic trees stretching off into an empty black horizon. Exiting the house, she cautiously walked the flagged path, and on the third step, she felt something strange. A distant cousin of pain, dull as a phantom. She stopped at the edge of the front lawn and felt her beautiful pageant-winning face slowly begin to alter under the artisanal craft of Sonny's knuckles, a razor, a bedpost.

Something caught fire inside of her. A quick eruption in need of sudden wrath. The wild beast within Dolores Ricci, which had for so long suffered under the yoke of docility, was opening its eyes.

Was she asleep? Had she been sleeping, revisiting this old house of bad dreams?

Whatever or wherever she had been, she was coming awake now.

And then something held her back. But what? It was a pulling sensation, too strong to break, holding her back, something intent on concealing certain parts of her character. But for an almost beautiful moment of passionate, crystallized hatred, she felt that core of defiance sitting heavy in her stomach, like a piece of iron waiting to be smelted into molten fury.

And then the sky opened. A titanic, almost-reptilian eye glared down at her as she slowly crossed her lawn towards the cul-de-sac's empty streets. She recognized the eye. Remembered the fear it had instilled within her. But right now, it felt as though it had lost some of its former authority. She stepped off her sidewalk and levelled her own death-gaze at the giant eye's warning. She felt her doll-mask mold about her face, shielding the mangled remains of her lost beauty. Her hands longed for something, clenching. She felt calluses on her palms that she couldn't recall ever earning, her moisturized and manicured hands developing into those accustomed to violent labor. The eye continued to glower at her with fury, and Dolores—no, Doll-Face—felt its presence searching through her mind swiftly, hastily locking away certain parts of her personality, reducing her. She tried to fight it, to will the eye to blink and look away. Banana Panic and her collection of murderous mannequins stood tall with her, but an almighty tide swept through her, carrying her volition away on a dark wave. Her picturesque home, the whole neighborhood even, her loving, caring dolls, and her every disarrayed memory all swirled around into a typhoon, drowning one and all and flushing them skywards, deep into the black vortex at the center of Charon's Eye.

All that remained was Doll-Face's cold rage and the Ferryman's borrowed power.

* * * * *

While Dolores was trying to find herself in her dollhouse, Nathan continued to walk the same old stressed-out blocks of the southeast Bronx. Paper bags and empty beer cans rolled down the sidewalk towards him, a voice carrying in their wake, spoken words carried down the crime-ridden street as if delivered by a ghost, their source a gentle voice, impelling, but far, far away.

Orphanage.

That final word split open the opacity clouding his skull like tar. Orphanage. The Lieberstein Refuge for Boys. Sometimes there are monsters so terrible in their deeds that they become almost impossible to imagine for the youthful and innocent. Their wickedness growing them all out of human proportions and into horrifying edifices of the collective mind.

But Nathan Moore had been a little boy at one point in his life.

Deposited into this life by unknown parents. A skinny mute, easy pickings for the bigger, rougher boys. There had been many beatings inside that supposed refuge, but he never looked at those bad times with self-pity. Self-pity was an alien concept to him and always had been. Violence, trauma, misery, they were just parts of existence, mere things that happened to people. And the violence hardened him.

Truthfully, the director of Lieberstein, along with the psychologist, the social workers, the visiting priest, the cooks, and even the janitors, had always sensed something untoward about Nathan, even as a seemingly harmless child. He was quiet, patient, and not prone to violence except for purposes of self-defense, yet there was always an intensity about him, as though he was never quite present or in the moment. He was searching for something he never quite knew or understood. But he found the first pieces of it as a teenager when he ran away from Lieberstein's. A homeless survivor doing what he had to do to survive on the streets. The first piece of the puzzle came when he made his first kill. Some big bad thug by the name of Henry Rooker, a dope slinger and killer for the Tremont Avenue Thrashers, found him squatting in what Nathan thought was an abandoned crack house and tried to entertain himself and his fellow gang-bangers with a little playful torture and execution.

It didn't play out as Rooker and the others had intended.

Nathan managed to fight the three of them off, having grown large since his departure from the orphanage. No longer a boy, puberty had shot him upwards into a skinny, starving man, but one with a wiry strength that saw him through Rooker's aggressive advances. Right up until Rooker was watching the blank, silent rage play out on Nathan's face as he garroted him with a length of old barbed wire he had found hanging from the chain-link fence in the backyard.

The word "orphanage" was like some magic trick, unlocking this whole patchwork of memories for Nathan. Suddenly, the maze of city streets seemed to swell and pulse like the flesh of some weakly-beating heart. The gang-tagged and filthy walls closest to him warped, shifting a little as if to provide him the right path out of this trap. The disembodied voice spoke again, a street name this time, the corner of an old block, and the barbs that seemed to snare-up Nathan's history slipped a little more, growing slack, and he felt the writhing mask of coils begin to slink from his face and head like a metallic snakeskin.

What was the significance of that street?

Looking around, Nathan found that he had left behind the repetitive but random streets and tried to recognize this new place. The urban ruin was no less severe, but he was now staring at a large patch of waste ground barely-lit by a few sparse streetlights, and the few ugly brown tenements that remained seemed to stare at this shattered spot of ground as if they too were fearfully awaiting the bulldozer's wrath.

And then there were people, shadows running through the night, racing across the dangerous trash- and rubble-strewn lot. A slim young man being pursued by a mob of taunting gorillas. The big males caught up to the smaller, weaker one as he cut through a desolate playground on the corner of Turnbull and Olmstead Avenue.

They worked him over, a dark huddle of grunts and nasty taunts that promised to end with a knife or a bullet.

Nathan remembered this now, but it was like trying to orientate himself in a dark room. And that voice speaking to him from the cloud-covered night sky, it was so familiar, yet as elusive as the smoke billowing from the trashcan fire burning in the waste ground.

He started to walk over to the vicious beating taking place, their shadows thrashing in the gloom like charcoal etchings.

And then the fight stopped. Literally frozen solid. It was as though a mental wall had hit Nathan from out of nowhere, robbing him of his purpose. The familiar voice, so liberating, had left him.

He felt the itch of something watching him.

Across the way, burning in a midnight alley was a single shining green eye, shimmering like the most beautiful gemstone in the world. Much, much too big to be a half-blind dog or cat. A swirl of stars circled around it like dust motes through a movie projector beam. Thoughts and images, not his own, he knew, but those from the eye in the alley struck him like bolts: faces, shuddery, flickering, but clear enough to understand. More agents of Hourglass. Four of them were specters, souls having wrongfully slipped Erebus. Three were flesh and blood, but two of them seemed to stand out as primary targets: a large white male Spark, and a young black male, not a Spark, but something unknown and potentially complicated.

Nathan was a powerless wanderer again, surrendering wholly to a force more powerful than his will: his master's. The hive of living barbs burst bloodlessly from his massive shoulders and neck, swallowing his head with a serrated twanging sound, tying themselves up into their usual mask, and in the end, the facial contours were those of complete blank subservience.

The Hangman felt his keen bloodlust stir. He had his targets.

* * * * *

The armored CSS van came to a gentle stop in the underground parking lot of its HQ. Boots hit the tarmac, the sounds of a keychain. With the turn of a key, the heavy locks clunked, the doors were pulled open, and the driver and his partner stepped aside.

Hangman and Doll-Face, oblivious to each other in anything other than the primitive awareness of shape and movement, walked quietly towards the doors and stepped down from the van.

The pair of armored guards were equipped with an assortment of non-lethal weaponry that could put an elephant down—just in case—and a further phalanx of guards stood waiting by the garage's elevators, ready to retrieve and escort Talbot's two pet monsters into the Citadel.

19

Clyde reached out tentatively, fingers flexing, down towards the strange ground beneath his feet. The colorful, densely woven tapestry of soul threads was as captivating as ever. His fingertips ran along them gently, their velvet touch tingling like small electric currents. The sensation of life.

He glanced up again, towards the slow pulse of that neon empire on the horizon, a halfway refuge between dreamers and the dead. His heart rate began to flutter. His lizard brain cognizant of his dangerous trespassing, awaiting the Median's authority to swoop in silently with alien methods.

He'd somehow done it again. Slipped through the layers of sleep. Drawn by this world of souls. He was tentative in his wandering, daring to edge closer and closer from the rugged fields and countryside to the mesmerizing city like a moth to a flame. With a hazy awareness he entered the limits of the metropolis, walking its wide avenues and staring up at the strange towers and buildings and other structures of fabulous architectural design. The city's beauty was almost matched by the eeriness of its empty streets. If some higher being or beings had gone to such effort to design such an aesthetically satisfying world, why wouldn't they occupy it? Besides Ramaliak, how many sleeping powers-that-be populated this staggering place? Clyde found himself drifting through a vast courtyard of almost imperial design, making him think of Ancient Greece and the Roman Empire by way of neon. Standing and feeling impossibly small and foolish before these heavenly constructions, he watched as an assortment of figures, rendered small by distance, assembled about a large balcony on the central municipal building. Details were impossible to discern, leaving them like indistinct cut-outs, but their various bodily shapes didn't lend them wholly to humanity. They quietly stood and stared at Clyde, and a profound dread swelled within him. He shouldn't be here. He really shouldn't. But paralysis had seized him.

* * * * *

Clyde stood in his kitchen, watching the coffee percolate in the pot, the wonderful aroma of the cheapest brand he could find on the store's shelf; he liked coffee as much as the next stimulant addict but was admittedly the furthest thing from a gourmet you were ever likely to meet. It was only 3 am, but after waking up he dared not roll over to try and pursue his fleeting sleep. He had awoken shortly after arousing the attention of those beings, and so startled was his waking that he was momentarily convinced that something had left the Median with him, to seize him in his sweat-damp bed, to hold him accountable for his repeated visits. Alas, the bed was empty, his dark room also. But not so dark that he couldn't make out the details of his pyramid of killers, and Hangman sitting there at the apex, staring at him, watching him, so vulnerable in his sleep.

And so...coffee.

The hours passed slowly, peacefully, allowing Clyde the chance to sit at his drawing board, not to sketch, but to watch the early sun rise with his washed-out eyes. After two cups of coffee and some scrambled eggs on toast, he showered, all the while pressuring himself to call up Spector at Indigo and divulge all this worrying information about his new nocturnal habit. But every time he had the phone in his hand, he would come up with some excuse: there's a two-hour time difference, don't want to chance waking him up—knowing full well that Spector didn't sleep much anyway; or it's only happened twice so far and that's not yet a pattern. But the worst excuse of all: I don't want to know what it all means. His life had been through some epic adjustments this past year, and he didn't think he could handle any more just yet. Because this...it felt big. Spector had classified him as a Level 1 necromancer during his training, meaning he could only anchor one other soul to his. In those terms, he was very limited, and so finding his way behind the curtains of dreamland should be something far beyond his capability. It took beings as powerful as Spector—*Ramaliak!*—to achieve such feats. So, what the hell was happening to him? He again thought about that mental presence he and Ace had experienced at the warehouse in Queens, an intruder feeling its way into his mind.

He was scared to learn who or what that thing was but believed it to be responsible for crafting the assassins. That meant he would learn what it was at some point, whether he wanted to or not.

So he postponed the call to Spector, did some push-ups to burn off a little nervous energy, checked on his home defense weaponry, got in a couple of hours drawing—just letting his subconscious mind guide his hand—and then caught up on the latest crop of comic-books.

Kevin entered at 7 am. No disguise necessary, all he had to do was make sure no neighbors were in the hallway and drift through the door. Clyde jumped at Kev's arrival, eliciting a weird smile from his friend.

'Looking a little edgy there, pal,' Kev said.

Clyde shouldn't have been surprised by Kev's visit; after all, he still skirted sleep and had been popping in around this hour each morning ever since Clyde became an early bird during training.

Clyde closed his issue of *Black Hammer*, placing it atop the latest *Deadly Class* and the small pile of comics on the table next to his drawing board. 'I must have been miles away.'

'Well, you seem kind of jumpy for a guy who had an early night.'

'Bad sleep.'

Kev glanced around like an amateur detective, checking for Clyde's laptop. 'You're not still haunting yourself with Hangman's highlight reel, are you?'

Clyde hit him with a sardonic look. 'I thought I'd try and ween myself off it. I'd hate for it to lose its impact, you know.'

'I hear you, brother. Don't you be breaking a sweat, though; any ass who has an issue with you has an issue with me.' Clyde appreciated Kev's effort and found a smile beginning to pry open his stern mouth. Kev leapt onto the couch, firing two-finger pistols that blasted a cushion across the living room towards Clyde. Clyde caught it and tossed it onto the nearby armchair.

'On a happier note, was it just me or was Nat seriously eye-banging you last night?'

Clyde felt a little more of the tension drain from his body at this new topic. 'I got a vibe,' he admitted. 'But...'

'But?'

'That girl seems wild. And that's cool. But I'm talking too wild. Too wild for me anyway. Some crazy punk chick: booze, rockin' out, a government-connected dad, and a Spark too!'

'I see you've thought about this.'

'A little. She's smokin' hot, but even if she was looking my way, and without all that other stuff, workplace romances are a bad idea in a normal job. And our job definitely isn't normal.'

'Yeah, no shit. There's a guy who kills people with barbed wire hunting us.'

Clyde's face dropped back into stress mode. 'You sure know how to spoil a mood.'

Kev giggled malevolently. 'Sorry, man. Just trying to prove a point.'

Clyde left the window seat and walked over to get another cup of coffee, knowing he'd regret it later. 'Which is?'

'Not to get too crude, but if I had working equipment and a hot girl like that giving me the come-on, I'd go for it. Never know when it could be your last.'

Clyde poured, then went to the fridge for the milk, thinking about what Kev said. He didn't want to think about it. 'I think you need to stop worrying about my equipment.' Lightbulb moment: 'Instead of banging your head against the wall with those vague old pages about the Null, why don't you hit up the archives at work about hitting up some ghost romances?'

'No thanks, lover boy. I got bigger things on my mind. They do involve the archives, though.'

'Whoa-whoa-whoa. I thought we agreed to give it a little time before we start digging into any restricted intel. We're still the new guys. Let's wait until we're a little less expendable, accomplish a little more before getting on the wrong side of Meadows, because I don't really enjoy his *right* side.'

'He is cagey, isn't he?'

'To be expected.'

Kev rolled his eyes. 'Not *that* cagey. He's borderline hostile about people asking questions.'

'He wants agents who take orders, not be openly suspicious about him and the agency. Go figure.'

'When did you drink the Kool-Aid? Listen to you.'

'No, I told you I'm with you on this. All the way. But you're so desperate to race in and find answers that you're only going to cause problems. Get caught, probably get our asses hauled off to some Hourglass black site. Maybe not something that sexy; he might call a few pals in the alphabet departments and have us—well, me—doing time in some ass-pounding federal super-max.' He stirred milk into his coffee. 'Ease off with the Spider Jerusalem act.'

'You lost me with that one.'

Clyde had regretted the reference the moment it left his tongue, knowing it to be too obscure for Kev, and despite not being a very big fan of Superman, he knew the Man of Steel and his associates were a much more recognizable brand of reference material.

'Stop being Lois Lane.'

'Ah! Gotcha.'

'Circle back. If they're sitting on any bombshells, we'll find them. I promise. But we gotta be ninja about it. And I need you to focus on the immediate problem, the one involving Talbot and his boogiemen. Cool?'

Kev sighed, long and almost obnoxiously. 'Fine.'

'You just need to get out of your head for a while. Read something besides them damn passages. Check out some fiction.'

'Our lives are stranger than... Seems a little pointless.'

Clyde wasn't lying, he really would do the unthinkable and cross a legit secret government department if Kev's suspicions about the Firmament Needle or the hoodoo and the House of Wise Stones were accurate. But right now, his head and heart were being pulled in so many directions. For instance, what would such knowledge really be worth? Even if Kev's loose theory about Hourglass's founders being connected to a house of the Order could be validated, would it change anything? In the end, the Null would still be there waiting for all of them. But most astoundingly, Clyde felt a quiver of trepidation about losing his job! He'd been stressing himself towards an early grave during all of this, his first official assignment, but it also gave him a quiet sense of purpose, a purpose he first recognized during his reluctant training at Indigo, which had developed from its nascency into an invigorating drive. He was a soldier who had wanted to be an artist, but the character in his blood had won out over the passion in his heart.

'Meadows...' Kev said ominously. 'Now there's a reason not to get mixed-up with Nat.'

Clyde gave him a *no-shit* expression and checked the time. 'Ace should have texted to say he's on the way by now.'

'Dude operates on his own time. He probably hit up a few bars after the rest of us bailed.'

Kev was probably right, but Clyde felt a small sliver of unease forming in his gut.

'Well, he's a dumb shit if he did.' Clyde pulled his phone out. 'Functional alcoholic or not, we can't afford to have him bringing his B-game tonight.' The call went through to voicemail.

Twice.

Kev wandered over to the drawing board, losing himself in Clyde's latest work. It was laid out in typical comic-book panels, but it wasn't part of his on-again/off-again indie project. Kev made a noise of curious recognition. The page was like a much more professional, jazzed-up version of the primitive pictograms he had photocopied from the *Dread Paradigm*. The apparent fall of paradise, the rise of the Order of Terminus, and the origins of Sparks.

'Shit! I think something's up,' Clyde said, his posture becoming stress-rigid, readying for action.

'Take a breath, man. Give him a minute, maybe he's in the shower or taking a beer growler.'

'Or what if Hangman got him?' Clyde's voice was cold. He didn't even like speaking that possibility out loud in case it tempted fate. 'I'll call Meadows, send out an alert. Then me, you, and Rose are—'

The phone in his hand started ringing, and Clyde felt a flood of relief flow through him. The caller ID said Ace.

20

'For real?' Clyde was riding shotgun in the van, with Kev leaning between the seats and Ace piloting them away from the island of Manhattan through a flush of morning commuters.

'For real.' Ace switched over from the fast lane, letting them cruise at a more sedate pace while they talked. He had a pair of sunglasses on to deal with the sun's glare and a mouth full of gum to try and mask any lingering booze. Ace had overslept, but it wasn't because of his boozy one-night stand.

'Details, details, details.' Kev was practically rattling Ace's seat in interest, but it wasn't regarding the barmaid Ace had hooked up with, or the fact he had misused company resources by foolishly banging her at an empty safehouse. It was the inexplicable events of Ace's misadventure that stirred such interest.

Clyde and Kev listened while Ace explained, starting with what happened at Elmore's Sports Bar. He had been focusing on his bottle one minute, trying to tune out a group of loudmouths getting heated over the Yankees versus Red Sox game on the TV, when his vision suddenly went spotty, like a half-dozen houseflies had taken up residence inside his eyeballs.

'Then it was like somebody jammed their big fat finger into the front of my brain and gave it a good old scramble,' Ace said. 'It only lasted a few seconds, nothing another bottle and some more nuts wouldn't take care of, but it's what I saw next that killed my buzz.' He told them of the chaotic scenes witnessed from someone else's point-of-view: all storming dust and thunderous skies, figures lighting up the cascading darkness and billowing dirt like megawatt angels, killing and dying in equal measure with hordes of fearsome creatures. The images all ran and crashed together, ending with one of the glowing beings, a fearsome but majestic sight, soaring down from the burning sky straight towards the viewer.

'And then just like that—' Ace snapped his fingers. 'It ended.'

Clyde, seriously unnerved, was left wondering if one of these episodes might sporadically blindside him. 'Like what we saw the other night at Willets Point.'

Ace gave Clyde a troubled look. 'And I'll take a swing at what it was we both saw. That slugfest, it was the Big One. The battle that changed everything.' His hand gestured to the world outside the windshield, dozens of cars sailing along the sunny highway. 'Turned all of this into the warm-up before everything really goes into the sewer.'

Ace had given them what he could, but Kev didn't look satisfied.

'Kev, I don't know what else to tell you. It was like living someone else's blackout drunk. I'd say what I remember is pretty fucking impressive. But I'll tell you one thing: I'm looking forward to letting my fists do the talking tonight.' Ace tapped a finger against his head. 'What kind of creepy asshole takes a look under the hood?'

Clyde was compelled to bring up his back-to-back descents into the Median now that Ace had kicked over this can of worms. Was this evidence of what he'd been mulling over during his coffee earlier on? Was this psychic whammy induced by whatever force was creating Talbot's assassins?

Clyde put it to Kev and Ace, looking at them and wanting to see support. 'That doll-woman wigged out like there was something inside her head right before something took a look inside ours.' He didn't recall the visions as strongly as Ace did, it was mainly just a blur, but he sure remembered the sense of helplessness as something entered his innermost self. He recalled the benign ruse of its inspection, the feeling that it was nothing more than a curious tourist taking a quick peek.

'Talbot's other killers all seemed okay,' Ace said.

'I think "okay" is a relative term here, mustache,' Kev replied.

'You know what I mean. They had self-control.'

'And no migraines or freak-outs,' Clyde added, staring thoughtfully at the interstate ahead.

'Could be she's just a basket case?' Ace suggested. 'A dud.'

'Maybe,' Clyde said. 'But whatever this thing is, it's sentient. Not some black-magic toy, but something with intelligence.' Kev sat there quietly, and Ace kept his hard stare on the road ahead. 'Maybe not even a some-thing but a some*one*.'

'The Boogieman Project might have an actual boogieman boss,' Kev posited.

'Between Hangman, Dolly, and Talbot, I thought we had enough boo-giemen for now,' Clyde lamented.

They drove for several minutes in silence, then Clyde took the plunge. 'The last few nights, since Willets Point, I've been falling into the Median when I sleep.'

Kev gave Clyde a slap on the shoulder. 'And you only mention that now? That's newsworthy. You called Spector?'

'Not yet.' Clyde grew fidgety. 'I might. But it might be nothing. Just this mind-hopping son-of-a-gun messing things up.' He paused, then quickly added, 'We should tell Meadows about all of this, though, see if he's got anything that can keep this asshole from—'

'Cloggin' your noggins,' Kev said.

'Yeah. Then we can focus on floggin' its noggin.' Ace hit play, and April Wine's "All Over Town" filled the van. He stepped down on the gas, and the van rocketed forth.

'Sure. Still need to find the thing first,' Clyde mumbled.

21

Rose put the last few holes in a target of King Kong she had printed out. She had gunned down a dozen since her high-protein breakfast and leg-day session at the Madhouse gym. Emptying the carbine's spent magazine, she laid the rifle down and pushed the button on the target rail, bringing the last damn dirty ape whirring towards her, minus its head.

Sarge had raised an eyebrow after seeing how much ink she had wasted on her prints, and throughout her entire time at the range he had barely lowered it.

'You working through something here, Private Hadfield?'

Rose tore the shredded print from the rail's clip. 'All better now.' She gave him a smile that was nigh on heartwarming.

'I see. You just have a problem with apes?'

'Only one.'

'Good, because I think they're magnificent creatures.'

'I agree, Sarge.' Darcy appeared, fresh from his downtime in the command center. 'Unless it's self-defense, anybody who guns down innocent animals should be hogtied and fed to them.'

'Doesn't your family own a farm? And sell cattle?' Rose removed her ear defenders.

'I don't take issue with people eating meat. But sport hunters are a whole different breed of asshole.'

Sarge folded his arms. 'That crazy lady with the doll mask really bunched your panties. You're a competitor, Rosie, I get that. But don't go letting that chip on your shoulder make any decisions about tonight's mission. Clear-headed, that's how you do your best work.'

Rose stopped what she was doing and listened to him, knowing he was right. The mission came first. Always. 'Loud and clear, Sarge.'

'Glad we're on the same page.' He nodded and gave her an almost paternal look of pride. 'And next time, instead of wasting company ink, why not just talk to that holographic quack Schulz. I'm sure he could create a few big monkeys for you to tussle with.'

'You could argue that that's a waste of ink too.'

'Okay, smart-ass.'

Rose gave a passing thought to Schulz, knowing that he might have heard Sarge's "quack" remark since he was essentially powering the whole facility, including all A/V. She'd seen some wild shit since landing in Hourglass, and done just as much, but she still found the variety of PLE forms stunning, though she wasn't entirely sure if Schulz qualified as a PLE due to his condition being the result of some type of curse. Though the subject of PLEs still remained a convoluted one. Herself, for example. Spector hadn't been able to attach a categorical label to her because technically she hadn't entwined the souls of Sarge, Barros, and Darcy to her own when they died but rather, somehow, had absorbed a tremendous burst of their psychic emotions upon death. Spector and his associates at Indigo Mesa had therefore declared her a type of spiritual empath to her dead squad, channeling their rage and grief from their point of death. And on top of all that hot mess came the endless species of demons and weirdos and bone-rattling magicians. It made her think about how much she loved this job.

Rose binned her targets and walked down the long aisle of firing lanes, empty rifle in hand. The range was currently quite empty, allowing them to talk at a reasonable volume instead of shouting at each other. Returning the weapon to the officer behind the bullet-proof glass, she went to walk through the automatic doors but found they wouldn't budge. The three of them glanced up at the electric eye in the corner of the doorway, and then to the handprint security scanner next to the steel-and-Plexiglas doors. Rose was about to voice her concerns to the officer back at the weapon lock-up when Schulz's fuzz-crackling face appeared on the scanner screen.

'Quack,' was all he said.

The doors slid open.

Sarge looked contritely at the face on the scanner. 'My apologies, Doctor Schulz.'

'Jizz on a donut and call it glazed,' Rose said, looking at Sarge. 'Talk about your social faux pas.'

Rose thought she saw Schulz give a good example of a harumph before disappearing. She led them out into a wide network of corridors and checked her phone, seeing the message from Clyde explaining that he was on the way with Kev and Ace.

Barros materialized beside the three of them as they approached an elevator. 'What did I miss?'

'Rose hates apes and Sarge hates ducks,' Darcy explained.

They entered the elevator with a couple of other agents and a lab coat. Rose pushed the button for the top floor, where Meadows was waiting with his report on the status of the CSS head office.

22

Clyde stared at the Free-Thinker in the palm of his hand. It was another agency gizmo cooked-up between the science and arcane divisions for the express purpose of keeping any psychic intruders on the outside of the cranium where they belonged.

'It looks like a triple-A battery with claws,' Nat said, tossing it from palm to palm before shoving it into a pocket of her leather jacket. 'What's in them again?'

Meadows had issued one to each of the team, including a variant for Kev and the ISU. 'Cerebrospinal fluid from a graklar.'

'These things definitely work?' Clyde asked. He still felt a bit shaky after the "psych evaluation" he'd just been subjected to, courtesy of said graklar.

Ace had gone through the procedure first, having fared the most explicit of the visions. He was still wearing a scowl, proving he had been no bigger fan of the procedure than Clyde.

'Of course they work, son. But if you'd rather try squeezing your eyes and clapping your hands over your ears, I won't be offended.' It was always difficult to gauge the line between hard-ass humor and frank indifference with Meadows, but Clyde thought he was slowly getting the hang of it. Meadows continued to stare at him, pondering something. 'You say you didn't get any clear images the other night?'

'Dust, light. Not much else.' Clyde had chosen to omit his Median detours when explaining how he had experienced a similar psychic intrusion to Ace's at Willets Point. 'There was no clarity. And it was over in seconds. I chalked it up to some minor side-effect of the doll-maker or Anselmo. It's why I didn't mention it sooner.'

Ace nodded in agreement, and Meadows returned his own fractional nod.

They were standing outside the sterile medical bay where Clyde and Ace had been subjected to a few of Dr. Schulz's irregular psychic evaluations. It had involved a piece of apparatus that neither Clyde nor Ace knew was on-site, and it was an experience Clyde hoped to never have to repeat. The procedure involved being seated in some type of dentist's chair and having his head fitted with a strange boxy contraption spilling wires and fitted with crystals. Clyde's vision had been compromised to a narrow tunnel, staring directly at the ugly thing opposite him: a solution-filled tank housing the large, severed head of a creature that lacked any discernible face, like a sculptor's unfinished head mold with a tremendously enlarged bottom jaw, and flesh resembling a dirty-yellow and brown mottled sheet pulled taut. Somehow, despite the graklar's head lacking any discernible eyes or means of expression, it had engaged Clyde in the worst staring-contest of his life, scouring his mind for the presence of any deceitful hijackers in waiting or other attempts at trickery. When the ordeal was over, a lab assistant separated Clyde from the equipment, and Schulz examined the data by way of transcribing some bizarre communicative output from the head-creature before declaring both agents had a clean psychic bill of health and releasing them back to Meadows. When Clyde had enquired about just what exactly a graklar was, Meadows described it simply as a reliable source and nothing more.

'It's a comfort to know you didn't pick up any earworms from this remote viewer,' Meadows said. Clyde concurred. Whatever these psychic disturbances were confounding him and Ace, at least they were after-effects rather than something taking up residence in their subconsciouses.

'The imagery Ace saw sounds a lot like the pictograms in the *Dread Paradigm*,' Kev said. 'What if this thing is some high-ranking flunky from one of the Order's Houses, working with or for Talbot?' Kev suggested.

'It isn't.' Meadows gave Kev his patented flat stare, giving no quarter. 'As you well know, Agent, there's a treaty. A balance that both sides uphold, us and every covert group that's fond of life as we know it, and the Order. If it is an underling of one of the monarchs creating the assassins, Director Trujillo would have heard about it. And none of the Houses would tolerate one of their subordinates working this side of the fence for some jumped-up black-magic peddlers like Talbot and the Cairnwood Society.'

'Maybe it doesn't have a choice? Enslaved somehow? Shouldn't we talk to Director Trujillo just in case he hasn't noticed this?'

'That will be all on the matter, Kev.'

'I'm just saying since they're a big part of this life/death balance, this possibility might have slipped by them.' He gestured at Clyde and Ace for back-up, catching a few discouraging looks from the ISU, but predominately Rose, who seemed to be calling him an idiot with nothing more than her eyes.

'And what vision did Ace receive, Agent Carpenter? Some dirt, some storm clouds, gilded god-types warring with another race. Do you have any idea how many wars there have been that sound exactly like that? How many just like that will be occurring right this minute in one realm or another? What Ace saw wasn't the end of heaven. It was just another war. And the war never ends, it just changes players and locations.'

'But I got a feeling about this,' Kev insisted.

'Are you telling me how to do my job, Agent?' Meadows's voice had an edge sharp enough to cut. 'I'm not sure what your problem with me is, and I don't care. We don't have to be friends. You're an asset, and you've proven yourself useful so far, but if this job isn't what you thought it would be, I'm happy to accept your resignation.'

Clyde stared wide-eyed at Kev, furious that he was being so forthright and quarrelsome, and his damn impatience in needing to know everything about the top-secret running of Hourglass and their history.

Kev stayed mute, his face unintelligible behind his shades and scarf. 'Won't be necessary, sir.'

Clyde quietly exhaled and noticed similar relieved looks on the rest of the team.

'Very good. Now, Kevin...' Meadows took a breath, 'can you forget about the Null, the Needle, and a long-lost war for one minute, and narrow your focus on our battles, on the mission at hand, so that we can try and maintain peace for the few people we can actually help?'

'Sure thing, boss.' Kev crossed his arms and leaned back against the wall, staring up and down the corridor somewhat petulantly.

The awkward atmosphere meant Meadows didn't waste any time in directing the team from the medical bay to an empty briefing room at the other end of the building.

Clyde tried talking to Kev on the way, touching base to make sure he had calmed down. It troubled him how obsessed his friend had become with chasing down objectives that, in his heart of hearts, he doubted they could accomplish. How long had it been since the Order had deconstructed paradise? How many all-mighty beings had perished trying to protect it? But a plucky bunch of agents with a few nifty tricks might accomplish what the Luminaries couldn't? Sounded like comic-book stuff to Clyde: awesome on the page and screen, ridiculous in reality. He hoped more than anything that one day they might do the impossible, but sometimes it felt ridiculously naive. But Kev had stopped seething by the time they reached the briefing room, a modest-sized lecture theater.

Meadows walked them over to a large table already laid out with surveillance photos, exterior plans of the CSS building, and most crucially, a printout of its schematics.

Before Meadows went into detail about infiltrating the target, he had other news. 'The pathologists have confirmed that the corpse that burned up in the Porsche was Brink, but most interestingly, they found traces of an undocumented non-biochemical explosive compound in his marrow, blood, and organs—that is, what little they could salvage.'

'When you say undocumented?' Clyde had a sneaking suspicion...

'The same mystical trace energy found in Anselmo and the Dukes of Purgatory.'

'So Brink was one of the hitmen in training.' Ace didn't look surprised. 'Why not? If some of his ex-military buddies were down for it, why not him?'

Rose drew up a very short list of motives for his explosive finale near FDR Drive. 'Then he was either clumsy with his new skillset, bored of living, or he pissed off his creator.'

'Boogieman,' Kev interjected, trying to lighten his earlier tension and make peace with Meadows. Clyde was just glad he was trying to become part of a conversation that wasn't fixated on the inner workings of the Null or politicking with its dead lords.

'Boogieman,' Rose corrected.

'Brink is off the table, but whatever the reason was for yesterday's building evac, it's occupied again,' Meadows said. 'The static surveillance teams witnessed a small convoy of company vans heading into the parking garage last night, and they never came out. Our spotters have reported that the building appears to be on alert. No suits and ties today, no clientele; all the employees are decked-out in tactical gear: body armor and assault weaponry. But so far nothing else has happened. It's as though the guards are waiting for a call.'

'Unless they're protecting something in there,' Sarge suggested.

'Maybe they're anticipating an attack?' Clyde added.

'Either/or, we don't have the luxury of handing this job to some-body else. Due to our recent history with CSS and their affiliation with Cairnwood, we have now been sanctioned to move in on the premises to conduct our search. On that front, the cyber team had some luck in breaching the CSS firewall, so you'll have the complete layout of the building, top to bottom,' Meadows said, indicating the building's plans. His shielded gaze swept across the team, and Clyde saw how it contained a small mixture of respect and faith in the team assembled before him.

Meadows checked his watch. 'There's still a lot of daylight to burn through yet, so I want you all drilling your roles ad nauseam. You're rolling out at twenty-one hundred.' His phone started to ring in his pocket. He checked the screen, but before answering and walking away, his eyes landed on Nat, and for the briefest moment he looked like a compassionate man again and not a stiff company bureaucrat. 'You're trained and you're ready for this, but you do what these do,' his finger swiped across the team knotted around her.

'Piece of cake,' Nat said with pep.

Clyde almost envied her seeming inability to be concerned about the gravity of preparing to enter a life-and-death situation.

'There's a coffee and snack machine down the hall. Check in with the Tactical Operations Center before heading out.' Meadows left the room before answering his call.

Clyde gathered a very strong sense that certain members of the team, namely Rose, wanted to have a few words with Kev regarding his bullheadedness. But he wanted to keep them all from getting distracted by backburner personal issues. He smiled at Nat from across the table.

'Welcome to the worst part of any operation...the wait.'

Nat seemed unfazed, returning his easy smile.

* * * * *

The hours had fallen away, bad coffee and sugar were consumed, and everybody knew their and each other's roles as though they were robots programmed to do nothing else but infiltrate Citadel Security Solutions. The new intel on the assassins' power source being a possible living and psychic organism was taken into consideration, but due to its ambiguity, the original plan remained the same.

Clyde sensed something funny within the team, the forming of a small rift among their usually cohesive number, predominantly between Rose and the ISU and Kev; they had taken leading roles in honing Kev's raw abilities, but their former military training and obedient attitude to chain of command hadn't rubbed off on Kev. Kev had rattled and tugged at that chain several times since finding himself under Meadows's command. It was mostly minor acts such as his frequent badgering about news updates on Konstantin Kozlov's quest for the Firmament Needle—updates that never arrived—or his incessant interest about matters relating to Trujillo's role in Null politics rather than any overt acts of rebellion, but it was starting to chip away at Rose and her need for unitary efficiency and morale.

Personally, Clyde was troubled by Kev's refusal to slow down. It was Kev who had been excited and curious to join Hourglass in the beginning, and Clyde thought if one of them proved to be unmanageable it would be him, not Kev. Instead, Kev's former excitement and curiosity had quickly developed into a restless obsession bordering on career suicide.

Fortunately, they all got through the pre-mission wait without too much friction.

Nat, for her part, seemed to hum along like they were planning a road trip. She even likened the awkward atmosphere to times when her band would argue, sometimes with fists, over beer, crap pay, or the occasional stolen groupie.

But they got through the practice runs, and once the late evening sun started its slow descent outside the briefing room's windows, the team headed down to the locker rooms and armory.

* * * * *

Clyde was putting his street clothes in his locker, happy to see Kev gelling with Rose and the ISU again, when Nat appeared next to him and slapped a big "Carpe Diem" sticker on the locker next to his.

'Looks like we're locker buddies.' It was Nat's first time in tactical gear, the latest generation of lightweight but robust body armor, over an all-black coverall.

Clyde was willing to bet she'd look good in just about anything and turned his attention to the big bumper sticker to keep his mind off any brewing physical attraction between them. 'You just been carrying that around with you?'

'Only for emergencies such as this. This is prime locker-room real estate, so I'm taking ownership of this here locker.' She unlocked it and shoved her bundled street clothes and various jangling chains inside and gave him that smile that made him feel lightheaded.

'It is, huh?' Clyde had already signed out for his weapons. He loaded his second Glock 19, fitted with a sound suppressor, and partnered it with the other on his tactical rig, along with several spare clips, his combat knife, several flashbang grenades, and even a few fragmentations just in case things went Hangman. He also had his usual sound-suppressed MP5 slung over his shoulder. 'Why is that?'

He leaned against his locker, wanting to look casual without doing anything stupid, like try and flirt with her. But every time they made eye contact, he felt that electrical tingle speeding around his entire body. And he reminded himself that this is what being alive felt like! Everything didn't always have to be terror and dread and gut-wrenching excitement. He found himself returning to the dark-hazel pools of her eyes for another drink. Nat didn't seem any more inclined to break the contact either. But Clyde knew any attraction between them, even if only physical, was a bad idea. Meadows might take his balls away from him. Their gazing had only been seconds, but Clyde was beginning to feel like they were both pieces of tinder preparing to ignite.

Nat glanced away, back to where Ace stood in the center of the room, strapping his old-school hockey serial-killer mask onto his head.

'Because geographically it's the furthest free locker away from Special Agent Midlife Crisis.'

Clyde's mouth curved into a wry smile, joining her in watching Ace's gruff but lovable charm pump the rest of the team up like a seasoned coach prepping his team to head out there and slaughter the opposition on the ice. 'He's pretty likeable when you get to know him. Take it from the guy who spent weeks getting a daily ass-kicking from him. Think of him as that asshole uncle who means well, and everything will fall into place. Plus, you're both Sparks and like beer...could be you're both kindred spirits.'

Nat gave Clyde a smug appraisal, baffled by his vouching for the big boorish hair-bag. And after a couple of seconds said, 'I'll give him a chance.' She turned back to watch Ace and Rose trying to out-bro each other. 'Should he be wearing a hockey jersey with his name on over his armor?' "TREMBLAY" was stenciled proudly across Ace's shoulder blades, over a big number 9.

Clyde gave her an uncertain look. 'It's got him this far.'

'Party dresses on, kiddies?' Ace vigorously clapped his bruising mitts together. 'Our chariot awaits.'

23

The Department of Defense supported the paramilitary activities of Hourglass in various capacities, supplying them with air transport, logistics, medical, and weaponry from the army, air force, and navy, therefore the Madhouse had a small fleet of armored jeeps, personnel carriers, motorcycles, boats, and even air support. None of which was currently required, as the team were loaded up in the rear of Ace's garish battle van. There had been some talk of whether an '80s heavy-metal album on wheels was the most subtle approach, with the consensus being that the operation should be as quiet and contained as possible, but seeing as how it would be parked out of sight of any ensuing drama, it was deemed irrelevant. And besides, Clyde knew it was only a matter of time before quiet and contained became loud and loose.

He was on the bench seat in the back with Nat at his side and Kev sitting opposite, sketching on a notepad to keep himself focused, holding off the nerves.

'Think you could design me a tattoo sometime?' Nat was leaning in to see his artist's impression of the nightmare quietly plaguing him, a giant shadowy figure looming ominously over the Ice Maiden, entangling it in a web of barbed wires.

Clyde thought the nerves might have gotten to her by now. He still had to fight like a motherfucker to keep from freaking out, hence his busy pen. But he found her ease and tranquility to be something of a calming influence.

'If we make it out of this with skin left to tattoo, I promise to give it a shot.' He'd love the opportunity.

'Awesome.'

Rose was riding up front in the audible danger zone of Ace's '80s metal and prog-rock assault.

Kev looked at ease, quietly composed instead of stewing over the earlier scene with Meadows. It was a relief to Clyde, who didn't want Kev sloppy or distracted, but he knew there was no reason why he would be; since getting inexplicably shot on his first outing by a CSS shooter, the bravado of being an intangible ghost had waned some for Kev.

'You got anything other than cock rock up there, frosty?' Nat shouted over Sammy Hagar singing "Heavy Metal."

Ace might have glowered at the comment, but it was impossible to tell since he already had his hockey mask pulled down into attack position. 'Game-face music, sweetheart,' he bellowed.

'Then can we play a different game?' Nat muttered, settling back against the wall.

'You build up an immunity to it after a while,' Clyde said.

He continued to sketch and went over the entry plan again in his head: with the cyber techs back at the Tactical Operations Center inside the system, they would initiate a blackout of the building on the team's word; Kev would enter through the elevator shaft within the parking garage and commence a sweep through the lower levels in search of anyone or anything resembling a psychic, super-hit-squad creator, a.k.a. the Boogieman Machine. Meanwhile, he'd enter from the roof with Nat and neutralize the security from the top down. And Ace, Rose, and the ISU would enter from the ground floor. They had all agreed that the soft-infil, church-mouse approach had a shelf life of about five minutes at best, but Clyde had learned that sometimes shock and awe was the best option.

Ace punched the roof of his van. 'ETA in two minutes.'

'Can you definitely jump us to the roof?' Nat asked Clyde. She didn't sound scared, only curious. 'Because it'll be a real fucking dumb way to die if you're just trying to impress me.'

Clyde almost smiled, feeling a little flutter in his chest. 'Impress you?' He scrambled to think of something cool to say and hoped it would sound convincing. 'You mean you're not already impressed?'

Kev, deep in thought, but not so much so that he could miss their flirting, groaned. 'I better not get shot a third time because two of my team are thinking about rubbing their crotches together.'

'Enough yappin', kiddies, or I'll turn this car around,' Ace hollered.

Clyde stared out the windshield, seeing the CSS HQ coming into view, its attractively massive glass cubes and polished steel rails and walkways, and of course, its scores of soft interior lights making the whole structure seem almost inviting beneath the indigo sky.

Ace expertly slid the van into a parking space in a side street. There were several covert agency vehicles parked in other side streets around the perimeter of the target site to provide back-up should they fumble the play.

The team started to slip their Free-Thinkers into the napes of their necks.

'Will you fit mine?' Nat asked Clyde.

He turned to her. The cool blue light of the van interior danced like sapphires in her dark eyes. He picked the alien device from her palm. She had tactical gloves on, same as him, but he brushed against her fingertips and felt their warmth. She turned her shoulder and lifted her ponytail to the side, exposing her smooth, tanned nape. Clyde gently placed it just below her hair and got the wonderful orchid scent of her shampoo, and noted that even if the scent was of spilled beer and cigarette smoke from a messy night-out, he wouldn't care.

She made a small wince as the device took hold, then turned and held her hand out to him. Clyde placed his in her palm and turned. He felt the brief pinch as it gripped the skin, imbuing the graklar's aura—on a spectrum invisible to the naked eye—throughout his central nervous system to shield him from any would-be voyeurs or puppeteers.

The TOC came through on the comm-frequency, announcing that local traffic and street cams had gone dark and would remain so for the next ten minutes until the team gained entry.

Nat piled out of the van with Ace and Rose, leaving Clyde and Kev as the last two to jump out. They both leaned in ritualistically, reading each other's taut expressions and understanding the dangers they were about to face. They quietly bumped fists, and Clyde absorbed a portion of Kev's telekinetic energy.

From their position, the big box of mercenaries seemed about as intimidating as a luxury hotel. For a place that was surely on some level of alert, nobody would be any the wiser unless chaos spilled out onto the streets.

Kev dropped through the pavement, cutting through the underground like an urban shark and heading directly for the parking garage elevator. Ace and Rose gave Clyde and Nat a silent stare full of unspoken sentiments, and Clyde solemnly returned it, hoping they'd all be walking away from this intact. Ace and Rose started across the Park Avenue traffic towards the main entrance, paying no attention to the startled looks of pedestrians and drivers.

Remaining by the van, Clyde grabbed hold of Nat around the waist, getting another encouraging smile from her, and propelled them both upwards onto the roof of the office building parallel to CSS.

Nat reacted as though she had just stepped off a roller coaster. 'Shit! We need to do that again at some point.'

Clyde didn't say no.

They ducked low along the roof's parapet. The cover of the night helped some, but there was only so much it could do in a city that refused to sleep.

And so...

Rose gave the TOC the go-word over the comm-channel, and Clyde watched as the cyber team dropped the security fortress into darkness. It wouldn't remain that dark for long; the schematic had mentioned a diesel back-up generator stored in the basement to power key components of the complex. There would be emergency lighting inside, but plenty of shadow still and, ideally, a worthwhile distraction.

Clyde glanced down at the sunken marble and stone courtyard of the security firm's main entrance, watching Ace and Rose hurry down the courtyard's steps, passing numerous large and meaningless geometric sculptures that grew upwards like stone and steel carbuncles. Bland art, but fair cover if needed. Moving through the shadowy courtyard, their gazes scanned the interior of the first several floors, finding no guards in the lobby or surrounding offices. Ace's hands started to channel the beginning of a deep freeze, the warm ambience of the night air beginning to plummet steadily in his vicinity.

Clyde was attuned to Kev, sensing his cautious mood. He would be in the lower levels by now, ghosting his way towards the elevator shaft, assuming the schematics weren't remiss in covering any PLE-prohibiting measures.

Clyde heard Rose in his ear: 'Ringing the doorbell.'

'That's our cue.' Clyde catapulted him and Nat in a silent arc across the considerable gulf of 62nd Street onto the CSS rooftop. Mid-flight, he glanced down at the exhilarating view, seeing Rose lift and throw what must be a 600-kilogram block of ice through the glass-fronted lobby of the building. The bullet-proof glass crumpled in and fell out of the frame. If the blackout wasn't a big enough distraction, then that should hold the attention of any ground-floor sentries for a few moments.

Clyde glided to a smooth stop on the roof of the largest and central building, his boots getting traction. The middle of the roof held a smaller glass-covered patio running around most of the perimeter. Its dark interior disgorged a big, dark figure in body armor, rifle raised. But Clyde was faster, using his telekinesis to seize the guard. He locked the guard's trigger finger in place and pulled him close, pinning his four limbs together and treating him as a potential human shield while drawing his suppressed pistol. He shot a second guard rounding the opposite corner of the boxy patio in an intended pincer movement, the quiet bullet taking him in the head. For a split second, Clyde found it ridiculous that these two guards had body armor but had only protected their heads with company caps, their bills pulled low. Did none of them expect nor care about headshots?

Nat landed and forward-rolled up into a stance, firing off several violet bolts. The concussive blasts were only mild, but sent a second pair of guards sprawling backwards like crash-test dummies into the metal stairway of an empty helipad; whether they would ever get up again remained to be seen, but it would likely be a day or two at the earliest.

Clyde's human shield couldn't work his mouth to scream or call for back-up, and with his limbs firmly locked, was unable to fight back. Clyde made it quick and painless for him, breaking his neck with nary a hand gesture. He tried not to think too much about his actions. This was war, and these were certainly not combatants to be sympathized with.

Clyde let the body drop. The whole thing only took seconds. He nodded at Nat, impressed.

'I guess Ace's jerk-off music has its uses,' Nat said, her hands charged with Sammy Hagar, of all things.

The building's back-up generator kicked in, and Clyde watched as red emergency lighting created blood-red shadows of the patio; inside, the stairway led down to the executive suite offices. The back-up power meant the locks would be back in effect. Clyde held out his hand, and the broken-necked guard's ID flew up and landed in his palm. He slid it across the patio's electronic sensor and moved stealthily with Nat through the glass doors, taking the stairs down into the top-floor offices.

They each took a side of the room, staying low, quickly moving from office to office. The whole floor appeared to be empty of any further guards, but from the distant yet furious sound of controlled gunfire, the lobby had unsurprisingly become a hot zone.

Clyde had just led them through the doors into a wide stairwell when a security officer sprung up from his cover behind the stairs' handrail. He was another large brute like the four guarding the patio above, cradling an automatic shotgun and swinging the mean barrel towards Clyde. Clyde seized him with an invisible hand, lifting and dangling him precipitously over the wide circumference of the stairwell's drop. Nat blasted him with a quick one-two, his armor absorbing what it could, but Clyde lost his grip, Nat's kinetic force propelling the guard through the stairwell's glass wall like a bulky missile.

Clyde gave her a disapproving look. They were supposed to be the quiet ambush team, picking off enemies during Rose and Ace's bombastic assault.

Nat gave him a shrug. 'Put a bit too much spice on that one.'

They both started down to the next floor. Clyde's mouth was dry, his heart a distant drum. He wanted to find the Boogieman Machine, be it living or mechanical, and destroy it with extreme prejudice. At the same time, the thought that the Hangman could be in here somewhere, protecting it, was almost enough to turn him into a trembling wreck.

He had faced some terrible odds and creatures in his brief time, but nothing with a body count like the Hangman. With his eyes now adjusted to the red and black gloom of the emergency lighting, he took the winding stairs carefully.

Neither he nor Nat noticed the large, shadowy figure slowly abseiling down the stairwell after them like a muscle-bound spider on a barbed thread.

* * * * *

Ace had resealed the shattered front entrance with a heavy sheet of ice seconds before the sniper gunfire erupted. Rose moved from pillar to pillar, each section of cover quickly becoming pocked with assault-rifle fire. The red back-up lights skimmed off and cut through hundreds of clean glass surfaces, doing what they could for visibility, but the enormity of the atrium—a vast channel bisecting the ten floors of offices on either side, the upper stories connected with walkways—remained a sea of cool shadows, intermittently held at bay by exchanges of rapid gunfire.

Rose popped out from behind a pillar, lined up her M4 carbine's rifle sight, and put a small burst into the chest and neck of a guard taking cover behind a large CSS sculpture in the middle of the concourse. The rest of the first floor was mostly open space with little cover but for a few benches, the odd piece of bland corporate art, and a receptionist's area. Frustrated with the remaining shooters crouched behind the giant logo of their murder-for-hire brand, Rose released her trigger and eyeballed a large metallic globe twenty feet away from her position. With the ISU supercharging her dense quads, she sprinted like a wild stallion out of the gate, straight towards the sphere. Ripping it from its supports, she raised it up and hurled it like a falling moon towards the snipers. The crash and collapse were loud enough to briefly muffle the sprays of automatic-weapons fire.

Meanwhile, Ace was skating around the perimeter, swinging a huge frozen mallet into the face of any enemy who popped out from behind cover. Whizzing past a bank of elevators near the central stairway, he glanced up at the series of glass-and-chrome bridges bisecting the atrium to connect the office blocks.

Shadows were running across the fourth-floor bridge from both sides of the building. Ace narrowly managed to forge himself a densely frozen shield before streams of starburst gunfire tore up the area around him.

Rose watched Ace speeding forth, absorbing the bullets with a spiky tortoiseshell of ice. The streaking hot lead chewed the shield up into torrents of hailstones, but Ace was a speedy craftsman, replenishing it on the go, moving closer and closer until he was directly under the enemy-occupied walkway, stifling the angle of the bridge shooters' aim. From within the ISU's command center, Rose heard Sergeant Connors declare a plan. It sounded risky, but what wasn't in war?

Weapons hot? Darcy asked in follow-up.

In what was still a relatively new development, the ISU had discovered that they could interact with the souls still housed inside of the living. Prior to their New York posting, their and Rose's Hourglass operations had tended to utilize Rose's enhanced brutish strength, but their new trick had become an interesting novelty.

Red hot, Rose issued.

She wished them luck and felt the ISU depart her body, taking to the air and drawing the enemy fire. They twirled and dashed, staying one second ahead of the bullets, which could very likely destroy them. They spread throughout the atrium: Sarge going left, Darcy going right, and Barros arcing straight over the bridge shooters; the perfect decoys. Ace stepped out from his concave shield, and Rose skidded to a halt next to him. Ace placed his boot on one of her dainty, iron-strong palms, his stomach lurching as she launched him upwards. Reacting quickly, he grabbed the bridge's handrail and swung himself over, and immediately set to impaling and beheading the guards with an axe that would surely make the frost giants of Jotunheim proud.

Needing no such boost herself, Rose leapt up to the bridge from a standing position, landing amidst the surviving shooters, her rifle and rhinoceros strength making short work of them.

Sarge and Barros had broken away, dispensing with their aerial cavorting, rushing towards more shooters positioned on either side of the fourth-floor mezzanine who were preparing to turn everyone on the bridge—including their own comrades—into Swiss cheese. Sarge waded into the pair of targets drawing down on Ace, while Barros took aim at the three drawing down on Rose. She moved like a cannonball dead-set on dragging their souls straight out of their armored chests in one powerful dash.

Except nothing happened.

No effect whatsoever.

Sarge and Barros had phased through their target groups without causing so much as a shudder. Still, it worked in a fashion as the two fire teams were now tracking them instead of their living allies on the bridge.

Rose burned through her first M4 clip, but the close quarters didn't allow her time to reload. Not that it mattered much. Bullets were good for long-range combat, but up close she was a human bulldozer. Through the melee, she dropped a broken guard and turned just in time to see an alarmed expression on Darcy's face, his attention fixed on something coming up behind her. Rose spun around to find a near-crippled guard fighting to his last breath, his rifle bearing down on her. She was about to charge him and finish the job, but Darcy was still moving swiftly, running straight through the bridge like a vapor and swinging a wild haymaker into the jaw of the aiming guard. Under less deadly circumstances Darcy and the guard's reactions might have been comical. Darcy stared in muted shock as his fist passed straight through the guard's jaw with zero effect other than buying Rose a few precious seconds.

Explanations could wait for now. Rose cleared the distance like a cheetah and kicked the guard so forcefully it was like she was trying for a field goal, sending him like a gridiron football up through a glass office cubicle on the fifth floor.

Darcy still looked confused as he said, 'That should have knocked the ghost right out of him.' Rose didn't know what to say.

Sarge and Barros had zigged and zagged from their own aborted assaults, trying to lure the rifle sights of the remaining mezzanine gunners away from Rose, Darcy, and Ace. While the gunners opened up in controlled bursts, chasing Sarge and Barros like possessed clay pigeons, Rose tore one of the new rifle models from a dead guard's hands and fired on the trio grouped by her end of the bridge. Her shots riddled them, punching holes in limbs, helmet visors, and even, occasionally, through their armor.

Ace took care of the remaining two gunners with a few well-placed frozen javelins.

'Are these guys already dead?' Darcy asked, still perplexed as to why he couldn't cold-cock the life out of the guard.

'It's a good question,' Sarge said. 'Same thing just happened to me and Barros. Dead or soulless.'

'Like they were puppets,' said Barros. 'You think they're connected to the doll-maker?'

'They don't look like her toys.' Rose gestured to the bodies littering the bridge and atrium. 'But if they weren't dead before you hit them, then they are now.' She admired the rifle in her hands from a purely technical standpoint, and not its current usage as a PLE exterminator. Quite frankly, the fact that they were being used to try and permanently silence her old army squad pissed her off no end. But the rifle was sleek and portable, not a bullpup design, thankfully, but standard, similar to the M4 carbine used extensively in the US Army. She ejected the clip, finding it half-full and fitted for common NATO 5.56x45 ammunition. 'And if this thing is loaded with Exorcist rounds, then these guys are so dead that even the Null can't claim them.' Her thumb grazed along the selector switch for single, three-fire burst, and full-auto firing modes. 'Think I'll keep hold of this. Meadows might like a closer look.'

Ace lumbered over the bloody corpses, scanning all around for additional back-up forces moving in. All quiet. He regrouped with Rose and the ISU on the bridge.

'We got bigger concerns than this fodder,' Rose said. 'Let's look for bigger game.'

'Clyde, rookie: atrium's clear. On the fourth-floor bridge and searching the mezzanine now,' Ace said. 'You got anything up t—' He never saw it coming.

Doll-Face, housed in her huge ethereal ape, dropped down onto the bridge and shoulder charged through him like a speeding bus.

* * * * *

Kev moved cautiously. Having exited the bottom of the elevator shaft, he found himself in a basement security hub. And the fact that the place was utterly deserted left him cold. The empty corridor led to an empty chamber filled with nothing but computer servers, while the next room down was nothing but unmanned security consoles and black screens. The whole level was as unthreatening as the blueprint he had studied.

Very strange.

What was most disappointing, however, was the lack of anything that could conceivably be a way and means of producing enhanced killers. Not a potential Boogieman Machine in sight, and he had been thorough in his investigation. No living creature—or any shade of undead—to work their mojo, nor any exotic doodad to do likewise. And pertinently, if there had been such a thing, then there wasn't a chance in hell that it would have been left unguarded down here. Still, Kev had swept the whole floor several times searching for hidden rooms, escape tunnels, *anything*.

Nothing.

But something felt off.

What were the options here? Either the means of creating the assassins was small enough to have been taken from the premises in a guard's pocket, or the means had never been here to begin with. And so, what had gone on between Harlan Brink, his finest contractors, and Talbot? Was Brink's death an accident, a type of mystical short-circuit, or could the power source also be used to destroy its own creations from afar, like a kill switch? Either/or, why were all the employees now kitted-out like an occupational force if there's nothing here worth protecting? Just because their computer system had been recently bypassed? Had they been anticipating a physical attack from Hourglass?

Or was this all some form of bait?

Kev was about to update Clyde and the team when he noticed his hand beginning to fade in and out of view. Not just his hand, but his whole form, flickering like a dying light bulb.

That meant only one thing. Clyde was in trouble. Wounded? Dying?

Kev speeded up through the floors, needing to get to his friend before he was killed.

* * * * *

Clyde never heard him coming. He and Nat had just cleared their way to the fifth-floor mezzanine when Clyde felt a tremendous push lift him off his feet, pitching him through the glass wall of an office. It was only by habit, and a little gut instinct, that he kept a thin layer of telekinetic energy cocooning him when on mission. It was draining if used excessively, but this time it probably saved his life.

Rolling over onto the carpet of jeweled glass, he turned around to see his attacker, and instantly felt his insides shrivel. After all these weeks of dread, the Hangman had finally surfaced.

And Clyde froze up.

He watched helplessly as the Spark killer easily restrained Nat's wrists, having bent them away from him to aim at Clyde instead and using them like a pair of sonic shotguns. It was her misdirected blast that had hit Clyde and almost killed him. And now the Hangman's greatly superior size and strength had him looming over Natalie as he forced her to her knees, rotating her trapped wrists until the bones threatened to break. Her gritted teeth shone in the red-strobed darkness, cutting off her pained groan.

Clyde felt like a statue, about to watch as the supreme killer bagged his fourth Spark.

Natalie wasn't going to go quietly. She gave Clyde a pained squint and a head tick, a subtle signal, one he intuited as to mean *keep your shield up*. With a grunt of effort, she released a small warhead of violet energy, the blast bubbling outwards and blasting the Hangman back into a wall of tempered glass. He cracked the multi-paned load-bearing wall, his head and wide back thwacking it with the sound of a large steak slapping onto a kitchen floor. It didn't seem to have much of an effect. He was up quickly, the face of slithering barbs glowering at Nat while lassos unspooled from both of his arms.

Clyde snapped out of it. He might not have what it takes to kill this son-of-a-bitch, but he wasn't going to let his self-doubt be an accomplice to his and Nat's death. He'd dropped his submachine gun after being flung through the glass wall. No time to search for it now. He had alternatives.

He took a breath, focused, and pinned the Hangman's arms to his side, realizing to his horror that even with his limbs immobile, the barbed lengths could still thrash around of their own volition. Holding the assassin's body in place with his closed left fist, Clyde used his right hand to pummel telekinetic shots into his chest and barbed head. The punches impacted like sledgehammers but seemed to do little against the wire nest. Clyde put more behind each strike, huffing with each shot now, and slowly, so slowly, began to break through the barbed helmet. Somewhere in that spiky maw, a human face was beginning to reveal itself.

Nat had been charging up another audible bombshell, one that might well burst the Hangman through the cracked glass wall if her expression was anything to go by.

But she suddenly stopped, a flicker of fear in her eyes.

And Clyde saw why.

Hands, maybe half a dozen of them, each one wax white even in the flashing red dimness of the back-up lights, sprouted from the floor like ugly plastic weeds. The mannequin arms dragged Nat through the floor like a trap door had dropped open beneath her, but in her wake, the ground remained solid.

'Nat!' Clyde shouted.

The distraction cost him. The Hangman broke from his hold and raised his bulging arms like a zombie ready to seize and chomp. Two cutting lines struck like snakes, and if Clyde hadn't managed to cover himself in his telekinetic sheath, the lashes would have bit deep and peeled him like a grape. For the second time in a manic minute, Clyde felt his feet leave the ground as the Hangman dragged him in, the barbs hooked onto his second ethereal skin, and with an incredible feat of power, pivoted and swung Clyde towards the dense corner of a glass wall. Clyde threw a hand up at the last second and pushed back, rebounding himself away a split-second before impact. The barbed wires slipped from him as he flew across the mezzanine, his hands out like an amateur flyer, doing what he could to guide himself to a gentler stop. The Hangman wasted no time in stalking after him, the red glow making rusty centipedes of his writhing head.

Skidding to a stop on the opposite side of the mezzanine, Clyde broke his gaze away from the pursuing killer and saw red light flashing across a plastic direction board on the wall, along with a big arrow pointing to "Armory & Firing Range." He sprinted in that direction, thinking that if this was his last night on Earth, he could perhaps die trying to destroy the Hangman. He knew it was absurd. But if he couldn't kill him, maybe he could at least wound him and slow him down for the others.

The Hangman was already on Clyde's side of the mezzanine, moving with a leisurely certainty that he would catch his quarry. Clyde drew his two sidearms, spun, and emptied two full magazines of nine millimeters into the Hangman's torso, but he just kept coming. Clyde holstered them and, still back-pedaling, used his telekinesis to lift Hangman into the air, intending to smash him off every hard surface he could find until he exhausted every last ounce of his loaned power, or this glasshouse collapsed on both of them.

But the Hangman was quick in mind and body, and lassoing upwards onto the sixth-floor bridge, he swung out and away from Clyde's hold, completed a tight arcing swing over the precipitous drop, and came back at Clyde boots first. Clyde had barely stepped aside before the stomp shattered a glass office wall. He launched a stiff right cross wrapped up in a telekinetic membrane into the killer's jaw. Hangman took it and fired back, his two huge fists wrapped up like barbed bushels, whistling through the air as Clyde continued to find himself on the back foot, slipping the deadly blows.

Clyde didn't know how much energy he had left and had no strategy to stop this advancing nightmare. The names of the dead team members called out in his head like an obituary roll call, and he knew his name was soon going to be joining that list.

Creating more distance, he pulled the pins on both frag grenades and both flashbangs, everything but the kitchen sink, and swept the four of them towards the unstoppable killer. The mezzanine rocked with blinding light, shrapnel, and boiling concussive winds. When the smoke cleared and the glass stopped raining, he saw the Hangman slumped over the twisted and scorched metal railing, his clothing torn and smoking, his head and arms sagging towards the lobby five floors below. Within seconds he was pushing himself away from the sizzling railing, hardly the worse for wear, and ready to continue his relentless pursuit.

Hearing the continued shouts and crashes of his teammates engaged in combat below, Clyde glanced over the balcony and saw the small forms of Ace and Rose fighting the doll-woman and her ape suit on the bridge.

He thought of mannequins and tried not to think of the possibility that Nat was alone with them somewhere, possibly dead.

They all had their hands full. He wasn't going to add the Hangman to their current problems.

This was his problem to deal with.

He turned and ran, heart pounding in his ears, racing down the long mezzanine past dark, empty offices and conference rooms until he found another corridor signposted with "Armory & Firing Range."

* * * * *

Natalie passed through what she could only think of as a tube slide from hell. The crazy passage dumped her out onto a plastic-topped table in the building's large cafeteria. In the eerie light, she watched the gangly, terrifying forms of living mannequins shuffle towards her with awkward mobility. Natalie told herself she wasn't going to be killed by a bunch of freaky asexual plastic dummies. The rough crash-bang of her entrance had topped up some of her audible reserves, and her hands shone with incandescent violet. With a single pulse she scattered them backwards into tables and chairs, the coffee machine, and the stainless-steel refrigerator. The resulting racket from their clacking and breaking bodies created a nice feedback loop, offering her more noise to absorb. She didn't know if they would get back up again, if it would take their absolute atomic destruction to end their lifeless threat, so she hurried out of the cafeteria, finding herself in the middle of the atrium. Her gaze cut across all the scattered bodies, searching for Rose and Ace. She was about to ask for a sit-rep over the comms when something caught her eye—Rose, falling into view from a steep height, one of the upper walkways. The impact was meaty, and Nat's mouth dropped open, fearing the worst. Rose seemed to have hurt the floor more than herself and was up again in no time.

Nat ran over to Rose, glancing up at the bridges connecting the mezzanines of each floor. She heard Ace's gruff voice hurling obscenities from somewhere above, and then spotted another worrying sight: a second bunch of mannequins, their frantic, jittery arm movements stringing Ace up precipitously in the middle of the atrium. A spindly waifish woman in a blank pale mask and some type of bizarre translucent ape armor was observing their craftwork.

'Who's that?' Nat asked Rose, the lilt in her voice highlighting her incredulity at the sight.

'The bitch who just put me down here. Come on.' Without asking, Rose grabbed Nat by her belt and leapt vertically. Landing amongst the bridge's littered bodies, Nat almost stumbled over a splayed limb or two before finding her balance. She channeled her energy into her bass guitar, the construct materializing in glittering, jagged violet. She turned around to see Ace strung up twenty feet away from the bridge, out of reach, thrashing helplessly as the silent idiot dolls jerked about to unspoken commands. The woman in the glowing ape suit turned her attention away from Ace, staring at Nat and Rose curiously.

Ace might not surf, but Nat had another question for him. 'You ever snowboard?'

Perhaps it was synchronicity, but Nat noticed that a fast-rising column of ice was already forming directly under Ace's feet, rising from the atrium, curtains of icy vapors pouring from it.

Nat's fingers raced across intangible strings, playing a bass solo that hit like rubber bullets and riotous energy, the vibrations ripping the mannequins apart limb from limb, pieces of them clattering on the bridge and the frost-misted atrium below.

Doll-Face was quick, the huge cartoonish gorilla leaping away from Nat's attack, its two large and clever paws grabbing the bridge's railing and swinging them underneath the walkway.

The puppet strings that had been holding Ace went dangerously slack, but the frozen peak, formed with such speed as to be absolutely exhausting for Ace, was now only a few meters beneath him. The strings vanished, much like the dismembered doll parts.

Rose treaded along the bridge carefully, her eyes constantly moving in search of the woman-ape combo clambering around the underside of the bridge, waiting for an opportunity to ambush her.

Another parade of dolls poured into reality from their unknown doll-house. Dangerous distractions for Nat, but she dealt with these fresh hostiles while Rose stepped over a dead CSS guard to peer over the railing. The ape suddenly swept upwards, balling one massive fist and blindsiding Rose. Rose managed to get her hands up, but the crushing blow readily discouraged absorbing too many of them. Rose's hard eyes stared into the black slits of the masked woman piloting the giant jungle animal, and she too appeared as robotic and dispassionate as her minions. Rose swung a big burly haymaker of her own, connecting straight into the simian's head. Despite its semi-transparent appearance, it was still physical enough to take a hit as well as give one. Rose continued to swing, eagerly trying to smash through the ape suit and get her hands on the woman behind the beast. But it still proved difficult to hit, nimble and extremely agile for its size.

Leaping from rail to rail, it kicked Rose in passing, and swung over and under the bridge again, leaving Rose guessing as to where the next attack would come from. A nice shiner was blooming around her right eye from the last hit-and-run punch. Such power. Whoever this madwoman was, she certainly ranked amongst the strongest opponents Rose had fought. The gorilla leapt up for another pass, a feint to anger Rose, but she had one advantage in this fight: she didn't have a silly cartoon business tie trailing behind her neck. Grabbing it out of the air, she yanked it in the hope of choking the thing out of existence, leaving the doll-maker vulnerable.

And it worked!

Rose pulled the tie hard enough to bring ape and master crashing back onto the bridge, their hefty weight mashing a dead guard in the process. Lying on its back, the greenish ape faded away, leaving its conjurer exposed and supine. As she stood over her enemy, a nasty little smirk spread across Rose's lips. She was going to settle a score.

Two sharp eyes peered up at Rose through the doll mask. Doll-Face flipped to her feet in a graceful, acrobatic motion, pulling two concealed blades from sheaths on her filthy white overalls. She moved like a ballerina on methamphetamine, launching at Rose with a beautiful choreography of fatal attacks. Rose had no choice but to circle and strafe on the wide bridge, hopping over an obstacle course of limbs and struggling to find an opening in the flurry of swishing attacks.

Rose was about to swipe another rifle from a dead sniper. Even if it was empty, she would introduce its stock into the doll-woman's face.

But something beat her to it.

A large chunk of ice whooshed past Rose's shoulder, cracking Doll-Face's mask and making her stumble. Ace's frozen column had now extended into a ridgeline, connecting him back to the bridge. His chest was heaving, his limbs sluggish, but with a frozen axe in his hand, he wasn't about to take a breather. Nat stood beside him, aiming her crackling bass like a rifle.

Doll-Face stared back at them, not moving a muscle. Red lights from the mezzanine continued to wash over her blank, cracked mask, glistening with the moisture from Ace's frozen projectile. Then she spoke. It was only a murmur, indecipherable, but the confusion and fright taking control of her was unmistakable. It wasn't fear of the aggressors before her, but something remote and unknown. She shook her head a few times as if trying to deny some terrible sight or knowledge, and backed away slowly, almost stumbling over a dead guard's splayed arm.

'If you're watching us, asshole,' Ace called to Doll-Face's quivering form, 'you won't be getting in our heads this time.'

Nat knew Ace wasn't directing his speech to the doll-maker but the psychic presence pulling *her* strings, the true puppeteer running the show. Watching the doll-woman's distress, Nat found herself very grateful for the Free-Thinker's uncomfortable pinch.

The ape suit engulfed her once more and, without preamble, she leapt through the air, the ape's huge paws swinging on puppet wires until they both crashed through a roof access hatch.

'That's twice that bitch has slipped me,' Rose grumbled.

'You guys okay?' Nat sounded a little shaky.

Ace was scanning the area, axe in hand, making sure no other nasty surprises were about to drop onto their heads. 'Nothing a few beers won't fix. Nice job, rook.'

Nat took a small, trembling breath. It was frigid and invigorating.

Rose switched communicator pre-sets, selecting the frequency for the back-up teams outside the CSS complex and telling them to keep an eye out for a big glowing monkey. Hopefully, they wouldn't lose her this time.

'Shit!' Nat suddenly took off running. 'We need to get upstairs. Clyde's with Hangman!'

Rose and Ace sprinted after her, Rose's incredible power and speed leaving them both in her wake.

'Clyde, hang on, kid. We're on our way.' Ace's mask could hide his face but not the concern in his voice.

* * * * *

Clyde found the armory, but it wasn't helping him a great deal. His telekinetic energy was sapped right down to the dregs, and the assault rifle in his hands was empty, the hot barrel pouring smoke. The armory was expectedly large and exceedingly well-equipped, with walls and cages full of everything from small arms for lighter celebrity bodyguard work to high-powered weapons to wage a small war for Citadel's more discreet, off-the-book clients.

And Clyde had used a dispiriting number of them so far, all with little effect. The barbs coiling around the Hangman's torso were better than the latest-generation Kevlar, it seemed, continuing to absorb everything Clyde had thrown at him. The killer had patiently followed him deeper and deeper into the armory, as if convinced of Clyde's inevitable death.

The red emergency lights continued their rapid blinks and swirling revolutions as Clyde urgently inspected the next weapon rack, then the next, and the next: another submachine gun, assault rifle, another semi-automatic pistol, even an automatic pistol—they all discharged death but seemed to pale before this true reaper. Clyde moved through the aisles of weaponry racks, listening to the Hangman's thudding footfalls over the tinnitus in his ears.

Locating a brutal combat shotgun and a box of steel-jacketed slugs, he loaded it with nervous breaths and trembling hands. Jacking the first round, he watched two wiry snakes slithering around the corner, and the Hangman soon followed, his big arms slightly limp as though being led by the barbed lines. The shotgun's first blast was practically ear-bursting in the confines, and the steel-jacketed round briefly staggered the Hangman. Clyde backed up, pumping round after round into the killer's torso and head until the long gun clicked empty. Each shot had stunned the Hangman, but with each interval, the paranormal killer had continued to push forward. Clyde dropped the shotgun, grabbed hold of an assault rifle he wasn't familiar with, his delayed reaction then recognizing it as one of the new variety of models the security firm had been supplied with.

Ace was suddenly in his ear, telling him to hang in there and asking him to confirm his location. Clyde told him, grabbing a rifle magazine and slotting it home. Were they Exorcist rounds? Did the Hangman even have a soul somewhere behind all that hellish armor? He quickly inspected the boxes of ammunition amongst the rifles and magazines, but the gloom made it difficult to read the box's information. Throwing it back, he saw the description NATO 5.56x45 caliber, but wasn't any clearer as to whether they were cored with ghost-destroying capabilities or any other unorthodox quirks.

Didn't matter. All Clyde could do was try until he died.

Clyde squeezed the trigger, the burst fire doing no better at stopping the Hangman than anything else he had thrown at him so far.

The rifle clicked empty.

He was running out of room. Out of ammo. With no place to run.

His back reached the glass wall with a view to a darkened firing range, but his eyes almost leapt from their sockets when he noticed a side door leading out of the armory to a check-out area. He charged for it, crashing through the door, and only realizing too late that the murky room wasn't empty. Three guards drew on Clyde, all big men of a strangely identical build and height, their faces lost in the shadows beneath their cap peaks. There was something else strange about them: they all stood there staring at him, but their postures told him that they didn't particularly want to shoot. Were they hoping to keep him here until the Hangman entered the room and seized him?

Unexpectedly, all three of the guards' heads twisted 180 degrees simultaneously, producing an awful crunching sound. Something else came speeding through the ubiquitous glass and red-strobing darkness: Kev, his expression one of absolute delight at seeing Clyde still in one piece. Clyde gestured at the three dead guards and gave him a look of gratitude.

'There's nothing here,' Kev said, sounding unsure of whether he was annoyed or relieved. 'No psychic big-bad, no means, no shaman, no enchanted McGuffin, curios, or chicken bones, no Boogieman Machine.'

'Oh, there's something here. No machine,' Clyde backed up towards him right as the Hangman walked into the room, 'but there's a boogieman.' Clyde quickly put his fist up for Kev to bump, needing another dose of power. 'The others are on the way. Maybe we can finish this fuck together.'

Their knuckles touched, fists glowing vaporously with eldritch energy. They both separated, moving into a pincer formation on the Hangman, when he suddenly stopped in his tracks, then stumbled about like he was on the deck of a wave-rocked ship, one barbed fist pressing to his barbed head. The deadly wires seemed to squeal in a shrill discordant harmony, pulling away one by one, beginning their retreat beneath his flesh and offering a tantalizing glimpse at the man underneath. But the wires stopped in their retreat and then recovered him once more. The Hangman swiped at thin air with a vicious backhand before racing out the way he came, smashing straight through the glass door.

Ace, Rose, and Nat filed into the room on the heels of his exit, catching themselves just before tripping over the trio of dead bodies.

Without comment, Clyde led the chase after the Hangman, the rest of the team right behind him. But the moment they made it out of the armory, he knew it was pointless. The Hangman was nowhere to be found.

For the next several minutes Kev and the ISU used their superior maneuverability to try and find him within the building, moving freely up and down the floors, but like Doll-Face before him, he had experienced a major psychological defect before abandoning his mission.

The team regrouped in the atrium.

'They both just took off,' Rose said, trying to make sense of it. 'That's the second time for ape-girl.'

'Probably wasn't for fresh air, huh?' Nat asked, staring about at all the bodies, a washed-out look behind her eyes. Ace's frozen mist still trailed about the place like a living carpet.

'Not going to get overly optimistic here,' Rose said, dabbing one finger at the swelling around her eye, 'but I'd say this is a small victory. We didn't find the source, but whatever it is that Talbot's using to cook these things, his recipe is far from perfected. They're dangerous, but they're liabilities. How long before they fuck up and stop following orders?'

Clyde went to pull the Free-Thinker from the nape of his neck, seeking relief from the removal of its tiny pincers, but had second thoughts, should there still be a psychic threat on the premises. 'Maybe we needed these things or maybe we didn't,' he tapped the device still on his nape, 'but can we all agree that there are some gnarly mind-altering methods at work here?'

It was not a contentious question.

Rose used the channel to talk with the outside teams, checking to see if they'd managed to track their fled targets.

'If all it takes is a few slaps to make those two fall apart, it shouldn't take too many more to break them.' Ace made it all sound so easy, but Clyde was thinking about how close he just came to being wrung out like a blood-soaked sponge upstairs.

He gave Ace a doubtful look. 'Whatever's controlling them, it'll take more than a "few slaps." Hangman just walked-off an armory. Whatever caused that, I don't think it was us.'

'Guys, look at this.' Kev had drifted away and was standing over one of the numerous corpses littering the atrium. He had lifted the guard's face into the meager light, examining it.

'Are you seeing what I think you're seeing, Kev?' Barros asked, inspecting another of the dead guards.

'Same here,' Sarge added, staring down at the body of a third.

'Yep,' Darcy agreed. 'I knew something was up when I laid into that one on the bridge. If he had been alive, he should have dropped like a soul with a glass jaw.'

'It's not that these fellas were already dead,' Sarge said. 'This is something else.'

Clyde and Nat walked over to where Kev was turning over a few more of the corpses. 'What is it?' Clyde asked.

Kev removed another guard's cap, tilting his face towards Clyde.

'Brink?' Clyde said. 'All of them?'

'All of them,' Sarge confirmed, sailing down from the upper floors. 'In this light and all the excitement, it was easy to miss.'

'What does this mean?' Ace asked. 'Has Brink got a truckload of brothers or a clone farm?'

The face staring up at Kev began to glow. Slowly at first, like an ignited road flare, it took a few seconds to reach full scorching brightness. The veins in the neck began to flood with a crimson-gold liquid, the throat becoming a furnace flue, and the eyes becoming a white-hot phosphorescence.

It wasn't just the one body. It was all of them.

'Fuck...' Clyde muttered.

* * * * *

Outside, the perimeter teams, who had by now sealed off the entire block with executive power, watched in shock as the head offices of Citadel Security Solutions went up in a giant chain of explosions and a hurricane of broken glass.

24

Brink flicked through the series of now obliterated CSS CCTV feeds from his phone, feeling a cold fury exuding from Edward Talbot.

'What the *HELL* happened to them!?' Talbot screamed. 'Running away!?' Talbot became incapable of standing still any longer, pacing about with far too much energy for the small room. 'They're supposed to be mindless drones who obey simple instructions. Kill! That's all. A fucking dog can be taught tricks, why not these two?'

Brink was more focused on the fiscal cost of this back-up plan. Blowing up CSS was going to be a difficult one to explain to Leonard, but if there was any consolation, it was the fact that the building's insurance policy had been recently updated to include an endorsement covering acts of terrorism. And at least he had been able to spare a lot of good personnel by switching them out for his duplicates.

'The blast will have taken the agents out for you,' Brink said, certainty in his voice. 'You wanted them dead, right?' It didn't seem to assuage Talbot's anger.

'If it did, it was too quick. I wanted them to suffer.' His nostrils flared, and he swept a hand through his neatly combed hair. He took a steadying breath. 'But dead is dead, I suppose. How long for confirmation?'

'I have an aerial drone at the scene.' Brink's attention was back on his phone, getting up the camera feed from the circling drone. The whole HQ was a ruin of broken glass and twisted metal beams, choking the streets with gouts of black smoke. He was about to call the drone operator to try and get closer and lower to confirm if anybody was walking out of that mess when he noticed a small convoy of vehicles—clearly agency personnel from the tight and fast formation they were travelling in—shuttling away from the scene, while a number of other suits and black-clad paramilitary types remained behind to coordinate the emergency service responders and crowd control. Talbot had gone from a close invasion of personal space to snatching the phone from Brink's hands, but not before Brink had time to notice that the small fleet of outbound vehicles had swiftly escaped the drone camera's field of vision. This pleased him, if only to savor Talbot's disappointment.

'All we have is a group of agents taking charge of the scene,' Brink said redundantly. 'No sign of the strike team.'

Talbot shoved the phone back into Brink's hands, his fingers nervously stroking his left eyebrow in thought. Brink almost thought Talbot's finger had become a pale shade of green for a moment, damp and scaly, but an eye-blink later it was back to its pale shade of white.

'I don't understand what's happening to him. Hangman started out as a rousing success. Obedient. Highly effective. He killed the entire previous strike team, no questions, no complications. And now...?' Talbot seemed to be talking out loud rather than to Brink, who was merely stuck in the same room with him.

Talbot shrugged hopelessly, and Brink thought he was acting like a naughty schoolboy afraid of being summoned to the principal's office.

'And that other one, the bint obsessed with the dolls,' he wagged his finger as if circling a point, 'she has been unreliable from the beginning. Two botch jobs back-to-back. Julius really fumbled with that pick. But the Hangman...?'

'It could be Charon, Mr. Talbot.'

Talbot glared at Brink for his interruption.

'I'll hold my hands up and admit that this isn't my area of expertise, but my new attributes seem to work okay.' He gestured to his phone and the drone's circling observation of destruction. 'And the men who all opted for the enhancement were, to my knowledge, effective and reliable up to a point, that point being their deaths. Could be it's only when Charon tries to get in here,' Brink said, tapping his temple, 'that it goes south. You admitted yourself that this Charon thing, no one knows what state he—*it*—is really in. He's just an eye, for Christ's sake. How effective do you think you might be if you were reduced to a severed finger and left buried in the dirt for a month of Sundays?' Talbot silently stared at him for so long that Brink was beginning to consider producing a few more of his chemically volatile imitations as a precaution. 'That wasn't a threat, just stating a fact.'

With a huff Talbot pulled his blazer from the back of the chair and eased into it, fussing with the cuffs and the fit. 'Keep watching that,' he said, pointing to Brink's phone, 'and update me if they drag any little identifiable bits and pieces of those bastards out of there.'

Brink saw something flash behind Talbot's eyes, and it wasn't those strange reflective green lenses of his. It was something he'd seen in the eyes of hundreds of men, but not Talbot's. It was fear. Without another word, Talbot swiftly exited the room. Brink called his drone operator and told him to shut it down.

He then texted a single vague message to Julius, signaling their success, and pulled a tiny plastic fob from his shirt pocket, the button of which had activated the tiny transmitters in the ears of Nathan and Dolores, playing them a prerecorded loop of Julius's specifically coded messages to cloud and usurp Charon's programming. Julius had made it clear that Brink had to make sure it looked good, convincing, by not activating the transmitters until at least a worthy struggle had transpired. That way Talbot, arrogant idiot that he was, would be more likely to assume that Charon's effect had diminished during the course of the fight, rather than the pair of them leaving Elzinga already confused and rebellious. For that wouldn't look good on Julius.

He grabbed the thin dossiers on the current Hourglass strike team from the desk. They were very light reading, containing little more than some surveillance photos and basic intel on each member, such as a name and their abilities. However, their photos, while far from perfect, were crucial bits of intel, each one taken from a drone or a member of Cairnwood's or CSS's network. But even if Brink didn't believe that was the strike team vacating the scene at speed, if they still happened to be in that bombed building, he knew there would be nothing identifiable about their corpses. He dropped the dossiers into a desk drawer and closed it.

Still drained from the production of so many duplicates, he reached for his rocket-fuel coffee and composed himself. He had to call Leonard immediately before he caught wind of this from the media or one of his many other sources. He still couldn't believe he'd just exploded their central office for that Talbot prick. Perhaps he should have just let his men die in there instead of filling it with his own explosive martyrs.

He tried to take some comfort in the fact that he only had to break his news to a business partner and not a superior, or whatever qualified as a superior to somebody like Talbot. He checked his watch: 10:45 pm.

He called Leonard.

25

'You're certain they were all Brink?' Meadows asked. There was no suggestion of incredulity in his demeanor, only a need for veracity. 'One hundred percent,' Kev answered. The ISU all nodded along in agreement.

Clyde and the team sat in Meadows's large office, feeling physically and emotionally depleted from the combat and the after-effects of adrenaline. The only reason they were sitting here in one piece instead of being scattered into three dozen smaller pieces across six city blocks was because of Kev's quick reaction in encasing them all in a bubble, seconds prior to the first Brink bomb going off. Sadly, even with the city block on lockdown prior to the explosion, Kev's defensive measures couldn't help those who still found themselves too close to the blast area. The glass and the concussive shockwave had created a number of casualties, not only Hourglass personnel guarding the block's four intersections, but numerous pedestrians who were unfortunate enough to catch a stray glass shard from outside the cordoned area, and the shock of the explosion had startled several drivers into, mercifully, only minor car pileups.

Despite this, the collective mood of Clyde, the team, and Meadows was one of glum professionalism.

They had debriefed Meadows on the mission's details following a once-over by the medics, who thankfully had nothing more serious to treat than a few bumps and bruises. Incredible really. After a much-needed shower to wash off the blood, sweat, and smoke, the team all grabbed coffee or tea from the cafeteria before joining Meadows. Rose had managed to pick up another of the security personnel's rifles before CSS went up like a glass-laden IED and had passed it on to Meadows before hitting the washroom. By the time the team knocked on his door, Meadows had already loaded a video on one of his screens, a hidden camera from the looks of it, likely pinned to a lapel or nametag. As it transpired, Meadows had managed to identify the rifle from Clyde's earlier surveillance photos, his contacts having provided him with footage taken from a private weapons expo recently held in Belarus for some eccentric types who dabbled in more untraditional, arcane forms of warfare.

According to Meadows and his industry spy, the newly unveiled model was the AB21 assault rifle, the latest product from one of the largest weapons manufacturers in the world, the Russian-founded Aristov Ballistics. The AB21: a lightweight polymer-and-steel rifle at 3.26kg, the weapon had a cyclic fire rate of 700 rounds and an effective range of up to 600 meters, with three selective-fire modes: single, three-round burst, and full-automatic. It was constructed with a rail mounting for various optical sightings, and under-barrel availability for an optional grenade launcher. It carried a thirty-round magazine of NATO 5.56x45mm ammo to cater to the largest market possible, with NATO's thirty member states constantly filling out orders.

The Aristov Ballistics portfolio was thick with the various expected models of tanks, attack choppers, fighter jets, armored vehicles, missile technology, as well as the more sophisticated aspects of modern warfare from drones, A.I., and experimental battle suits. But that was all for the public to read about. Aristov Ballistics also had one foot in the realm of the mystical. Hence, the AB21 and their patented Exorcist ammunition.

But even taking all of this into account, Aristov Ballistics was just another arms dealer with no known loyalties, not even to the Cairnwood Society. Meadows did, however, mention that he'd have R&D retroactively investigate how they produced the PLE killers.

'No hint of anyone or anything that could be accountable for the assassins, only a building filled with combustible copies of Harlan Brink.' Meadows chewed it over, watching live aerial footage of the scene's destruction. 'Nothing but a death trap with an explosive failsafe, and I sent you all in there. Unconfirmed number of civilian and agency casualties...' He muttered something angry under his breath.

'Not the result we wanted, but we had to cross that place off the list at some point,' Rose said, pointing at the zoomed-in satellite view of the obliterated CSS. 'I'd say it's crossed off.'

A second screen rolled footage of oblivious reporters on the scene, scrambling in the dark of a media blackout, where they would remain until Hourglass sources decided to drip-feed them some typical and fabricated nonsense about domestic terrorist plots or disgruntled CSS employees taking up arms against each other. The latter possibility could then lead on to some further journalistic think pieces about the danger of metropolitan-based paramilitary security firms, which might prove uncomfortable for Leonard Sharp's conglomerate.

Meadows stared at the team with his everlasting moody countenance, but somewhere in those hardened, craggy features his eyes seemed to soften. Was that a touch of pride Clyde saw in them? Meadows's roving appraisal stopped on him, and then Natalie to his right.

'It's no small thing that you both managed to survive an encounter with the Hangman. He got away, but so did both of you, with all your pieces intact.' A pause. 'Well done.'

Clyde sat there, replaying the black-and-red-painted memories of the Hangman stalking him through the armory—relentless, unstoppable.

Rose reached across and punched Clyde on the shoulder with a big white smile. 'Nice going, nerd.'

'You too, rookie,' Ace said to Nat. 'You play a mean bass solo.'

There were a few strained attempts at bravado and humor from the rest of the team, but it all sounded so hollow in the aftermath that it practically echoed.

Kev threaded the cheap high-five optimism with a pertinent point. 'They managed to walk away because the psychic entity, whatever it is, seems to be losing control of the Hangman and Jungle Jane. In fact, I'd say it's *lost* control of them. I hope Talbot's ripping his hair out over this setback.' He huffed a little as if in preparation for what he was going to say next. Holding his hand out to Meadows in a show of peace, he asked, 'Trujillo got any updates on the energy signature of our chief boogieman yet?'

Meadows's demeanor was not that of a defensive man, but one who only seemed relieved to have not lost another strike team. 'Trujillo and the hoodoo are still looking into it. But it'll require a little more patience, it's a sensitive process.'

'Patience? Fat chance of that, huh, Kev?' Darcy remarked, getting a few tired chuckles from around the table.

Kev smiled, but Clyde knew it was false even if the others didn't. He had to keep Kev busy. Kev, who never slept and spent every night obsessing over the larger picture he couldn't see: The mysteries of the Null. The mysteries of everything.

Clyde sat up in his seat and cleared his throat, which still felt raw and parched from some of the smoke he'd inhaled exiting the bombsite. 'So...Brink exploded a decoy of himself in his car because he knew we were watching him and wanted to throw us off his scent, or to project the illusion that the firm would be in a weakened, vulnerable state with the sudden loss of their leader, drawing us into a trap with Hangman and the doll-maker. Option A or option B, the ruse is over. We know, unequivocally, that CSS are still pulling triggers for Talbot. Meaning we still have one lead to try and find the Boogieman Machine.' He watched how Meadows's jaw bunched up in thought, and Clyde had a feeling Meadows had already been pondering his forthcoming suggestion. 'We need to start looking into Leonard Sharp personally.'

Meadows picked up a small remote from his desk and turned off the screen depicting the satellite view of smoke and glass. 'We're on the same page, Agent Williams, though this will require a strict hands-off approach. Observation and investigation only. Mr. Sharp will be facing some unanticipated media exposure over this, to which he will inevitably feign ignorance, and hey, perhaps that's still true, perhaps it's not. You're all entitled to make your own conclusions about the man: pawn or patsy. If it's the latter, we don't officially exist and therefore can't attempt to pursue him through legal channels, and as you know, the FBI can't link him to his suspected criminal activities, so we won't be prying intel from him with plea-bargaining. And if he's a patsy, then we owe him the common courtesy of separating him from Talbot and Cairnwood if possible.'

Ace groaned. 'Great, so we got a whole lot more sitting around doing fuck-all until we stumble onto a break.'

'Luck and patience have always been facets of the job, Ace.'

'This mean we all wear big shades and trench coats, snap photos of this dude until he leads us to where the Boogieman Machine is?' Nat asked. She almost sounded enthusiastic about the idea, though Clyde thought he could still hear the slight strains of stress in her voice.

'That's a romantic idea,' Meadows admitted, 'but the modern age has taken a lot of the fun out of such cloak-and-dagger activities. But not all the fun. A good place to start would be his office. I'll order a few surveillance drone passes to get glimpses into his office, see what we can see. If he keeps a laptop in there, I'll talk to the cyber team to see if they can access remotely. But that won't be enough.' He looked at Kev and the ISU. 'We're going to need to get inside there to take an old-fashioned look around: desk drawers, notebooks and such.'

Barros perked up. 'Being the owner of CSS, it's a safe bet that the geek squad downstairs won't be able to crack his computer from here.' Her floating torso may be dead and ravaged but the shimmering light of interest and curiosity in her eyes was vigorous. 'Unless this guy is embarrassingly amateur hour, he'll be protected from RDP hacking.'

Clyde listened to her gloss over something called remote desktop protocol hacking for the IT-challenged like him, Kev, and, well, most of them, really, except Meadows, who had some degree of familiarity with the concept. RDP hacking basically involved leaping onto a user's computer via the Internet if it was attuned and waiting for an RDP signal. If RDP is enabled on the target computer, the signal can be duped by an outsider, allowing them access and the opportunity to turn the computer into their own private little zombie, granting the intruder access to run riot through the system: peruse all contained files therein, install malware, whatever tickled the hacker's fancy. Clyde had to agree with Barros: such ease of access would be incredibly amateur hour for somebody owning a lucrative security firm.

'Pretending that the CEO of a security firm isn't a complete disgrace to his profession, if we get into his office, I can walk Kev through a few more hands-on things. I talk to the tech guys downstairs now and then, and they've mentioned that they've been toying with the latest generation key-logging hardware. They say it can even bypass basic biometric locks with some quite literal computer wizardry. Impressive stuff. So, I'm thinking we slip the computer's USB port a little plastic roofie, skip any biometrics, and retroactively find out what his password is and, voilà, check out the files. Anything of value we can instantly send across to the keyboard warriors down in the basement. And hey, if it's a bust and there's no computer or it's empty, I'll encourage Kev to ransack the place like a Prohibition-era Fed.'

Kev blinked a few times, clearly surprised by her nomination of him as a novice gray hat. 'Walk me through it?' He gauged the reactions of Clyde and the others, perhaps hoping for a better alternative. None were forthcoming. He huffed. 'How long will that take?'

'Do this,' Barros said, making a USB-sized pincer with her thumb and index finger. Kev obliged. 'About that long. There's nothing to it. The hackers have done all the hard work already. All you need to do is put the key-logger into the port, let it do its trickery, and away we go.'

Meadows considered Barros as though she had suddenly increased in market value. 'You know, if you ever get tired of fieldwork, I could find you a place on the cyber team.'

Barros lifted her arms, splayed her fingers, and wafted her hand clean through Rose's coffee cup on the desk. 'No touchy-touchy, remember? I have as much use for a keyboard as I do a pair of pants. But it's okay, that's why Kev can be my hands.'

Kev looked at Barros, chock-full of curiosity.

Meadows thought it over for a moment or two, looking a little haggard. 'That's enough for now. You've all had a long night.' He finished his gone-cold green tea and placed the mug neatly back on his desk. 'Go get some rest. Or whatever constitutes rest for you people.' His glare focused on Nat and Ace specifically, then found the others. 'Don't cause any trouble.'

* * * * *

Out in the corridor, Clyde heard Meadows call Nat back for a private word. Nothing serious, it seemed, for they both stood openly in his office doorway. Clyde and the others waited a little way down the corridor for her, seeing some of the agents switch shifts. Ace muttered something to one of the passing guys, and the disgruntled agent handed over a small wad of dollars.

Ace pocketed it with a wily grin, and upon seeing the curious stares he was getting from the team, answered, 'Fantasy hockey.'

Nat caught up to them, giving a somewhat tired smile. 'Uncle M's just checking I'm not going to have some type of breakdown after my first taste of action.'

'And are you?' Rose joked. 'Schulz still has his original office on this floor.'

'Ask me again tomorrow. Right now, I want a lot of beers. We all in, or are you all going to pussy out on me?'

'You got some mouth on you, darlin',' Ace said, patting the winnings stuffed in the pocket of his sleeveless denim jacket. 'How about I buy you a bottle to stick in it?'

Rose scoffed and nudged him, telling Nat, 'If you want to pop his eardrums, I'll square it with Meadows for you later.'

'I'd probably be doing the old dude a favor with the shit he listens to.'

Clyde gave Nat a resounding high-five, always happy to throw a dig at Ace, and everything about it felt good: the physical contact, the joy, but more so, the simple and pure vibe of still being alive.

'I'm lookin' at two assholes who just high-fived their way out of a free beer,' Ace said, looking pleased to be having a few more dollars for himself. 'C'mon, ladies, the night's wastin'.'

Clyde was debating calling it a night, maybe even crashing here in the sleeping quarters to save him the trip back to Brooklyn. But there was an expectant glow in Nat's eyes that told him it would be the wrong decision.

And why would he want to sleep anyway?

The thought of sinking back down into a shining kingdom of soul threads and hidden dream gods still troubled him.

26

Nathan Moore never returned to Elzinga Asylum. That once powerful voice, an unyielding commanding tone, tried to impel him from somewhere deep within his mind, to box him back into that maze of urban blight and confusion, but Nathan couldn't stop hearing a second voice looping through his head. So familiar, it echoed all around him, through the streets and alleys of his mind, pulling the whole manipulative artifice down brick by brick. Saving him. And by focusing on the words spoken by this second voice, he felt the former's imperative begin to fade away, its power waning.

It wasn't until some time had passed—how much Nathan wasn't sure—that he realized there was something physical in his ear. Pulling out the small transmitter, he stared at it like it was some fat bug that had crept inside while sleeping rough; an occurrence that his younger self had experienced from time to time. In the transmitter's absence, he suddenly feared losing himself again, a stomach-clenching dread, and that's when he heard it. The controller's voice. Back. But now…it sounded weak, like an old radio signal sent from some faraway city. Nathan blocked it out easily enough, mentally repeating the words of that second voice.

A friend's voice?

Forgetting the transmitter for a moment, he looked around at his incredible surroundings. It was a dizzying height. Where was he? He had fled Citadel Security's big glass building and scurried across the city like a spider. Bits and pieces started to rise in his memory like bodies bobbing up from a river. Who had he been fighting back there? He thought about the face of the young black kid he was chasing; he couldn't have been any older than his mid-twenties. Tough little bastard, though, and good survival instincts. And that power of his.

What was that?

Wait... *What am I?*

From the ledge of a Manhattan high-rise, Nathan Moore examined the infernal changes that had altered him, feeling the barbed mask writhing around his face and across his eyes like a thousand millipedes.

FUCK! They were coming out of his arms, using his veins and arteries like a fucking subway route. Nathan's chest heaved with frantic breathing; the horror of what he was, and what was living inside him, was too much to handle. He resisted shrieking into the canyons of Manhattan. He was just another lost soul singing its plight. Trembling, he understood that these things, these *wires*—Henry Rooker appeared in his memories, dark skin flushed pale and lips tinted blue from blood loss—were not part of some bad dream, and they were not his undoing. They were power.

A body full of barbed wire and a head full of broken memories. He needed to piece them back together.

That's when the identity of the second speaker revealed itself to him with a jolt: Julius Sharp.

How could he possibly forget? Like a broken fire hydrant, the memories began to gush and spill forth a stream of history. He revisited the last memory he had been pursuing before that strange watchful eye in the psychic alleyway had found him, luring him back into darkness. In the memory, he had been watching a young kid being chased through the park. A gawky teen with big glasses, straggling and gasping as he was pursued by some of the thugs from the Tremont Avenue Thrashers.

Back then, Nathan was a white boy with no gang affiliation. For him, he was surviving the streets alone. But he'd made a reputation for himself. A Bronx urban legend complete with silly rhymes and rules made up by kids swigging 40s and passing joints. The psycho who wore a stupid rubber skull mask and carried a length of barbed wire. Hiding on the fringes, watching, biding his time, and then leaving the shadows to kill members of the Thrashers, robbing their corpses of drug money and jewelry to finance a living. Over the years, Nathan had grown strong. The blood money from his stalked and garroted gangsters provided him with plenty of food and cheap hotel rooms, even a gym membership.

He remembered this scene now with sharp clarity. He'd gotten the drop on the gang as they beat the kid senseless. He mangled the hoodlums, relieving them of their valuables, and in a rare moment of compassion, reached out a large bloody palm to the young kid trying to find his broken glasses.

The kid's name was Julius Sharp. The soft target of a notoriously hard and mean brother.

That was how all this had started for Nathan.

The layers of barbs unveiled Nathan's head with a chitinous rasp, the soothing breeze scraping across the blonde stubble on his scalp. Like a living statue, he stared out at the streets and lights 150 feet below him, perplexed as to how he got up here. Then it became obvious: his new talents.

An image seemed to hit him in the side of the head. The basement of Elzinga. Kneeling on the tiled floor, a big spooky eye staring deep into him from its platform, hypnotic. It felt like fingers running across his brain, squeezing it, testing it. But there was someone else in his periphery. Another kneeling figure. A woman, he thought. He couldn't make out her features, but hadn't he heard her name? One of the things Julius's voice had been whispering to him?

Dolores Ricci.

Who is that? He didn't know yet, but it felt important.

Give it a little time. Not everything was back yet; parts of his history remained obscured in the dark alleys of his mind. But that great, glaring eye in his head was no longer watching him. Next time it did, he felt confident he could tear it open, letting its mess rain down onto the lost and hopeless streets below.

Leonard. I need to see if he's okay. Julius too.

Nice work, Jules.

27

Dolores was finally out of the house. Funny how she had fought so desperately to escape its luxurious confines, only to find herself now standing on the *real* front lawn of her one-time little slice of suburban paradise.

But it was somebody else's home now.

Probably contained a loving family, trying to live the lie that was the American Dream. Dolores had been sold that same dream by her own mom. A big Rockwell-esque advertisement poster full of domestic bliss, but as Dolores had gotten older, wiser, and more bruised, she found the corners of the poster to be torn and yellowed, the colors faded, and the expressions on the wholesome family's faces to be those of tension and wrought nerves.

Her hand reached up to the mask hiding her carved-up face, and she slowly removed it. Taking a few steps onto the neat lawn, she decided to take a few more, down the side of the house, stopping by a window drawn with a curtain. It was the study, she remembered. But that was of little concern to her now. She was more fascinated by the deep scars crisscrossing her face, the tip of her once perfect nose now a rough nub. She used to be such a beauty. Winning pageants and drawing the eye of every man—and even more than a few women—as she walked down the street. She had had her pick of potential husbands.

And she had picked Sonny.

She felt as though she ought to shed a tear, not for Sonny or the ruins of her fake life or her time in prison, but for whatever had been done to her since then. The loss of time and identity. Her eyes remained dry as dust. There was no pity in her this night, certainly not for herself. She had buried that side of herself when Sonny had performed that one final, terrible act upon her.

She wondered if the family in the house now had any idea of the things that had gone on in there. The lingering haunt of terror and pain. She wondered if the real estate agent had managed to get all of Sonny's and his good time boys' blood out from between the floorboards of the game room, or if new clean wood had been laid down. She suddenly remembered the hunting knife in her hand as she slowly finished Sonny off. The bodies of his drunken, coke-nosed and shark-eyed friends bleeding out throughout the house.

Look at me now, Mom. Your little princess is doing man's work. Had she really said that to her mom as she was dragged away in handcuffs, a big triumphant smile stretching across her recently disfigured beauty, flashing her still perfect but bloodstained teeth?

Cheerleader. Arm candy. Trophy wife. Scorned, novice hit-woman.

Not bad for her first job. A houseful of wise guys.

She tried to recall who had taught her such violent methods but came up blank. Curiously, her heart seemed to soar at the missing memory. Did she used to have feelings for her teacher?

For some reason, an image of a skull rose in her mind before diving back into darkness. Whoever it was, she was grateful. They had taught her strength. No, that wasn't right; they had told her that the strength was already in her. Of that she was certain. But they had taught her how to find it and use it. Guns and knives. And of course, herself, a weapon of hate crafted by their secret love.

A cat leapt from the tall tree onto the roof of the house. A fellow hunter driven by instincts it didn't understand.

Dolores thought about how powerless she had felt in that basement. The asylum. What right did they have to take her mind from her? To make her submissive? Sonny had done that and paid the price. What right did they have, whoever they were? They'd done something to her in that place. Made her even worse than she already was. At least they had given her some new friends. That was their mistake. She needed to find out who "they" were, and when she did, she would make them *her* puppets. Her dolls.

But first, she needed to find a quiet place to sit and think and to try and find out more about who she was, and who she now is. It was late, the moon the only bright eye in the sky tonight, shining like a smooth skull. Remembering these streets well, she slinked off into the bushes and trees of the leafy suburb to think, and all the faceless mannequins crouching low on rooftops and hugging the tall oaks quietly slinked after her.

28

Clyde wasn't a big drinker and wasn't even attempting to try and keep up with Ace and Nat, both of whom seemed to be making up for lost time. It was past midnight, and the Bottom of the Barrel only had a few hours of serving time left. Part of him wished he could be the brooding, surly, beer-chugging tough guy like Wolverine but that just wasn't his role. Thankfully, Rose was keeping it moderate right along with him. And Kev, well, he was doing a damn good job of staying positive despite being sober. The Barrel was considerably busier than it had been last night, packed almost wall-to-wall with hard drinkers and punks young and old, with Wasserman and a few other surly and thick-skinned punks slinging beers and shots, much of which was ending up on the bar and the floor.

Ace slammed his empty pint glass on the table, eyeing the jukebox through the sea of bodies—well, maybe sea was too generous, as stagnant pond might have been more apt. 'Is there anything on that juke that isn't poser anarchist noise?'

Nat matched his movements, slamming her shot glass down. She waved a finger about the bar like a helicopter. 'Might want to check the room, snowball. You forget where you are?'

'I'd like to hear something that's more than three chords and a chant.'

Clyde watched Nat compose herself. 'Nobody here wants to hear some gay six-minute ballad about elves, or Foreigner. I'm already losing face being seen in here with a guy wearing that.' She pointed at Ace's chest and his Triumph T-shirt, the *Thunder Seven* album.

He leaned his hairy, muscled arms onto the beer-sticky table, showing his gap-toothed smile in an attempt at charm. 'I'd be more than happy to teach you what you're missing.'

Clyde's beer paused at his lips, wanting to see if Nat was being worn down by the rough braggadocio of Ace. Wasn't too far-fetched of an idea. They were both consenting adults, and just look at some of the people in this place.

Nat leaned towards Ace seductively, her lids half-lowered, dripping sex appeal. 'Unless you got a jerk-off sock with my face on it, you won't be teaching me a thing.'

Clyde was surprised by the twinge of relief he felt and laughed it off.

Rose whooped. 'Put some ice on that, big guy.'

'I'll make a metalhead of you yet, darlin',' Ace said.

Nat derided him with the briefest of expressions. 'Metal sucks!'

'You kill with a bass guitar made of glowing light. That's the most metal thing I've seen.'

Agent Orange's "Bloodstains" brought out the rowdy side of Natalie again, setting her head bobbing to the energetic beat. She referenced the attack of the song with a declarative finger, getting charged up on it. 'Nothing beats this.'

Ace took it on the chin and leaned back to mourn his empty pint glass.

Having come face-to-face with the Hangman only hours earlier, and surviving, Clyde was feeling a little better about his self-worth on this team, perhaps even a little carefree. Still, the last thing he wanted was to be dealing with a pounding headache and nausea in the morning. At least that was the lie he kept telling himself. But the *real* reason he was carefully checking the time on his phone was because he could practically feel Nat's intent whenever she looked at him. His groin was telling him to shut the fuck up and enjoy himself, but the consequences of such attraction could only mean a whole heap of complications to both him and the job when they sobered up.

Clyde patted the road-sign tabletop and sat up, keen to get away from this raucous environment and the gorgeous pile of trouble sitting near him. 'Well, it's a school night, and some of us have to infiltrate the corporate head office of a possible mob kingpin tomorrow.'

Kev turned to Clyde, his face a concealed enigma—it was surprising Wasserman continued to allow him into the bar with his blatantly suspicious style of dress. 'You can relax,' he said, subtly tipping his head to indicate the rising flirtatiousness between Clyde and Nat. 'It's not until late in the pm, and you're only the lookout. The ones doing all the actual work will be sober and rested.'

'Yeah, stop being a pussy, kid,' was Ace's sage advice. He gestured to everybody's mostly empty drinks. 'Everyone still looks thirsty.' He climbed out of the booth and made his way towards the bar. Because of the late hour, some of the meaner, unhappier drunks were spoiling for a fight, one of whom found himself between Ace and the bar. The steaming young man was a tall guy with red liberty spikes and an outfit patched together with safety pins and chains, who was beginning to thrust his head aggressively towards a would-be peacemaker, goading him into taking a swing. Ace moved with surprising agility and grace for such a large drunk, and without breaking his stride, slapped a wrist lock on Liberty Spikes with just the right amount of *don't-fuck-with-me* pressure to make him compliant. The rest of the drinkers, even the toughest-looking customers, stepped aside, forming a quick channel for Ace to walk the instigator through before tossing him out on his ass with a minimum of violence. Ace even got a bonus shot of whiskey and a nod of approval from Wasserman on the way back in. Ace knocked it back, ordered another round, and was expediently back at the table holding a tray with four more pints of Riot and four shots of whiskey.

Nat accepted the drinks from Ace with a big carefree smile, practically hoisting them onto Clyde before grabbing her own.

Looking burdened, Clyde raised his shot glass. 'I'm going to regret this. To surviving another day,' he toasted.

They all downed their shots, and Nat grabbed Clyde's hand, pulling him out of the booth, dragging him towards the rowdy dance floor of slamming and pogoing bodies. He tried to protest, he even playfully begged a little, but it all felt so useless.

Clyde wasn't much of a drinker, but, small mercies, this wasn't music that required him to be much of a dancer either. The warm, sweaty bodies hurled into each other, they shoved and pulled, but it was all in a tribal sense of savage good-natured catharsis. But best of all, it meant Nat's body was repeatedly thrown up against him, her body heat and scent and rebellious smile all-dominating Clyde's awareness, drowning out everything else, all his anxieties and the meaningless noise in his head.

This wasn't his scene, but he was happy to brave it all for her tonight.

* * * * *

Last orders came and went, and as Clyde and the team tried to flag a few taxis on the street corner, Nat shared a cheery goodbye with Wasserman while his other barkeeps pushed, dragged, or yelled the last of the paralytics out the door. While Clyde watched the drunks shamble off, laughing and singing in every direction, he was finally able to flag down a Yellow cab.

Clyde felt a hand on his arm and turned to see Nat. She had an expectant look on her face, like she was about to drop some big news. 'Afterparty at my place?'

'Your place?' Rose overheard, arching an eyebrow. 'Didn't you say your dad is some mover and shaker in the consulate? I'm sure he'd love a bunch of drunken dickheads piling into his place.'

'They're out for the night,' Nat said. 'It's cool.'

'Nah, you guys go ahead.' Rose was shuffling her feet and ready to go. 'I'm calling it a night while I still got no regrets.'

'Shit, Rosie, and just when I was beginning to think you were cool.' Nat winked at her.

A tipsy smile formed on Clyde's mouth, and he gave Ace a meaningful stare. 'What about you, handlebar? Another safehouse rager?'

Ace smoothed down his mustache proudly, pulling his phone out. 'I'm booked up. Promised a nice lady a mustache ride.'

Rose tried to sneak a glance at Ace's phone. 'How much are you paying for this broad?'

Ace looked pleased with himself but didn't divulge, dialing up his booty call and breaking away from the team with barely a farewell wave.

The waiting cab driver was becoming impatient, leaning out the window to beckon them. Clyde gave him a "one-minute" gesture. He wasn't sure if he was prepared to go back to Nat's yet, but he didn't want to just stand here all night—or all morning, rather—either.

Rose started off in the opposite direction, then stopped, seemingly remembering something she had forgotten to say earlier. 'Kev, I love you, man, but you need to stop trying to shake Meadows out of his tree.'

Clyde closed his eyes slowly. Knowing there was no way the cab driver was going to wait around much longer, and this wouldn't be a brief topic of conversation.

Kev, stone-cold sober, tensed up a little. 'Meadows can stay in his tree, I don't care.' He sounded defensive, and Clyde could tell he'd gone along with this beer session for the sake of group morale, but really he'd spent most of the night in his own world. He shrugged and appeared to remember something of his own that he'd been wanting to say. 'I remember a little conversation we once had in the library at Indigo. I was searching for anything I could find on the Null, and you were giving me all this talk about knowing the enemy, the *big* guys, the ones behind it all, and how one day it'd be time to lead a resistance against them; all or nothing.'

'And I meant every word,' Rose said. 'But I also told you that that day would be when I've got a one-way ticket to the Null. And I'm not dead yet.'

'We already have one-way tickets to the Null,' Kev said. 'Why wait until we're dead before doing something about it?'

Rose rolled her eyes, the conversation evidently more complicated than she was prepared for right now. 'That's why you've been a hemorrhoid on Meadows's ass, because he hasn't called up Director Trujillo to assign us to some half-cocked suicide mission?'

'You make it sound so stupid,' Kev said, his sarcasm bordering on the wrong side of friendly. 'Look, I'm not big on suicide missions either, it's just...' His arms went limp. 'Don't you feel like this whole arrangement between Hourglass and the Order is weird?'

Rose looked at him like he was the dumbest asshole in the whole tri-state area. 'Weird? It's fucking nuts. Is this your first day on the job or something?' She took a breath. 'It's weird, and it's also a predictably boring aspect of warfare. Two opposing forces with a healthy dose of respect for each other's power. It's called a stalemate.'

'I'm referring more to the—'

'The Firmament Needle, yeah, I know! You and that Needle. You're convinced it's a real thing and that you're being lied to. But why *would* the brass lie about something like that?'

Clyde stayed quiet, almost grateful that somebody else was having this discussion with Kev for once.

'I don't know...' Even Kev sounded doubtful now. 'But Trujillo has been cagey since the moment we saved Kozlov from Talbot's big energy deal. I know you noticed this. And Meadows is just as quick to shut down any talk of it too. Look,' Kev glanced around, not wanting to get any further into this in the middle of the street, 'I've been thinking: what if the hoodoo belong to one of the houses of the Order? The House of Wise Stones.'

Rose looked exasperated. 'Just because they're made of stone, you're accusing them of being part of the Order.' She flashed Clyde a solicitous look, needing support in talking sense to his friend. 'So this is all some big conspiracy. Are the lizard people and the Illuminati also involved?'

Kev stayed quiet, his posture sagging, losing the energy for this fight. 'I never said the hoodoo or Trujillo are working with the Order, just that maybe there is some sort of connection. Maybe that's why they don't want anybody going into the Null after Kozlov. They might be hoping the monk gets himself killed over there, body and soul, in his search for the Needle. Hush him up.'

'Or maybe they don't want to throw valuable assets into hell to help some crackpot Russian necromancer search for something that doesn't exist.' Rose folded her arms, the bulging muscles almost tearing her tight T-shirt. 'And tell me this: If the Needle did exist, and Hourglass wanted to keep it quiet for some reason, why wouldn't Trujillo have the hoodoo send in a covert retrieval team to track down and capture or kill Kozlov?'

Clyde shared an awkward glance with Nat and listened to the strained silence between Kev and Rose, the distant ocean sounds of Manhattan traffic washing over them.

'Maybe they have,' Kev finally answered.

Rose massaged her tired eyes. 'Kev, you were a civilian not long ago, so I understand why you're seeing need-to-know information as this big sinister secret. But we're here to follow orders, remember? You joined up wanting this. A purpose. I remember the excitement on your face when I was training you. You fucking loved this shit, this life. I don't understand why you're turning on it now, all because Meadows isn't spilling his guts to you about every company secret. That's not how this works, because that *can't* work. We're the hitters, the problem-solvers. We can't go into dangerous situations with heads full of official secrets because what if an enemy got a hold of us: Talbot and Cairnwood, or some other group, or some lone madman with enough power to be trouble?' Kev had no answer, or at least he wasn't sharing one. 'Please, don't we have enough to be dealing with right now? Can you not go searching for enemies in our own camp?'

Clyde was certain he had regained his sobriety by now, mortified that Kev's suspicions and restless behavior might now finally erupt into a brusque, cold resignation.

'I'm sorry, Rose,' Kev said.

Rose's sigh of relief matched Clyde's, and she walked over to Kev, a lopsided smirk on her face. 'You were making me worried there.' She slapped him on the shoulder, light enough to keep her hand from swatting his coat deep into his ethereal arm. 'Asshole. So are we good?'

Kev, hunched over a little, aloof and embarrassed for their bickering, said, 'We're good.'

Clyde gave Kev a concerned look but was happy that the air had been cleared a little.

But he had been so wrapped up in the slowly-heating discussion that he hadn't noticed the cabbie had taken off with another bunch of leftovers from the Barrel.

Nat was a little slow on the uptake too. 'Awesome, now we need another two cabs.'

'Forget it, McKay owes me a favor.' Rose got her phone out. 'Agent McKay runs a safehouse not too far from here. I'll call in a lift. We can get him to drop you guys off in the Village.'

* * * * *

Ten minutes later, Agent McKay dropped them off outside a brownstone in Greenwich Village. He gave Rose a put-upon look, a weary dog disturbed from its sleeping basket, and waited for Clyde, Kev, and Nat to bail out of the back.

'Good time tonight, boys and girls,' Rose said, having regained full control of her tipsiness. 'Enjoy the walk of shame.'

The car drifted off down the street, quiet as a whisper.

Nat took the steps up to her front door, unlocked it, and deactivated the alarm. Clyde was about to follow her up when he noticed Kev still rooted to the spot, raising his arm for a farewell fist bump.

'I see where this is going. I don't know how kinky she is, but I don't think she wants a piece of dead bread in her sandwich.' Kev pulled his scarf down to give Clyde a quick peek at a spectral blue smile. 'Besides, I need to clear my head.' He glanced about the quiet street, almost wistfully. 'And it seems like a nice night for a rooftop hop.'

Clyde tried to say something, anything to encourage him to stay for a while, but realized that even a blind person could see where this was going. Nat had been all over him all night, and there were limits to friendly playfulness. The "after-party" was just to get him here; anybody else could entertain themselves.

'See you back at the apartment.' Kev took his time in walking past the pleasant row houses, drinking in the lonely, peaceful night.

Clyde called after him, 'Be careful.' If Kev had heard him, he didn't respond, already deaf to the world.

'Is he okay?' Nat had reappeared at the top of the steps, the hallway lit warmly behind her.

'He gets restless, can't switch off. Drives himself a little crazy now and then.'

She leaned against the doorway, a small sympathetic smile dimpling her mouth as she copied Clyde in watching Kev walk out of sight. 'He'll be okay?'

Kev had rounded a corner, probably already up on the flat rooftops by now.

Clyde nodded, unsure whether he was trying to convince himself or Nat. He had hoped, deeply and sincerely, that Kev might have found some solace when he agreed to join Hourglass, but such solace was evidently short-lived. Kev wanted answers, and Clyde did too, but for a personality like Kev, knowledge was ravenous.

'I'll know if he gets into any trouble,' Clyde said. He forced his legs to move and slowly went up the stairs, following Nat inside.

It was a very neat home, expensive but understated, and not without warmth. If Clyde had expected some beige and restrictive world to be the culprit for Natalie's untamed and rebellious manner, then he was pleasantly surprised. He noticed some intriguing cultural items posed about the living room: ancient weaponry and art, possibly expensive. He curiously roamed about the room while Nat lit a bunch of candles on the coffee table and windowsill. His eyes found some framed photographs of Mr. Mondragon posing and shaking hands with various official-looking types. He leaned in for a closer look.

'Looks like important work.'

'He enjoys it.' Nat backed up into the hall, asking, 'Beer?'

Clyde didn't have another one in him right now. 'You got any coffee?'

Nat gave him a friendly scowl. 'Damn, dude. I don't want to drink alone.' She sighed deeply, wounded. 'Coffee it is.'

The sound of a coffee percolator could be heard coming from the kitchen and the clink of cups.

Clyde spied another photo, this one of Nat, her dad, and, presumably, her mom, smiling and carefree on some exotic beach. The Philippines, he presumed. 'Nice-looking beach,' Clyde offered. 'That the island where you go surfing?'

Nat appeared in the doorway again and walked up beside him, glancing at it fondly and nodding. 'You traveled much?'

Clyde returned a cynical smirk. 'Nothing quite like that,' he answered. 'Been to the Null for a spell, though. That was nice.'

Nat gave a throaty chuckle, unbidden and completely alluring to Clyde.

'Does your mom work in government too?'

'Nope, she teaches high school math.'

Clyde winced. 'Shit, I hate math. I'd rather go back to the Null.'

Nat's eyes widened in jest, playing along. 'What if there's a place in the Null that's a 24/7 math lesson?'

Clyde shivered. She brushed his arm, asking, 'Milk and sugar?'

'Just milk, thanks.'

Nat returned to the candlelit living room a minute later with two cups of coffee. She passed one to Clyde and, to his surprise and perhaps a little disappointment, sat cross-legged on the window box instead of next to him on the couch.

Had he somehow read this situation all wrong?

'So...how did your dad get involved in the consulate?' he asked.

She tipped her head back and smiled as if suddenly wise to a trick. 'You heard how Meadows and my dad have history, and now you want to know if there's some sexy origin story, huh? Some sixties occult spy-craft and that kind of stuff?'

Clyde laughed a little self-consciously. 'I'm all about those jazzed-up serials. But sure, I suppose I'd like to know if there was ever a normal laidback kind of guy buried somewhere deep in Meadows.'

'I'll give you the radio-edited version. A long time ago, back in the Philippines—I'm talking, like, way back when the Spanish had just finished colonizing it—my family made some powerful enemies. One of my ancestors, he developed his Spark. It got him some attention from the other clans in the village, becoming a local celebrity, and a pariah. Word got around, as it tends to do, all the way to the wrong people in China and Japan.' She slowly rotated her back towards Clyde and pulled up her baggy, torn-up T-shirt, revealing a full-back tattoo shining in candlelight, of a scene too detailed and complex for Clyde to process all at once: Komodo dragons with fearsome riders, some ghastly figure that looked like a mushroom had grown up into a samurai, tentacles and sharks and other stuff. He had no clue what any of it meant, but if nothing else, it was great work.

'The Komodo Clan.' Nat dropped her shirt and rested her elbows on her knees to face him. 'A very old sect of Pan-Asian necromantic warlords. Total dick-bags. Ever since they learned that the Mondragon family had a little extra spice in their blood, they wouldn't leave us the fuck alone. Every generation has had to put up with their bullshit at some point. Before my dad had the good sense to move here and raise a family, he had his trouble with them. Luckily for him, a young Hourglass field agent called Frank Meadows, fresh from the army, was stationed in China at the time, digging into this same group of dick-bags. One thing led to another, and he became acquainted with my dad, filed some paperwork, made a few phone calls, and Hourglass shipped him over here to start a life free from all that bad mystical kung-fu-movie wire-fighting shit.'

She tried her coffee, and Clyde found it impossible to ignore how the candlelight worked to enhance her beauty further. 'But my dad's no fool.

I am, but he isn't. He persuaded and bribed and threatened me to train my abilities, just in case one day those people find out about me. Those old-timey vendettas can be petty.' She smiled, but her eyes were diamond hard. 'Some people just can't let shit go.'

'So he finally wore you down.' Clyde sipped his coffee. 'Probably for the best.'

She paused before answering, reflecting, and Clyde felt the atmosphere dip ever so slightly in the way it tends to when preceding a harsh truth.

'He didn't wear me down.' A pause. 'I accidentally killed my band and a bunch of my friends.' Nat's matter-of-fact tone left Clyde speechless. 'We were partying in this old warehouse, having a fucking good time too. And then I felt it. The music...it felt as though it was actually passing into me, through me, like under my skin. Racing through my veins. I thought I had been drugged or was dying or something. Then...' her hand opened like a flower, 'boom. I was drenched in their blood and the roof was caving in.'

'Shit,' was all Clyde could think to say. Dumb but profound at the same time. 'What happened?'

'My dad made that call to Meadows.' She looked ashamed. 'I wasn't proud of it—and my dad, he didn't do it because he worked in the government and thought he could get away with it. He had to do it for confidentiality. It's not like I can just make an official statement about my private life as some walking sonic bomb. So he made the call instead, and some people picked me up from the warehouse, cleaned me up. And just like that, I was never there. And the last I heard the local cops who were looking into the mess had no idea what happened. I don't think I'll ever not feel shitty about it. Having to have my friends hosed off of me, bits of them in my hair. You know what it's like to be responsible for the death of all your friends? Just because you were born with some stupid power you didn't want.' A look of guilt fell across her face. 'Sorry, I didn't think.'

'It's cool. I'm not responsible for Kev's death, but it is my fault I dragged him back here. Even knowing that the Null is there, I still wonder sometimes if he might have preferred to stay over there and face it. Whatever happens,

happens. I don't think it's much of a life for him here.' A wry smile twisted his mouth. 'Our problems aren't like a lot of other people's, are they?'

'You got that right. Not all bad, I guess. At least I can do this,' she said with a hint of bitterness, resting her cup beside her as the shimmering bass guitar appeared across her lap, her fingers plucking out some flashy and high-energy run up and down the neck.

Clyde found it fascinating that each note she plucked was tonally accurate—as far as he knew, anyway—with her manipulating and forging each soundwave into the correct pitch and frequency.

'Real talk. How much did it fuck you up when you first learned that all the dead get dropped off in the Null?' Nat clutched onto the bass like a piece of ethereal driftwood, her usually tough and deflective eyes now wide open and searching for something, a trust maybe, in his. 'Especially since you've been there in person.' Clyde's solemn expression did the talking, and Nat moved on with what might have been a fatalist's sense of satisfaction. 'Every day I wonder if my buds are still okay over there, or if their souls are dead now too. It's another reason why I put money into Wasserman's bar. To keep my memories of them alive.'

Clyde leaned forward and put his empty cup on the coffee table, making sure to use a coaster, something that Nat hadn't bothered doing. He thought about how often he had tortured himself with thoughts of his brother and dad stuck over there. Perhaps fighting to survive, perhaps running, or perhaps destroyed absolutely.

'I think it's best not to dwell on it,' he said.

In the ensuing silence, Clyde stared through the window netting behind her, seeing the peaceful tree-lined street.

He felt something between him and Nat. He had only known her a couple of days, and while he was certainly interested in her despite his best intentions, he wasn't sure if the feeling was mutual. But right now, it felt inarguable; there was a hum of excitement, of potential, charging the air between them. They were both a little drunk, and despite the growing urges of his body, he was worried about what came next. Would it be a mistake? What was the expression? Don't shit where you eat.

'It was late an hour ago. I'll call an Uber, or maybe McKay.'

'You not staying?' Her dark eyes bored into him. It was a beckoning and a challenge.

A test.

He felt his heart kick up its pace. 'You talking about—'

'Fucking.' She uncrossed her legs. 'We nearly died tonight. We'll almost die every night...until the night we finally do. Shouldn't we have some fun while we can?' She seemed to know that she had him. Removing her T-shirt, she moved over to an iPod dock in her bra and jeans, the candlelight illuminating her athletic curves and ink in golden light and shadow. Something mellow and pretty started up, not what Clyde was expecting from her: Peter Murphy's "I'll Fall With Your Knife."

Clyde felt his body responding, and unsurprisingly, his mind was quick to follow.

29

Clyde woke up to sunshine, in a bed he didn't immediately recognize. Then two things occurred to him: it was Nat's bed, and he was alone in it. Naked under the sheets, he fumbled around for his jeans and phone. The display said it was 6 am.

After very little sleep, and a bloodstream still struggling to resist the effects of alcohol, he still felt remarkably good. He laid his head back on the pillow and could still smell her on him: a dizzying scent of citrus body wash, perspiration, and sex. After having spent so much of his recent life battling evil and fixating on death, it felt incredible to be reminded of life's simple pleasures.

It was only as he lay there listening to the pigeons cooing outside that a third, and most startling, thing occurred to him: he hadn't visited the Median last night.

And it was such a relief. His life had altered drastically enough already, he didn't need to become some anomaly for Spector to puzzle over. He was just fine being a lowly Level I necromancer with access to guns.

Satisfied, he rolled out of bed and got dressed. He was about to call for Nat but remembered whose house he was in.

Shit.

Would her parents take kindly to her bringing a stranger to their home?

Double shit.

Would her dad, a friend of Meadows, appreciate a team member of his daughter's doing some filthy but amazing things with her last night?

He padded gently through the hall, guided by tranquil, meditative music. Surely not Nat. Even last night, after she played that gentler, downright romantic song as they started off on the couch, she changed it up again so that they were fucking like animals to some loud and rowdy punk.

But he heard no voices, no TV, just the soft music. He followed it to a room before the stairs and was shocked to find Nat, wide awake and well into a yoga routine.

He sniggered in surprise, catching her in some pose that looked borderline masochistic. She looked untroubled by the flexibility. It certainly explained some of last night.

'Yoga...? You're just full of surprises. I'm beginning to think this whole reckless punk thing you got goin' is really just you frontin'.'

With her long hair tied back, she wore short-shorts and an old baggy halter top. A light sheen of perspiration gleamed on her face and made her tattoos glisten.

'All about balance, dude.' She shifted to something called Warrior One pose, but it made Clyde think more of a surfer than any form of combat. 'My body is a temple, but the monks like to drink. Thought I'd sneak this in while you were snoring.'

'Shit, I snored?'

She laughed softly at his naïveté. 'Little bit.'

'Sorry.'

'It's cool. I don't regret our unbridled animal fuckery because of it. It was your farting that was the problem.'

Clyde was astonished, humility burning his cheeks. 'You're fucking with me?'

'Am I?'

'I hope so.'

Her teasing smile lit the already sun-drenched room up. 'Err, I'm not one for making breakfast, but I do a mean bowl of cereal if you're sticking around a little longer?'

Call it the sobriety, but Clyde thought she seemed a little more aloof, considering the things they did last night, and had to accept it for what it was. Fun. And nothing more. There was nothing wrong with that, but he couldn't help but wonder if there would be any more fun at some point. He certainly hoped so but had to remind himself of why he had been so reluctant to indulge in the first go-around: it complicated things. He got out of his own head, enjoying the fact that they were easy around each other. It felt nice.

Clyde thought about a bowl of cereal with her and grinned. 'I'm down for that. Your mom and dad still out?'

'They both have busy schedules.' She finished her pose and gave him her full attention. She was radiant. 'We're alone for a while longer. Shower?'

30

Clyde got back to his apartment around 7:30 am with a spring in his step and was sliding the key into his lock when he glanced over his shoulder at Kev's apartment.

Knocking on the door, he called, 'Kev?'

'Come on in.'

Clyde used his copy of Kev's key and entered to find a surprising scene: Kev sat before a laptop with Private Barros already schooling him on the dummy basics of computer coding and hacking. Something Clyde would have been in no mood for even if he'd had a solid eight hours sleep and a strong cup of coffee. It made him feel a bit guilty for enjoying himself last night—and this morning—while Kev had started doing this at...what ungodly time?

'Early start, guys?'

Barros hovered over Kev's shoulder, not taking her eyes from the screen, too focused on guiding Kev like the apt pupil he tended to be when motivated. 'He needs practice. I don't think I've ever met someone of our generation so computer illiterate. He doesn't need to be capable of bringing down governments or financial institutions, but this can only go a little smoother if he isn't a total noob when we enter Sharp's office.'

Clyde joined them around the table, his attention momentarily drift-ing to a book: *Pragmatism as Anti-Authoritarianism* by Richard Rorty. Clyde didn't comment on it but pondered how much anti-authoritarianism material his friend had been reading in the late hours.

He pushed past it. 'I thought the Moloids in the cyber team had some gizmo for you? This looks pretty intense.'

'Sure, their little toy will do all the heavy lifting for his laptop, but just in case that's a bust, we should skim through the building's computer servers too,' Barros explained. 'So a little experience can only help his computer-illiterate ass.'

'Illiterate is a bit much,' Kev said defensively.

'I was being generous. Luckily for all of us, I'll be there to coach you through this.'

Clyde would only be providing a lookout during the operation, but he felt it was only right that he should express at least a passing interest in their roles too. Teamwork. But it became quickly apparent that hacking was a skill he neither possessed nor cared to. He couldn't tell what the hell was happening on that computer screen. And then he found himself wondering, 'Where did you get this laptop?'

'I took it from the Madhouse last night,' Kev replied.

'Took it?' Clyde asked wearily, thinking about Kev walking, floating, or hitching a ride out to HQ in the dark hours. Swiping himself in, and then loitering about the complex. 'As in signed it out?'

'No. It was collecting dust in lock-up. Confiscated from some extrem-ist cell of Clark's jarillians who were planning on making waves on the black-market magic amulet scene.' The Clark's jarillians were a sub-species of alloyus jarillians, a species of innate mages with a fondness for metallurgy. And D.T. Clark had the honor of being the first human explorer and crypto-taxonomist to discover the beings.

Barros gave Clyde a look that told him to leave it alone. Already well-trodden ground. 'Rose was going to drop one off on the way to training this morning,' she answered. 'Kev saved her the effort.' Clyde glanced for some type of reaction from Kev. Had he and Rose been cool this morning after their talk last night? 'And it's clean, the tech guys wiped it like a baby's ass when they took it.'

Kev leaned back from the computer and took a needless breath. 'Shit, wouldn't it be swell if Leonard has just left a little black address book with a pentagram on it sitting in his desk?'

Barros made a low throat-clearing sound. 'We should be so lucky.'

Kev was squinting at his work, keeping up with what Barros was explaining. Though he managed to find a quick opening to ask Clyde, 'You and Nat, huh?'

Clyde tried not to let his face split into a very satisfied grin. It was difficult, but he managed. 'I don't know. Maybe.'

'Maybe? What, did you just sleep on the couch?'

'No...but—'

Barros wasn't buying it either. 'I'm betting if I still had a sense of smell, I'd be smelling a whole lot of pussy on you right now.'

Clyde thought about it for a minute. 'I think it might have just been a bit of fun.'

'Probably not for her,' Kev said.

Barros cuffed Kev over the back of the head, knocking a laugh from him, and continued pointing to the keys she wanted him to hit. 'Pay attention, shit bird.' She side-eyed Clyde. 'If you're tapping our team's new big hitter, you better not compromise her—or *your*—focus. Don't need no bullshit sit-com romance getting us fucked when we're in the thick of it.'

'We're all adults.' Clyde held his hands up with an easy-breezy manner. 'And I don't think she's the soft-hearted, giddy schoolgirl type.'

'No, but you are.' Kev was getting a bit better, managing to burn Clyde while keeping up with Barros's instructions.

Clyde smiled, feeling exhausted. He needed to get a little more shut-eye before the evening's mission. He tapped the table in farewell. 'I'll leave you to it. I'm going to get some rack time.'

Back in his apartment, he found his eye drawn helplessly towards the drawing board positioned by the large window, soaking up the morning light. No matter how much he had been through these past months, staring at the drawing board was like staring at another ghost. His old life. His old ambitions. His old dreams.

He walked over to the pages of sketches. The topmost one was his comic-paneled recreation of the *Dread Paradigm* pictograms; still a work in progress, and taking some artistic license, it was shaping up to be a far more cinematic and dramatic retelling of the end of heaven, and hell's ultimate victory.

And the subsequent creation of Sparks, those mysteriously powered people wandering the earth.

Ace.

Nat...

He pictured her, her lustful smile, the heat and touch of her body. And her calm, at-peace smile.

He flipped past the page to his creator-owned characters, a few warm-up doodles of poses, renditions of classic superheroes, and a sketched view of the city from this very window. Would there ever be a day in his mortal span where he could add a little something of himself to the comic-book world? He could end his service to the agency at any time; that had always been the case since day one, but it seemed like such an unimaginable option right now. Say they managed to put an end to this trouble with Talbot and the power behind the Hangman and the others. What then? No matter how many big, scary threats they stop, he was still going to end up in the Null along with every other dead thing. Talk about pissing into the wind.

He put the artwork back in a neat pile on the table beside the drawing board. Kev was right. The only logical endpoint for all of them, the agency, every damned living thing, was if they somehow confirmed the existence of—and then found—the Firmament Needle. Maybe the Russian monk Kozlov would beat them to it. More power to him, Clyde thought with sincere admiration. It would certainly save him and the team having to circumvent the tight lips and red tape of the agency.

Giving the drawing board a parting tap, he headed off for his bedroom. Collapsing on his bed, he tried not to think about an unstoppable psychopath wrapped in barbed wire, or if sleeping next to Nat had been the only thing keeping him from falling into the Median for a third night in a row.

He concentrated his mind, thought about Nat, and was out cold in minutes.

* * * * *

Kev and Barros sat quietly around the laptop, taking a short break. The silence was pensive, his eyes on her, hers fixed at some point in Kev's mostly bare apartment.

'So...? Are you in?' He broke the silence.

Barros continued to stare off into space for at least ten more seconds. 'What can I say...I'm not surprised you want to do this?'

'So is that a yes?'

Barros looked trapped in a box, uncomfortable at what Kev was suggesting.

'The others don't need to know. And if we strike oil, I think they'll be okay with getting off of our backs,' he encouraged.

Her eyes met his. Cool, calculating.

'We both know I can't do this without you. At least not this way.' The long, quiet stretches were now getting to him.

Finally. 'We get this thing with Sharp out of the way, and if we have a breather...' she jammed her eyes shut and sighed, 'then yeah, okay. I'm in.'

Kev excitedly slapped a hand down on the table, flashing his teeth in an almost feral look of success.

'But what happens if you're right?'

Kev's eyes had attained a level of seldom-found peace. 'Find out when it happens, I guess.'

31

There were a few minutes where Leonard was beginning to think Julius wasn't going to show up, standing him up again, and probably in the middle of texting him some succinct and vague excuse. Leonard had already rescheduled his day's meetings with shareholders and investors for this meal, and after Brink's wholly unwelcome news that the CSS head office had been reduced to a scorch mark and some unwanted publicity, he didn't particularly feel like having his time wasted. Taking a liberal slug of his martini, he considered the fact that, if nothing else, he wouldn't mind this brief reprieve from another day of board meetings, quarterly projections, and charts and figures.

Right now he couldn't give a damn if his whole professional life fell apart. He'd roll with it and rebuild. But his personal life, his *family*, that was a worry that enervated even the most driven of individuals. All he wanted was to see his brother, but why should something as easy as that be allowed to happen? So imagine Leonard's surprise—his relief!—when he glanced impatiently across the sea of occupied tables to find Julius arriving at the maître d's station. And for once, he didn't look preoccupied or harassed by Talbot's meddling.

Even this early in the afternoon, High Steaks was busy. It was seldom quiet, being one of the busiest and most sought-after restaurants in all of Manhattan, but getting a reservation was never an issue for Leonard. He owned it. It was a revolving restaurant named for a bad pun, but that delivered views as stunning as the food.

Julius gave him a small nod as he approached the table, and again Leonard noticed how at ease his brother looked today. He hadn't seen him look this relaxed in weeks, and found himself smiling at the sight of him. Even after last night's bullshit, simply knowing Julius was okay made everything seem alright.

'I was thinking about ordering without you,' Leonard said, watching Julius acknowledge Zeb, seated at the table across from them, before settling into his chair.

Julius kept it simple, ordering the house red from the waiter while he picked up the menu for perusal. On closer inspection Leonard reevaluated Julius: he did seem a little preoccupied, but not agitated.

'I got held up,' Julius apologized, his tone light. 'Actual, legitimate work, if you can believe it.'

Leonard sipped his martini. 'After last night's fracas, I'm sure Talbot is busy having a lot of explaining to do to his people. With a little luck maybe they'll kill the prick and we can go back to normal.'

'It worked,' Julius said cryptically, a hint of pride on his face.

Leonard was confused. 'What worked?'

'The last thing Talbot said to me was that something went wrong with Nathan and Dolores again. He thinks Charon is damaged goods.'

Leonard felt a peculiar bout of excitement and dread deep down in the pit of his stomach. With a subtle crack of his neck, he leaned in a little closer, hands folded on the white tablecloth. He mumbled an affirmation. 'Brink said Nathan had some type of freak-out and left right in the middle of fighting those spooky Feds. So would you care to enlighten me on what exactly worked?'

The waiter returned with Julius's wine, but Julius politely told him he needed more time to consider his meal. 'Trigger words. Unique trigger words. I've been researching some classified military files on subliminal programming; quite hard to get a hold of, but persistence can be rewarding. And so I've been working on finding a specific sequence of emotional triggers for Nathan and Dolores's personal histories. It was a crapshoot for the most part. I had no idea if the tailored sequences could actually interfere with Charon's programming to any significant degree.' He gave an excited grin. 'But they do.'

'All this time, these episodes of Nathan's, that's been you?' Leonard's voice took on a tone of disapproval.

'Isn't it great?' Julius was now positively merry, and Leonard didn't think he'd seen him look this happy since he earned his doctorate. 'When Talbot first took Nathan and made him his great white hope against Hourglass, he seemed unstoppable. But I'd been busy too, and now I've removed Charon's leash. Like you, I know the man behind the mask. I knew which threads to pull to make him remember who he was, to varying extents of course, but it was enough to keep him sidelined for weeks. Oh, he's performed the odd task here and there when I chose not to interfere with Charon's influence, cautious of Talbot's reaction to repetitive failures. But at most they were tasks that were only auxiliary to Talbot's plans: like sorting out your recent Triad trouble, for example.'

'No. It's not great, Jules.' Leonard sat back into his seat and immediately rebounded forward as though the seat back was rubber. 'What if Talbot finds out you've been fucking with them? What about that...*thing?* The Eye, Charon. Could that know what you've been doing? Can it *think?*'

Julius seemed saddened at his big brother's reaction, surprised almost. 'Charon. It exists in a weakened state. I believe that's the only reason the trigger words are helping Nathan and Dolores in overriding some of its control. Their memories are helping them find themselves again, like breadcrumbs.'

Leonard dropped his voice even more. 'Jules, you're going to get yourself killed. Probably all of us. You—' His frightened eyes cut to Zeb taking his time with a club soda, then back to Julius. 'You need to get out of town.

Now, while Talbot's busy with his people.' Julius was already shaking his head firmly. 'Miami, Chicago, shit, go to Switzerland, but you need to go, right now.'

Julius took a hearty taste of his wine and set the glass back down. 'I'm not going anywhere without you.'

Leonard was fit to burst but kept his composure, his huge fists balled up on the table. 'I can't believe you'd do something so reckless. Damn it, Jules!'

'I did this for us.' Leonard tried to interrupt but Julius cut him off. 'All our lives I've been the weak one. Always needing you to watch over me. I did this to help us. By undermining Talbot and his grand plans, we can make a fool of him. He's tried to hide it behind all his swagger, but I know he has a lot riding on this project of his. He's scared. This might make his bosses lose faith in him. Give him a little demotion even. Maybe a transfer six feet under.'

Leonard watched the Midtown skyline slowly rotate by and gave Julius a remorseful glance. 'The only reason I ever had to look out for you was because of the choices I made. The *mistakes* I made. You don't owe me a damn thing. Shit, even now you've got assholes like Talbot hanging on your shoulder, and it's all because you're related to me.'

'Lose the self-pity. It wasn't as though our young lives were rife with opportunities, now was it. With Dad and his cancer, and Mom doing everything she could to scrape five dollars together, what else could any of us do? No jobs, no prospects. You, Leonard, you stepped up and made the ugly choices. Now look at us.' Julius cast his hands and eyes about the high-class restaurant.

Leonard didn't need to see such fruits of his labor, for even this particular establishment was plucked from a diseased tree with bloody roots.

'You got us out of that place. All of us, even now, even the younger guys.' Julius discreetly gestured towards Zeb. 'Now look at you, you got our family name on the side of your own tower overlooking Wall Street.' He picked up his glass of red, staring at it thoughtfully. 'I'd say you made the right choices.'

Leonard quietly pondered the path that had led him here, led *them* here. It was a path littered with dead bodies and all manner of unpleasant acts and situations. It was this very restaurant in which he, Nathan, and Zeb had been sitting with the late heads of the mafia when the bullets started flying. In fact, it was this very table where Frank Ricci, father of Sonny, had been sitting before Leonard tossed him through a glass pane of this giant revolving discus.

'Is that why you picked Dolores Ricci? I mean, I never would have picked her as being capable of doing what she did to Sonny and his guys, but...still an odd choice for Talbot.'

'I thought her presence would dovetail in corrupting her and Nathan's brain-scrambling.'

Leonard huffed and actually managed a fraction of a legitimate smile, which Julius returned. 'Spare me your technical lingo, Jules.'

'It worked, didn't it?'

'For now. But this isn't one of your carefully controlled studies. We don't know what can go wrong with the things you're messing with. What if Nathan ends up thinking we're the enemy? What if, and I need to stress this again, that *demon*—and that's the world we live in now, with demons—what if that demon you're tricking gets wise to what you're doing?'

Julius folded his hands, letting the clinical professionalism take over. 'It's a risk. What else is new? This could be our only way of lessening Talbot's leverage over us.'

'And what happens to Nathan and Dolores now? Will they return to Elzinga?'

'I'm not entirely certain. I haven't been able to gather any clear data on how long their personas remain in control once liberated from Charon. But if we create enough confusion and complications to get Talbot out of the picture, perhaps we can track them down when they're compos mentis, and I can conduct a full work-up on them. And keep them far away from all of this until Talbot's replacement, or Talbot and his burned fingers, decides to abandon this assassin project of his.'

Leonard grew thoughtful, running through logistics of leading his men to Nathan and his terrifying x-factor, and getting him to a quiet place far from Talbot's ken. But first, 'How would we track them down?'

Julius retrieved a small GPS locator from his pocket and passed it to Leonard, the digital map showing two disparate and distantly separated red markers. 'Harlan provided me with two tracking chips to attach to their clothing. Unless they somehow find the tiny things, you'll know their whereabouts. But if you go after them, I still recommend extreme caution, and I don't want you to make any move on either of them until I'm with you; only I know the sequence of words should Charon regain control. And I consider them my patients.'

Leonard still felt penned in, uncomfortable with such a high-risk, unforeseeable strategy, but with a slow nod, he acquiesced. He didn't want to think of problems right now. For weeks he'd wanted to see his brother, to catch up with him in a situation that wasn't somehow being manipulated by Talbot.

He raised his martini, clinking glasses with Julius, and signaled the waiter over. He was starving.

32

E dward Talbot rolled his pride and joy, a British Racing Green Jaguar
F-Type, to a stop outside the Westchester mansion. It was a dual-
winged palace of marble, porticos, and verandas settled within many acres
of private land. A beautiful property, one that Talbot had had the pleasure
of residing in temporarily, but the person responsible for authorizing such
long-term visits was also the reason Talbot quietly resented coming here.
And right now, that person—Mr. Gabriel—had requested a tête-à-tête
with Talbot to discuss last night's complications.

One of Gabriel's men met Talbot outside, offering to valet the Jag.

Talbot replied with a churlish, 'Piss off,' and kept tight hold of his car
keys, leaving the vehicle parked on the gravel near the entrance. He was
very familiar with such minions, Cairnwood foot soldiers, same as the
bunch he had borrowed to watch over things at Elzinga, and was well
accustomed to feeding them a steady diet of abuse and spit.

Talbot knew where Gabriel would be, sparing him the effort of asking
one of the several dozen lackeys for directions or searching the manse's
many rooms. He would be in the treasury, which was a comfort to Talbot.

He didn't relish the idea of the coming discussion but would much rather it transpire in a room of otherworldly delights than in the kooky little owl fortress Gabriel had built within the surrounding woodland. Those owls never sat well with Talbot. It wasn't long ago that he had callously murdered one of them to make a point to that Russian slag of a monk Kozlov—behind Gabriel's back, of course—but somehow Gabriel had learned of the act, and ever since Talbot had felt the unwholesome itch of being observed from time to time, from what he wasn't sure, but it caused him to watch the night skies with a flutter in his chest.

Steering himself away from the copious number of owl statuary and oil paintings of former Cairnwood Society alumni, some of which also contained owls, Talbot reached the engraved double doors of the treasury. He raised a hand to knock, but before his knuckles were halfway to the door he heard, 'Come in, Edward.'

How terribly disconcerting.

Talbot was in no mood for this horseshit and just wanted to get it over with. He entered the room, which was large enough to showcase an art gallery or museum exhibition. All about the huge room were pedestaled glass cases holding an assortment of the wondrous and the terrible, and the high ceiling was propped up by archways and veined marble pillars.

Gabriel seemed to be amusing himself with some piece of parchment, his saucer eyes hooded a little in reading, the gray hair at his temples sticking out from his balding dome like feather tufts around a veined ostrich egg. Physically he was trim and healthy, in ways that went beyond those of mortal standards.

'This wasn't easy to get a hold of.'

'What is it?' Talbot inquired.

'This...?' Gabriel angled it ever so slightly to allow Talbot to glimpse it. Like everything else in the treasury, it was evidently ancient. He was known as the Curator for a reason. 'It's a rare testimonial about Charon the Ferryman. Scribed by an ancient being of unknown origin. One of our members plucked it from their archives after I made mention of what you had brought back from that shore in Erebus. He translated this himself,'

Gabriel said of the text. 'Many occult scholars and philosophers only understood Charon to be a coxswain across the Styx, unaware of the much larger role he played.' He lowered the parchment slightly, regarding Talbot. 'As you've witnessed yourself, Charon is more than a mere drudge, some fancy transport minister for the Order of Terminus. We believe he was closely affiliated with the monarch of the House of Fading Light. A regent perhaps, or at least a noble in some military capacity.'

'You're telling me that all this time, I've been treating a House loyalist like he was some knickknack? And that's *after* we crossed his sovereign's border to rip him off?' Talbot might have blanched, but with skin so close to ivory it was difficult to tell.

Gabriel appeared less concerned, delicately lifting the parchment up again as though he was trying to chart a course with a map. 'I'd hardly say it's worth losing any sleep over now. There was a time when he was undoubtedly a fearsome entity; now he's not much more than a disembodied organ sitting in the basement of a mental institution. Suffered quite the fall in status, I'd say. Still, very handy. At least he was for a short while there...'

The formalities had been adequate, but now here comes the brunt of it.

'Yes, the assassins haven't been quite as dependable as I first projected,' Talbot admitted. 'The Hangman's slaughtering of the previous Hourglass team was perhaps a case of beginner's luck. But I believe if we stay this course, Charon might once more find his sea legs. His influence remains lethal to many of the candidates placed before him, but other than that, the only complications that have cropped up have occurred when Charon tries to impose himself into certain minds, rebellious subjects such as the Hangman and Doll-Face.'

'Still entertaining yourself with fun little nicknames.'

'It's not my business to coin colorful sobriquets, but—'

'No! That isn't your business! Very astute, Edward. It was your one and only task to produce a new line of talented killers to keep Hourglass out of our affairs and stop our endless quarrelling. But everything seems to be turning to so much shit as of late.'

'Sir.' Talbot felt the desperate animal in him beginning to snivel. It wasn't a pleasurable feeling, and he thought such cowering was now behind him, having since climbed up to this position within Cairnwood. How fast could he lose it all?

'Do you remember the day I first selected you to be my protégé?'

'Of course, Mr. Gabriel. I'll never forget it.'

'Drop the formalities.' Gabriel allowed the parchment to roll up slightly in his talon-like hand. 'I saw something in you that day. A hunger that, if sated just right, could become an appetite for great things. Perhaps I chose wrong. Maybe you've since reached your full potential.'

Talbot shook his head so hard it looked like he was snapping awake from a doze. 'Absolutely not. I will return to our organ grinder Charon and the monkey in charge of recruitment. I'll ensure that from now on every subject is a *willing* participant, grateful for the opportunity. No more loose cannons like the Hangman and Doll-Face. And to account for the fatalities of incompatible subjects, I'll ensure the cattle line is doubled, *tripled*. We'll get an army to irreparably smash Hourglass, or to keep them busy until Judgement Day. We may still manage to turn a profit from this when the assassins begin to tally up.'

Gabriel smiled, but it was far from photogenic, and made all the worse by the glow radiating from a gemstone-laden mantel, which cast him in an infernal light. 'That's what I wanted to hear, Ed. Commitment. Fall off the horse, you dust yourself off and climb back on. Which is why I have something interesting to share with you.' His wide, shiny button eyes alighted on a specific passage, and he quoted: '"And the dreaded architect of Death's cargo removed one of his penetrating eyes from its housing of mineral and shadowed light, affixed it to a great and vital spinal scepter, and raised it high into the dusky twilight of burning lights and warring figures born with the powers of demi-gods and beyond. From the scepter's apex, the reaper's eye swept its chaotic gaze across a legion of souls of weak and poorly stock, reading their worth, and watching as they galvanized into a battalion of foul horrors eager for the battle raging on."' Gabriel cocked his head, wanting Talbot's two cents.

'It's a bit Lovecraftian for my taste. Very insightful, though.' He clasped his hands before himself, pondering Gabriel's interpretation of the author's account and feeling highly dubious of the conclusion he'd arrived at. 'If we're on the same page: by finding this vague scepter of Charon's, we could implant his Eye onto it and increase productivity by an order of magnitude.'

Gabriel's silence wasn't encouraging. 'The scepter was a spine, according to this. Perhaps it was unique. Perhaps its previous owner had been one of the great and powerful Luminaries warring against the Order. Or... perhaps it was merely the remains of a once-living being.'

'You want to transplant the Eye onto a living vessel, have Charon use their soul like some type of battery? But who is to receive such an honor?'

'I'll leave that decision to you, Edward.'

Yes, very insightful indeed. This would give him something to chew on as he drove back to the city. Still...

'I'm keen to see what might happen, but is this something we should gamble with? Far be it from me to be the squeamish type, but I'm still a trifle concerned that for months now we've been mistakenly treating one of the biggest boys in the schoolyard like some two-bit magician, and now we're to potentially...awaken him? If that were to happen, I would imagine we'll learn sharpish that he doesn't share our interests.'

Gabriel the patient but expectant mentor had left the room, leaving only a bored and very powerful member of Cairnwood's inner circle. Talbot pressed his lips into a firm line, setting his jaw and rolling his shoulders back proudly. The posture of someone who would get the job done.

'Great success requires great risk,' Talbot said.

Gabriel's chin drooped a tick, proud of his protégé. In testing moments such as these, Talbot could practically hear Gabriel chortling to himself, patronizing him as though he was regarding some entertaining fool.

And so, with his skin still intact, and a choice—possibly disastrous, but possibly promotional—to make, Talbot nodded farewell and turned on his heel, his eyes doing their usual dance between the various items of the reliquary. Approaching the double doors, he waited for it.

Any second now.

'Edward?'

Every time.

Every. Bleeding. Time. He stopped, turned, seeing the aging bird-man at the far end of the museum.

'You fall off the horse this time, I might just kill your horse. Understand?'

Wordlessly, Talbot left the mansion with a fantasy of burning the whole place down one of these days, with Gabriel trapped inside.

33

Clyde awoke in the late afternoon, swimming out of a dream that clung to him like tentacles.

Again.

He went there again.

Alone.

To the Median.

He sat there, watching the sun stream through the windows of his bedroom, snatching at the coattails of the dream. He could still see that impressive building behind his eyelids, imposing, imperial, sacrosanct, its balcony slowly filling up with an imperious parliament of mysterious beings. He tried in vain to think of the possible cause of these trips, but one thing was now certain: three incidents were not arbitrary. Either the psychic presence he was hunting had done something to him, something deep-seated but hopefully not irreparable, or there was more to him than Spector knew.

Both possibilities left him cold.

If Spector had wrongfully designated him as a Level I necromancer, what did that mean going forward? Reclassification? Was he losing control over what little power he had, or was he gaining more?

The specifics didn't really matter. Clyde now had no choice but to take this to Spector before he took one accidental trip too many and found himself unable to wake up.

He glanced at his phone. Noon.

But the talk would have to wait for the moment. It was almost time for work. He could still smell the sweet scent of Nat on his T-shirt. After a quick wash and change of clothes, he did some stretching, a few sets of push-ups, and knocked back a few egg whites and his second bowl of cereal for the day. He was about to leave his apartment when he was met by Kev, already wrapped up in his usual alter-ego disguise.

'If it isn't the future of cyber terrorism. You ready for this?' Clyde asked.

'Hope you had a nice nap while I've been getting spoken to like a fucking caveman by Barros.'

'You're not normally shy about being verbally abusive.'

'Yeah, well... She can't hit a keyboard anymore, but she can still hit me.'

'It's a quandary.'

They started down the hallway to the stairs; it wouldn't do for Clyde to accidentally get trapped in a faulty elevator before an assignment.

At the top of the landing Clyde mentioned the dream, and even with Kev's face hidden, he knew what his exact expression would be: that dopey one where his eyebrows sprang up into horseshoes, eyes filled with so much wonder.

'You seriously need to tell Meadows about this. Actually, screw that, just call Spector privately; seems like more of a personal issue than a team one anyway. Well, bi-personal...don't forget this involves me too, old bud.'

Clyde could feel his brows sinking into worry lines. 'I swear I'll call him after this job.'

The pair always tried their best to stay loose before an assignment. You never knew when it might be your last one. Kev tried to ease the burden. 'So, you and Nat? I don't get it.'

'Get what?'

'What she sees in you.'

Clyde took it on the chin and chuckled. 'Fuck you, man.'

Kev wriggled his gloved fingers before him like a pianist warming up, then gave a big hearty guffaw. 'You know I'm teasing. You banged her, though, right?'

Clyde answered as respectfully as he could. 'Do I need to remind you that she is a part of our team now?'

'Funny you mention that because that's what I was circling around to. I can tell by your evasiveness that you both paired up pistol to holster, so I'm wondering if it was a one-time deal. I'm glad you had your fun, but don't go getting any complex emotions about her. Don't forget you're a boring introvert like me.'

'Again, fuck you, man.'

'That's a compliment. This doesn't apply to Nat, so don't start defending her honor or anything, but extroverts are all full of shit anyway. Big mouths who do a lot of yammering and no listening, always pretending their lives are so much cooler and happier than they really are in private. They need to raise themselves up by boasting to everyone in earshot.'

Clyde glanced back up the stairs as if he'd left the stove on. 'Did we just miss your point?'

'Ha-ha, fuck you. But yes, that was a tangent. My *point* is that you're not the type that enjoys going to dive bars and getting fucked-up, doing whatever other crazy shit she does, or used to do.'

'I also wasn't the type to pull triggers and work for covert ops, but here I am.'

'Touché.'

'And she's not as wild as you think,' Clyde said. 'I mean, she is, everything you said is accurate.' He thought about what she told him about accidentally killing her band and the calm center behind the storm front of partying. 'But there's a quieter side in there too.' They were nearing the last landing before the lobby, and Clyde realized how ridiculous he was sounding. 'Look, it doesn't matter anyway. It was just a casual thing. Just physical. Nothing more, I don't think. But what do I know?'

'Well, unless it's comic-book related, not much.'

'True dat.'

They pushed through the doors into another bright afternoon. Ace was waiting outside in his van for them, bothering the sidewalk with Cinderella's "Nobody's Fool."

* * * * *

The floor plans for Sharp Industries had been easy enough to obtain. Copies of them were now pinned to the wall of Safehouse 16; based in the Financial District, it was the natural choice for staging an operation so close to the objective's doorstep. It was a large open-plan office space, barely furnished, but the windows were fitted with one-way mirror glass. The team were going over one final run-through of the impending assignment. Rose was tooling about with a peculiar sniper rifle not available on the market—an Hourglass prototype made for a very specific purpose.

Clyde checked the digital clock on the wall: 19:00. 'The conference rooms and all the upper floors of the building should be empty by now, with just the skeleton crew of security in the lobby and the cleaners working the floors. Now, since we don't want either of you,' his attention bounced between Kev and Savannah Barros, 'giving some innocent janitor a heart attack, we use the prayer bead.' He pointed at the prayer bead floating a few inches above Kev's open palm.

The R&D crowd coined the name prayer bead during its development: a small rubber ball inlaid with microscopic incantations and covered in an outer layer of soft adhesive gel.

'You guys get cozy in there, and Rose will deliver you.'

Rose raised her scope-fitted rifle in confirmation. Barros had the new-fangled key-logger on her person: a semi-corporeal flash drive that emitted a faint foxfire glow. The semi-corporeality was the result of the mystical components built-in with the chips, granting it the esoteric ability to "read" and replicate the physical memory of any biometric security within the laptop; the semi-physical nature also gave it another unique feature that allowed Barros to grasp it and phase it through any physical barriers such as walls and windows.

'You two enter Sharp's office directly and start the search.' Clyde tapped the long-shot of the tower, which loomed impressively over much of its surrounding buildings. 'Since there are no nearby rooftops of a similar height for the rest of us to station on, and we don't want to advertise our presence with a flashy skyline entrance, I'll be your only back-up should you need it, but some dude float-scaling up a tower block without a harness is still a bit eye-catching, so remember, it'll be emergencies only. If shit goes sideways in the extreme, then you two get out of there. Failing that, the low profile gets scrapped and we'll all converge on your position. We all clear?'

After several previous in-depth breakdowns, everyone was more than clear on the objective. Still, Kev rotated the small, rubberized ball shot in the air, an uneasy look on his face. 'This will be the first time I've stuck myself inside a gimmick. Must be like getting buried alive—*undead*.' He dropped the analogy. 'You know what I meant.'

Barros, Sarge, and Darcy all watched him spinning the prayer bead.

'Not a completely new experience for you,' Sarge said. 'All four of us went inside that Russki monk's fucked-up soul hive. You can bet your bottom dollar that little bead will be more welcoming than that experience.'

'Apparently they have all the comforts of a Marriott hotel,' Darcy interjected. 'That's how the R&D folks advertised it to me.'

Kev looked from the ISU back to the prayer bead, stoking himself up. 'No time like the present.' With a huff and a thought, he ran a ghostly finger across the near infinitesimal markings, causing them to glow with a soft red light. With the door open, so to speak, he and the ISU were painlessly pulled inside of it like a rush of vapors escaping down a vent.

Clyde used a small thread of his loaned power to pull the prayer bead to him before it hit the floor and fired it to Rose, who snatched it out of the air and loaded it into the bespoke polymer rifle, which resembled some sort of futuristic toy gun. Since meeting up at the safehouse he had shared a few stolen glances with Nat, but she was still playing it aloof, slouching in a fold-out chair and acting strictly professional, the way an agent should. So what the hell was he doing, feeling like some dopey teenager with a crush? He needed to get his head in the game.

Ace finished shoveling down his can of chili, dropping the fork in the empty container. 'I still wish we could just grab this asshole and dangle him from a roof until he talks.'

Rose zipped up the leather bag holding the rifle. 'If this is a bust, you still might get your wish.'

'I'd put three months' salary on him knowing exactly where Talbot's working from. Sharp might be getting used like some temp agency for quick and easy muscle, but our sources show how often they meet in that office.' Ace's hard stare thudded into the printouts of Sharp Industries. 'He'll know enough. You think a smug little prick like Talbot would be afraid of saying the wrong thing to a glorified thug in a suit?'

'Is it weird that you can't chill?' Nat asked him, one eyebrow raised sardonically. Her headphones were around her neck, the ill-tempered power chords only loud enough for a dog's ears, but still enough to bask her with a passive charge.

'Real funny, darlin'. Maybe I just prefer a good old-fashioned punch in the face instead of a knife in the back.'

'Like last night's rousing success?'

'We got the job done, didn't we?'

'You got me there.' Nat put her headphones back over her ears, one black-and-white Chuck Taylor tapping on the floor.

Clyde looked out the windows. The evening sun was creating a chiaroscuro of the stone and glass valleys with brass tones and shade. 'Rose, good to go?'

She was already heading for the door. 'This would be a lot easier with a chopper. Quick fly-by, one shot from this baby.' She patted the rifle bag's strap.

Clyde followed after her. 'Next time we'll try and get Meadows to leave us one in reserve.'

'Maybe it's time I learn to fly one myself. It might come in handy, beat the morning traffic.'

Closing the door behind him, Clyde caught Nat's eye. Was there any deeper meaning in her parting glance? He looked away and caught up to Rose.

34

Kev had to admit, the interior of the prayer bead was certainly cozier than the once demonically corrupted soul hive of Konstantin Kozlov. For starters, it wasn't brimming with an army of damned tar-black souls trying to tear him apart. The interior had impressive square footage, and the miniature red-lit incantations scrawled along the walls were now enormous in size, giving the huge round chamber a near-occult aesthetic. It got even weirder when Kev noticed that there were some creature comforts in here with them. Sarge rolled himself into a swinging hammock, while Darcy rested himself and his dangling guts behind a table to play a game of solitaire. Barros scooped up an ethereally-lit basketball and began to take free throws at a net. All materials were composed of eldritch fibers.

'Take a load off, Curly,' Sarge told Kev, a somewhat occasional reference to his hair. 'No use in standing there like some jackass waiting to charge the hill.' He had a point. Clyde and Rose needed time to get into position without drawing attention to themselves.

Kev found a second hammock and dropped himself into it. 'Is this what your other place is like?'

'What, the command center?' Sarge smiled, facial muscles raising up the shards of bomb shrapnel. 'A little bit. This isn't half bad, though. Though we got a nice big portal window at our place, lets us see out at the world around Rosie.'

'Not in a creepy way,' Darcy added quickly, placing a card from the stockpile down on one slowly building card sequence.

Kev allowed his eyes to admire the surroundings, the minimalist decor doing nothing to rob it of its wonder. He ran his fingers along the netting of the hammock holding him, feeling the strange energy between his fingers. 'What else do you think they could build with this stuff?'

'I already put in a request for a beach resort,' Barros said, sinking the ball through the net.

'Makes you think, though, doesn't it. How something like this is done. Incredible.'

'You're getting that idiot-look in your eyes again,' Sarge said, his own eyes half-closed in comfort. 'Too much of anything will make a man crazy, including knowledge. I don't need to unravel every mystery in the universe, I just need to find my place in it. And I'd say I have.'

Kev thought about that. The sergeant's philosophy wasn't without its merit, but Kev quietly and respectfully disagreed, at least when it came to acquiring knowledge. How could anybody not want to know about the design possibilities of the energy currently supporting his ass in the air, or crafted into playing cards and a basketball?

But maybe Sarge was right after all. It wasn't like Kev could just waltz on down and start asking the Madhouse geek squads about their projects. The power of bureaucracy being what it was, and as irritating as it was, he didn't want to risk inciting any disciplinary action against himself. Especially not with what he was planning to do with Barros. Looking at Sarge and Darcy, he wondered if Barros might have mentioned any of it to them. He doubted it. But they'd all know soon enough.

Before too long, Kev felt a tingling. It was Clyde sending a Morse code message along their conjoined soul thread.

Showtime.

* * * * *

The shot wasn't as tricky as Rose had expected. Hunkered low against the stone parapet of a modest thirty-story building a few blocks over from the southeastern side of the Sharp Industries tower, there was just enough distance between them to keep the shot's angle manageable. When they had been in the initial stages of selecting a rooftop, her concern had been finding a safe location that wouldn't require her to crane her neck too badly, or aim skywards at some impossible five-degree angle. But this was perfect. She glimpsed through the scope, zeroing in on the main office windows at the pinnacle of the building. With her finger on the trigger, she slowly squeezed. The shot was barely audible, a rather typical *phut* much like that of any suppressed rifle. The prayer bead pierced the evening air, hitting the top right-hand corner of the floor-to-ceiling window of Leonard Sharp's office with a sound barely louder than that of a hurled piece of chewed-up gum.

* * * * *

With utmost care, Kev tentatively peeked his head out from the bead, only to be met with the sight of human specks and ant-sized cars seventy-plus floors below. It would have been terrifying if he wasn't a gravity-defying ghost. Maneuvering around the exterior of the bead, he found the polished glass of the private office. The place was empty. Debouching from the bead like steam from a pipe, his body regained its normal dimensions and passed through the glass with the ISU right behind him. The office was large and tastefully understated, but still exuded the commanding presence of a professional and powerful individual, as was to be expected for the CEO of a conglomerate and possible linchpin of the criminal underworld.

Sarge and Darcy crossed the office and gingerly phased through the wood-paneled walls to watch for possible security threats outside in the corridor.

'That was easy. About time we caught a break,' Barros said, eyeing the laptop waiting on the large mahogany desk.

Kev stared at the sleeping computer. 'Okay, let's get this over with.' He settled in at Leonard's desk, turning the power on. 'At least I can remember how to do that,' he said, giving a small smirk for Barros's benefit.

Kev inserted the key-logger into the port and, as advertised, it worked its strange tech-magic, unlocking the desktop, and within minutes, Barros had Kev dancing about the keyboard, searching every digital nook and cranny for any pertinent files relating to Talbot's assassins. It didn't take them long to sift through the laptop, at which point Barros schooled Kev on accessing the building's servers, but before long their hopes were dashed, with Kev sensing the budding frustration in Barros's voice and seeing the growing expression of someone on a pointless pursuit.

'Forget it,' she finally said. 'There's nothing we can use here.'

Kev let his hands rest on the desk, staring at the drawers by his legs. He tugged the handle of the topmost one, working his way down, but each one was locked. It wasn't over yet. He'd undertaken some lock-picking training at the Madhouse, sparing him from using any noticeable brute force. He wouldn't be cracking any bank vaults anytime soon, but surely a basic desk, even a very nice one such as this, wouldn't be fitted out like the Federal Reserve. And so, after some concentrated fumbling, he popped the top drawer open and quickly floated several files and notebooks up in the air, lining them up before him and Barros, and peeling back the pages in unison as their eyes skimmed for anything of note. Again, nothing. The drawers below, also nothing.

'I think Ace might get his wish. Looks like we're going to have to get a little more hands-on with this guy.' Barros stared at a framed photograph of Leonard and the mayor hanging on the wall, something about charitable works.

'I guess.' Kev got up from the seat, disappointed this hadn't paid off, when Sarge pulled himself out of the wall with a serious look on his face.

'Sharp's here!'

'What?' Kev looked undecided for a minute and was about to send a message to Clyde when he had a better idea. 'He alone?'

'Affirmative.'

'Screw it, we need a little chat with him anyway. This saves us the effort of knocking on all of his front doors.' Kev walked around to the other side of the desk and casually leaned against it. Barros was next to him, with Sarge and Darcy still flanking either side of the doorway.

Leonard Sharp entered the room, his size and natural dominance owning the space instantly. If he was fearful of four ghosts occupying his private office, he was doing an admirable job of hiding it. 'I was wondering when you lot would turn up. You here to blow up my office too?'

'We didn't blow up shit, that was your guy,' Barros corrected him. 'Remember?'

'Your guy, my guy, Talbot's guys; all I see is a bunch of fucking freaks disrupting my life and my business. What do you want?'

'We want to know where Talbot's making his "fucking freaks,"' Kev said. 'Then we're going to shut his little Boogieman Project down. But if you're in a quiet mood, I don't mind breaking your fingers one by one.'

Leonard's wry grin was there and gone in a heartbeat. 'You won't need to break my fingers unless you're that way inclined. I want Talbot as dead as anybody. But you'll need to make a deal with me before I tell you anything.'

'We don't need to make a goddamn thing with you, son,' Sarge grumbled off to Leonard's left. Leonard didn't deign to look at him, keeping his eyes firmly on Kev.

'He's right,' Kev referred to Sarge. 'But first, let's hear what you're dealing with.'

'My brother Julius works for him, not by choice.'

'He's the top shrink, right?'

'He's the head of clinical psychology at Elzinga. Talbot has him running recruitment, selecting the most violent but mentally pliable patients for the procedure.'

'What about Bai Li, Charles Niedermeyer, and the Dukes of Purgatory? They weren't patients, they were criminals and prison inmates.'

'That was my influence. I wanted to take some pressure off Julius, so I pulled some strings to get Talbot some other potential subjects. Neither of us volunteered for this shit, but Talbot isn't something I can stand up to. Unlike you freaks, my people and I are a bit mismatched in putting an end to that fucked-up Eye thing.'

'What fucked-up eye thing?' Darcy asked.

'Some demon leftovers that used to belong to something called Charon. That's all I know, but that's the cause of the assassins.' Leonard lowered his guard ever so slightly, offering Kev a glimpse at the compassionate man hiding behind the wall of violence he displayed to his enemies. 'I want assurances that Julius is kept safe. In his own confused way, he's doing what he can to help stop Talbot.'

'What do you mean?' Kev asked.

'I understand all of you met the Hangman last night, and a masked woman who plays with dolls. I have history with them, mainly the Hangman, but I never liked that stupid name. He's called Nathan. Talbot had him turned into that thing just to prove a point. Until recently I had no idea who the hell Talbot or the Cairnwood Society was. Still don't, truthfully. He just showed up one day with an interest in CSS and wanted to show me that what was mine could be his. He changed Nathan against his will, but that was a slight misfire. According to Julius, the Eye needs to continually exert its control over Nathan because of his resistance. And that's how Julius has been risking his life, by secretly feeding Nathan control words that can trigger memories, helping him recall who he was, who he is, helping him fight back and retake control.'

'So that's why he ran off last night,' Kev said, mainly to himself.

'It's also the reason why Julius selected Dolores Ricci, the doll-woman. Talbot isn't aware of this, but she had a fling with Nathan before her life turned to shit. She has her own trigger words. She left the fight early too, right?'

Kev looked to Barros, then Darcy and Sarge, seeing the silent agreement behind each of their eyes. 'You tell us where Charon is, and if Julius is there you have my word we'll protect him.'

Leonard sized him up, and Kev found it impressive how defiant a simple flesh-and-blood person could be in the face of phenomena they didn't fully understand, especially when it came to matters of the heart. 'They're in Elzinga. A sub-basement of the old, abandoned buildings on the north side of the grounds.'

Kev held Leonard's stare for several moments, reading him, searching for truth and trust. 'Okay,' he said. 'We'll look into it.'

'Let's go.' Barros quickly turned back towards the window and the prayer bead, Darcy and Sarge joining her.

Kev drew a piece of notepaper and an expensive silver pen from the desk blotter, scrawling down a burner number. He sailed the paper square over to Leonard. 'You think of anything else, call me. Maybe we could help each other in this.'

Kev was about to join the others in the bead, but in turning, Leonard said, 'You'll protect Jules for me?'

Kev nodded. 'I will.'

Being shunted back into the prayer bead, the markings lit up softly, and the tiny vessel returned along the invisible energy trail it had originally blazed above the city, back to where Clyde and Rose waited.

35

'So that complicates things.' Rose shoved the rest of a protein bar into her mouth in a very unladylike fashion, tossing the wrapper onto the cheap table in the center of the safehouse. 'Engaging the enemy on the hospital premises, we're going to have to find a way to vacate the surrounding populated buildings. Trip the fire alarm or report some suspected viral outbreak.'

'A viral outbreak would cause them to be locked under quarantine,' Ace said. He was lining up a penalty shot with his hockey stick, readying to whack a puck into an overturned trash bin on the far side of the safehouse. 'Fire alarm, though, I like that.' He shoots, he scores.

'Couldn't we get Julius to smuggle in a bomb to take out one-eye?' Nat asked. She was quietly playing along to "Barbed Wire Love" by Stiff Little Fingers, her bass lighting up the corner of the room.

'The place will be crawling with Talbot's own security,' Kev said. 'Let's operate under the assumption that Julius isn't trusted enough to breeze in and out with suspicious packages. Besides, we don't know if a bomb would do the trick. What size would it have to be? I'm backing the fire alarm idea. Evacuate the place long enough for us to gain access to the abandoned buildings and find the sub-basement. Once down there, we should be able to keep everything contained.'

Clyde wasn't convinced. 'I'd rather make sure we have a totally clear zone, free from any possible casualties. We don't know anything about Charon, and even less about what other killers it might have down there. We've seen how much damage some of the others can do.'

Kev's burner phone vibrated on the table. He pulled it to him and read the text. 'We might be in luck. It's Leonard, says he wants to help.'

'Fuck that!' Ace whacked another puck, practically denting the inside of the bin. 'You talk to the guy for five minutes and now we're supposed to trust him? He could be lying about the Eye being in the nuthouse.'

That bought a few seconds of irritable contemplation. And just when they all thought they could be getting somewhere.

'I don't think he's lying.'

'You're not a lie detector, Kev.' Ace walked the long office space to retrieve his pucks.

'I agree with Kev,' Barros said. 'Leonard seemed genuine. I think he and his brother are getting used. The Hangman was just some dude—not saying he was a good one—but he was a buddy who Talbot took and turned into a rabid attack dog. Talbot's like a mosquito getting fat on Leonard's resources. It doesn't make sense that Leonard would be lying about him wanting Talbot snuffed.'

'Unless he's acting a part under duress,' Rose posited. 'He might not have even sent that text.'

'Well, we need to do something here, guys. I say we hear him out. Even if we're taking a risk, it's a lead,' Clyde reasoned. 'What else does the message say?'

Kev read it again. 'He's talked to Julius, and they both want to meet us at Leonard's penthouse tomorrow to plan this out.'

They all exchanged looks with varying levels of enthusiasm.

'Cool, I'm in,' Clyde said, his expression set.

'Okay, but if I see an army of ka-boom clones, I'm backing out,' Nat said.

'It won't be an issue. Tomorrow gives them time to plan an ambush, but it also gives us time to prepare for one.' Rose's stool legs scraped along the floor as she got up quickly, motivated once more by the thought of meaningful action. 'I'll drop Meadows a line.' She quickly tapped out a message bullet-pointing the evening's proceedings and the meet with the Sharps tomorrow.

'What now then?' Nat checked the clock: it was early, not even 9 pm. With only the standing lamp in the far corner lit up, the young evening light was bathing the office space in tones of purple dusk, complementing her neon bass. It was obvious what she was veering towards: a rowdy beer session.

Clyde wanted a peaceful night in his apartment, doing nothing more exciting than throwing a movie on and doing some drawing. He waited, though, just to see what Nat's suggestion might be.

'It's a weekday, isn't it,' Ace asked rhetorically. 'I'm sinking a few.'

'Early one for me,' Rose said. 'I want to get an early workout in.'

'I'm shocked!' Nat said. 'Those guns not big enough for you?'

Ace was already grabbing a bottle from the fridge, leaning his hockey stick against the wall as one of his chosen White Snake power ballads started up on the playlist he had made in a compromise with Nat.

Nat looked to Clyde. 'What are you doing?'

He thought he saw the promise of something in her eyes, but he didn't think he could be bothered knocking back beer all night just on the off chance that he got another drunken lay, not that it wasn't worth it.

'I'm taking it easy. Going to chill out, maybe get a pizza.'

'Sold. I'm in.'

'What?'

'Ace, you're on your own,' Nat said. 'Maybe next time.'

Ace downed half his bottle and belched, 'White Snake.'

Clyde glanced at Kev, who seemed bemused by the rapid shifting of plans.

Filing out the steel safehouse door, Ace punched in the alarm code and locked up. As they all filtered down the empty hallway, Nat was casual to a fault, sidling along with Clyde and Kev, saying how much she couldn't wait for a pizza and, in fairness, offering to pay for both of them. Clyde admired her presumptuousness, but found himself in the bizarre predicament of not knowing what was most appealing: having some quiet "me" time and putting pencil to paper, or more potential sex?

Maybe he could try designing her that tattoo she had asked about.

Moving down to street level, Kev pulled his scarf up over his mouth and, one-by-one, the ISU vanished into the command center. Before Barros vaporized, she said to Kev, 'Nice work earlier. I might make a cyberpunk of you yet.'

Clyde thought he got a vibe from Kev. Was he into Barros? Did they have a thing going on? He felt bad thinking it, it was pure gut reaction, but it grossed him out a little. Being what they were, their mortal wounds were on display at all times, and Barros's were a few degrees worse than Kev's single clean gunshot wound. Could ghosts even do anything? Surely not. Companionship, though. He put it out of his head and focused on the pizza to come.

And then he suddenly remembered. The Median. He had to call Spector. Tonight.

Hands in his hoodie's pockets, he followed Rose and Ace out onto the sidewalk, Nat and Kev at his side.

36

Leonard was restless. Standing on his penthouse balcony, he watched the island of Manhattan illuminate itself against the fallen night. He often got this way when large events were moving too slowly for his liking. It was the difficulty of being born and raised as a man of action, and not knowing the blessing of being able to sit comfortably in anticipation. Over the course of his years, he had learned to dull the sensation some, and it had started with boxing. He had been an anxious youth, a trait of his dad's, and as such, his dad had been quick to recognize the seemingly bottomless well of pent-up energy within his eldest son. Having boxed at a place called Colt's as a young man, before his twenty-a-day habit wrought its damage, Leonard's dad had forged a good bond with the eponymous trainer, staying in touch even as his health deteriorated, and decided to introduce him to Leonard. Leonard had been predictably twitchy at first and, upon arrival, deeply hesitant to walk through those double doors and up the old flight of stairs. But his dad gave him the courage to try.

Which he did.

And the experience changed his life. It worked like some miracle drug. Fumbling through his first attempts at skipping, basic punching technique, and push-ups, he felt incredible. Focused, his head clear, and his body responding in the sweet joys of movement, no matter how ungainly their fledgling attempts. Leonard had taken the bus home with his dad that afternoon, feeling completely at peace. For a short while, at least. Until the big anxiety monster came stomping around the insides of his head again.

So he kept going to the gym. Each and every day without fail. Doing a few odd jobs about the place to help Colt out in lieu of a month's dues when times were tough, but Colt was understanding and wasn't too much of a hard-ass with him. He mostly just made Leonard pay it all back in blood and sweat until he had the cash on hand. The routine shaped him. Every morning before training, he'd feel himself slowly getting worked up, his hands restless, his foot tapping and bouncing, until he was in the gym, throwing punches.

The lead-up to his first amateur fights used to be unbearable, but in good time he was in semi-pro bouts, and then finally professional fights.

Each battle slowly taught him to temper the caged animal inside him, honing its instincts, conserving his energy for when it was needed to strike.

But it wasn't only boxing that helped instill patience within him, it was also the inherent risks of the streets.

By the time he turned semi-pro, he was already a name in the South-East Sovereigns, and as a contender with a promising future, he was running the gang and making big moves, his equanimity and forethought keeping him from the sort of rash actions that would have caused unnecessary bloodshed and police, perhaps even federal, interest.

Yes, he had developed patience in his time, but right now he felt its virtue slowly dissolving.

Ghosts in his boardroom. Brokering deals with one set of freaks to fight another. And in the middle of it all, his brother. The last of his family. He had become so powerless, Talbot taking liberties with his empire, making him an assistant in his own operations, but now it felt as though he had a chance to turn the tables on Talbot. Leonard didn't know the depths of that pale bastard's connections, but a part of him believed that none of them could care less about Leonard Sharp. Only Talbot seemed interested in sticking to him like an opportunistic leech. If these creepy Feds could take him out, then Julius, himself, and his whole life's work should be off the hook.

He just had to wait.

He cast his eyes down at the two GPS signals flashing on his phone. Dolores was still lying low somewhere out on Long Island. She wasn't an issue right now; her collection could wait until after he and Julius concluded their tentative arrangement with Hourglass. Nathan was another story. Leonard had noticed how his signal had been encroaching ever closer to this penthouse since just before he himself had arrived. There was a cautiousness to Nathan's approach, working his way closer in smaller concentric circles. Leonard could picture his movements, stalking and moving from one rooftop to the next, losing himself in the shadows.

Having watched his blip get nearer, block by block, Leonard felt his stomach tighten. Was he coming here as Nathan or as Talbot's brain-damaged monster? Rolling the dice, Leonard decided not to call Brink or Zebra. The blip was honing in with speed now. Any moment now he would know whether this decision not to call for back-up or a pick-up had been a mistake or not.

Behind him, he heard the intentional scuff of a boot. Turning about, Leonard saw death waiting for him. Nathan, barbed armor unbidden, was perched on the flat roof of the patio, the swimming pool light painting him in silver wavelets.

'Are you...*you*?'

'I think so.' Nathan's voice was unexpectedly soft for a man of his imposing stature. A quiet voice for a natural predator. He gestured at his forehead. 'The noises up here are gone.'

'Why are you here?' Leonard reflected on what Julius had told him at lunch, how his own experimental manipulations had accorded Nathan his independence. But cynicism had its merits for survival.

'Jules. I don't know how he did it, but he helped. Helped me remember who I was. Who I am. But...' He held one large arm out, a barbed wire slowly coiling up around the muscles. 'I'm still this too.'

'And you're thinking for yourself? You're certain?'

The murderous wire shot back into his arm like a startled adder. 'There was always a pressure, pressing out everything that was me. I had no way of fighting it. But I remember everything now. That pressure's gone. And now I want to know what we can do to butcher the motherfuckers who are responsible for this.'

'We might not have to. If you remember everything, as you say, you'll know about the powered-up Feds you fought at Citadel.'

Nathan nodded. 'I killed a bunch of them a while back. Now they want payback?'

Leonard almost gave his head a shake. 'Sort of. They want Talbot and all of his shadowy friends buried. Most importantly, right now, they want to find Charon's Eye and put a spike through it. Me and Julius are meeting them tomorrow to talk strategy, then they're going into Elzinga to clean house.'

'You're working with them?' Nathan's voice was calm, but a note of judgement reared its head.

'Temporarily. They might focus on problems bigger than organized crime, but they're still Feds. I don't trust them, but I don't see any other options in getting out from under this shit pile we're in.'

'They'll still come for me. Payback.'

Leonard leaned back onto the rail in thought. 'Yeah, they will. Or maybe we can arrange some sort of deal with them. You didn't kill their guys. That thing in your head did. Or maybe they will just turn on all of us if they manage to pull this off. Speculation can't help us now. We have one option: use them to kill our enemies. After that...see what happens.'

Nathan was reflective for a moment. 'Dolores? Jules helped me, did he help her too?'

'He told me he did. And Brink watched the Citadel security footage: she took off not long before you.' He held up the tracker app for Nathan to see. 'She's on Long Island now.'

'You've been tracking us?' Nathan began to slowly pat himself down.

'Only since last night. No one knew how you two would react to the latest deprogramming.' Leonard indicated the belt loop near Nathan's right pocket. Nathan found the tiny tracker chip and held it up, rolling it between his fingertips before closing it in his fist. 'We'll find Dolores when this blows over. She'll be okay. Jules will help her. She's out of this for now, though.'

'No, she isn't. She won't let this go. I know the anger inside her. They tried to control her, fucked with her. She won't just disappear.'

Leonard knew all about Dolores's wrath. It was Nathan who had forged it into a blade after Sonny had learned of their trysts and thought he'd make an example of her. 'No, I expect not. If you remember everything, then I'm guessing she does too. She might try to find you.'

Nathan sat quietly with that for a minute. He hopped down onto the flagged patio of the balcony, passing the pool and deck chairs with a purposeful stride. 'If they're going in there to kill Charon, then so am I. I'm owed too.'

Leonard weighed it up. 'Julius's life is in the balance here. I don't want additional hostilities complicating matters. If you're getting involved in this, it needs to be brought to the freak Feds' attention tomorrow. Make it clear that you've got your head on straight and aren't an enemy, and make sure that they're not going to let personal grudges get in the way of killing Charon—hopefully Talbot too—and getting my brother out of there.'

Nathan didn't appear fond of meeting the agents. He moved beside Leonard, resting his arms on the glass parapet and staring out at the magnificent island. 'You remember that day at the steakhouse?' There was only one steakhouse worth mentioning in their shared history: the former mob-controlled spinning wheel of High Steaks. 'The five heads of the Families called you in to talk terms. Start a ceasefire, join up.'

'Course I remember. I own the place, don't I?'

'They were scared of us. Scared that we'd cornered the Chinese heroin market. Scared that we'd got all this dirty ex-military muscle. Scared that we'd pushed the Bratva out of the arms deals. Most of all they were scared of us. Because we made all that happen.'

'And they tried to kill us. A nice meal became an ambush.' Leonard recalled the pivotal meeting. The day was overcast and felt like one endless rainstorm, turning an otherwise spectacular 360-degree view into a wall of lashing water and streaky lights. The gathering of rarely glimpsed dinosaur wise guys had been set amidst a sea of empty tables in the restaurant, laughing and joking as they sipped wine and smoked cigars, owning the establishment allowing them to break the rules for the private get-together. On the way to the meeting, Leonard had joked with Nathan and Zeb about how they all looked like bad cartoon stereotypes, ugly gangsters to be roughed up by Dick Tracy. He still remembered them now, the names and faces of the five dead Cosa Nostra patriarchs: Anthony Gigante, a middle-aged man on the slide between doughy and globular with a graying side parting; Arnold Remini, a wizened, ratty-looking piece of work with a hook nose and receding hair, his glass eye—a tale from his younger glory days involving a back-alley knife fight—always rolled about inside his head and made Leonard think of a shark about to bite; Dominic Costello, a tanned, sleazy man with a permanent five o'clock shadow, gaudy amount of gold jewelry, a perpetual reek of cologne, and a permanent toothpick rolling from one corner of his mouth to the other; John Moretti, who had the appearance of a bookish turtle with accountant glasses, but who cut an imposing figure and had the kind of reputation that quickly put such cute comparisons to bed; and of course, Frank Ricci, a preened mustache, black eyebrows almost as thick as his upper lip hair, and about as charming as gonorrhea. Just like his son.

'They had that Jewish hitman,' Leonard fished for the name, 'Iceberg. You left him hanging over the bar with his own ice picks in his chest.' Meyer Feldberg had been a feared presence within the underworld, on a par with the rising Hangman. His ancestry had kept him from becoming a "made man," but the big five kept him as a favored confidant.

'And you beat Gigante's capo to death in a brawl while the bullets were flying.' The capo was Paul "the Ox" Corozzo, a well-respected boxer whom Leonard already knew of from the local circuit, who had fists like concrete blocks and a fighter's face that looked as though it couldn't say no to a good punch, which was true since Leonard had out-boxed him a number of years back to a unanimous decision. The only reason the Ox managed to stay vertical during his painful twelve-round education was because he had a chin every bit as tough as his fists.

'All those dangerous men, they learned to fear us. They turned on us because of their fears. These new players, I butchered a lot of their agents. And now they fear me. They aren't going to trust me. And I don't trust them to keep Jules safe. Let them handle what they can. I'll get Julius out of there.'

Leonard stared into Nathan's dark eyes, so dark they were almost voids. He had depended on him so much in his life, and vice versa. What if Charon could somehow get back in his head and take control again?

It was a risk. But he trusted him. Always would. That was the reason he had taken a bullet for him from Iceberg's gun that day at the steakhouse and watched the panic and rage in Nathan's eyes as he finished off the Jewish hitman with a concerted effort towards maximum pain. And when the thunderous violence was over and all lay dead, apart from Frank Ricci, who lay crippled with two shot-up legs courtesy of Zeb, Leonard had cemented himself as the city's criminal kingpin. And with short, labored breaths, his lungs filling with blood and knuckles scraped raw from his deathmatch with the "Ox," he had managed to stay standing long enough to issue a diktat. 'Old man Manzella was a baller back in his day, uniting all of your families. A smart move. I don't want to bring it *all* down, Frank. I'm just relieving you of it.' Slivers of blood had been running down his chin, coloring his teeth and accompanying his words with red flecks like celebratory confetti released during the unveiling of a new king. 'You and your boy Sonny can get in on the ground floor of a new company. Or you can have a little one-to-one time with Nathan.'

Frank Ricci's eyes had remained steely and wild. 'You're fuckin' out there, pal. No fuckin' nigger will head the families,' he spat.

Leonard had made a small attempt at pretending to look around. 'Doesn't look to me like there is much of a family left. But what's left of your wop empire'—the blood was really filling up his lungs now—'can call me daddy. This is a *new* family. I'm not some street-corner banger...content to buy...shiny rims and gold teeth. I already have the police commissioner's ear; he knows a sure thing when he sees it. I have vision...weight...and nobody is taking this from me, you hear?' A cough of blood had misted the air. 'Nobody!' At that point he had looked at Nathan, covered in mobster blood. 'Make the call.' And Nathan hit speed dial. Ricci senior's face was a waxy pallor of hot discomfort. Leonard had felt the room starting to spin, weakness pulling him down, blood pressure beginning to drop. His fortitude was unshakable as he hung on. 'That call just ordered a series of hits. Every...underboss, advisor...and capo from every family... has just been greenlit. Every family...but yours. In about ten minutes... Sonny, your brother, your crew...will be all that remains. You're my bitch now. And you're going to sign over...your construction firm to me...as a huge fuckin' thank-you...for letting your rat fuck ass...live.'

And history was made.

Yeah, Leonard had always trusted Nathan. And he still did.

'Okay. Me and Julius will talk to them tomorrow. You stay low, and I'll get you a new burner, give you the details after we've finished.'

They stood in peaceful quiet, watching the city lights from one of their several blood-bought luxury towers.

Leonard still felt restless.

37

Julius checked his watch again and couldn't help but grumble. His nerves had been on edge since his talk with Leonard at lunch, and the tuna steak and asparagus were now roiling around a bellyful of wine. For some reason, it had taken talking to Leonard, and seeing the concern on his face, to really hammer home the risks he had been taking since that first night he spoke into Nathan's ear. Perhaps all his time spent sequestered in Elzinga's basement, poring over the raw and lethal personalities of wards of the state and recidivists, had made him more detached than he'd realized. Even in his professional life, on those occasions when he had discussed with colleagues and board members and state legal officials, he had begun to feel a step removed, like an actor reading lines he didn't fully understand.

Leaving the confines of his Mercedes, he shuffled about Elzinga's parking lot. Waiting. Worrying. The night was a warm cloak, reflective in moon shimmers, but Julius felt cold inside, staring at the possessive black woods peeking over the hospital walls.

It was a little after 6 pm when Talbot had rung him in a tone of near breathless excitement, ordering him to be here tonight at 10 pm. For someone who only last night had been in such a pique of rage over the random departure of Charon's remaining pupils, Julius thought Talbot might be visiting just to kill him in a blind fury, and all day long Julius had hoped Talbot's bosses might have recalled him, or better yet, killed him. But then he got the call. And without divulging any specifics, Talbot stressed how imperative it was that Julius be on site tonight at the requisite time. Naturally, Talbot didn't deem it necessary for him to practice punctuality.

Julius felt alone out here and glanced over to the main building's lobby. He couldn't see Talbot's guards from this vantage and didn't know if that made him feel safer or more vulnerable. Finally, a growl started up from somewhere deep in the belly of the black woods.

A Jaguar.

Trying to look casual, Julius strolled towards the large iron gate between the cobblestone walls. He watched through the thick bars as a pair of headlights sped down the country road, loping towards him. Talbot's arm popped out and swiped his pass across the electronic lock. He eased into the space next to Julius's car and stepped out with a calculated expression, a look of surface-level good humor.

'Julius.'

Julius nodded, not feeling any safer in the man's presence. Like Pavlov's dog, he immediately began his usual regurgitation of work-related noise. 'If this is about the candidate list, I haven't whittled it down to any absolutes yet. Still searching for those who won't overtax Charon. We're still in agreement that if Nathan and Dolores are the litmus test for unruly personalities, then we need to steer clear of any further forced participation, yes?'

'Correct.' Talbot closed and locked his car, sounding very amicable. 'I learned something very promising this afternoon. Let's go inside, and we'll put it to the test.' He started off without Julius.

'Put what to the test?'

This didn't bode well with Julius. What exactly would they be testing? Nerves quivered throughout his body. He looked at his Mercedes and almost bolted for it, carried away on an escapist's flight of fancy, speeding from the asylum grounds, never to return. But then what? Try to convince Leonard to flee with him in the time it would take for Talbot and his forces to find and kill them both? Placing his shaking hands in his blazer pockets, he tried to catch up to Talbot, noticing the purposeful speed of the other man's stride.

Circumventing the large, eerie complex, they cut through the dark gardens towards the abandoned buildings, entered one such ruin, and descended down deep into the lair of Charon.

Talbot stood before the dormant fist-sized Eye, seeming to be gathering up his courage, pale hands primed and flexing. He stopped and cupped his chin in thought, the sort of pose perfected by executives trying to look important and wise. Julius listened to the wall of quiet expanding throughout the large dungeon cellblock, the guards as soft-footed as mice.

'I had to see a man about a horse earlier. And, well, as it turns out, I might have discovered a way to rejuvenate this old boy, here. It turns out his power might be magnified through direct contact with a soul.'

Julius's knowledge of souls was as hazy and uninformed as it was on quantum physics, but he would have wagered a large sum of money on Talbot not being in possession of one for his beta test. 'I thought we were already doing that. Isn't that what this whole study has been, him feeding on the souls of his subjects?'

'Nibbling. But if he's to regain his full strength, that could take a long time. I'm talking about a three-course meal. His Eye can be grafted onto things. Some jazzy scepter in a once-storied incident. But really, I suspect it's anything that holds a soul: repositories, esoteric items and the like... living beings. As long as there is a soul involved, the implant should take.'

'Are you sure?'

Talbot snorted in derision. 'If I was sure, I'd already be wearing the thing like a fancy headdress.' His hands went to probe the Eye again, as though testing it for electrical shocks. 'Rather, I'm sure it's true, but I don't know what happens to the soul donor. If I can help restore some of Charon's weakened power...' Julius could tell Talbot was talking to himself now, his eyes aflame with the possibilities of a bigger, brighter future. 'But it wouldn't do me much good if I end up a shrunken husk.'

'Well, that's how these Faustian bargains tend to go.' The Eye was plenty powerful in Julius's opinion, and he had no ambition to see it develop its dreadful capabilities any further. 'I know you have enemies you want to be rid of, but is it worth potentially destroying yourself in the process?'

Talbot was a one-man staring contest, a laser focus directed at the closed Eye of a dismembered devil. His pale hands shot out, seizing the Eye, inspecting its almost beautifully bizarre alien textures. And he trembled. Julius had seen the Eye handled with bare hands previously, but this had never happened before. This wasn't transformation, this was something else. Talbot's eyes fluttered as if wracked by an epileptic fit. Julius glanced about at the guards, seeing how those who were in sight of this situation were slowly tensing, but indecisive. Talbot backpedaled a step, catching his balance as if awakening from a falling dream. His eyes shot open, spearing Julius, and there was nothing but hatred inside of them.

'You son-of-a-bitch. It was you.'

Julius stared at him, aghast.

'I suppose I should have known, but I never took you for the sort to be in ownership of a spine.'

Julius felt as though the ceiling was coming down on him, a nervous sweat racing down his back.

'You've been meddling with the Hangman and Doll-Face's treatment.'

Julius almost denied the accusation, knowing how ridiculous it would have sounded before such a cast-iron judgement. Charon: it must have communicated with Talbot in its way. The large Eye seemed to swivel about in sleepy confusion before seeking him out. Three eyes now drilled into Julius, and he knew he was done for. He wouldn't even have time to warn Leonard. Talbot moved so swiftly, he was almost a blur, and Julius felt the grave-dirt chill of one hand raising him into the air as though he weighed no more than a patient's pillow. Choking, the long, pale fingers didn't increase their pressure, nor did they take on that almost-reptilian hue he had seen them do when sucking the life out of bodies; no, they just continued holding him aloft, and when Julius saw what Talbot intended, he was sure it was going to be a fate worse than death. With a murderous smirk, Talbot raised Charon's Eye towards Julius's perspiring forehead.

'Eye for an eye.'

Julius felt an explosive sensation as the strange coppery tendrils— wires, whatever they truly were—inserted themselves around his skull like compressing bands and electrodes. His consciousness was swiftly obliterated in an ocean of memories, none of which were his, but those of his new guest. He quickly became host to many worlds, countless galaxies of moons and multiple blazing suns, and what must be an infinity of species and alien races, their one common denominator being the souls that left their carcasses to travel into what Julius knew to be Charon's true home, that nightmare realm of death, slavery, destruction, and the dark merriments of horrifying potentates.

All that and a war.

So many snatched glimpses of righteous wrath raining down upon the dead domain by glowing creatures, bright as blue embers. No, not embers...sparks. Their bodies coursing with electricity, a power surely divine as they performed staggering and varied skillsets on the heinous creatures fighting for Charon.

Julius snapped to—at least physically—but his mind remained preoccupied.

For a few bleak seconds, he had learned the truth of what Charon truly was. And then his guest was in full command, his body now a vessel.

Julius's two eyes now shared the same emerald galaxy swirl of Charon's, which sat unblinking from the top of his forehead. Talbot gently lowered Julius until his leather soles touched stone.

'What is this place?' Julius asked. His voice had altered, modulated so it seemed to carry up from a deep well of echoes. He wasn't Julius anymore, he was Charon.

'You've shored up on Earth, Ferryman. Allow me to guide you.'

38

'You want the last slice?' Nat asked.

Clyde did, but he was too focused on the latest drawing task set for him by her and Kev. 'I'm good.'

Nestled at the other end of the plush white couch, Nat started in on the last slice.

What had started out as Nat's admiration for his artwork had quickly become a fun series of dumb and off-the-cuff drawing challenges, which Kev was only too happy to join in on, turning Clyde into something of a police sketch artist instructed by a deranged person on LSD. So far he had sketched a growling armchair wearing a jetpack, a house cat made of yarn and wielding a pair of scissors in one tangled paw, and a bipedal pizza slice strangling a fat guy.

Clyde, for his part, was having a ball, only too happy to have a pencil in his hand, and with the added bonus of spending a bit more time with the girl he couldn't quite get a read on. Normally when he was drawing, he would listen to podcasts or chill-out music, but Nat had kept the atmosphere lively with some speaker-bruising music.

Finishing the timed five-minute doodle, Clyde called, 'Done,' and displayed it to Nat and Kev. He was quite pleased with his cartoonist impression of Ace done up as an '80s-era heavy-metal bimbo straddling the hood of a muscle car.

Nat threw her head back in sheer, unbridled laughter.

'Shit, Ace never looked better,' Kev said. Nestled in the armchair, he was lazily floating coasters about the room.

'Can I have that?' Nat asked.

'I don't think it'll ever be worth anything, but sure.'

She used a wet wipe on her hands before accepting it. 'This could be my next tattoo.'

Having seen every inch of her the previous night, Clyde wondered whereabout she might get such a large tattoo. He almost made a tacky flirtatious comment about it but thought better of it. It was getting late, and he wasn't sure what was going to happen next. Was she going to clear out like they were just friends? Nat stood up and, with perfectly casual timing, made her bass appear and ran through a sweet little fill with the song before letting the bass vanish again like it was no big deal. She made a bored, meandering circuit of the apartment, ducking Kev's flying coasters, and stopping at the rough pile of sketches bundled about by his drawing board.

'This part of a comic-book?' She held it up.

'Just scribbling.' Clyde glanced at Kev, then back to her. 'Kev found this book older than rocks at Indigo Mesa called *Dread Paradigm*. It had these pictograms showing what might have been the origin of, well, people like you—Sparks. Some big war between a bunch of flying night lights and things with lots of teeth. It ended with the glow-people losing, and a load of sparks or energy raining down across the planets. No idea how many; could be the whole universe.' He shrugged.

'I guess that makes me part light bulb then,' Nat said.

'I wouldn't feel too bad about it,' Kev said, catching the coasters in a neat stack. 'That big sexy broad with the dress and the hockey stick is part light bulb too.'

'Speaking of Indigo Mesa...' Clyde checked the time on his phone. New Mexico was two hours behind them. Not too late to call Spector, especially with his sleep patterns being less than conventional. Clyde had put the call off after getting back to the apartment, even stupidly toying with the idea of waiting to see if he accidentally fell into the Median again tonight.

He stared at his phone, scared of what he might learn. The thought of just hearing Spector's disembodied voice didn't make the decision any more appealing, and Clyde could practically hear the dream walker's voice becoming cold, distant, and concerned over the line. So he went for the FaceTime option, believing that seeing his facial reactions might make it a little easier. Nat lowered the volume of her tunes.

Spector's face flashed up after several rings. With a strong stubble-bristled jaw, a good haircut, and wise eyes behind his Buddy Holly glasses, he was attractive with a roguish bent. He appeared to be outside somewhere, a starry desert evening twinkling over the boulders and cane cholla cacti behind him. 'Clyde, how the hell are you doin'?'

'Still alive. That's something.' He gave an easy smile. 'This a bad time? I thought you'd be in your office.'

'I do have a life outside of that boxy little room.' Spector showed off the vista of his rocky plateau perch. It wasn't too high up, with a stony trail sliding down a fairly steep gradient towards a small satellite desert town in the distance. 'Going for a walk. Clear my head. Then probably get stinking-ass drunk in that town over yonder. Find me a nice lady to keep me company.' He winked playfully, and Clyde got a good clear view of the roguish conman and master thief of rare and eclectic items that existed before Hourglass picked him up.

'Cool. I'm with Kev, and the new girl, Nat.' He turned his phone around to finish the pleasantries and knew he was on the verge of digressing, chickening out. He just had to get this over with. 'Look, err, the reason I'm calling is...' He knew it was best to just spit it out. 'I've entered the Median three times in as many days, and I don't know how, or why, and I've been seeing this super-ominous-looking group watching me from this big imperial balcony, and I'm quietly freaking out over it. And I'm sort of needing you to tell me that it's no big deal and that I shouldn't stress over it.'

Spector stopped walking, his eyes suddenly piercing, concerned. He held up his index, middle, and ring fingers. 'Thrice?'

Clyde was right. He knew he wasn't going to like Spector's disconcerted tone.

'That's a tricky one, Clyde. I wouldn't want to misinform you, and sure don't want to give you anything to worry about, but...' He bit his bottom lip in thought.

'But?'

For a moment he wriggled like a worm about to be stepped on. 'Let's say there's a *slight* possibility that there's more to your situation than first appeared.'

Clyde covered up one eye with the heel of his palm and groaned. 'Jesus, Specs, couldn't you give me a vague answer?' He sat up a bit, positioning his lower back against the arm of the couch. 'What are we talking about here, the limitations to my soul binding? My Level ı status?' A thought bolted through Clyde's mind, of him revisiting the possibility of finding the still-intact souls of his brother and dad in the unknown limits of the Null; not entirely unreasonable with their former lives spent as US Marines.

'I'm not going to throw around pseudo explanations or give you false hope here.' Spector rubbed his chin, working something out. 'That "ominous-looking group" will be the rulers of the Median, my— *Ramaliak's*—colleagues, you could say.'

'But none of them have mentioned this to you over the last three days?'

'I have a complicated relationship with them. The first time you entered, alone, was there anything significant you can think of that might have triggered it?'

'Yes and no...maybe?'

'Who's being vague now?'

'Me and my team are dealing with something, psychic we think; it's being used by Cairnwood to create assassins. I felt something slip into my thoughts a few nights ago during an op, but I had already dropped into the Median a few hours before that happened. But that psychic presence, I don't know, it still feels like it's connected to it all somehow.'

Spector was adding something up. 'Like maybe this psychic force has been rubbing off on you, through your engaging its assassins?'

Clyde hadn't thought of that. 'I'm kind of asking for your expertise here, Specs.'

'Have you any suspects of who this psychic entity is, a name? Anything at all?'

Clyde glanced at Kev, his mind briefly drawing a blank before recalling the name Leonard Sharp had mentioned. 'Charon.' Spector's curious face went slack, just for a moment. 'Who's that?'

Spector took a moment to respond. 'It's nothing, a mistake from the sounds of it. Let me look into this, okay? In the meantime, if you enter the Median without me again, keep out of the city, okay? They don't ap-preciate unsolicited visitors.'

'You can count on it.'

'Then I'll sleep a little easier tonight.' Spector winked and started slow-walking, shoes crunching on grit and stone. 'I'll be in touch soon. You and Kev—oh, you too, New Girl Nat, take care.' He signed off.

Clyde let his phone hand drop limply to the couch. 'That cleared that up.'

'Awesome. You're a bigger weirdo than me, and I'm part light bulb alien.' Nat waved about his comic interpretation of esoteric scripture.

Kev hurled a scrunched-up paper ball at Clyde's head. 'The shit we've been through so far, you better not wimp out on me and die in your sleep like some punk-ass Elm Street kid.'

'I wouldn't sweat it. It's more likely Charon will kill us all before that happens.' The offbeat comment landed a bit harder than Clyde intended, causing the three of them to ponder what they might be going up against in the asylum.

Nat turned the tunes up again, but before the fun, chatty atmosphere could return, Kev floated up from the chair. 'That's it for me. I got video games to play.' He raised his hand to Nat, who mirrored him, and he cracked a telekinetic high five with her.

Clyde caught his speedy exit at the door. 'Dude, you don't need to go,' he said quietly.

Kev gave him a friendly punch on the shoulder. 'You're not fucking me tonight. I'll leave you two to figure out whatever this'—he wriggled a finger between Clyde and Nat—'is. Two caveats, though: No mopey swooning shit, because it's repellent, and seriously, don't die in your sleep. I'm too young to die a second time.'

Clyde humored him. They bumped fists, and Kev phased through the door.

Clyde dropped back onto the couch next to Nat, who had lowered the music's volume a little.

He tried to think of something casual to say before the moment became awkward. 'You miss being in a band, don't you?'

Her expression was one of surprise, and her face lit up with fond memories. 'A little.' She must have decided she could do better than that. 'Fuck yeah! It was awesome. One big party. Responsibilities always find you, though.'

'Why punk?'

'Why comic-books?'

'Okay, you got me there.'

'I love the energy. The urgency of it. It's about grabbing life, the moment, by the nuts and fuck everything else. That's why I paid Wasserman and the guys to keep the Barrel open. For the people who need to ride that wave to get through the day.'

'You paid them? Like, bailed them out?'

'I loaned them some of my rainy-day savings. My parental unit went seven shades of green shit when they found out, but I wasn't going to college, and with the exception of a few band van repairs, beer, or new guitar, I wasn't spending it on anything else. And Wasserman paid it back soon enough.' She angled her face to Clyde's, the lamplight turning her eyes to dark liquid amber. 'I'm not the rich girl acting the rebel. Punk just spoke to me, made me not care about the constant worrying and anxiety of being part of an endangered family. Maybe if I took the family responsibility seriously a little sooner, I wouldn't have burst my bandmates like they were water balloons filled with ketchup. Lesson learned, I guess. But you shouldn't get too hung up on past mistakes, knowing what we know.'

'I think there's definitely some value to saying fuck it from time to time. I barely know you, but I look at the way you handle yourself and I just think, shit, I wish I could be all carpe diem like that. I even worry about worrying,' he admitted bashfully. 'I seem to have spent most of my life chasing a dream of drawing comic-books, and I think it took joining this psychotic, fucked-up group to make me realize I've actually been hiding in a fantasy. I never wanted to be any type of soldier, and now I can't seem to relax until I'm in that moment, with the team around me, a gun in my hand and some monster in my sight. I sold out my ideals. So yeah, I think you're right about the punk rock stuff. Stop thinking, start doing. Right?'

'Now you're getting it,' she said. 'You might not be drawing comics, but look at our job. You're living that shit.'

Clyde felt a warm satisfaction coursing through him from her words.

Nat slowly inched in closer towards Clyde. 'I lost my old band, but I'm starting to like the one I'm in now.' She leaned in, her passion suddenly attacking Clyde like an animal, and he had no intention of fighting her off. Carpe diem.

39

'Thanks for not standing me up.' Barros was waiting for Kev in his apartment, standing ineffectually beside the laptop he had taken out of the Madhouse lock-up.

Kev's good cheer had diminished, his expression sanded down to one of hardened determination. He fired up the laptop, its glowing screen the only light in the apartment. 'You still good for this?'

She nodded. 'You having second thoughts?'

'Of course not. But I can't do this without you. I'm just making sure you're not getting cold feet.'

Barros smirked, but it barely concealed the deeper sadness beneath. She glanced down at her stumpy legs. 'No feet here. Cold or otherwise.' She paused. 'It's strange, I do want to know, but am also scared at what we might find. Can you imagine breaking this to the others if we do find something? Sarge will be cool, I think. He used to butt heads with brass in the army. Darcy...I don't actually know, but at a guess, I think he'll be okay too.'

'But Rose?'

'You know how she is. She's kind of an open book when it comes to obeying orders.'

'I hope she'll make an exception for this.' He glanced away from Barros to the home screen and sat down before the keyboard.

Without another word Barros moved in, huddling over Kev's shoulder, and they began. Kev had no idea what he was doing, simply typing and pointing and clicking at what Barros told him to. Using a virtual network provider in conjunction with a browser that anonymized the computer's IP address by relaying it across the globe, they slipped past the Madhouse firewall and breached the building's servers. Kev had heard her mutter a curse of contrition as he did this. He understood; he wasn't enjoying himself doing this, but if there were any suspect secret dealings between the agency and the big soul-suckers at the end, then he needed to know. They all needed to know.

If he had flesh he knew he would be getting a nervous sweat-on by now. But feeling alive on the inside didn't change the fact that he was dead on the outside. His hands weren't even shaking.

They were inside the agency database and found themselves facing a wealth of restricted, top-secret files, but since none of them were slapped with big convenient titles, the dirt-digging became even more daunting. Time passed, and Kev's patience began to wane, but Barros, being more experienced in such activities, retained her hyperfocus. File by file, they opened and skimmed contents, finding no trust-breaking information relating to Trujillo's hoodoo being connected to the House of Wise Stones.

Then, a couple of files later, they found something equally earth-shattering.

Kev's face went slack, his eyes running across the same paragraph over and over as though he was trying to burn it onto his eyeballs.

'It's real.' His voice sounded hollow.

Barros stayed speechless.

'It's real!' Kev sounded on the edge of mania, the revelation changing everything.

The screen started to crackle, a yellow pixelated fuzz clouding it like digital froth. A face started to appear, contorting with a blizzard of yellow electricity. It was Schulz, and he didn't look happy.

Out of sheer knee-jerk reaction, Kev crushed the laptop better than any trash compactor could, reducing it to a pile of broken plastic, glass, and chips. Together they both stared at the crushed pile for several nerve-wracking beats.

'You think he saw us?' Kev asked. Barros remained speechless.

40

Central Park was heaving with life and activity in the beautiful morning sunshine. Kev received a few of his customary suspect looks, dressed as he was for such balmy conditions. Clyde, on the other hand, wore baggy shorts that concealed a small 9mm pistol and a Deadpool T-shirt. They sat on a bench, people-watching and waiting for their meet.

'You feeling okay? It's like somebody hit your mute button,' Clyde said, his eyes doing constant recon of the surroundings.

Kev had seemed distracted all morning. Several times since leaving their apartments he had verged on starting a conversation before lapsing into a sullen quiet. 'I just want to get this over with.'

Clyde left it at that. This was hardly the time for chit-chat anyway. He checked the time on his phone and was about to grumble about being stood up when he saw a brute of a man coming down the jogging trail towards them. Leonard Sharp, his impressive form straining his dark jogging gear, slowed down and took a seat next to them. Clyde noticed several other track-suited men dotted about the area, doing their best to seem casual and not overly interested in the bench meeting, but they all gave off such distinct tough-guy vibes that Clyde thought they might as well be wearing colorful henchmen outfits; one of them even had an almost arresting pigmentation condition that left his deep-ebony skin lashed with pale stripes.

'Discreet doesn't really suit you, does it?' Leonard said to Kev, keeping his eyes on the jogging path and sipping his vitamin water.

'It's my understanding that they don't make fashion lines for ghosts.'

'You're the one who changed your mind and wanted to meet in public.'

'We came to our senses,' Clyde interjected. 'So where's your brother?'

Leonard squinted through his sporty sunglasses, irritable. 'I can't get a hold of him.' He took another sip of his sports drink.

'Then why the hell are we here?'

'It's nothing new. Getting a hold of him is like chasing a riled-up chicken. But he knows about the plan. I'm expecting him to give me a call later on today, giving us the green light to move in.'

'Us?' Clyde's tone made it clear that Leonard and his associates were to play no part in what was to come. 'We didn't agree to a team-up.'

'We didn't agree to much of anything other than to meet up and discuss how to deal with the sick shit going on at Elzinga. Let me clarify: I'm not talking about sending my men in there to help you.' His offhand gesture encompassed the dangerous-looking thugs stretching and warming up nearby. 'But I want Brink to go in with you. He's got the means to help your crew, as you well know.'

Kev hacked out a laugh. 'The guy who tried to blow us all up the other night? Pass.'

'We go in alone,' Clyde added. 'Our team, our back-up. That's all. All we needed from your brother was entry options so we could strategize a safe way to remove civilians from the premises. And since he couldn't be bothered showing up, we'll just do it ourselves. Enjoy your run.' Clyde stood up to leave, seeing the black-and-white-striped man with dread-locks slowly tense up in his periphery. 'Tell your guys to relax, for their own sake. You're a smart guy, right? I know you don't think we came here without our own back-up.'

Leonard remained ice-cold, talking to Clyde without bothering to look at him. 'Look here, son, I know you got some...*irregularities* going on, but unless you're bullet-proof, I'd show me some fucking respect. It's a big old city we live in here. A lot of people to lose yourself in. A lot of guns. A lot of rooftops. You never know who could be watching you walk down the street.' Now Leonard did deign to turn his neck and stare at him. 'Are you bullet-proof?'

Clyde held his stare, not backing down. Leonard was right, of course, but Clyde had been confronted by far scarier things than a big man with a gun, and wasn't about to give Leonard the satisfaction of believing he had intimidated him.

Leonard's mouth twitched a fraction in what could have been either good humor or impatience. 'We could sit here all day, trying to prove how big and scary we are to each other, or you can accept my one-time offer of a partnership. Brink was under orders of Talbot that night, not mine. And he didn't push you in any ways he didn't think you couldn't handle. We all want this shit to blow over. And, respectfully, it isn't that I don't trust a bunch of supernatural federal agents,' he mocked, 'but I'd feel a lot more comfortable about my brother's well-being if I have one of my most trusted guys going in there with you. The alternative is Brink goes in alone, or not so alone, if you catch my meaning. He's a highly-skilled former special operator who can create a small army of walking Semtex. I trust him to get in there, pull Julius out, and blow the rest of the place to rubble if necessary. And I can live with that.'

Clyde exchanged a look with Kev and heard the voices of Rose, Ace, and Nat in his ear, all in reluctant agreement to allow Brink to join the party.

'For the record, I'm sure you're wearing a wire, that's how you snakes like to conduct yourselves, but I know you can't make what I just said public. Hourglass,' Leonard mulled it over, '...is that a chartered department? Because I don't ever recall hearing of it until I was sucked into this end of the sewer. And before you threaten to pass it over to a more reputable agency, I want it on record that I, Leonard Sharp, my brother

Julius Sharp, my businesses, and my associates have all been held hostage and are acting under duress.'

'This isn't being recorded,' Kev said. 'We don't give much of a shit as to what you're normally involved in. We'll let the "more reputable agencies" worry about that.'

Leonard was impassive. 'So, what's it going to be?'

Clyde acquiesced. 'Fine. But bomb-boy's going off on our schedule.'

'I'm okay with that.'

'If Julius decides to get in touch, tell him to set the fire alarms off and give us an advance warning. But we're not waiting around all day for him. If he's out of touch, we'll come up with a new solution to clear the area. Make sure Brink is ready for tonight.'

'He will be.' Leonard sipped his berry-flavored vitamin water. 'It's the basement beneath the original asylum building. Near an old chapel and a big botanical greenhouse. Maybe you can all fast-rope in like you're fucking Tom Cruise or something.'

Clyde tilted his head to Kev and they both started to walk away.

'No bad blood here.' Leonard left the bench and started to bounce on the balls of his feet. 'You guys fancy a run?'

'Maybe next time.' Clyde watched Leonard, Stripe-Skin, and the few others in his entourage set off at a brisk pace down the path.

Clyde and Kev rendezvoused with the rest of the team outside the Central Park Zoo. They walked and talked, discussing the new, unwelcome elements of their plan, and spit-balling hypothetical ways to gain entry into Elzinga Asylum that may not require instigating an evacuation of the patients and staff. They looked like just another bunch of tourists enjoying a day out, grabbing coffee and ice cream, visiting the grizzly bears, red pandas, and snow leopards.

But it was as they stood about watching the sea lions play and swim with acrobatic poise that Clyde thought of a potential entry point into the asylum.

41

The computer monitor in the situation room showed some very old and rough prints of an escape tunnel leading outwards from Elzinga Asylum to the eastern shore of Hunter Island. It wasn't too long a tunnel, a mile at the most, but considering it had been hastily excavated by a group of men who were far from their right frames of mind at the time, a few miles could very well seem like an eternity in practice.

Having arrived back at the Madhouse, the team had updated Meadows on the talk with Leonard Sharp, the as-yet-unreachable Julius Sharp, and the unwanted partnership of Harlan Brink. These issues had been considered and, inevitably, accepted by Meadows, leaving them all with the more pertinent issue of gaining access into the abandoned building without alerting Talbot's security or Charon, and therefore ensuring no civilians got caught in the firing line.

At least, that had been the plan.

'Shit.' Clyde and the team were watching a complication reveal itself on the big screen.

Schulz had decided to be a presence in the room today, allowing Meadows to act hands-free, and had brought up a satellite image of Elzinga's 770 acres of land and its sixteen buildings. Five of them constituted the original abandoned hospital, one of which—Charon's, presumably—had small groups of civilians being marched into it by Cairnwood underlings.

'This doesn't change the plan, does it?' Clyde asked Meadows. 'We do this right, we can bring those people back out.'

'No, the plan remains the same,' Meadows said. 'There's no time to debate other options when we have no idea how many civilians are already being held captive in there.'

He gestured to Schulz, who angled the shot away from the prisoners, zooming in to a small quadrant of grassland and rock beyond the limits of the forest, to the old tunnel's mouth along the shoreline.

Clyde noticed how Kev's tense silence had only become more prominent in the presence of Schulz and Meadows.

'I'll have the cyber team access the hospital's network when you touch down,' Meadows said, making reference to the satellite image of the cave. 'They'll remain on standby as a precautionary measure. If the tunnel remains accessible, you can proceed discreetly and gain the advantage on the enemy. If the tunnel is inaccessible, you'll fall back on a more direct route, and I'll have the cyber team trip the fire alarms to evacuate the rest of the buildings before the fighting breaks out and potentially spills out of the containment zone; I'll also contact the local fire department, telling them to stand down.' He must have picked up a milkshake from a drive-thru on the way down, and his sipping on it somehow humanized him a little more for Clyde.

'If the tunnel is sealed, I'm sure between us we have the power and the ordnance to blast through,' Clyde said.

'Only after me and the meatless bunch have scouted ahead to see what we're up against in there,' Sarge emphasized the ISU.

Clyde nodded. 'Either way, even if we have to get noisy, the tunnel seems like the best route. If we're loud we'll lose the element of surprise in hitting Charon, but if we meet resistance on the way inside, the tunnel could keep the enemy bottled in front of us. We could cut them down until we push on through into the old cellblock.'

'Do we really need an element of surprise?' Nat asked. 'Apart from having a literal eye for talent, what's Charon going to do, wink us to death?'

A faint smile played on Clyde's lips, but he evaporated it before Meadows accused them of not taking this seriously. Meadows, however, seemed to have stopped paying attention entirely, his eyes distant and troubled.

'Sir?' Rose said.

Meadows cleared his throat. 'I have something to tell all of you about Charon. Something I only received confirmation of,' he checked his watch, 'thirty minutes ago. When you first mentioned the name to me, I thought—I *hoped*—it must be some mistake. Or something else with the same name. Schulz?'

The static figure of Schulz opened up a waiting conference call with Director Trujillo on the large screen. The part-flesh/part-mineral countenance of the Hourglass founder was large and imposing on the screen, and his expression severe. He was in his large bespoke suit and standing somewhere in the rocky desert surroundings of the Indigo Mesa facility. The humanity of his Native American heritage was still just about discernible through his mystical stone countenance.

'Good evening, Agents.' His dark eyes moved favorably across their faces, and Clyde recalled his late introduction to the director. Hot on the heels of his first-ever live combat mission—an unofficial mission, and something he had never wanted to experience in his life, but fate had seemed insistent—Clyde had an eleventh-hour meeting at Trujillo's ghost-road diner inner sanctum, where he and Ace gained access to the Null to stage a daring rescue of Kev, Rose, and Konstantin Kozlov.

The team greeted the director warmly, but Clyde couldn't help but notice how Kev continued to act a little more coolly than the others.

'The hoodoo and I have concluded our investigation into the source and nature of the trace energies obtained from the cadavers Meadows shipped.' Trujillo's face became impassive, the pleasantries now over with. 'What we found is nothing short of dire. That energy signature hasn't been seen in a very long time, and I'm saddened to see it has arisen at all. It belonged to an incredibly powerful being. He's had a different name in every culture, on every world, but the ancient Greeks called him Charon.'

'We already know this,' Kev interjected, a little too prickly. 'The Ferryman. He created the soul nexus system that runs throughout the Null.'

Trujillo, to his credit, didn't try to close Kev down. 'Yes, that's correct. The last he was seen, he was obliterated, and it was assumed that there was nothing left of him, but these recent events state otherwise.' Trujillo paused on the edge of indecision in disclosing the nature of the Ferryman. 'He's more than just the creator of the Null's entire soul nexus. Charon was—*is*—the monarch of the House of Fading Light.'

The whole team exchanged various troubled looks, even a few of mock bravado.

'You shitting me? Pardon the language, sir.' Barros was shaking her head. 'A monarch of the Order? How does something like that end up in Talbot's hands?' As soon as she said this, it became blindingly obvious. 'Oh yeah, how fucking silly of me.'

'Cairnwood,' Kev answered for all of them, staring down at the table. 'Their souls-for-profit gig. Acton Mortis must have brought something back for Talbot when they were sneaking through the back door into the Null. So what are they doing here, trying to reassemble him?'

'I have strong doubts about them reassembling him. All relevant authorities agree that there was nothing left of him.'

'And yet here we are.' Kev sat up a little straighter. 'What if the next time Cairnwood finds a way to slither into the Null they unearth another piece?'

Trujillo matched Kev's stare. 'If the Cairnwood Society found anything, you can be assured it was pure luck.'

'Assured? Okay, sure. So how can we stop him?' Kev asked. Clyde was practically cringing at Kev's flat-out belligerence towards Trujillo.

Trujillo offered an uncertain look, which didn't do much for team morale. Intelligence operatives had a way of being overly possessive of their intelligence, but Trujillo pursed his lips, ready to parcel out some sensitive information. 'The House of Fading Light subsisted on the weakest souls throughout Erebus because Charon is able to take something weak and convert it into something truly formidable, should he desire.'

Clyde envisioned Vor Dushi, that nightmare guardian of the Eidolon Trench. A multi-headed horror atop a collection of snaking necks guarding that giant soul repository of the House of Fading Light, marked for Cairnwood siphoning.

Trujillo continued, 'In his prime, Charon could create a legion of obedient warriors to use as he saw fit. With the mind and soul being one, he could manipulate complete control over his subjects, allowing him to exert pressure on their forms, cause pain, govern their will, even tear their soul apart should he choose. And Charon isn't the only member of the Order of Terminus who can strip a being of their volition. The other monarchs have been known to dabble in possessions, creating drones to carry out their wishes from time to time; but it's something that Ramaliak and his cohorts monitor and regulate within the Median, cracking down on it when discovered.'

'We're all somebody's puppets,' Kev said.

'And speaking of Spector, Clyde...' Clyde didn't like the expression on Trujillo's face. He felt bad news coming and waited with bated breath. 'He's explained your situation to me and has confirmed that your repeated exposure to Charon's energy signature has disturbed something latent within you.'

Clyde braced for the worst, his flat and clinical voice asking, 'What do you mean? Latent what?'

'It's nothing to worry about right now. But I'd prefer to discuss it with you in person. When this is over.'

'Fine.' Clyde stared down at his hands. Whatever Trujillo's news was, Clyde knew it wouldn't mean anything if he died before he could deliver it. 'If Charon's that much of a threat, shouldn't we be calling in every big gun Hourglass has? Every domestic office, every international ally we have?'

Meadows gave him a lugubrious look. 'As of this time, this isn't the only major threat facing our company. Trust me, this level of despair you're feeling, you get used to it.'

'So it's just us and Brink.' Clyde said it aloud to try and make it sound more encouraging.

'Fuck.' That was Nat, being a realist, not an optimist.

'And there's no way this could be a mistake?' Rose asked.

Trujillo shook his head, a little dusting of stone falling from him like dandruff. 'The hoodoo don't make mistakes about these matters. It's Charon.' His gaze switched between Ace and Nat, on a screen so large it was impossible to misinterpret his focus. 'Two Sparks.' He paused. 'It took a lot more to destroy him in his original form. But he isn't in his original form. Your power, coupled with the rest of you,' he nodded to each of the other agents in sequence, 'might be enough to stop him.'

'Cool.' Ace belched and finished his bottle of Moosehead but didn't reach for a second. 'He's playing with a handicap. We find him, bring our A-game, knock his teeth out of his ass, and have a few cold ones.'

'I hope that's the outcome here, Ace. I really do.' Meadows's narrow palette of expressions settled on a variant of his broodiest one. 'But if this thing slips the leash, I'll have to initiate the failsafe.'

Clyde knew what that meant and tried not to think about himself still alive in Elzinga when the failsafe was activated. 'USAF airstrike. Bunker buster.'

Meadows quietly sucked on his milkshake.

'Then we won't let it come to that,' Clyde said. He tried to rally a supportive look from Nat and Ace.

'Good. Because I don't want a high tally of civilian casualties on this. Not to mention having the air force and the NSA harassing our department like a bunch of overzealous babysitters would only create more problems for us.'

'And you'll be emotionally overwhelmed with our deaths, of course?' Nat asked, cocking an eyebrow.

Meadows levelled her with a serious look, a deep sincerity that he then shared with the rest of the team. 'That goes without saying.'

Kev stared unflinchingly at the brass, then singled Trujillo out. 'I know there's pay grades, and I know there's privileged information, but since we've suddenly jumped up a notch by preparing to go up against one of the Order, I think you should cut us all some slack and give us a slightly bigger glimpse of our big dark world.'

Meadows folded his arms in thought, exhaling through his nose. At first, Clyde thought he was going into shutdown mode again, but instead, he was letting Trujillo handle it.

Trujillo's craggy features seemed to soften in understanding. Decades of operating and delegating in such otherworldly catastrophes had taught him when to push and when to yield. The team seated before him had impressed him in their short time together. Sadly, so had many other teams, ones whose souls now wandered the potentially limitless miles of Erebus.

'I consider myself a being in the know, but even I'm unclear on the beginning of everything. But before things got this bad, the Order of Terminus were kept in check by a now-extinct race known as the Luminaries. And they were successful for a very long time until the Order managed the unthinkable.'

'The Null. The death of the angels, depicted in the *Dread Paradigm*,' Kev said, his eagerness at hearing some straight, official answers wearing off some of that morning's edginess.

'They were not angels per se, not in any Judeo-Christian sense. However, they were essentially demi-gods. When the dead lords and their armies finally razed paradise and defeated them in the greatest military defeat in existence, the Luminaries' last battalion sacrificed themselves to avoid imprisonment. In doing so, they emitted their energies across all the planes of existence, sowing the seeds for future revolutionaries. Sparks.' An evasive glint crossed the director's eyes. 'A noble act, but shortsighted and desperate, sadly. Such a revolution could never truly succeed.'

'Why?' Kev pushed.

'When the Luminaries themselves had lost the capability to stop them, what chance do a bunch of mortals with some flashy parlor tricks have?'

'With respect, sir,' Clyde leaned forward, the beginning of a scowl on his face, 'if that's the way you feel about our chances, what's the point in us going on a suicide run into Charon?'

'It's risky,' Meadows jumped forth, answering for Trujillo, 'but it's a fight that I believe can be won. Charon is a spent force compared to what he used to be, the Luminaries saw to that. If he was at full strength, we would have a lot more than only a handful of enhanced killers coming after us.'

In the background behind Trujillo, several of the hoodoo started communicating in their voiceless way, the large sentient rock beings expressing their meanings and messages through the sharp scrapes and clunks arising from rubbing their stone digits together. The director turned to them, his sleek black hair threading more sparsely through the back of his head's pebbled flesh.

'Meadows, Agents, excuse me: I have some other matters to attend to. I'm counting on all of you to put this fire out before it becomes a funeral pyre. Good luck.' The screen went dark.

Meadows nodded to Schulz, who closed the conference call, leaving only the satellite image of Elzinga on the screen.

'Time is of the essence here. We need to eliminate Charon swiftly. The state he's in, he won't be returning to the Order anytime soon, but if word of our taking up arms against him somehow found its way to the other monarchs, they'll see his coming destruction as an act of war. The fallout of which would be nothing short of apocalyptic.'

'And if we stop him, we're expected to just go back to existentially spinning our wheels,' Kev said with a shake of his head.

Meadows, brusque and tight-lipped, appeared on the verge of a dilemma between upholding hush-hush agency policy or disclosing company secrets to a team who were about to come face-to-face with a being whose existence partly provided the impetus for the very creation of Hourglass. He stared at Kev for so long that Clyde began to anticipate Meadows demonstrating some as-yet-unseen psychic powers. That didn't happen; he merely used his words.

'There's an arrangement, remember. If the Order learn that there are forces on this side fooling around with the remains of one of the imperialist big boys, they won't take kindly to it. I'm talking total annihilation. Bluff and posturing are sometimes the best weapons an army has. And for us and our allies, it's helped us keep them wary of pushing back too much and turning our world into one big cattle pen and slaughterhouse. Hence the truce.'

'Huh... So that's the reason?' Kev gave him a thoughtful look, with an air like he had a trump card in his hand. 'And is that also the reason why Director Trujillo has buried the fact that the Firmament Needle is, in fact, real, at least according to Case File HG 21-1-6388?'

The glass cubicle seemed to become pressurized. The clacking keyboards and beeps and the various communications outside the glass chamber sounded so very far away.

'To keep this war cold? Having all of us do nothing more than act as peacekeepers and diplomats for a status quo stacked in the Order's favor?'

Clyde and the team didn't know where to look, rapidly switching back and forth between Kev and Meadows.

The deputy director wasn't the first to speak, however; he was still busy glaring at Kev when Schulz broke the silence, his crackling electronic voice loaded with recrimination. 'That was you last night?'

'And me.' Barros straightened her shoulders, receiving a similar look of doubt and anger from Meadows, but somehow worst of all from Rose. Sarge ran a rough hand across the shrapnel in his chin, and Darcy stared downwards as though to inspect his shoelaces or maybe play with his bulging intestines.

The incident of the security breach was obviously not news to Meadows, but confirmation of who the culprits were was very disappointing.

Rose's hands balled into fists, her shoulders hunching up, then relaxing. She gave Meadows a blank stare, held it, and then seemed torn between Kev and Barros. 'You both hacked into our own agency?' Disgust dripped from her face while Meadows quietly stood there with a murderous glower in his eye. 'We're trying to keep this ship afloat here, Kev! But all you seem to do lately is try to make holes. You're more interested in picking a fight with your own side than doing some good with the time you have.'

'Ever the dutiful soldier,' Kev replied, eyes derisive at her blind obedience.

'What the fuck would you know about it? Don't we have enough to deal with than having our own camp turning on each other?'

'Rose—' Barros began.

'No! I'm not surprised this dipshit wanted to go rooting around, but you?'

Meadows intervened, having no time for in-fighting, even if the cause would otherwise demand it. He threw the remainder of his milkshake over their heads, the carton thudding against the glass of the doors, painting them with a thick gout of strawberry.

'It's a complicated situation you can't fully grasp, Agent Carpenter. And I don't need to divulge any further details to you.' The silence was a white roar. 'The truce is delicate and must be maintained. The Order and their forces are a nuclear deterrent unto themselves. Hostilities could see them going to war not only with us, but all of our allies, and I'm not convinced we would come out on top. They'll invade every living world, grinding every last one into submission, and our short lives would be just as miserable as our long eternities.'

'If seventy-odd years of an up-and-down life is the consolation for the Null, then I say fuck it. Kozlov has the right idea, and if sending quiet patrols into the Null to try and find the Firmament Needle starts a war, then what are we really losing here?'

'Focus is what we're losing!' Meadows snapped. 'Right now, we need to concentrate on finishing off Charon while he's weak.'

Through the dense atmosphere, Clyde gave a solemn nod to Meadows's call for a rapid response, even if he couldn't quite believe what Kev had done. Worse, he couldn't believe what he and Barros had managed to discover. He wasn't sure where the hell he was going to land on this issue of the Firmament Needle when this was over.

Meadows leaned over the table, and Kev bore the full weight of his smoldering gaze. 'After this mission, both of you,' his attention cut like a swishing dagger between him and Barros, 'will be facing disciplinary action.'

Clyde's mouth was dry, his heart a sickly bump in his chest, thinking about what that could mean for Kev—no, for both of them going forth in the agency. And he noticed that at some point during all the flying expostulations, Schulz had disappeared. Kev's rebellious bent didn't seem to be in the mood for backing down from the deputy director's stare, but Rose created the distraction that ended the tense stand-off.

'Let's go, shit birds. While some of us still have jobs.'

The team quietly got up and filed out of the cubicle.

Clyde stepped over the dented milkshake carton and paused at the door's threshold. He turned to Meadows, unsure of what he was even going to say, but the deputy director was leaning on the table, his back to him, staring at the aerial view over Elzinga and deep in thought. Clyde felt a nudge on his arm and found Nat standing there. He nodded and followed her and the rest of the team out to what could be the last night of their lives.

42

It started with the staff. The orderlies, the doctors, the administrators. And once it started, it moved very quickly. After that, the patients were collected from their rooms, dragged, beaten, or cajoled until every living soul was amassed in the huge dungeon complex of the original Elzinga Asylum.

Charon, still in his Julius flesh suit, had grown. It was a complicated form, the meat puppet held aloft by a framework of flexible semi-transparent scaffolding. The pipework was greatly reduced in size and complexity compared to the gargantuan nexus pipelines he engineered eons past, the staggering undertaking that fed souls from each and every world into the vast and endless provinces of his underworld. But there could be beauty and sophistication in smaller creations too. Mobility, for example. Though able to retract these smaller pipes at will and capable of walking the psychiatrist's body around like a spidery stilt-man, Charon chose to keep the tubes at a length sufficient to raise him above the second-floor catwalks, allowing him to stare down at his rapidly spawning power base. One side of the hellish cellblock was already a swelling of organisms stripped of their erstwhile humanity, and even if they retained some of their greedily gnawed souls, they were now forever spotted and unclean with the sputum of an arch doom-bringer. As for the other half of the cellblock, it was grouped with the sobbing, the sallow-faced, and the medicated, all boxed-in by the silent Cairnwood suits and waiting their turn to be granted purpose by the horror standing tall over them.

Through the paralysis of shock, even the numbest of the hospital staff knew which fate awaited them, for Julius—or the thing that *wore* Julius—had initially only seemed interested in converting the inmates into the things that hopped and climbed and slithered with tongue and claw, while everyone else had been impaled by one of the numerous feeding tubes extending throughout the basement, reducing them to husks as the ethereal light of their souls flowed through the pipes from bloody, impaled corpse to corpse eater, sustaining Charon, replenishing his diminished state. He may still lack his original form, but he was learning to adapt.

Talbot stood and watched from the catwalk, hands gripped tight on the railing and staring down at the soul banquet below with absolute delight. Gabriel and the Cairnwood Society wanted an army to slaughter Hourglass. Well, Talbot had provided them one, by Christ. Through the excited crashing of his thoughts, he briefly pondered on finding a way to do in Gabriel should he attempt to take credit for this magnificent accomplishment.

Several of the guards he had installed within the asylum to watch over this project during its fumbling infancy had joined him in watching the transformative feast unfold. None of them were strictly human themselves, but they were not born of Charon's talents, and unlike Talbot, they emitted a primitive, cautious sense of concern.

When the last of the devils had been ripped out of their useless meat shells, Charon kept a battalion close, guarding his newer inner sanctum, and turned the others away, sending them out to occupy the wings and grounds of the empty asylum. Every one of them was now his eyes and ears.

You could hear a pin drop in the ensuing silence, and Talbot continued to stare, gobsmacked, at the deformed oddities waiting patiently throughout the cellblock: some with multiple limbs, segmented bodies, talons, scorpion tails, wings, or multiple faces, so many things wicked and obscenely beautiful. After a few indecisive minutes, he started for the spiraling iron staircase to the cracked cement floor and gingerly approached the stilt-man Julius, Charon's Eye blazing hungrily in the center of his forehead like a galaxy roaring to explode.

'Charon...?'

Julius slowly regarded Talbot with a look he knew well: it was the same one he himself wore when noticing a cockroach or some piddling nobody, and in that moment, Talbot silently begged not to have this whole endeavor backfire in his face. Not now.

Charon remained silent, staring down at Talbot with his three eyes.

'*Lord* Charon...?' he tried. That produced some minuscule reaction from the once and future monarch, so Talbot pressed on. 'If it is no burden to you, would you see it in your own interests to honor our previous engagement?' Talbot felt like such a weasel. Some fumbling prick adding airs to his speech and manner to implore the help of this arsehole. If it wasn't for him—okay, if it wasn't for the late Acton Mortis—this thing would still be nothing but an eye without a body, buried in the Shore of Eternal Storms at the outer limits of Erebus.

'The agents of the Luminaries.'

Talbot was taken off course by the statement. Agents of the Luminaries? If Charon didn't swat him like a fly in the next couple of minutes, he would have to report that to Gabriel; surely he or one of the inner circle would know what that meant.

Talbot took a stab. 'We know them as Hourglass, if we're still on the same page here. But yes, those. I believe it would be in our collective interests to continue our collaboration in destroying them. Something of a shared enemy, it would seem.'

'There will be no collaboration. Yes, the disciples of the Luminaries must be located and made to perish. They're lesser but are still a dangerous and powerful lot. You will serve me to this end. You have proven quite useful.' Julius's voice still sounded as though it was falling out of a dead man's chest, which wasn't too far from the truth. He was still alive for the moment, but how long could that last?

Talbot tried damn hard to keep the outrage from contorting his features, and then, with bitter irony, he realized he had just been spoon-fed a great dollop of his own medicine and pictured Leonard Sharp holding the spoon.

'It would be an honor, my liege,' he said and curtsied, suspecting that such an alien life form wouldn't be familiar with sarcasm. 'I have many spies and resources,' he bragged, needing to stay useful, 'but our enemies abide by certain mortal rules and morals. I believe the best step now is to lure them in. Set the bait and they'll be compelled to play the hero.' As he said this, he found himself thinking about how the rest of the Cairnwood Society would view this historical turn of events. The inner circle would have surely known that Charon wouldn't care for throwing in with their collective, but did they care about such eventualities, or did they have their own plans for getting an old dead king back on his throne?

'In this, we are in agreement. And this will make a fine battleground to commence my new reign. When the local bastards of the Luminaries are gutted and their souls are ripe to be devoured by my kinsmen in the Order, I shall retreat from this pitiful world.'

Talbot made a face at what sounded like an anticlimax, and once more, just like that, he envisioned all his careful management and dreams going up in smoke should the Ferryman set sail for home after harvesting the latest crop of Hourglass agents rather than burning and salting the field in which they had taken root. And what about the profitable army of devilish assassins he had hoped to bring to Gabriel, and those on the rungs above him?

'Do you only refer to the agents you have encountered recently, my lord? Because there are many more than that. I don't know how many of them are these "Luminary" types, but Hourglass exists across this entire continent, and their reach intertwines with other like-minded groups across this whole world. Might I ask, why stop with the death of this one team?'

Julius's face sneered down at Talbot. 'That is not the way of our covenant. Shedding the life force of diluted Luminary warriors is acceptable, tolerated. Open warfare on legions of the living is not.'

'Covenant with whom?' Talbot reprimanded, immediately regretting his tone.

'Do not forget your station, insect. Make no demands of me.' That swirling cosmic Eye seemed to alter its color from bottle green to amber, and his whole posture was that of a man whose interest had been piqued. 'You are no longer mortal, Edward Talbot, but you still carry a soul I'd be willing to remove from you if you continue to speak out of line. All you need to know is that it is the nature of the living to kill themselves if death doesn't move quickly enough. And the bellies of Terminus remain sated by this. We do not need to risk losing our endless feast.'

Talbot felt the psychopomp's gaze staring at him from the multitudes of eyes surrounding him.

'As for our enemies, there will be no waiting for death's chance to claim them. I will end them, and use the souls of these Luminary pretenders for sport, and then I shall make my departure.'

43

Clyde stood in the heliport, double-checking his gear as, in the distance, the waters of Oyster Bay gently rolled to and fro from a horizon settling down into a canvas of pink and deep blue, the warm evening air scented with the sea and diesel fumes. The heliport at the rear of the Madhouse was a vast concrete square outfitted with armored hangars filled with sleek military birds and VTOL aircraft. The north and western perimeters of the airport jutted out into the waters of the bay, surrounded by an electric fence and manned guard towers. The jetty of a private dock extended outwards from the cove of the Madhouse's internal vehicle bay.

Clyde tapped his finger against the Free-Thinker embedded into the nape of his neck and couldn't help but muse on what Charon had triggered inside of his subconsciousness. What anomaly lay hidden inside his soul? He regarded the rest of the team finishing their own gearing-up routine in stony silence. Since leaving Meadows at the situation room, they had said very little to each other, limiting any exchanges to brief declarations or meaningful glances as they all tried to process everything they had just learned.

The Firmament Needle was real. If found, there could be a new heaven. But was the cost of seeking it out too much? Clyde was conflicted, not viewing the potential eradication of all life and its limited peace as a minor sacrifice. But the more he batted it around in his head, the more he was beginning to change his mind on the matter.

And what about Kev? Barros too, of course, but mainly Kev. What type of disciplinary action would be awaiting him if they made it out of this? What would Kev do? What would I do? Clyde thought.

Kev had retreated into his own headspace, standing away from the group, keeping away from Rose, and staring at the whitecaps of the bay and boats bobbing on the edge of the world.

Clyde felt eyes on him and pulled his attention from Kev. Nat was giving him a troubled smile and tossed him his pump-action shotgun before quietly checking her playlist and the battery life of a small but potent speaker system housed in her belt. Clyde smirked fondly at her unorthodox weaponry. He stared at her for a long moment. Sleeping next to her last night had once more kept him from diving into the Median. But was it actually her doing? Something about her presence, her Spark energy perhaps? Was it the peace and happiness he felt around her? He wouldn't know for sure until he visited Trujillo and Spector. He glanced at Nat to try and keep the worries away, thinking about their second night together. It was amazing, and the way she somehow made him feel so centered was unprecedented. He never was the sort to get all woozy about women in such a short space of time but being around her was different. He felt at ease in a way he had seldom experienced with other girls in the past. But was it wise to keep fooling around with her, and potentially developing feelings for someone who was going to be throwing themselves into life-and-death situations with him on a regular basis?

Nat glanced up from her playlist and caught Clyde watching her. 'My power's more fun with my own soundtrack, you know? And it's not like I can fuel-up on all of this sparkling repartee.' Her hand made a small presenting gesture to the tense stoicism of the others.

Clyde smiled, his eyes becoming distant. 'Bring the noise.'

She regarded Ace briefly, the big guy's inventory as sparse as her own, outfitted only in his hockey jersey-clad tactical armor and hockey mask. 'All the years my family has known Meadows, I thought he and this agency were doing the right thing. Whatever that means. Keeping people safe, stopping monsters and all that stuff. I never thought they'd be so…I don't know—'

'Pointless?'

She didn't rush to agree, but nor did she deny it. 'Is that how you feel?'

Clyde shrugged in resignation. 'I was the same as you when Rose first knocked on my and Kev's door, giving us the big recruitment-drive sell. I only went along with it for Kev's sake. I wanted no part of this, but then I started to think that maybe this really was the place for me. That Hourglass might be a good thing after all. The good fight, and all that. And then it turns out that all they're really doing is wallpapering over the cracks. And now Kev, of all people, is the one who's pushing back.'

They both glanced at Kev, who continued to stand and stare out at the water like a condemned man.

'You know Meadows better than anybody here. What will he do to Kev?' Clyde asked.

Nat wasn't quick to answer. 'Honestly, I have no idea. I know Meadows has all the lovable charm of a hemorrhoid, but when it comes to this business, your guess is as good as mine. Anyway, it'll be the big cheese handing out the bad report cards, not Meadows.'

Kev's ears must have been burning, for he started to drift over to where they stood, his expression sullen. Clyde didn't know what to say to him. Did he really have a right to be pissed off at his subterfuge when it had unearthed something as monumental as the existence of the Firmament Needle?

'I don't know where we go from here. What happens next?'

'We deal with Charon,' Kev answered. 'There might not even be a next after that, so don't break a sweat over it.'

Clyde nodded stiffly. 'Whatever it is, I'm with you, you know that, right? Whatever the punishment, we face it together.'

Kev stayed silent, but slapped Clyde on the shoulder.

Ace's gruff voice rasped like sandpaper in the warm dusk; he had wandered over without them noticing. He checked over his shoulder to make sure he was out of earshot of Rose. 'I'm three kinds of fucked-up about where I stand with the agency's choices, but I get what you and Barros did. But right now, it doesn't matter. Fuck the politics of the situation. Up until thirty minutes ago, we fought this fight because it was our job, and we understand that life is short and death is long. Hate to sound like some sappy poetic cunt here, but we're the flickering campfire in an endless night. We do this to keep that fire lit and as inviting as possible before it goes out. That's not nothing. This job still means something. Remember that.'

A grateful smile struggled upon Kev's mouth. 'Thanks.'

'And when the fire does go out, at least there'll be some big swinging dicks like me and toothless here to be a spark in the dark,' Nat added.

'Did you just reference an Alice Cooper song?'

'If I did it was unintentional.'

'There's hope for you yet, rookie,' Ace said, staring at the speaker system built into her armor. 'At least tell me you got some hard stuff on that playlist for me. This is a contact sport.'

Nat gave him an enigmatic smirk, queued up some punk—and punk-adjacent—favorites instead, and hit play, turning the volume up and soaking up the sounds of "Happy House" by Siouxsie and the Banshees.

'Guess I was wrong,' Ace said. 'There's no hope for you.'

The back-up teams started to rally around and clamber into a trio of Black Hawks. A fourth awaited the strike team.

'Let's go!' Rose hollered. Her blood was still up, and she could barely stand to look at Kev as she led the way towards their waiting aircraft. A few mechanics had detached the Black Hawk's M134 Minigun for her to carry into combat. She handled it like it was a Nerf gun.

Nat started walking, paused, and stared at Clyde as if she was about to say something. The moment stretched, and Clyde thought she might kiss him. But instead of a public display of affection, she reconsidered and followed Rose and Ace, cranking up the volume a little more.

Clyde and Kev hung back for a second longer.

'If we do make it through this, you're not thinking about going AWOL, are you?' Clyde asked. 'We don't need to make this situation any worse.'

'Suppose I'll wait and see how much detention the principal gives me.' Kev shared a troubled look with Clyde and raised his fist to him.

They bumped knuckles, the surge of power coursing through Clyde and making a temporal X-ray of his hand. 'Let's go see a man about a boat.'

* * * * *

The interior of the Black Hawk thrummed with the vibration of the rotor, making it a roaring barrel of sound. Clyde and the team were the only quiet things inside, focused internally on what lay ahead for them. The flight path took them across the deep-green waters of Hempstead Bay towards Hunter Island.

Ten minutes out from the landing zone they received word from the TOC informing them that the cyber security division had encountered a problem. Having accessed the asylum's security cameras to keep an eye on Talbot's suited stooges and to gauge their current activity of patient and staff pressganging, what they discovered was positively dire.

Every room and corridor of every building was eerily deserted, but the staff parking lot remained mostly full. Unfortunately, but hardly surprising, Talbot's green Jaguar was absent.

While exact figures couldn't be determined, it seemed that Charon had a great deal of hostages, or perhaps something much worse, down there with him. Too bad the older building's dungeon was devoid of cameras.

The Black Hawk formation separated as the island neared, each chopper banking left or right to deploy their armed agents at different points around the asylum's perimeter, the troops fast-roping down into pre-chosen glades amongst the surrounding forest canopy. The strike team's bird descended close to the large flat platform of slate rising from the shallows of the eastern shoreline, the rotor wash rippling the green water into shuddering ringlets.

Clyde slid the chopper's door open and spotted Harlan Brink already waiting for them, sitting on a rock near the black throat of the tunnel. The chopper's thermal imaging had displayed no other body-heat signatures waiting for them, but Clyde couldn't help but survey the tableau with suspicion. He hopped down from the chopper, and the team followed. They cautiously met with the mercenary, his reddish hair and light skin seeming to catch the last rays of the falling sun.

Clyde and Brink eyed each other with naked contempt, and with no pleasantries to exchange, they got right down to it.

'Are you at the wheel?' Clyde asked.

'Would you believe me if I said yes?'

'I could just take a few steps back and shoot you,' Rose said, lowering the minigun's six barrels at him.

Brink quietly appraised the pretty young woman, ripped-up and elephant strong with a six-pack and machine gun fit for an attack chopper.

'You had a look in there yet?' Clyde asked him, referring to the cave.

'Not yet, I just got here.'

'Then let's not stand around with our dicks in our hands.' Ace started marching towards the cave and switched his flashlight on. His body was generating an aura of frost, causing the torch beam to create a halo effect when it bounced back and hit him.

'Hold your horses, snow angel,' Nat called, catching up to him.

Clyde and Rose crowded in close to Brink, with Kev and the ISU backing them both up.

'Before you try and fuck us over,' Clyde said, getting in his face, 'I want you to think about the fact that me and Rose here have each notched one of your super-powered asshole lieutenants. You could make a hundred dupes of yourself, but we'll still take you down with us.'

Brink didn't react, and Clyde knew that the cutthroat's line of work must be low on sentiment for their fellow contractors.

Brink inched forward a little closer, taller and heavier than Clyde but obviously respectful of his abilities. 'I don't give a fuck about you or your agency, you're all just as dirty as anyone in my line of work, so don't delude yourself. That's how your cloak-and-dagger shit works. I'm only here to ensure the safe return of my business partner's brother.'

With the air crackling between them in static animosity and nothing more to say, they moved into the cave, where Ace was trailing a frigid slipstream, shining his light like the North Star with Nat close behind him.

Since the tunnel was only approximately a mile in length, they knew they were nearing the end after the fifteen-minute mark. Luckily they hadn't encountered any natural or man-made obstructions, and just up ahead they found a sealed iron door, rusty from the elements, and probably a quick job by the building's owners.

Brink rubbed his brow for a few seconds and squinted as though beset by a coming migraine.

Ace shone his torch about the iron door, seeing how it was welded tight into an iron frame set into the rock. 'Hope you had your protein today, Rosie,' he said, backing away to let Rose pass.

'Please.' She sounded mildly offended by such a paltry use of her strength.

Brink grunted, pulling all eyes onto him. He had become a lifeless automaton, staring straight ahead with glassy eyes, not at any of the team, but as though he was seeing what waited beyond the door. The whole team knew what was coming next, but Clyde assumed the betrayal would have at least come a little bit later, like after they had finished helping him rescue Julius Sharp from Charon's clutches. Alas, it wasn't to be.

'Motherfucker,' Ace mumbled as Brink's skin began to glow reddish-white like an electric torch beam shining out through blood and tissue.

Kev threw up a force bubble around Brink, sealing the blast within. The containment orb lit up into a white-hot furnace, the blast trembling like a bottled storm. Kev carefully peeled back an area of the bubble, allowing the smoke and char to drift out back towards the tunnel's entrance.

'You think that was his choice?' Kev asked.

'That, or Charon just took his deposit back.' Nat flicked her Free-Thinker for luck.

'Fuck it, let's go find out.' Rose thrust the sole of her boot out, ripping the iron door from its frame.

The team stepped into the dungeon. It was huge, cold, and heavily populated. Standing there, waiting, was the mass of hostages, now a horde of vile creatures of all descriptions, and standing high amongst them all, like the regent of doom that he had become, Julius Sharp, raised by a strange translucent scaffolding that flowed with the ethereal soul feed of numerous catatonic human husks, and a great burning eye of cosmic light bound about his forehead.

'Well, shit. Anyone feel like calling in that airstrike?' Ace asked.

Clyde had his rifle up, Rose her minigun, Nat unpaused her playlist, her bass crackling in breakneck rhythm to the music now pumping out of the speakers, and Kev and the ISU stared hard at the fiends before them, and at the terrifying and despicable ruler partly responsible for the Null.

'Guess not.' Ace pulled down his hockey mask. 'Game time.'

44

There hung a great iron bell from a wooden bandstand in the grounds of Elzinga Asylum, out near the northwestern wall in the lee of a copse and not too far from the derelict chapel. The bell was forged from the melted-down chains of those grotesquely stigmatized for their psychological maladies by an older, less enlightened society, the bell being a perfect symbol: a gong, a beacon, a wake-up call to increase social awareness and respect for such unfortunate individuals. It had been commissioned by Julius and the hospital board five years ago and had come with a big unveiling and lots of media attention.

Pressed against the corner of the old abandoned medical lab, listening to Julius's looped code words, Hangman stared at this bandstand, letting another fragmented memory rise up from the blackness of his mind to fit together like grinding tectonic plates: a recent scene, the private office of a very classy Chinese restaurant—he saw his bulky, wire-wrapped arm dangling a Chinese mobster out of a broken window. The cursing, thrashing mobster had a large black horse tattoo on his chest, which invoked a name to the front of Hangman's mind: Charlie "Horse" Shen.

A torrent of other memories collided, these of people he had no dealings with in his former criminal life, but whose apparent abilities and deformations quickly clued him in to their identities. In one such memory, he used two barbed lassos to stretch out and tear the arms from a man who had turned into a wolf-man, a big two-legged snarling beast, all fur and teeth, but only after he had expertly ripped the secrets and whereabouts of his teammates from him. A wall of blood-drenched scenes sped through his mind.

His savage, impersonal slaughtering of an Hourglass team. Talbot's wishes.

The dizzying kaleidoscope of carnage slowed down, slower, slower, settled, stopped on a scene in an office. Leonard's office. A pale, handsome man entered without invitation, somehow overpowering a few very dangerous members of the South-East Sovereigns without even mussing his hair, and drained the life out of them until they looked like rags of rotting vegetation clinging to soiled bones. He remembered sneaking behind the intruder, Talbot, and slipping his concealed wire length around his neck. And then being sent flying across the office like he had been plucked up and flung by a giant.

Waking up in some old prison, ancient-looking, like it belonged in a castle from a history book he'd seen in school. A glowing Eye, staring deep into him, beyond the windows of his eyes and deep into his skull, reading the electrical mush housed within.

A whipped dog had been made of him. What he wouldn't do to get another shot at Talbot.

But now wasn't the time for revenge fantasies.

Nathan Moore approached the bell, his shadow tremendous under the bloodied sky. He inhaled deeply, basking in the wonderful scents of elms and pines, always grateful to be away from the urban reek, and when his eyes caught the lithe cat-slink of Dolores as she stalked towards the very same bell, he felt his slow, cold heart thud. Leonard had texted him before he entered the grounds, mentioning that Dolores was closing in on the location, but seeing her now, what she had become, was jarring. And beautiful.

She stopped in her tracks, noticing him, possibly reconsidering her actions. Nathan was pleased that she never backed away from him, but also fell speechless, fearful of talking to her again. She still wore that mask, hiding the things that greasy piece of shit Sonny Ricci had done to her. Nathan had accepted his partial responsibility in those ghastly wounds long ago, but the sight of her mask still gave him pause. It was small consolation that it was he who had trained his forbidden lover how to kill a man. He had wanted to be the one to skin the jealous Sonny for what he had done to her, for trampling on his rose garden. Such a retaliation would have gone against Leonard's wishes, but Nathan wasn't going to let business interfere with justice. However, when the raw and battered face of Dolores spoke to him in a voice as ambiguous and deadly as black ice, he knew how much she wanted to do the dirty deed herself. And he was more than willing to help, to nurture her blunt edge and make it keen.

But he never saw her after she went to prison.

And now here they both were, a couple of rejects from nature, or Hell, brought together again, not through synchronicity, he knew, but a shared need to spill the blood of the thing that tried to own them.

They met inside the bandstand, slowly coming to a stop at the foot of the dark iron bell. Neither spoke, unable to find the words that could possibly sum up their feelings or the impossible events that had beset their already twisted lives.

Nathan reached out a large hand tentatively, not sure how she might react. Dolores didn't move, didn't flinch, but let him take her hand in his. It was still warm, and soft too, despite some of the hard work it had been through in murder, prison, and mental bondage.

He could only recall her face as a vignette of bruises and stitches behind her doll mask, but the eyes staring back at him through the oval openings were still the same sparkling crystal blues that hit him in the stomach like a shotgun blast. They were the *only* things that had ever been capable of eliciting such a response in him; even the rabid orphanage cubs or the bigger animals on the street had never made him tremble in the way her gaze did. All that other stuff was do or die. It was simple.

And the women he had been with before Dolores—though sparse in number—had merely been playthings, purely physical, the rutting lust of jungle beasts in heat. For only Dolores Ricci had somehow found a way to snip through the barbs of his armor.

'Dolores, can you hear me? Do you recognize me?' He wasn't sure if she was even present right now. She might not have been so lucky with Julius's counterprogramming.

'You think I wouldn't recognize the one person who helped me remove my blunt edges?' It sounded like she was smiling.

'I'm sorry,' he whispered, his voice heavy with shame. 'I should have visited you in Bedford.' He held her quiet stare, waiting for her to rip her hand away, perhaps even sic some of her dangerous creations upon him.

'It doesn't matter now.' She squeezed his hand. 'It's good to see you again.'

'I know why you're here...but this thing isn't Sonny.'

'No, it's just another thing that trapped me inside my own head, walled me in with nightmares and made me a slave. Just another monster.'

Nathan was proud of her strength. Who'd have thought a vanilla, born-and-bred housewife could have such steel inside of her? 'I'm here for Julius. I need to get him out of here. But there's still plenty of slaughtering to be done while we're here.'

'Sounds fun.' She squeezed his hand once more and released it, watching as a tsunami of barbed wires burrowed out from under his face and bullish neck, twining once more into a writhing skull mask.

Nathan heard the drone of helicopters somewhere nearby and figured it must be something to do with those agents who'd want his head on a wall when all of this died down. 'There's going to be some complications. Turns out we made some enemies when we were playthings.'

'Those people.' Doll-Face regarded the sky and the white noise of the rotors circling somewhere out of sight. Her dark hair twisted loosely in the wind. 'The ones with the powers.'

Together they slinked from the bandstand past the chapel and into the off-limits medical labs. He pulled the heavy chains from the rusted doors of an access tunnel that sloped down and fed into the central passage connecting to the other old buildings, including the dungeon.

In the earth below them, madness and monsters burned the air with violence and soaked the centuried flagging with blood and ichor.

Now two more were joining the party.

45

Brink was along the northern perimeter, crouched low behind the bole of a lofty elm, when he felt his rendezvous and tunnel scout explode.

It wasn't patently obvious what had triggered the premature detonation, but what was clear was the fact that these self-important and pushy Hourglass dickheads were playing nice for the time being, which was conducive to Brink and therefore conducive to Leonard's wants. On the losing side of the coin, however, neither he nor any of his other doubles had spotted a single living thing anywhere on the grounds or through the windows of the buildings. Not a single Talbot goon posted or on patrol. This was definitely a bad-news situation. But after a career as a Navy SEAL, followed by what felt like several lifetimes as a no-questions-asked soldier of fortune, bad-news situations were all he felt comfortable with. He had learned to depend on shit going sideways, and it was as reliable as wet water and cold steel.

"The Only Easy Day Was Yesterday," as the SEAL motto went.

But did that mean Julius was in trouble? He didn't look forward to reporting this potential SNAFU to Leonard. He listened to the relentless beating the air was taking from the circling Hourglass birds and paused to check through the eyes of his back-up team: an entire squad of himself, ready to get in and get out, put the enemy down hard or at least go up like the Fourth of July in their faces. Each viewpoint showed him various angles of the main castle-cum-asylum. Unfortunately, one set of eyes in the parking lot found no trace of Talbot's Jaguar. It would have been truly something to get an opportunity to test whether he was bomb-proof or not; perhaps by eliminating that stuffy prick, he and Leonard's syndicate could step away from Talbot's elite power players and get back to focusing purely on earning money. But no Talbot. Not tonight. But another set of eyes did spot something, and it was a beautiful sight indeed: Hangman and Doll-Face, brains unscrambled and bolting into one of the ramshackle brick buildings. He hoped they were on their way to take the payment out of Charon's ass and not find a quiet space to fuck in.

With a deft command, Brink converged his soldiers like chess pieces towards the original and heavily dilapidated main building. They too would take the fight down into enemy territory if necessary. But the job must be thorough, a full building clearance with no stone unturned. Julius Sharp was his only objective tonight, and for his safe retrieval, failure was not an option.

He thumbed the transmission button on his radio and updated Leonard. Then, with his suppressed assault rifle in his hand, he darted low and quick towards the water-damaged asylum entrance, a company of his duplicate commandos falling into his arrow formation. The violent combatant in him hoped he'd get to see some action inside the complex.

46

The mouth of Hell had opened and spewed forth its corrupted minions by the rank.

The basement block was enormous, the width and vaulted ceiling providing plenty of room to maneuver, but that worked both ways, and for Clyde, it meant the enemy had space to try and flank him: long arms and slashing claws like razor winds, elongated skulls and protruding jaws gnashing only inches away from his face and jugular. A former doctor, his white coat flapping behind him like dirty, off-white bat wings, leapt fifteen feet into the air over the surging carnival of demons, his blood-red eyes snarling at Clyde, his fingers now mutated into five silver scalpels, his whole head hideously reconfigured and now resembling a gray, hairless, pulsing brain. Clyde blasted off several shotgun rounds, then used one hand to seize the inhuman shrink in mid-air, locking his arms out to the sides and spinning him downwards into the shoulder-rubbing legions, the finger-scalpels slicing through meat and scale and protoplasm like a miniature tornado.

'Kev, you want this?' Clyde shouted.

Kev was holding up an invisible chest-high battlement around the team, trying to hold back the rush, but the infernally-powered hordes were mighty. Casting a glance at the dizzying Scalpel-Fingers involuntarily clearing a gory space through the crowd, he accepted Clyde's offer, taking control of the monster and firing him back into the air like a runaway top towards a figure somehow affixed to the wall, a patient once known as the Peeper in the sensationalist trash media, a voyeur who watched young women for days at a time before acting out his heinous fantasies, which always culminated with him removing their eyeballs. Now Thomas "the Peeper" Burden was a physical freak to match the fantasies in his soul: his head had become a large, vein-swollen eyeball within a hood of bruised and blotchy flesh, while his body and limbs were a seething and blinking network of eyes. Before the gleaming-fingered doctor could spray the room in a viscous shower of Burden's aqueous humor, another of the devils interceded, a giant troll of a thing, snatching the doctor from the air in one huge, callused hand and, by either accident or intent, burst him into a wet mess that seeped through the hulk's fingers.

Holding down the trigger on the M134, Rose thrust the six-barrel rotary assembly through an embrasure in Kev's bulwark, hosing off a few thousand rounds of 7.62-caliber belt-fed death. It was a brief but effective opening gambit, reducing the front waves into chunky vermillion mists and bursts of chthonic hues. The apocalyptic roar of the machine gun shut off all too quickly, the rotating barrels no longer producing a steady rain of brass cases, producing only an ear-piercing shrill as they whirred about emptily. Misshapen corpses were now stacked around the battlement like a small gory hill, coating Kev's invisible defensive wall in blood-spatter. Rose jammed the heavy column of the gun into a very hungry inmate, a notorious cannibal in life with a particular fetish for bone marrow; Milo Wren now had a double-hinged jaw and grossly swollen neck, bulging with florid glands brimming over with an acid capable of liquefying bone in seconds. The machine gun's six-pronged jab sent Milo stumbling back onto the bed of chunked corpses. Unshouldering the heavy battery pack and placing the weapon down, Rose made to reach through the battlement and drag Big Mouth Milo over to her, where she could ball him up and toss him like an origami football straight into Julius. That's when she saw the twelve-foot-tall steroid junkie and ex-Mr. Olympia-turned-serial strangler Shawn Keesee, his enormous left hand still dripping with the ruptured innards of Scalpel Fingers.

Pulling Big Mouth towards her, she spun him around to face the oncoming Keesee, watching the titan brush through the melee like an unstoppable wave. Between the looming giant and the endless crash of hell-spawn hammering away at the ghostly rampart, it wasn't clear how much longer they could hold this position. Kev fired the wall out like a battering ram, sending creatures flying backwards, deeper into the cell-block. Not Keesee, though; the wall seemed to break around him.

'Hold the line,' Clyde yelled, and the team did, moving forward in lockstep as they put more freaks down.

'Big guy's mine,' Rose stated, keeping a firm hold of Milo Wren, his struggles useless in her grip. And with a horse-out-of-the-gate sprint, she leapt high, and once close enough to see the hatred burn in the red-skinned hide of Keesee, she crushed her hands into Milo's distended neck and the acid glands therein, spraying a fountain of corrosive muck into Keesee's face. Landing at his huge feet, Rose sidestepped and hopped about to avoid his blundering steps as the flesh, and then muscle, sloughed off Keesee's face, leaving behind a huge steaming skull with a buzz cut for several seconds before even the bony dome of his skull collapsed in on itself like wet tissue paper. The huge body broke the stone flagging as it impacted the old dungeon floor. Rose searched for her next target.

'Something seem off about Julius?' Clyde yelled between shotgun booms.

Still watching the event unfold from his ethereal stilts, the vacant psychiatrist wore his glowing Eye, a crown as beautiful and deadly as a collapsing star.

'He looks taller,' Ace barked. His frozen sword was cutting a swath through the turbulent and shadowy figures climbing out of the back and shoulders of a paranoid schizophrenic.

Clyde unleashed a ripple of telekinetic force from his left hand, sending a group of beasts sprawling backwards. Using the space, he burned through his last shells and allowed his combat knife to race ahead of him, skewering and slashing as though it was being wielded by an invisible man. 'It might not be too late to save him if we focus on the Eye.' Between the teeming bodies, he spotted what he thought were civilians at the far end of the room, transparent tubes connecting them to the Julius-Charon hybrid. 'And those drip-feeds he's moving about on.'

'Need to get over there first,' Nat added. Her bass slaying was blowing holes through the swarm of hellions but the holes were quickly refilled by more gibbering psychopaths with satanic gifts. She threw a look at the iron door Rose had kicked out of the sealed tunnel, lying crumpled but whole near the wall to her right. 'Kev, how about surfing me over there?' She was already hopping onto the door when Kev caught her meaning. He obliged.

Clyde saw Nat rise up on the floating door like some theatrical stage show, a firework display of audio kinetic bombs showering down on the roaring and shrieking heads below.

Ace beheaded the jittery man, ending him and the chattering shadow-men who lived in the corners of his mind. Turning to Clyde and Rose, he asked, 'You both got this?'

Clyde head-banged a nod over the noise. 'Go! Help Nat!' His knife continued more of its grim work while he squeezed off pistol rounds with his right hand.

The intended strategy of the ISU, slugging and tearing the afflicted souls out of the cursed bodies, was to no avail. The work of Charon was not so readily disposable, with each blighted soul a black and thorny pip secured fast to the diseased bodies. It was a frustrating realization for the ISU, but they were not lacking in tactical purpose for long. Sarge floated up to get the lay of the battleground and spotted another complication they didn't need. He shouted down a stark warning to Rose, who was busy using Kev's spectral wall to mush the head of a female pharmacist whose torso had come alive with thrashing tentacles, each ending in a hypodermic needle filled with unknown impurities. She turned to where Sarge pointed, watching through the shifting tide of bodies as two more figures emerged on the second-tier walkway: Hangman and Doll-Face.

Rose let the brained druggist fall into a dead slump. 'Fuck! Clyde, Kev, up top, eleven o'clock!'

Clyde stared up through the grated walkway above, only seeing fragments of whom Rose was pointing at. But then he saw them, and his blood seemed to cool. Hangman, standing up on the walkway, staring down at him, his presence as terrifying as certain death. Clyde thought about an armory not even denting his barbed-wire armor and being pursued like a helpless bunny to his ravenous wolf.

Doll-Face stood as still as one of her plastic dummies, matching stares with Rose.

Their arrival shouldn't have come as a surprise. No matter how screwed-up Julius had made them, it was hardly a guarantee that both of the supreme killers had permanently severed Charon's link, to vanish on the wind.

But here!

Now!

With a seemingly endless wave of mutants pouring at them governed by a netherworld big shot, could things get any worse?

As if in answer to his inner freak-out, Clyde watched in stunned amazement as Hangman and Doll-Face acknowledged him, Rose, and Kev, and raced along the walkway towards where Charon was preparing to engage the incoming threat of Nat and Ace. Amazingly, it seemed that the Hangman and Doll-Face had little interest in stopping the Sparks from fighting their creator, choosing to wade in and help, using their fatal talents to tear apart the mindless minions scrabbling about to defend their hellish king in a rumpled $3,000 suit.

* * * * *

Nathan and Dolores moved swiftly along parallel walkways, largely ig-noring the bounty of beasts boiling below them. One or two of the things, seemingly cognizant of the independent thoughts now guiding Charon's former converts, flew or sprang or clambered up onto the second tier of the cellblock to try and stop them.

Nathan eviscerated something that resembled a fat, sickle-handed, melting man, his gloopy head atop a neck and torso that rolled like a shiny sea of flesh. Dolores didn't shield herself in her Banana Panic totem just yet, but allowed her dummies to appear, arrest and render the things bounding along the walkway in an attempt to impede her.

Nathan saw how two of the Hourglass agents were almost right on top of Julius: the big hockey-masked bruiser skidding to a graceful stop on his ice floe, and the young woman's flying-door ride coming to a stop, the heavy iron dropping and crushing a snarling terror guarding Charon. Seeing that Eye blazing upon Julius's forehead, and his body atop those flexible glassy stilts sucking the energy, the life, the *soul* out of so many inert victims, made him feel that familiar hollow pit of hatred. He couldn't stomach the idea of Julius dying in a place like this.

Call it woman's intuition, but Dolores called out, 'We might not be able to save him.'

Nathan didn't answer, but mutely kept pace with her, reaching the end of the walkway. Without hesitation, he leapt over the railing, hands reaching out in the hopes of grabbing hold of the Eye and ripping it from Julius's head if he had to.

But something happened. A head rush. He felt, or thought he felt, time slowing to a crawl.

He could feel his barbed wires growing cold from the localized tem-perature drop emanating from the icy agent.

He heard the rowdy beat of the female agent's music slow to quarter-time, her guitar's violet light barrage becoming a gentle cascade.

And he watched as his large hands closed in, only inches away from the Eye. Saw how Julius, slack-jawed as a somnambulist, looked up straight into his eyes. And then Nathan felt it—Charon skewering straight through his thoughts, his wants, his very *self*. In the blink of an eye, the recorded loop playing in Nathan's ear was nullified, and he had lost himself again, the efforts of Julius no match for the empowered Ferryman, glutting on the flotsam and jetsam of so many souls.

Dolores experienced the same thing as she leapt over her railing, watching as Charon whipped his head around like a snake, shifting focus from Nathan to her, aiming the full manipulative force of his stare directly into her. She tried to surround herself in her ape armor like a knee-jerk reaction.

Too slow.

Charon was back in control. Dolores landed amidst a collection of crystalline prisoners, each one locked away in a membranous sheath as giant mosquito stems slowly drew their souls from them into her lord and creator. Before Charon, her pose almost genuflecting, she rose and covered herself in the full might of her crushing simian, and with Hangman beside her, the killer couple turned to face Ace and Nat.

Charon had them hold their position for a moment, his attention briefly looking beyond the two Luminary scions, beyond the gradually thinning mass of his forces, and stopped on the young black man fighting like a demon himself. Currently lacking a face of his own, Charon's concern at seeing this mysterious warrior was nevertheless apparent on Julius's doped-up features. There was recognition there, from several nights ago when Charon first looked through Doll-Face's gaze at the two intruders at Willets Point. Saw briefly into their minds, and souls. This one who battled on the side of the Sparks was an unknown quantity. But there was something about him that disturbed Charon.

He transmitted a simple and vital instruction to Hangman and Doll-Face: *Kill him!*

Obediently, the pair ignored Ace and Nat, and with impressive agility and speed, they dodged around the pair and made for Clyde. Doll-Face charged like a bus through the crowd of lesser beasts on her way to fulfill her master's command.

Charon focused his attention back on the confused-looking Sparks.

'Bastards of the Luminaries, let's take this upstairs.' He propelled himself up towards the high ceiling, his transparent legs growing and more of the alien appendages emerging from the ether to punch through the layers of concrete with ease, carrying him up into the murky, rubble- and dirt-strewn hub of the asylum, dragging behind him some of the sheathed victims whose whole lives had been reduced to batteries; the rest were left behind, drained completely by Charon with one last great quaff.

Without hesitation, the Sparks obliged. Ace pulled Nat close and, with grit and determination, quickly sculpted a frozen column beneath their boots, raising them to the dark mouth in the ceiling.

The surviving converts of Charon were quick to pursue.

* * * * *

Clyde ejected his last pistol mag, now down to his loaned telekinesis, his knife, and his wits. That's when he saw Hangman bounding and swinging towards him over the heads and shoulders of the dwindling beast mob. Instantly he knew that this time, the cause of his recent anxieties—the destroyer of a three-Spark strike team and the thing he couldn't even scratch the last time they'd fought—was aiming to kill him.

'Rose!' Kev called out, creaming one of the lesser creations against wall, floor, and ceiling. 'Get the ISU. I have an idea.'

Rose clobbered a thing that bore no resemblance to anything human and nodded. Sarge and the privates rallied around her just as Doll-Face broke through the growling and barking throng, going full-tilt and swing- ing a giant ape fist towards her. She was sent hurtling into a wall, leaving a crater in the brick.

Rose got back to her feet, worked out a kink in her back and popped her knuckles. 'Getting sick and tired of you, bitch.' She charged.

Kev told his ghost comrades what he had in mind: that perhaps by destroying Charon's food source, the imprisoned he had taken with him upstairs like impaled travel snacks, they might help weaken him for Ace and Nat. 'I know these freaks are too strong for you to wrestle the souls from, but the captives are only human.'

'Worth a shot,' Sarge said. 'Let's move.'

Kev declined, seeing the threat of Hangman closing in on Clyde. 'I'm staying behind.'

The ISU didn't argue, saw Rose giving as good as she got from Doll-Face, and sped up through the ceiling.

* * * * *

Brink shot the rusting padlock from the double doors, the gun's report loud as a bomb in the quiet wing of the original asylum. From somewhere deep within the bowels of the wing came a din he knew intimately: it sounded like a storm brewing on the horizon, but what it really was, was the noise of a warzone shaking the dungeons below. Priority one was to rescue Julius, but he knew there were certain limitations to his actions, such as making sure to try and establish a safe distance from which he could engage Charon without risking having his bomb clones—and probably himself—self-destruct. With a safe zone established, he would help Nathan and the Hourglass team any way he could.

He led his team of doppelgangers through a shadowy corridor into a large former cafeteria, lit by pale moonlight through barred windows set high in the walls. Rats voiced their displeasure at the intrusion into their claimed kingdom, but they were only garden-variety creatures, and Brink was prepared for much deadlier game.

Spotting the belfry as he passed one of the cobwebbed windows, and over the quiet rhythm of five pairs of careful footfalls, Brink heard something skitter. It sounded too large to be that of a rat. It must be the size of a full-size human body at least. Brink's five pairs of eyes stared about the large high-ceilinged room and found ten pairs staring right back. The Peeper, half-hanging out of a broken, dust- and grease-coated ventilation duct, the large capillary-shot orb of his head blinking wetly in the gloom.

One of the clones slowly scanned his torchlight about the room, checking what else they might have missed. The beam shimmered off something slowly rolling down the wall, several things actually, small things, and then he spotted several more rolling through the dust bunnies on the floor. They were eyeballs, crawling along on dark vestigial limbs like baby octopi. One dropped onto the top of the Brink clone's head, a gentle, moist weight clotting his hair. That's when the pain and darkness obliterated his thoughts, the small eye-octopus lashing its mini spoon-limbed appendages around the sides of his head to puncture his gaze and blind him.

Brink Prime quickly shut him down before the blinded and screaming clone pulled his own pin and killed the rest of the team. As one unit, they all directed a fusillade of assault-rifle fire up towards the Peeper, the priority target. The voyeuristic sadist moved with aplomb, skittering cat-quick out of the hanging air vent and somehow able to run along the ceiling and walls, his feet squelching and adhering like glue. Four torch beams and a blizzard of lead chased him about the room, shredding the place into chipped stone, wood, paint, and gouts of dust.

The wave of small octopi continued to quietly slither and roll in towards the Brink quartet from all sides. Slapping in fresh mags, the team of one split into two: two shooters—including Brink Prime—going after the big one capering about the dark room as though it was loving the chase, and the other two shooters focusing their bullets and stomping boots on the black-and-red slimeballs creeping ever closer, trying to surround them.

Another of the mobile eyes landed on the shoulder of one of the crowd-control shooters but quickly found itself skewered with a blade before it could do any damage. The Brink copy then felt another one rolling up his leg, smooth and swift, as another slithered down the back of his neck, its sucker finding purchase as it quickly slithered around to his throat and up his chin, past his lips and nose. And then the agony of permanent darkness as the damp, rubbery eye blinded him.

Brink Prime didn't bother shutting this wounded clone down. He led his two remaining troops in pursuit of the Peeper, climbing over old tables and stepping on eyeballs as they moved from cafeteria to kitchen, putting enough space between them and the two blinded clones. Then he lit them both up, the duplicate pair rocking the room behind them like an airstrike, blowing a substantial hole in the brick walls. Moonlit dust and smoke wafted across the largely atomized remains of the all-seeing, all-eye-gouging creepers.

The kitchen layout had hindered the Peeper's maneuverability but also impaired the Brink trio's lines of sight. Large countertops and old metal shelving units cluttered the space. Somehow, the thing still eluded them in here. Was there another vent it had scurried into, or a door they hadn't noticed in the gloom?

A ragged shape sprang out from under a large stainless-steel shelf, squeezing Brink Prime about the waist and dragging him down to the tiled floor. It reared over him, legs straddling his hips, one giant eye glaring at him as it prepared to rob him of his vision. The two Brink clones grabbed one arm each of the Peeper and hauled him away, only to find themselves beset by another quiet cluster of eye-squids as they rolled out of the creature's arms and shoulders, back and legs like fish eggs, each one squirming and racing up towards their victim's bulging and disgusted eyes.

Brink Prime rolled backwards onto his feet and skidded around the corner of a stout kitchen island, and detonated his last pair of soldiers, blowing the staring horror straight back to hell.

Tinnitus was nothing new to Brink, but the blast certainly didn't improve his hearing any. Waving his way through the veils of smoke and cooked blood particulate, he searched for the first exit out of the kitchen, trying to focus on the continued sounds of warfare that could only lead him to Julius, Charon, and, in a perfect world, the agents delivering a fatal blow to the latter.

* * * * *

King Charon and Prince Julius had crashed through boarded-up doors and took blind turns until crashing through the gray-smeared windows of a large Gothic greenhouse. Ace was doing all he could to freeze hell over, and the botanical greenhouse was now chillier than the Devil's own heart, lit by moonbeams that resembled dirty ice as they strained to pour through the filthy glass panes of the vaulted ceiling.

Charon was adrift in the air, trailing his captured morsels around like ethereal ball and chains. It wasn't that Ace wanted to kill Julius, it was more a case of pragmatism. With every second that he was bonded to Charon, the stronger the monarch became. And the Eye was a relatively small target, and a moving one at that. He formed an icicle in his right hand, ready to throw it like a javelin, when three murky forms rose out of the stained checkerboard flooring like smoke.

Nat momentarily swung her bass towards these newcomers, expecting more of Charon's back-up, but stayed her nimble fingers when their faces revealed themselves to be those of the ISU.

'The feed bags,' Darcy called out cryptically. 'Hit them, it'll weaken him.'

Ace's eyes zipped and zoomed about like agitated hornets, moving from one undulating captive to the next. Each one looked to be on the wrong side of healthy, skin graying, and some beginning to shrivel with most of their souls now tapped. He knew there was nothing they could do to help them now. At this point, it would be considered a mercy killing.

'Fuck. Do it!' Ace yelled.

Darcy led the charge of the Scare Unit, floating up to rattle and pound at the luminescent pipes. But it was no good; they were out of bounds to the ISU's thrashings, like so many materials. So Darcy made the tough call. Rearing back, he delivered a wild looping left hook that passed harmlessly through the carapace of a withering female staff consultant, knocking the soul right out of her body. Liberated from its mortal shell, her soul dissipated, away from Charon's clutches but into the deadly wilds of Erebus. It wasn't much of an improvement, but Ace had to settle on the fact that at least she was no longer aiding a god of death. Some days you really had to struggle to see an upside.

Julius's mouth wrenched open like a broken jaw, emitting a noise like a banshee's screech. Charon's Eye fixed on the ghostly interlopers, and with a swift motion, the membranous tentacle dropped the empty sack of female meat and lashed out for Darcy. Darcy couldn't help but shut his eyes and await the inevitable.

The inevitable never came.

A sonic blast swept the protoplasmic spear aside, eliciting an enraged shriek from Charon. The Eye turned to Natalie, squinting with outrage. The glowing iris rebounded dizzyingly between her and Ace as fresh tentacles fired out to snatch them both with crushing python strength. Nat's bass vanished from her restrained hands.

'You think you can stop me?' Charon called out. 'Your progenitors were slaughtered as their refuge burned. The fearsome defenders of an everlasting peace left only a legacy of everlasting shame.' The tentacles squeezed more tightly, stealing pained grunts from Ace and Nat. 'Yet neither of you are fit enough to match even their pitiful standards.'

Sarge and Barros had joined Darcy in chasing about after the other flailing soul food-bags, finding their quarry too quick and elusive.

'Big talk, asshole,' Ace gasped through the tightening vise around his chest. 'Look at you! Look what the Luminaries did to you. You're in fucking pieces!'

Julius glared at Nat, all three eyes squinting in frustration, incapable of solving a maddening riddle. 'The filth in your blood, your soul...I can't shape it!'

'Can't mess with our souls, can't mess with our heads. Who's pitiful now, limp-dick?' Nat sneered, cheeks flushing from the squeeze.

'If I can't enslave you,' Charon said to the Sparks, 'I'll settle for crushing your innards to pulp and conjuring a hundred ways in which to torment your soul when I return to my kingdom.'

Barros snagged hold of another flailing limb, trying in vain to steady it for Sarge to drag the soul from the unfortunate prisoner. Impatient from such insolence, Julius snapped his head around, and the Eye shone a terrible intention upon Sarge. His very essence began to burn from within. Lacking a physical form meant nothing; all Charon required was the engine that powered the flesh to build a beast. He had produced armies to wage war upon the Luminaries with such raw material. The pain was such that it stole the voice from Sarge, and the terror at the realization of what was occurring to him bulged his eyes.

'No!' Barros grunted, seeing what was about to happen to her commanding officer, her family! And with a death grip, she held onto the impaled man slowly losing his mortality and reached inside him, exhausting herself in trying to hold on to the thrashing skewer while fighting to unmoor the soul from the body. With an exclamation of righteous anger, she managed it, distracting Charon and sparing Sarge's soul.

At least for the moment.

* * * * *

Clyde kept a trained eye on Hangman as he swung towards him on barbed vines.

'Ideas?' Kev asked, alighting next to Clyde.

'We need to find a way through those barbs.'

'How hard can that be?'

They watched as Hangman dive-bombed straight towards them with lashing barbs. Clyde reached out, telekinetically seizing and pulling him straight into the ground, where he hit like a falling boulder. He was up in seconds.

'Any other ideas?' Kev was trying like hell to push down and hold the killer onto the broken flagging but was losing the battle.

'Heads up!' Rose yelled. Clyde quickly bounced to one side as Doll-Face went blurring past him to smash upwards into the walkway, collapsing it in a screech of old steel. Rose was straight back in the mix, popping mannequin heads like zits and twisting their bodies into pretzels before continuing her slugfest with the spectral ape suit.

Clyde had one idea. He reached his hand out to where Hangman was pushing himself back to his feet and, with a thin stream of telekinetic energy, filtered through the mesh of razor wires writhing around Hangman's head. He clutched at a single wire wrapped deep within and pulled. It was like trying to uproot an old tree, but slowly, he felt something start to give.

Kev copied Clyde's strategy, reaching into the snarling skull of barbs and gripping a wire of his own. Together, they dug their heels in—Kev metaphorically—and began to unwind the barbs, which seemed to squeal like a nest of devilish snakes.

It was arduous, but a hole was slowly being pulled open, revealing a glimpse of the man within. A flare of pain raced up Clyde's ankle, an unseen wire having slithered like a sidewinder across the ground and over the bodies to snatch him. Clyde felt his boot begin to well with blood. The pain only enhanced his resolve. He tore at the nestled wires so hard that he ripped the whole mask open, exposing Nathan Moore's dazed expression, and with his right hand, he fired off a stiff right cross that covered the space between them like a telekinetic piston. The Hangman's nose burst open like a spoiled tomato, his eyes rolling back. But even the flesh and bone of the man beneath the mask had been made more durable by Charon. He focused his starry, hateful eyes on Clyde and shrugged off his and Kev's best efforts, his mask beginning to reseal itself. Whips whistled through the air, seeking out Clyde. He pushed off from the ground, launching himself up onto the walkway, trying to mitigate the rough landing but feeling his ankle ignite as he alighted. The wound wouldn't cause any lasting damage, but it was quick reactions on Clyde's part rather than a lack of trying on Hangman's that had kept his foot attached to his leg.

Hangman paid little mind to Kev, his blood lust reserved only for Clyde. Kev used the killer's ignorance to his advantage and swatted him up into the air for Clyde, who followed up by blasting him through the railing of the opposite walkway and into a section of wall between two empty cells. The impact was devastating, but Clyde continued to push and mash like he was grinding a spider with the heel of his palm, pushing Hangman deeper and deeper into the brick. Kev scooped up a broken piece of handrail from the collapsed walkway, drifted up into the air, and hurled it straight for Hangman's chest. It stuck fast in the barbed breastplate. Together, Clyde and Kev started to strike the tip of the broken railing over and over like invisible hammers pounding on a giant nail. Clyde grunted in exertion, running low on energy, sweat seeping down his face while blood continued to squelch in his boot. Finally, he felt the rail tip slip between the barbed coils. From the depth of the hole in the wall, Hangman could no longer be seen. Neither could the lash that left the crater with the velocity of a lizard's tongue, winding around Clyde's exposed neck.

Clyde had just enough time to feel the barbs beginning their bite into his tender throat, centimeter by centimeter. In seconds it would be tight enough to shred through his neck and pop his head from his shoulders like a champagne cork. He managed to ward off the killing noose with a reactive sliver of energy, just barely protecting his neck in time. But that wasn't all. Everything started to slow down, each second becoming a crawl, and Clyde felt as though he was leaving the world, not consciously, but physically, and for a few drawn-out seconds he thought he might have been too late in his reaction and that he was already dead, his body becoming lighter, insensate. Was his brain using up its now finite oxygen reserves before blacking out?

From Kev's shocked expression, he knew that wasn't the case.

Clyde was very much alive. He stared across the cellblock to where the Hangman was climbing out of the wall crater.

A turbulent force jarred Clyde's psyche, and a deep sense of vertigo pulled at him. His thoughts—astonishment, relief at still being alive, rapt confusion—were intercut with jumbled glimpses of the Median, of field and tree and towering spire and places he hadn't seen before. It might have been some ancient wisdom that allowed him to do what he did next, some dormant alien reflex or autodidacticism, but whatever the root cause, Clyde realized his physical body had remained frozen in place, but the hand of his immaterial counterpart clutched the Hangman's garrote. Clutching the barbed wire delicately between immaterial fingers, Clyde's dreaming-self felt Charon's dark presence thrumming through it like a direct channel to Hell. He felt the Hangman trying to retract his killing spool to no avail; it remained where it was, held in place by Clyde's immaterial form, the noose still circling the neck of his physical body but denied his blood. With a single smooth and graceful motion, Clyde's dream-self shuttled along the barbed wire and was upon the Hangman in seconds. He slipped his hand through the screeching outrage of carnivorous wires, through the flesh, the muscle, and the bone of their host, and somehow seized that priceless force that drove him: his dark, oily soul.

Dream snippets flew like confetti through Clyde's awareness, too hazy and swift to garner any meaning or true understanding. Then he saw structures beautiful and mysterious. A glowing loom, tall as a mountain, and a pair of pyramids, one gold, one winged and black, stacked on top of each other, point to point in defiance of gravity. He saw ceremony, ritual, treaty, Ramaliak and dream guardians, and he felt a marrow-deep foreboding at some of the bizarre and vile creatures in attendance.

The Hangman shuddered, releasing a drowning man's gasp, but Clyde's Median avatar didn't see the enemy standing before him; all he saw was his soul thread in his hands as he used it like a guide-rope to traverse the kingdom of dreams and psychic rest. He could feel the diseased growths festering along the surface and deeper fibers of the Hangman's soul, the ailments of Charon. Hand-over-hand, he followed the thread's infection deeper, seeking out its source within the Median. In the physical world, the whole process only took moments, but the faraway look in Clyde's eyes proved how his subconscious aspect had somehow reached in beyond time and space and conscious life itself, zeroing in on the root of his enemy's soul thread. It was a tattered stitch compared to many of its neighboring weaves, gummed upon by Charon's corruption. With a magic touch Clyde couldn't possibly fathom, he cleaved off the worst of the sullied soul fibers and released Nathan Moore, the sleepwalking Hangman, from Charon's influence.

Tangible and panting, Clyde suddenly found himself back in the moment, back in his physical body, with all the urgency and shock of receiving a bucket of freezing water to the face. The telekinetic sheath about his throat vanished as the barbed noose fell slack, retreating to its owner. And Clyde found Kev staring at him, bug-eyed.

'What did you just do?' Kev asked in quiet awe.

'Let's circle back to that later.'

Across the way, the Hangman stumbled about drunkenly for a second or two, his mask unpeeling and all the writhing barbs slithering back into the impossible space within his body. He glanced over at Clyde and Kev, but not in animosity.

'Take me over,' Clyde said.

'You sure?' Kev asked. Clyde nodded, and his boots took to the air, coming down gently on the adjacent walkway, next to Nathan Moore.

Nathan stared at Clyde for a moment. Finally, and with some grudging deliberation: 'Thank you. You cancelled out the noise,' Nathan said. 'I've never been a saint, but I want you to know, all that shit I've done, all that damage, since the change...it wasn't me.' He gestured to the wild brawl that was, by now, getting close to collapsing the cellblock, with Rose and Dolores demolishing the tunnel like a pair of wrecking balls. 'She's a victim of that motherfucker too,' he said of Dolores. 'Can you help her?'

'Dude, I got no idea what I just did,' Clyde answered.

Nathan looked glum. 'This isn't the real fight,' he added. More booms and shudders were coming from above them than below. 'It's up there.'

'I know,' Clyde said. feeling sore, tired, and flying high on enough adrenaline to induce a cardiac arrest.

'I need to get up there and stop Julius from getting killed. I owe him.'

'Best you stay out of the way,' Kev told him. 'Who says Charon can't take you over again?'

'I ain't asking for your fucking permission.'

'And I'm getting tired of you trying to kill my friend. I've had enough bullshit for one day.'

'That's enough!' Clyde acknowledged Nathan and couldn't believe that he was siding with him. 'Like he said, the real fight's up there.'

'Whatever,' Kev snapped, staring hard at Nathan. 'Just don't get too close to that bastard this time. You turn on us again, we'll finish the job.'

Clyde turned to Nathan, shutting out the pain in his ankle. 'You still able to fight?'

The barbed wires burst forth again in answer, crafting their familiar death's head.

* * * * *

The ISU were proving enough of a distraction for Charon that the bind around Ace had slackened a little, just enough for him to rotate his hands around and press them palm-up into the coil. Something had ignited a surge of righteous fury within him, right down to the molecular level. It felt like a great six-pack of beer buzz. He knew it couldn't be his proximity to death, for he had come closer to biting the bullet than this in his life. But he had never been in the vicinity of a member of the Order before. Part of Ace suspected that this stupid, trash-talking ass-hat had somehow amped-up his Luminary power in its vain attempt to demonize him.

A gust of sub-zero pressure jetted from Ace's palms, solidifying the air around him, pushing against the semi-spectral tentacle and creating an ever bigger wedge between them until the tentacle released him. Dropping to the floor, Ace felt his knee jar on impact, but it was nothing he couldn't walk off. In seconds, his frozen sword was back in his hand, and a sensation unlike anything he had ever felt before was coursing through him. It was the feeling of tapping deep into the core of his power, and Ace looked to be standing within a giant snow globe, his sword taking on an alien light. He started skating, a moving target for the new array of crystalline tentacles shooting out of Julius's body.

Frozen flakes stung Nat's cheek, and she watched excitedly as Ace weaved and sliced through the until-now impervious limbs. The beat of angry punks still tingled through her nerves, yelling in her ears, goose-bumping her skin as it mixed with the sounds of combat: the whistle of Ace's sword, the split of limbs, the angry marshalling of the ISU as they cautiously circled the fight seeking a target, and best of all, the angry bellows of Charon.

'Ace!' She reached for her iPod, hitting up a preselected song. 'I got something for you!'

Heavy metal!

The intro riff to "Rock Out, Roll On" by Triumph started out quietly, but she was a beer can being shaken-up, waiting to have her tab popped. Her eyes were sparkling from the power boost Charon had mistakenly induced as he had tried to convert her soul. When the song's drums and bass kicked in, she went off like a crate of flashbangs, falling from the entwined limb. Landing in a crouch, she jumped to her feet, bass guitar materializing in her hands as she raised its headstock, carpets of dry ice shifting around her knees. She watched as Charon's last minions scurried up out of the basement like spiders from a plug hole, and smiling, her fingers struck the strings, playing along with the song as she machine-gunned her bass. The audible bullets stymied the desperate creatures, and right as the big sing-along chorus came in, she whirled around towards Charon and dealt a concussive sound wave that threw Julius's head back in a jarring whiplash. The last of his converts stumbled about, confused and directionless. One by one they abandoned their master, fleeing the battle like startled animals.

It took a moment, but Charon shook off the daze, his Eye burning with rage and disdain, but now something else too.

Fear.

* * * * *

Rose was getting tired. Her arms were ready to fall off, her thighs filling with acid. It was the reason why two of the mannequins had managed to secure her arms, stretching her out in a crucifix pose while the big ape wound up to pulverize her exposed abs. Grunting from exhaustion, she dug deep and broke free, ripping the arms off her two captors in her escape and dropkicking Banana Panic into the wall. The ape armor blinked out, and Dolores slowly fumbled back to her feet, one hand on her mask like a drunk fighting for balance.

Clyde and Kev dropped down from the walkway and gathered about Rose while Hangman leapt the distance to Dolores's aid but found himself being warded off with a gentle hand.

'Something...something's hurt him,' Dolores said. 'He's lost control.'

'Jules!' Nathan blurted. His eyes met Dolores's, and urgently, they turned away from the three agents, racing towards the gap in the ceiling.

'Come on!' Clyde said, running after them, his ankle spilling blood, with Kev and Rose right beside him.

* * * * *

Charon had grown. That was Clyde's first thought upon leaping up through the crater in the floor. But he hadn't grown so much as he had become a desperate barrage of tentacles, a cornered Kraken, each limb spinning around the axis of Julius and the flickering Eye. Ace and Nat were a flurry of awesome power and capability, cutting down and blasting the spectral limbs apart like ethereal powdered glass while the ISU darted in and out to euthanize the remaining souls of the bodies still hopelessly fixed to the ends of certain limbs. That was no easy task, though, as each time one of the ISU tried, Charon's stare seemed to find them, making them reconsider their actions before losing themselves to some nefarious redesign.

Rose watched the great struggle unfolding in the middle of the huge botanical garden of wild weeds and stone statuary, strategizing the best way to engage. It started with her pulling the ISU out of there before they got themselves destroyed.

'The Sparks have this one,' she told them from the sidelines. Sarge, who looked a little paler than usual, didn't seem happy with Rose's decision, but he didn't question it.

Clyde saw the way Hangman was poised next to him, tension keeping him taut as he watched Ace and Nat getting closer and closer to the mind-controlled Julius flitting about in the middle of the soul-siphoning tubes.

Hangman turned to Clyde, eyes as dark and sketchy as an old Bronx basement. 'This is me talking now: If they hurt Jules, your side's going to have two more dead bodies.'

Clyde didn't respond. Ace and Nat were not bloodthirsty murderers, but if their only choice to stop this involved having to kill Julius, then he knew one of them would do it. Clyde knew he would do it too if the moment presented itself. But that didn't seem likely. He didn't know what the hell he could do right now; the final stage of the fight offered no place for him. Nat was bass-gunning another limb into submission, and Ace lopped off another with the strange visual effect of shattering frozen fog as they continued to whittle down the limbs. Clyde saw the last remaining pair of soul-batteries being held close to Julius in a protective embrace. And knew then what he could do.

'I'm going for the Eye,' he said to Kev. Kev gave him a look that clearly asked "are-you-fucking-nuts?" But after what Clyde had managed to do with Hangman, he didn't know if it was nuts or brilliant. Clyde sighed anxiously, his stomach flip-flopping, his ankle still a blaze of soaking-wet pain, and his body exhausted.

'Okay.' Kev got behind the idea, accepting how he wasn't going to talk his friend out of it. 'I'll try and pull those last few captives from him.'

'I'll help,' Hangman said.

'No way.' Clyde stood in front of him, still smaller but feeling so much bigger now. 'What if he turns you again?'

A whip of barbs fell from Hangman's clenched fist, trailing the floor. 'I never said I was getting in close.'

Kev glanced at the poor state of the dying captives, their souls being consumed more rapidly now by Charon's sheer desperation. 'They're as good as dead.' He nodded at Hangman. 'Get them away from him, any way you can.'

The three of them moved in, carefully circling the thresher of tentacles, ice, and rock music. Charon was visibly fading. A weakened force against what had somehow become overwhelming odds. But a cornered animal was a dangerous animal.

Kev found an opening in the rotating-limb assault and found purchase on one of the imprisoned bodies. The attempt got Charon's hackles up, this latest offense proving to be too much of a distraction for him. A barbed wire was cast through the storm of battle, tying itself about the midsection of the second body like a prized catch. Charon bellowed in what could only be described as despair.

Kev pulled.

Hangman pulled.

They each found themselves in a tug-of-war with a possessive limb. Back and forth they went, with Kev feeling his own strength quickly giving out. Ace stepped out of the blizzard, cleaving the tentacle in half to Charon's shriek of anger. Kev hauled the now partially desiccated body from the fray and laid it down to rest in the corner of the room. Hangman dragged his catch away from Charon's enfeebled grip and, without the same level of respect or care, slid it across the floor like a rolled carpet.

Clyde chose his moment well. Having telekinetically raised himself high above the battle, he dropped down from the ceiling, palms down, carefully slowing his descent with his erratic telekinetic pops and shudders, until he was right on top of Julius. His hands slapped onto the sides of Charon's large Eye. Julius thrashed about, mouth slack, skin ashen, and his own two eyes rolling back to show their whites. Julius's hands beat and groped furiously at Clyde, frantically trying to dislodge him. Clyde lost his grip of Charon's Eye, and his balance, almost toppling from Julius's shoulders. He just barely managed to lock his arm around Julius's neck, holding onto his position, but Julius continued to claw at him until something, *somethings* seized the possessed psychiatrist's arms. Clyde gritted his teeth, not knowing what was coming next. A pair of mannequins, dangling on invisible wires, had each wrested one of Julius's arms. From his bucking, lofty perch, Clyde could just about make out Dolores Ricci through the frosty mists and chaotic light, standing on the sidelines of the battle, marshalling her two minions. Unopposed, Clyde took tight hold of Charon's Eye, his fingers quickly going cold and numb from the temperature. He still didn't know how he was doing it, or what exactly it was he was doing, but he felt his whole nervous system lighting up like cold fire trailing along his spinal column to explode out of the ends of every nerve fiber. Another hazy sequence of imagery beset him, scrolling through his head: more of the Median's grand architecture, more indiscernible flashes of strange faces and forms, and again, that great spinning loom, shining bright as an electric rainbow, steadily spooling out a vast and endless sea of threads. Were these somebody else's memories?

'You...' Charon choked out. 'One of them? Usurper!'

Clyde's hands blurred briefly, flitting between tangibility and intangibility as those of his sleepwalking form phased in and out from the flesh, and igniting with white fire, these dreaming fingers sank under the physical matter of the Eye, tearing and digging at its untouchable bed. Charon wailed like a wind tunnel. With the Eye's psychic molding gouged and ruined, the burning sleeper's hands vanished and Clyde's physical grip strengthened, and slowly, he tore it from Julius's forehead.

'You won't be...enough. You're...still...mortal!' Charon spat with rage, but behind this, Clyde also sensed the half-god's fear. 'You'll never...be enough! The Order...is...eternal. Nothing...escapes death.'

Sensations moved like a river through Clyde's subconscious, thoughts and ideas he could only barely grasp. More visions, but were they forgotten histories or flat-out delirium? He saw the conjoined pyramids again, the gold one a thing of purity and beauty, housing a glass city and rows of impressive and fearsome statues; and the inverted black pyramid, flapping its great raven wings above it like a terrible omen. He saw the indistinct gathering of ruling parties beneath a stormy void.

As he tore the Ferryman's Eye away from Julius, the imagery instantly ceased, like pulling a TV's plug from its outlet. The giant cephalopod of translucent limbs faded out in sections, and an unconscious Julius toppled precariously from his stick-insect limbs. Clyde caught him, holding him in his arms as they both plummeted for a messy impact forty feet below before he managed to use his last ounce of strength to break their drop speed, lowering them to the frozen stone flagging.

Boots on frosty grit, Clyde stared at the lightless Eye of Charon and dropped it on the ground. Ace and Nat appeared on either side of him, standing over it as though waiting for it to devise one last trick. It didn't. Ace buried his sword clean through the half-shut iris.

Everybody checked on Julius, but Hangman had beaten them all to it. Cradled in Nathan's arms, Julius resembled a corpse dragged in from the Arctic, a goatee white with snow and ice. Nathan gently pressed one hand to the raw, painful marking on Julius's forehead.

Clyde didn't like the quiet stillness of Nathan and was expecting his counterpart to erupt into a killing frenzy at any moment. It never happened. Instead, Nathan reverently picked up Julius's body. He turned to Clyde and the team.

'We're sorry. We didn't want it to end like this,' Clyde offered.

Hangman's dead eyes burrowed into Clyde's. Without any verbal response, he and Doll-Face turned around and made to leave.

'We can't let them go,' Ace said.

'Another time,' Rose said, bruised and panting. 'They were victims in this too.'

Nat stepped in, holding the impaled Eye. 'Our job's done, right?'

Clyde noticed the small flickers of electricity deep down in her eyes. Exhausted, he nodded, wanting nothing more than to get out of this place. But did he really want to sleep again after all that Median business? Even with Nat at his side?

Helicopter searchlights continued to pass through the dirt-rimmed glass of the vaulted ceiling, turning the last snowflakes silver in their passage, accompanied by the distant droning of engines.

A gunshot rang out, making the team jump. A set of padlocked double doors screeched open in the corner of the room, revealing a stout silhouette. It was Brink, looking a bit worse for wear himself. Nathan spared him a look, nodded along in gratitude to the friendly face, and exited through the doorway with Dolores at his side.

'About the tunnel—' Brink called over to the agents.

'Yeah, we get it,' Kev said. 'Everybody's had a head fuck tonight.'

'How about a peace offering?' Brink suggested. The team tried to appear as cordial as possible under the circumstances. 'I have a pair of eyes on the road. Guess who's on his way here right now. I'll try and hold him for you before he gets spooked.'

Brink turned on his heel and left them standing there in the ruins of a battle that had, unknowingly for all, turned the tides.

But the ocean was a callous and unforgiving thing.

* * * * *

Talbot stopped his Jaguar a hundred yards from the entrance to Elzinga. The wooded lane obscured much of the night sky, but what he had mistakenly first assumed to be a passing helicopter had proven to be a hovering circle of them sweeping the asylum and the surrounding grounds.

Panic started to make him edgy, wondering what had happened in his brief absence. He had come here to see how Charon was doing with his new skinsuit, and if his new army would be up to snuff, capable of drawing those Hourglass cockroaches into a worthy fight.

But he hadn't expected this. Had Charon decided to renege on their arrangement, instigating an asylum breakout? No, that wouldn't be it. Surely he would have spotted something untoward on his way down here if that was the case. So, instantly, his mind latched on to the only inevitability it could find: Hourglass. It was their presence troubling the skies right now. But how did they learn of Charon's location?

Fear started to etch away at his innards, imagining how Gabriel and the inner circle would view this latest flop of his. He should be so lucky that they merely turn him away, disown him...disavow him. That would be punishment enough, to lose not only everything he had achieved for them in his long climb up the ladder but to find that the ladder had been cleaved away from his grip.

He put the car in reverse and made it halfway through a three-point turn when he noticed a dark shape step out of the tree line. Startled, Talbot's hands began to show their true form, shedding their human make-up to become reptilian talons clutching the wheel. He stared at the figure's cautious approach, entering the gleam of the headlights with cocksure certainty. At first he was surprised, but then it all made perfect sense. Brink, or one of his explosive idiots, stepping towards the driver-side door. Brink had turned his coat.

The Jaguar lit up the dark road with a tremendous fireball.

47

For three days Leonard had sat on the balcony of his luxury condo, watching the yachts and jet skiers enjoying themselves on the pristine blue waters off Miami's South Beach. The stunning visuals barely registered with him. Neither did the contents of the wet bar he had been steadily working his way through.

After the private service held for Julius, Leonard had taken his brother's ashes and hopped on his jet for here. Before scattering them, he had spent a good deal of time drinking and talking to the urn as though he was expecting the spirit of Julius to talk back. It never happened, but those mournful soliloquies had allowed Leonard to revisit some of the good times he had had with his brother right here. Back when he was climbing the ranks and making waves in the criminal fraternity, resolving to reach the top.

Well, here he was. The top. Was this the top?

From his yacht, he had scattered the ashes into the depths of the Atlantic and thought about eating a bullet while he was out there, positioning himself so to topple over the side into the same dark waters. After a long struggle, he placed the gun on the deck and sat in a catatonic state until the sun bled along the horizon's blade.

There was still some of that old iron-core ambition inside of him. He only had to figure out what to do with it.

In the brief lead-up to the funeral, he had been expecting Talbot to show his face and enact a swift and violent retribution upon him, at the very least on Brink, Nathan, or even Dolores. But it never happened. It could be that Brink had managed to kill him that night, but the survivor's instinct in Leonard told him not to believe that. The absence of Talbot had proven useful so far, however. With Leonard on vacation, he had left Nathan and Brink in control, having Zeb and the Sovereigns reporting any issues directly to them to sort out in Leonard's absence. They called him every day to check in. So far the other factions had remained obedient, not just out of fear of Leonard's now three supernatural enforcers, but of Talbot and his backers, wherever they may be.

But with his board temporarily running Sharp Industries, and the Sovereigns manning the illegal side of trade, he had time to think. He knew that his next move couldn't be as small-minded as merely making money. His life was smaller without Julius, but his world was now so much bigger. Guns didn't cut it anymore. Not with such terrifying powers circling. If Talbot was still lying low, he wanted to find him, and have the means to rip his guts out.

And the same went for Agent Clyde Williams and his team.

What he needed was knowledge. But that would take time and money. So it was a good job he had plenty of both.

Sitting there soaking up the evening rays, he breathed in the salty air, staring at the palm trees and the stars slowly beginning to pierce the evening sky.

He topped off his drink.

And he imagined Julius was sitting there with him, talking over their next moves.

48

Clyde hobbled along Coney Island's boardwalk, his recently stitched ankle throbbing, but nothing that painkillers, a few weeks off work, and the company of friends couldn't sort out. He had gotten the hang of the crutches quickly enough and knew that they were only a temporary requirement. Coming to a halt on the warm, sandy boards, his phone to his ear, he stared out at the beach and the slow walkers enjoying the pink sunset. He was subliminally enjoying the lights and sounds of Luna Park: the rides and the arcade, the laughter, and the boardwalk aromas of salty air and fried food.

'Yes, it's healing well,' he said. 'Still looking around the two-week mark before I'm fit to return to duty.' The Cyclone rattled behind him to a chorus of whoops and screams.

'Very good, Agent,' Meadows replied. 'Ace and Rose can hold down the fort in the interim. You just heal up.' An awkward pause settled over them. 'I still don't like how we left things the other night. I don't want distrust or clashing perspectives causing friction. Whatever you feel about our central policy, don't let it interfere with your and your team's victory.

What you did should be in the history books, if such a thing *could* be in the history books. It's a shame we must hide in the dark because you all deserve a damn parade for what you pulled off. I'd even go as far as saying a national holiday.'

A brief silence filled the line.

'But pride comes before the fall.' Meadows huffed down the line, touching a still sensitive topic. 'No matter what you think, and no matter what you accomplished that night, Director Trujillo is not about to authorize a Hail Mary run into the Null in the hopes of finding the Firmament Needle. But I'm sure you'll discuss this when you see him at Indigo. But when you come back, I need to know you'll be focused on company tasks.' Clyde's jaw bunched, his eyes staring down at the plaster cast loaded with well-wishes, bad language, and friendly put-downs. 'Never in my tenure as an Hourglass official have I commanded a team with such potential as this one. I believe we can wipe out the Cairnwood Society for good before their ignorance, stupidity, and greed inflict the sort of damage that can't be undone. Can I trust you with that, son?'

Clyde gave it a moment. Still trying to wrap his head around what he did that night. What they all did that night. And he thought about how, on his own, and without Trujillo's hoodoo, he lacked the resources and the know-how of how to enter the Null, short of killing himself.

'Yes, sir.'

'Excellent.' Meadows was about to hang up when Clyde caught him with a question.

'And Kev?'

A troubled sigh. Meadows was a man of many sighs. 'To be decided.' He ended the call.

Clyde pocketed the phone and shuffled his tripod act over to where Nat was waiting for him at the wooden fence, the soft wind teasing her hair, the evening glow burnishing her tattooed skin.

She was giving a death stare to some of the gulls wheeling through the sky, guarding her hot dog like she was a mama bear protecting her cub. 'If one of them steals my dog, I'm gonna need you to avenge it,' she told him. 'None of these rubes will know what happened. Make it a seagull heart attack, telekinetic style.'

'I swear to wipe out its entire family,' Clyde assured her and accepted the large mocha from the bundled-up form of Kev to his right, leaning his elbows on the fence and reading something on his phone. 'Thanks, man.'

'No problem,' Kev mumbled. He glanced back at his phone and asked, 'Does he miss me?'

Kev had been suspended from duty. But what was surprising was the fact that Meadows, via the lofty decree of Director Trujillo, had decided not to incarcerate him. There was some brief but heated mention of a place called the Fish Tank deep in the East River, a black-site name if Clyde had ever heard one. Alas, the agency brass had granted clemency to Kev for his part in helping to destroy Charon, an event that, although already classified, buried, and all but brain-scrubbed from the collective consciousness, was one that had quietly, unknowingly sent ripples throughout Hourglass, their allies, and their enemies. A monarch of the Order, once presumed destroyed, was now truly so.

Doling out punishments was a surprisingly complex issue in this instance. Clyde knew that Kev knew—or at least suspected—that the department was hamstrung from the get-go. They couldn't lose Clyde right now, especially with whatever the hell was going on with him and the Median, but whatever that complication may be, they needed him and Kev for field assignments. And without Kev, Clyde would be reduced to a regular agent with a gun, at least until his new erratic talents could be understood.

There was also the small fact that Kev, while clearly the engine behind the digging and scraping into the secrets of Hourglass, couldn't have acted in such an illegal manner without Barros and her skills. And she couldn't be disciplined by way of vacation in the Fish Tank or anywhere else as, being a member of the ISU, she was a component of Rose's brute strength. There would likely be some terse comments and pissing between Barros and Rose in the foreseeable, but eventually the hatchet would be buried, and Rose and the ISU would be back to its powerhouse top form.

And so, Kev was to steer clear of the Madhouse until Clyde was field-ready, and he was by no means allowed to talk to Meadows.

'He grumbled a lot,' Clyde answered.

Kev smirked and continued skimming the news article pertaining to the freak fire that had broken out at Elzinga Asylum the other night, gutting the entire complex and producing a terrible death toll. The ongoing investigation had now come to an end, tightly regulated by the agency throughout. They had swiftly sealed and swept the entire area for any secrets best left hidden, burning the basement cellblock and several key buildings before propagating their false report to the local media. The stories had all mentioned the mournful death of Julius Sharp, who was on the premises during the time of the tragic blaze, along with the large number of staff and patients who had also perished. Hourglass had now filtered the details of the last of the missing victims—sans corpses—to the media, who had leapt on each morsel like a pack of ravenous dogs upon a T-bone.

One seagull wasn't getting the hint, still coming too close to several people strolling the boardwalk with cotton candy and ice cream. Its head and neck suddenly and inexplicably bent sideways during its dive as if hitting an invisible barrier; nothing fatal, but enough to confuse the hell out of it. Several passersby too, for that matter, appeared baffled by the invisible wall it had thudded into. Kev chuckled to himself, his mirth muffled by the scarf, and turned to watch a life-beaten clown loitering further down the boardwalk by the Thunderbolt, vaping his blues away.

Nat watched the stunned gull sail away and quickly finished off her hot dog in a very unladylike fashion, washing it down with her Coke. Clyde smiled at her unbridled lack of self-consciousness. 'Anyway, don't be stressin' over Uncle Meadows. I wouldn't push him again for the next couple of decades if I were you, but it'll smooth itself out, you crazy, mad fuck.' She raised her can in cheer. 'The Boogieman Project is officially out of business. Case closed.'

Every now and then Clyde would catch a small flicker of light, like a Fourth of July sparkler cutting burning traces and figure 8s deep in her eyes. Right now, in this nerve-tingling romantic setting, a boardwalk at sunset, he found the sparks in her eyes magnificent, like swirls of diamond dust coating pure amber. But the rational part of his mind couldn't help but pick at the cause of these fleeting light shows. He didn't doubt her allegiance or the state of her mind or soul, but it made him think again about what they were all becoming in this war. He had spotted a similar coruscation in Ace's steely gaze that night at the asylum before they had all parted ways.

At least her complexion hadn't paled in Charon's folly, unlike Ace, who had become a little paler than usual, with skin like an arctic snowdrift.

Clyde tapped his mocha to her soda can. 'The Ferryman has taken his last toll.'

'Any leads on Talbot?' Kev asked.

'Nothing yet. I'm sure he'll turn up. Rats always do.'

Clyde sipped his mocha and thought about Hangman, and Doll-Face, and Brink, and Leonard Sharp's own threat about rooftop snipers. Hourglass would be monitoring their threat levels, of course, but since examining Talbot's smoking car, nobody expected them to show their faces for a while. Clyde and his team were no longer the only ones with their necks on the block.

He leaned in and gave Nat a socially acceptable kiss, earning himself a blood-rushing mischievous smile. Putting his back to the water, he propped his elbows on the fence and found his eyes magnetized to the Wonder Wheel, lit up splendidly against the drowsy purple-blue sky. It made him think about the giant loom he had envisioned during his tussle with Charon, except that wheel, whatever it was, was immeasurably more impressive in dimension and structure. But what was its purpose? He thought he had some vague idea of what it might be, but until he flew back to Indigo to see Spector, he was stuck with assumptions. A lot of them.

But perhaps not for long, as Spector practically materialized out of thin air like some attractive book-smart beach bum, catching Clyde off guard, sidling over to him with a casual gait, just another easygoing person out for a pleasant stroll. He greeted Kev, introduced himself to Nat, and then shook Clyde's hand, appraising his leg cast and crutches.

'Hi, Clyde. I'm sorry for pushing up our schedule, I know you wanted to rest a little before flying out to see us.' The red sun flared across Spector's lenses. 'But it'll be safer if we start this right away.'

'Start what?'

'Protecting you from the rulers of the Median.'

EPILOGUE

The monk's boots waded through the deep muck, a composite of unknown minerals in hues of almost pleasant pastel. The functional fatigues beneath his sacred necromancer armor had seen better days: torn in parts, frayed at others, soaked in sweat and ichor and, for the last half-mile, bog water. But the stains were barely noticeable in this world of near-perpetual dusk, lit by varying moons and even distant suns of peculiar color, none of which could light the way much better than a winter solstice back home.

His former master, now his equal, slogged along beside him in his visitant state. The Arkhitektor: a once brave and noble head monk of the Rising Path, necronauts set on traversing the great unknown lands of Erebus for the Firmament Needle. An item somewhere between myth and wishful thinking, but worthy of their sacrifice.

The Arkhitektor had been killed some years back, his soul diseased by Charon's palatial guardian Vor Dushi, but now restored by his once prized pupil.

Konstantin "Gulag" Kozlov shared a look of weary pleasure with the Arkhitektor. Through all their unknowable days and nights in these lands without time, the thrill of possibility had yet to fade. They had walked, climbed, and hidden, and hunted when necessary, and of course, learned.

And now they waded through thigh-deep swamp water, eyes scrutinizing every mossy tree, hanging root, and alien light for a potential predator.

They had left the Eidolon Trench many miles back, the place that had played a pivotal part in their lives, and for the Arkhitektor, also his mortal death. But the road was slow going, searching for clues and knowledgeable sources about the dread lieges of these vast lands—the Order of Terminus—and most importantly, the possible whereabouts of the Needle.

Slow going indeed, with an end nowhere in sight.

But the effort was worth the sacrifice, even if their souls were destroyed in the process.

The canopy overhead was like a tangle of blackened cables, lit by a green sky somewhere between bleach and infected putrefying flesh, burning with yellow stars. None of the giant skulls—whether moons or sentinels of the Order, Kozlov and the Arkhitektor still hadn't decided—had appeared overhead in a while.

They pushed on through the cold water, focusing on the next stop of their journey. Crossing the borderlands of the now obliterated Charon, into those of a House whose king they knew nothing of.

The House of Strange Fates.